THE MOON SHONE ON D'ARTOIS'S FACE.

"Why did you have to show up here tonight, Jeffrey?" he asked, his voice sounding almost petulant. He scowled at Jeffrey's bloody back.

"I never wanted to kill you, although for seven years you had the woman I wanted. Yes, I've stood by and watched you possess the woman I think of as mine." D'Artois leaned closer. His voice blazoned his suffering.

"Do you know how hard that was, to see you in my place?"

Jeffrey grunted, trying to speak, but the pain was too great.

D'Artois stiffened. "Now I must kill you, something I hate to do." His voice croaked. "But I have no choice—like the times before—I have no choice."

The Last Lover

Tish Martinson

WARNER BOOKS

A Warner Communications Company

WARNER BOOKS EDITION

Cover photo by Jim McGuire

Warner Books. Inc., 75 Rockefeller Plaza, New York, N.Y. 10019

A Warner Communications Company

Printed in the United States of America

First Printing: August, 1981

10 9 8 7 6 5 4 3 2 1

I wish to dedicate this book to
my husband, who dared me to write
it, and then bore with me—and,
to my children who loved me through
it.

The Last Lover

Prologue

Colombier, Côte d'Azur, September 1975

In the courtyard at Colombier, under the blazing, hot September sun, a grotesque statue of Mephistopheles cast its elongated shadow over the small garden. Everything around it had been burned to the ground. The flowers were dead, the birds had flown away. At the end of the statue's shadow, a woman stood looking up at the twisted face. She was wearing a white piqué suit, and her long blond hair was carefully brushed to one side of her head, coming around her neck to rest on her shoulder. Except for the faint scar on her left temple, her face was as beautiful as the flower she wore on her jacket. Her green eyes glistened like two large emeralds, and it seemed as if there were a blazing fire within each one as she studied the stone figure. She stared at the statue, and whispered softly to it: "I've conquered you, haven't I, demon? You're a living ghost, robbed of name and fortune. We both breathe, but you're a walking dead man, and I—no matter what you've taken from me—I'm alive and will live my life. You never had one, did you? All you could do was destroy—you even destroyed yourself. But not me. Rosalie La Farge Farahet Guthrow lives, do you hear?—lives and *will* live!"

A crunching of gravel behind her roused her to the approach of the sport-coated young man with a sheaf of papers in his hand. She turned to face him. "Gerard, it's possible, then?"

"Yes, madame. It'll cost all kinds of money, but it can be done; Colombier can be rebuilt as it was before the fire."

"Good. We're told in the Bible, 'Blessed are the peacemakers,' but it's always seemed to me that there was never enough notice given to the builders. To build—that's to fight decay and death, isn't it so? So let us build, create, leave something solid, eh?"

"As you can afford it, yes. May I say"—the young man turned slightly pinker than the sun might have caused—"that I respect profoundly your decision to establish the foundation? I read of it in the newspapers, and I am thunderstruck—a quarter of a billion francs for the relief and care of those fleeing totalitarian states. Few nations would be as generous."

"If the money is there, why not use it?" Rosalie said. "It is the most fitting memorial I can imagine"—she cast a glance at the statue—"for one who was such a friend of my family."

Chapter One

Paris, August 1962

In August of 1962, an event of international social significance took place at the Paris mansion of Commandant Armand La Farge.

The guest list included some of the most powerful and influential men and women in the worlds of government, entertainment and high society. Every year at this time, such a gathering would be hosted by this famous multimillionaire and philanthropist, but this one was of special importance.

Present at the affair were many representatives of the press. Their interest centered on one man, the tall, handsome La Farge, powerful-looking in an almost frightening way. As he spoke, his strong hands moved back and forth, skillfully emphasizing the importance of his words. Beside him stood a strikingly beautiful brunette, his wife Jacqueline. Her bare shoulders reflected the dancing light of the hundreds of tiny candles flickering quietly in the four huge chandeliers hanging from above. Her dark hair, combed back and gathered at the nape of her neck, curled around in a ponytail effect and flowed down her left shoulder to the tip of her left breast. The strapless emerald green dress clung tightly to her body, molding her slender waistline and clinging to her narrow hips.

La Farge abruptly dismissed the group, and Jacqueline moved off into the crowd. He glanced at his watch and snapped his fingers at the butler standing nearby, who hurried over.

"I see that you are filling in again for Oscar. Where is he? Sick again? Or drunk?"

"Yes, monsieur."

"Well, which one?"

"Both, monsieur."

"I see. Very well, I shall have to take this matter up with you later. But now, would you please see to it that Berthe gets that daughter of mine dressed and down here before her party is over?" La Farge laughed as he thought of his daughter's sense of time. "She's always late," he said, turning to his guests. "Not like her mother, I should add, who is *almost* always on time."

His guests chuckled at this remark.

La Farge turned to the butler. "Max, go and fetch Rosalie. She is already thirty minutes late."

The man bowed slightly, clicking his heels as he turned to leave.

"Damned Germans. Why do they always have to do that? It brings back memories, bad memories. Fourteen years I've been trying to get him to stop doing that, and still, every now and then, he forgets himself—and bang, Hitler is back."

Some of his guests smiled, amused by La Farge's exasperation.

"Well," he went on, "I've lived with it for this long, and I haven't fired him yet. I don't suppose I ever will, now."

He took a puff from his Havana, held it for a moment, then exhaled.

"Mademoiselle?" Max knocked on the door at the head of the stairs. There was no answer. Louder: "Mademoiselle Rosalie, your father would like you to join him in the ballroom at once.

The guests have already arrived and everyone is waiting for you."

The door opened and Rosalie La Farge emerged.

"Oh, mademoiselle, you look simply beautiful," the butler said. "Your papa will surely be proud of you tonight."

"Max, you are always such a love. Where did you say Papa was?"

"In the ballroom, mademoiselle. Everyone is waiting for you there."

"How do I look?"

"Magnificent, mademoiselle!"

Her white silk dress shimmered in the soft candlelight as she floated down the curved staircase. At the bottom, she stopped to check herself in a mirror.

"Oh, *zut!*" She had left her gardenia upstairs in her room. "Max! Max!"

"Yes, mademoiselle?"

"Max, would you please ask Berthe to bring me my gardenia? I left it upstairs."

In a moment, a neatly dressed middle-aged woman came down tne stairs carrying in her hands two creamy whire gardenias.

"Oh, Zalie," Berthe said. "How forgetful you can be at times! I reminded you before you came down to put on your gardenia. What would you do without me, I wonder?"

Rosalie's laughter rang out like a bell.

"Berthe, you know I could not survive without you. Why, I sometimes think that if you left me, I would not even know how to get out of bed."

She twirled around once for Berthe to admire her.

"Is Maman already in the ballroom with Papa, Max?"

"Yes, mademoiselle. Now hurry before he becomes angry."

At that moment the door to the ballroom was flung open and the sound of La Farge's voice boomed through the house.

"Max! Berthe! Where is that daughter of mine? What's taking her so long?"

"Here I am, Papa—I'm coming."

A lump stuck in La Farge's throat. Was this breathtakingly beautiful woman approaching him his daughter, his little girl? She had grown up so suddenly—first a baby, then a little girl, then away at school, and now a young woman. Where had all the years gone? He felt a stinging in his eyes as he lovingly admired his daughter.

"Oh *chérie,* I cannot find the words to tell you how pleased and proud I am tonight. You . . ." His voice faltered, and he cleared his throat. "You look simply lovely tonight." He kissed her forehead and made a face at her in an attempt to mask his emotions.

"Come, *chérie,* let us show you off to our guests. Let's not keep them in suspense any longer. After all, this is your debut, and everyone is eager to see you."

"Wait, Papa. Just a minute, okay?" She beckoned to Berthe to hand her the other gardenia.

She arranged the flower on the lapel of her father's dinner jacket. "There now. Doesn't that look better?"

La Farge glanced at himself in the hallway mirror. "Well, maybe a little big for a boutonniere. But tonight, anything for you, my sweet." He backed away and bowed. "Will the lady take my arm?"

She giggled, amused by his playacting, and responded by curtsying. Her face lit up in a twinkling smile as she took her father's arm. When they made their entrance into the grand ballroom, a murmur rose from the crowd, as everyone turned to look at Rosalie and her father.

The press charged up to them, taking pictures and throwing a barrage of questions at Rosalie.

La Farge raised his hands. The noise faded immediately, the crowd responding to their host's aura of authority.

"*Mesdames, messieurs,* I would like to present to you my daughter, my treasure, my lovely Rosalie. *Reine de la soirée.*"

Jacqueline La Farge stood watching, envying her daughter's youth and freshness. Until tonight, she alone had reigned as the queen of fashion and flair. Her flawless beauty had been acclaimed throughout the world. Now she could see that her daughter was to be the new darling of the press.

Jacqueline's thoughts drifted back to when she had first married the mighty La Farge. She had only been twenty then, twenty-five long years ago. She fidgeted for a moment with her small, beaded purse, her face twisting in an unbecoming grimace as she became engrossed in her thoughts. Was it truly possible that at one time they had been so much in love? Where had it all gone, that love she had once felt for him? She had her lovers. Did he have a mistress? How silly of her, she thought, after all these years to start wondering. Hadn't he been a good husband to her? Hadn't he always shown her more respect that she deserved?

She glanced around the room, and her eyes lingered on the tall, graceful young man in the velvet jacket. Paul. How handsome he looked standing there, and how young. She watched as her husband introduced Rosalie to him. The look in Paul's eyes—was that just admiration for someone so beautiful or was it something more? A surge of jealousy rose and stuck in her throat, almost choking her, as she watched him take Rosalie's hand and kiss the back of it. Was it her imagination or did his lips seem to linger just a little too long?

But why was she so afraid? They didn't even know each other. And after tonight, with Rosalie going down to St. Tropez for the rest of the summer; they'd probably never even see each other again. She would make sure of that. *Merde*, why couldn't she have had a son instead? That way, Armand would have had the male heir he'd wanted so much, and she would not have to contend with a daughter as a rival. She studied Rosalie's figure as she went about shaking hands and curtsying to the more distinguished guests. Jacqueline had to admit the girl was striking. No, *dazzling* was the word that suited Rosalie best. She compared the girl to her father. They were alike in so many ways: the way their presence demanded attention; the way they both held their heads when they spoke or laughed. Yes, at least in Rosalie, La Farge had some of what he had wanted in a son, even if she *was* a girl.

Jacqueline's thoughts were interrupted as La Farge and Rosalie came over to stand beside her.

"Oh, Maman, how beautiful you look tonight! As always, you are the belle of the ball."

Jacqueline flinched, not knowing what Rosalie had meant. Did Rosalie really believe that? Or was she already exercising her superiority?

Rosalie threw her arms around her mother's neck in a spontaneous embrace. "Oh, Maman, isn't this exciting?" She stopped to catch her breath for a moment. "I mean, the people and my dress and the press and all. Would you believe the editor of *Femme* magazine asked me to be the January cover? Why, I'm so excited, I can hardly stand it."

Jacqueline had never been a physically demonstrative mother, and she felt embarrassed at her daughter's unexpected embrace. She could see Paul in the distance, looking across the room at the family scene—and obviously, she thought bitterly, registering the difference in their ages. She pushed Rosalie away.

"Now, now, Rosalie," she said. "You will get your dress all wrinkled, and your gardenia. You shouldn't be so careless, child. After all, you are now almost eighteen, and that makes you officially a young lady. You should start acting like one."

It was evident to La Farge that his wife's concern at that moment was neither Rosalie's dress nor the corsage. It was the perfection of her own appearance which concerned her. God forbid that one strand of hair fall out of place, or that the pink lipstick on that perfect mouth be smudged. Already she had whipped out her compact and was reapplying powder, checking to see that all was well and holding fast on that royal face. He smiled, remembering how his wife sometimes used the royal "we" when referring to herself. Some royal cunt he'd married!—and it was, at that, when he was allowed in it. He wondered whether her breasts had yet begun to fall, and whether her once-tight little bottom had yet begun to sag. If there was one thing he couldn't stand, it was a woman with an orange-peel ass and droopy tits. He leaned forward and stole a glance down the front of her dress; the round, pink, undulating bulges looked quite good for a woman of forty-five. It had been a long time since he had grabbed hold of them and kissed them—exactly eighteen years and seven months ago: that day in Martinique. She had not let him touch her since. He wondered how he had put up with it this long.

The sharp snap of the closing compact brought him back to the present.

Jacqueline's callousness, it seemed, had gone unnoticed by Rosalie. "You look beautiful, Maman. Don't worry." There was something in the way she said it that made La Farge wonder. Was it his imagination, or did Rosalie sense her mother's fear of competition? But he could never be sure of anything he ever read in a woman's words. She might say one thing and mean something quite the opposite.

His thoughts of his wife troubled him. Was it possible that after all this time he still felt something for her? Was he still aroused by the thought of her nude body?

He promised himself that he would surprise her one day soon, when she did not expect him, and was in her bathroom bathing. Once and for all he would see for himself how the bitch was holding up. And if he liked what he saw, he just might help himself to some of it. After all, he still had his rights, and like it or not, she wouldn't be able to do very much to prevent it. He chuckled, glancing at her cool, sophisticated face. He would have given a lot right then for her to have known what he was thinking, just to see her reaction. He turned to face Rosalie.

"Well, young lady, let's get back to our guests. We don't want them to think you're hiding from them. And I promised the press you'd give them an interview and some pictures for their papers. Jacqueline, are *you* ready?"

It was a little dig at her constant primping, and she knew it.

"Aren't I always, Armand, my love?"

Arm in arm, the three made their way across the room to join the others.

Rosalie did not know many of the people in the room, only a few close friends of her father's whom she had met from time to time in St. Tropez during summer vacations. Others she recognized from their pictures in various publications.

President de Gaulle, an old friend of La Farge, was standing in front of the huge rose marble fireplace, directly under one of the magnificent chandeliers. He was leaning against the mantel, sipping a glass of champagne. His tall figure stood out among the others, emphasizing his stately appearance.

Seeing his daughter's obvious fascination with the President, La Farge teased, "Hm, isn't he a trifle too old for you? And with a nose like that, just think what your children would look like!"

She grinned at him in mock disgust. "Oh, Papa, you are the most horrible person I—"

"I have not yet given you permission to speak, young lady. Now, as I was saying, should you, however, still be interested in an old man, in spite of my warnings, how about this one? He is a fine figure of a man. He has a strong, but reasonably sized nose. He is handsome and tall. And he has lots more money than the President."

"Who are you talking about, Papa? I see no such man here." She knew quite well that he meant himself, but chose to go along with his game. It was one which, in one form or another, he had played as far back as she could remember.

"Why, mademoiselle, I am most grieved to hear that I do not suit your taste. A little plastic surgery, perhaps? And a couple of inches topped from the height?" He stooped. "Like this, maybe?"

"Oh, Papa, you're always joking; do be serious. Is there anyone else I haven't already been introduced to?"

At that moment, a lanky, silver-haired man with piercing gray blue eyes came over to them. Jacqueline turned and walked away as he approached, making it clear that she did not wish to speak to him.

"May I introduce myself, mademoiselle? I am Jean, Duc d'Artois, a longtime friend and business associate of your father. You probably don't remember me, but we've met before, at your father's villa in St. Tropez."

Rosalie nodded. "Of course, Monsieur le Duc, I remember you quite well, as a matter of fact. The last time I saw you was on the day of my twelfth birthday. You took me shopping with you that day and you said I could have anything I wanted in all of Paris."

She laughed and paused for a moment, recalling that day's events.

"And I made you buy me—unbelievable, no?—a duck."

"And your mother made you take it back!" D'Artois laughed, bowed gracefully, took her hand in his, and kissed it lightly. "Yes, time does fly. I can hardly believe how you've grown up in just a few years—and into such a beauty."

His bony fingers clasped tighter around hers. The ring on his finger cut into her flesh.

"Come, Rosalie." It was her father. "Let's go over and meet some of my other friends. Jean you can see anytime. In fact, he will be joining us on the Côte."

D'Artois released her hand, but his eyes still held hers compellingly.

"Well, let me congratulate you on your soirée. It is charming," the duke went on. "I'm sorry I missed you earlier, but our good friend Sheikh Farahet had you monopolized at the time, and I did not dare intrude on your conversation."

A man with a potbelly and a shock of drab, gray brown hair came over to join them. "Ah, I see that you have finally met our young hostess, Jean. Isn't she gorgeous?"

Artois nodded. "She is, indeed."

Rosalie extended her hand. "Senator Buchin, it's nice to see you tonight. I'm sorry Philip couldn't come—I remember we were such good friends when he visited us in Martinique when we were both little."

Senator Buchin—from Connecticut, Rosalie recalled, such a quaint name!—laughed. "I suspect you'd better not stress the good-friends note that much the next time you see him. Now that he's out of law school, he's about equally occupied with clerking in a Wall Street firm and sparking a young lady named Claire Streeter. I suspect that he's going to be pretty thoroughly married in the next few months, and from what I've seen of Miss Claire, I doubt she cares much for the idea of my boy having had good friends who look like you, no matter how long ago it was."

The music was beginning, a slow, tempting beat. La Farge took Rosalie's hand and kissed it.

"Shall we dance, my darling?"

Rosalie glanced across the room at her mother for approval. Rosalie thought her mother should have the first dance with him, but saw that Jacqueline was, by this time, completely wrapped up in Paul.

La Farge guided his daughter onto the dance floor, and pressed her young body gently to his own. He held her like a flower in his arms and twirled her across the floor, showing her off to all.

An admiring remark about the handsome pair caused Jacqueline to turn and look at her husband and daughter. Moments before, Jacqueline's only thoughts had been for Paul. Now her gaze concentrated on her husband's body. She felt a pang of jealousy as he pressed his face against Rosalie's and whispered something in her ear.

Why, she thought, anger rising inside her, why does he continue to ignore me?

Jacqueline looked away and turned to face Paul, whom she saw was looking with great interest at Rosalie.

A woman standing nearby leaned over and whispered to Jacqueline, "Armand is still one handsome *type*. If only my Gaston looked like that!"

Jacqueline gave her a catty look.

"Looks, my dear Cécile, can be very deceiving."

"Can they now?" The voice was Armand's. "Looking at you, my dear, I wouldn't say that was true. You are everything you seem to be: intelligent, *warm* and *loving*."

He put stress on the last two words, smiling slyly as she fought to keep her composure.

"Where is Rosalie?" she asked, her voice almost hostile.

"There!" He pointed to the dance floor. "There she is, our little girl, dancing with the President. You wouldn't, by any chance, care to dance with me? I don't think Paul would mind."

She looked up angrily at him, her dark eyes flashing and moist with restrained rage.

"No, thank you," she said. "I think I can deny myself that pleasure."

She turned her back on him and walked away, leaving the two men standing alone together.

La Farge stepped away from Paul and focused his attention once again on his daughter.

Rosalie winked mischievously at her father as she waltzed by in the arms of her distinguished partner. La Farge winked back.

He stood watching the two dance, touched that his old friend had chosen to come to Rosalie's soirée. Ever since a serious illness six months earlier, the President had not been very active, except for attending to the compulsory affairs of state. La Farge felt that in the President's own refined way, he was showing the depth of his gratitude for all the help and support La Farge had given France. In World War I, La Farge had become, at the age of twenty-three, France's top ace, having shot down seventy-two German aircraft. In World War II, La Farge had given a fortune to support the cause of de Gaulle's Free French.

He watched approvingly as the two waltzed away, twirling round and round to the lively Strauss music. The President's figure towered over Rosalie as they danced, making her seem like a tiny doll. La Farge could see her lips moving, and he wondered what she was saying to her austere companion.

"My father and I admire you greatly, and I would vote for you if I could. But I promise to do so as soon as I am old enough."

"I can hardly believe that your father admires anyone else but you, my dear, but it is indeed a great honor to know that one as lovely as yourself thinks so highly of me. I am flattered."

They were brusquely interrupted.

"Excuse me, Monsieur le Président, but would you allow me to dance with this charming young lady?"

The voice was a familiar one. Rosalie froze, almost afraid to look around. They stopped dancing. The President turned to face the intruder.

"Well, that is up to the young lady to decide. Who will it be, mademoiselle?"

"Well, Monsieur le Président, I would so love to dance with you again, but I am afraid that the rest of the ladies present would not appreciate that, since they are all hoping to dance with you at least once this evening. I think, as a good hostess, I should allow them the privilege."

The President smiled, amused by the girl's tact.

"I can see that you are as charming and tactful as your father, perhaps even more so where charm is concerned. Might I say that is the nicest dismissal I've ever had? I even enjoyed it, coming from someone as lovely as you, my dear."

"Oh no, Monsieur le Président. I didn't mean to—"

He did not let her finish. "Shh, my dear. Don't be disturbed. I am pleased to have had the honor of this one dance. I shall treasure the memory always."

Rosalie felt she might have hurt the President's feelings. He was her idol, a man she respected more than anyone else except her father. She held the President's hand tenderly in her own.

"I would love to dance with you again, *mon Président*, tonight or any other night."

He smiled again and patted her hand. "I will be sure to hold you to your promise, Rosalie."

The intruder tapped the President once again on the shoulder.

"I beg your pardon, sir, but the music has begun."

The President smiled. "I will leave you now to the prince," he said.

Rosalie turned to look at the young man standing beside her. "I imagine he confused you with someone else, eh, Ahmed? Surely no prince would be so ill-mannered."

He ignored her comment and without a word took her in his arms and whirled her rapidly across the floor.

"Rosalie, how beautiful you look tonight! How charming. I'm truly happy I came. I wouldn't have missed it for the world." He bent his head and pressed his cheek tenderly against hers. "Do you remember the last time we saw each other?"

"Yes, I remember." How could she ever forget that glorious evening? The night they had spent together in the Beverly Hills Hotel, locked in each other's arms. That had happened almost eight months ago. She had been with her father to the premiere of a film in New York. They had gone on to attend a New Year's Eve party in Beverly Hills. Ahmed had been her first lover, her only lover up to now.

His eyes locked with hers as she looked up.

"Oh, Ahmed. Please let's go out into the garden."

The orchestra was playing "La Vie en Rose." It was a favorite of hers, and she melted in his arms as he danced with her, leading her out the door and into the garden.

He pulled her hard against him and kissed her passionately. "Oh, Zalie, my sweet, why don't we go away someplace together, just you and me? I've missed you so. Ever since that night, I can't put you out of my mind. I want you every night. I want you every day." His voice changed almost to a whisper. "I want you now."

"Ahmed, I want you too; but not here. Someone might see us. Let's go to my room."

"But your father! And what about Berthe? She never lets you out of her sight."

She thought for a moment, and then her face lit up. "I know what. I'll ask Papa if I can leave now with you for St. Tropez, instead of in the morning on the plane with him and our guests."

"Will he let you? Drive all the way to the Côte? Alone with a man? At this late hour?"

"Oh, come on, Ahmed. Tonight I am only two glorious months away from being eighteen. This is my debut, and I'm sure that I can be trusted alone with a man, now that I am a grown woman." She winked at him and he laughed.

Chapter Two

Paris-Valence, August 1962

The silver Porsche streaked through the narrow Paris streets. The sunroof was open, the wind blowing their hair as they sped through the light traffic. The air was cool, not a typical August night; but the stars were bright and the moon almost a perfect circle in the dark blue sky. From the car's radio came the sound of Charles Aznavour's voice.

"Can you sing, Ahmed?"

"What, me? Sing? Of course. Who do you think I am?"

"A man who can't sing, that's who." Rosalie giggled as she pulled her feet up under her.

"One day I'll sing you a song, young lady, that'll make you never want to hear Aznavour again."

"You mean it will actually destroy my eardrums? I didn't think you would be *that* bad."

Ahmed gave her an exasperated look. "Would you stop clowning, please? I can't drive with all this noise. It's distracting me." He switched off the radio. "There. That's much better.

Just the two of us again, less one much-overrated, sawed-off Basque tenor."

"Aznavour is not just a tenor. He's a genius, a real artist. And he isn't that tiny either. You'll see when you meet him. Papa has invited him to Colombier, and I hope you will try to be polite when you meet him."

"Hmm, I think I will have a headache that day or maybe I'll even break a leg. All I know is that I won't be around for the big event."

"I can't believe it. Do I get the feeling that you are jealous, Ahmed?"

"Ha! Me jealous? That's a laugh. Listen, my dear, if you believe that you can make me jealous, you're crazy. I must admit though, it did bother me some the way you and that old goat were dancing together."

"You can't mean the President, can you? No, you couldn't be jealous of him, too. Could you?" Her tone was teasing.

"Oh, Zalie, why don't you just be a good girl and let me concentrate on my driving?"

She leaned over and kissed him on the cheek. "I love sports cars, but why do they have to make them with seats like these? I can't even get close to you." She ran her fingers through his hair. "Ahmed?"

"Yes?"

"Oh, never mind, now isn't the time."

"Come on, tell me. What were you about to say?"

"I'll tell you later when we come to our first pipi-stop."

"Our first what?"

"Pipi-stop, silly. You know—boys and girls both do it."

"Oh, for heaven's sake, where'd you get that word?"

"I made it up. Don't you like it?"

"Rosalie, will you please stop talking? I just made a wrong turn. I knew I should've taken the Autoroute instead of these back roads. The next town I come to, I'm getting back on the highway. At least then we'll get to Lyon before dawn."

"Lyon? Why Lyon? Why are you taking that route?"

"Do you know a better way, Miss Michelin of 1962?"

"Maybe I do and maybe I don't, and then again, maybe I'd tell you if you asked me nicely."

"I'll stick to my own plan. With yours, we might end up on the Atlantic coast instead of the Mediterranean."

"Okay, okay, but promise me we won't stop in Lyon. It's all factories in Lyon—you know, mills and things. Couldn't we stop in someplace like Givors or Valence? I know the cutest little *auberge* just outside Valence, and it's right on the Rhône too. It's really beautiful there. Lots of weeping willows and swans and things. There's even a little park nearby." Her voice was filled with excitement as she spoke. "Oh Ahmed, let's. I *know* you'd like it."

"By *just* outside Valence, do you mean a couple of miles? Or halfway to the Italian border?"

"It's just a few miles *before* Valence, I think."

"You think? Rosalie, look, we're tired, and I myself am even a little hungry. Couldn't we just stop in Lyon, where we'd be sure to find someplace open, have a snack, and then go to bed?"

"I don't like Lyon. *You* can sleep in Lyon if you want to. *I'm* going on to Valence, even if I have to walk."

Ahmed burst out laughing. "You know, you are the funniest person I know, even when you pretend to be angry. All right, I give in. We'll drive as far as Valence, but only on one condition—that we stop in Lyon first for something to eat. I'm starved." He turned to look at her and frowned, trying to look menacing. "You know, of course, mademoiselle, the only reason I'm giving in to you is that I have an ulterior motive." He growled and looked cross-eyed at her. "You get the picture yet, mademoiselle? Of the motive?"

"Look *out,* Ahmed—you almost clipped that Peugeot. Now who's being silly?"

"I didn't even come close to that car. From the passenger's seat, it's well known that one's perspective is distorted."

"If you'd come any closer, we'd have been on the meat slab in the morning instead of in sunny St. Tropez."

"Bah, what a horrible thought to have on such a beautiful

night!'' He reached over and fumbled through the glove compartment, looking for the right tape to play.

''Here, let's listen to a little Mozart for a while, okay?''

Rosalie nodded. She liked Mozart. She leaned back against the black leather seat, relaxing in anticipation of the music. It was the haunting andante of Mozart's Concerto no. 21, a favorite of hers, with its romantic violins and the airy sound of the harpsichord. She wondered what he must have been like, that boy genius of music. She toyed with his name, repeating it over and over again in her mind, in rhythm with the andante: ''Wolfgang—Amadeus—Mozart.''

She stole a glance at Ahmed; his face was rigid, eyes fixed on the road. This was the perfect music for lovers, she thought. She smiled, remembering the kiss she and Ahmed had shared earlier in the courtyard, and stretched languidly in her seat, like a cat stretching itself before a fireplace. She closed her eyes once again, her mind clinging to every note of the andante, and fell asleep enraptured by the sweetness of the music.

People were preparing to leave the ball, standing in line for their hats and wraps, exchanging promises to see each other on the Côte. The moon shone through the ballroom windows, paling the shadows cast by the chandeliers. The few remaining people on the dance floor seemed to gather some of the moonlight around them, like a halo of magnetic energy, as they whirled in a last wild tango.

La Farge felt like retiring. He had to be up early the following morning—this morning, actually—to leave for his estate on the Côte d'Azur. He stifled a yawn as he instructed Max to attend to his guests' needs, and then went upstairs.

He undressed slowly, carefully creasing and folding his trousers. He hung them over the back of a chair along with his tie. He hung the jacket over the mahogany valet stand next to his bed and threw the shirt, along with his socks and underwear, into the brown leather hamper next to the bureau. He rummaged through the drawers of the bureau and decided on a pale blue pair of pajamas. He placed the jacket over his left arm and threw the bottoms angrily across the room.

Damn that valet! he told himself. I'll fire him yet if he doesn't start doing what he's supposed to do. James has been with me for nearly thirty years, and he still doesn't know his ass from a loop. He should know by now that I never wear the damn bottoms; keeps me too confined. I can't breathe with the damn thing tied at my waist all night.

He rang the small white buzzer next to his bed.

He was still muttering angrily to himself when James entered, carrying a tray with a large bottle of Vittel mineral water on it.

"You rang, sir? I am sorry. I did not know that you'd already left the party. I was not expecting you to come up until much later, sir."

"Stop the damned babbling, man, and put that tray down. The way you're just standing there, you make it seem as if it were stuck to you permanently."

James could tell that his employer was not entirely pleased.

"Is there something wrong, sir?"

"Wrong? Yes, there's something *wrong*. I'll tell you what's *wrong*. Just put that damned tray down first."

The valet did as he was told. La Farge resumed speaking.

"How long have you been with me now, James?"

"Thirty years, sir." He raised a finger to quiet La Farge, who was about to speak. "That is, twenty-nine years, ten months and one week, sir."

La Farge looked at him sourly. "Well, I can see that you *do* have a memory. No matter how small or insignificant, you *can* remember—that is, *when* you want and *about* what you want. Isn't that so? Speak up, man. Have you lost your tongue?"

James was glancing at the brown leather hamper. He could see the blue pajama bottom partly hanging out of it. He did not have to guess why his employer was so upset.

"I see that you found another pajama bottom in the bureau. I'm sorry, sir. It was an oversight. It won't happen again. It's just that since Mademoiselle Rosalie bought that pair *especially* for you on your birthday last month, I thought you might have wanted to keep them. Just this once."

La Farge smiled, touched by his daughter's thoughtfulness. "You mean *she* got me those? I don't remember her giving them to me. I wonder *you* do with a memory as bad as yours."

He cocked an apologetic eyebrow at James. James pretended not to notice.

"Don't you remember, sir? You were in Geneva on the day of your birthday, and Mademoiselle Rosalie was still in Cap d'Antibes with Madame. She bought them for you on the Côte and sent them by parcel post. I put them away in your drawer with the card she sent." He walked over to the bureau and poked around searching for the card.

"See? Here it is. Just where I put it. I just forgot to tell you, sir. You only got back yesterday."

La Farge patted him on the back. "Okay, *mon vieux*. Let it go. I am dying of thirst. How about pouring me my brandy?"

The bottle of Rémy Martin, along with two large snifters, was standing on a small silver tray on the bureau. James poured the brandy to about one fourth the capacity of each glass, and wiped the rim of the bottle before replacing the cork.

He handed one glass to La Farge. "There you are, monsieur, your cognac."

He waited quietly as La Farge sniffed the bouquet. "Hmm, delicious! Nothing like a cognac to perk you up before going to bed."

"And nothing like a tall glass of Vittel to keep the bowels open." That was James's ritual joke.

"That's right, old boy. Nothing like the two to keep a man perked up and regular." He squinted in the darkness at James, the small night-light barely lighting the room enough for him to see him.

"You could use a little of the same yourself, my dear fellow. I find you a little on the greenish side lately. Here, have a sip of brandy." He handed James the second glass. It'll do you good. You can have your Vittel later, on your own time."

James nodded and raised the glass to his lips. This had been going on since the first night he had come to work for La Farge.

"Keep it warm, James. I'll be back in a minute."

La Farge showered and shaved and dusted some powder between his legs. He hated getting chafed. "All that dancing and the tight pants,'' he muttered. ''I'll have to have a talk with that damn English tailor. The next time that infidel asks me, 'What side do you carry on, sir?' I'll just have to show him that I'm well built and carry a damn lot on both sides.''

The yellowish bristles of the shaving brush squatted out in the cup in front of him. He wondered why he went to all the trouble of shaving twice, especially since he did not have a very heavy beard. Habit, he supposed. When they were first married, Jacqueline used to complain about the roughness of his beard against her skin, and he had got into the habit of shaving at night. He wondered what the hell good it had done him lately. The closest he had come to Jacqueline in the past eighteen and a half years was tonight, when he had imagined her naked.

James appeared in the doorway of the bathroom carrying the blue pajama shirt. ''Your pajamas, sir.'' His face bore a slight smirk.

La Farge gave him an annoyed look. ''Is the brandy ready yet?''

''For some time now, monsieur; it is almost too warm.''

La Farge trudged barefoot across the blue carpet to the brandy-warmer on the night table by his bed. He dunked his little finger into the liquid. ''Brandy is never too warm, James; just as a good valet is never too indispensable.''

He got into bed and pulled the light satin sheet up over his legs. ''Damn it, James, you tell Madame La Farge or Berthe, or whoever the hell it is that takes care of these things, that in the summer I don't want any more damned embroidered satin sheets on my bed. I'm a man, and I want to be able to sleep on material suited for a man. In the morning you can pack them up and send them over to Archbishop Lernier's. I'm sure he'll find them to his taste.''

James drained his glass and disappeared into the bathroom to clean up a bit. He washed the brush and cup and replaced the old razor with a new one.

He grinned as he pictured Archbishop Lernier's pink, puffy face. A satin-sheet type, that one, true enough. He wondered what La Farge would say or do if he were actually to send the sheets. After all, he said, ''James, when I say *do* something, *do* it; don't ask me again, just *do* it." James chuckled at the thought. When he had finished tidying up, he left by the door to the dressing room, assuming that La Farge would be asleep by now and taking care not to wake him. His hand closed over the doorknob.

"Good night, James. Stop sneaking around like that. You might wake up the whole neighborhood."

"Good night, monsieur, I thought you were already asleep."

The door closed softly as James left. La Farge turned out the light and plumped up the feather pillow.

It was late and he was tired, but too many thoughts were swimming in his head for him to fall asleep.

He reached for a cigar on his night table beside him and lit it. He lay back on the pillows, his hands folded beneath his head, his eyes following the coils of smoke as they rose and dissipated. In the drifting smoke he pictured Jacqueline and Rosalie at the ball.

How beautiful they were tonight, he thought. Zalie's a miracle, no doubt about it. And Jacqueline's held up pretty well over the last twenty-five years . . . though she's ice now, not fire, the way she was in Martinique. . . .

Chapter Three

Martinique, May 1937

He sailed into the harbor of Fort de France at exactly 3:00 P.M. that Sunday afternoon. The sun was hot and cheerful on the shimmering bay. A group of young black men had gathered on the old cement wharf to greet the disembarked tourists, and stood huddled together beating out a glorious tune on their cut-down steel drums. Crude straw hats and bandanas of bright madras fabric adorned their heads, and they smiled broadly as they played.

As La Farge took a deep breath, the salty air filled his nostrils. He held it a long time, trying in one breath to capture and hold the mood and mystery of the sunny island. He handed the waiting porters some money and told them to take his bags to the Hotel St. Jacques.

The Matouba, where he had stayed during two of his previous visits, was no longer his style. He was now an extremely prosperous gentleman. He had arrived with his valet, his car, his trunks laden with dozens of fine white suits and his pockets filled with Havana cigars. He had enjoyed Cuba, but something told him that he would find what he was looking for in Martinique.

His spectacular flying career during the Great War had brought him in touch with many prominent and influential men—including Charles Buchin, an American industrialist serving as liaison officer with the French forces—and some of them had seen that it would do them no harm to be associated with and to help one of France's most decorated heroes. Though just twenty-one when the Armistice was signed, he was burning with ambition and dreams for the future, and used his contacts and his reputation shrewdly, going from success to success.

He had used a small legacy from his father to buy some rundown vineyards in newly liberated Alsace-Lorraine, and with great determination and a generous share of luck had managed to produce some of the finest wines that ever came from that region. He soon bought other vineyards, and then bought into a gold-mining scheme and a real estate project in Paris. Before long, his wealth had grown enormously; enough so that he could now lie back and relax for the rest of his days if he wanted to.

But La Farge was not completely satisfied with his lot. He wanted more, and his dreams were far bigger than his accomplishments thus far. Now, at forty, he looked thirty. He had traveled the far corners of the earth, had bedded Italian princesses, had had affairs with several ladies of the Parisian aristocracy, and had amused himself with attractive women wherever he had roamed. But he had not found a woman he wanted to marry. It was not that he hadn't considered it on several occasions; it was just that in the end they had never measured up to his expectations of what the woman he was to make his wife should be.

He had come to Martinique this time to stay—until he had succeeded in his dream. His desire was to become a planter. He had grown tired of the frenetic, pompous ways of the great cities of Europe and wished to live for a while in the relaxed surroundings of an island, at the same time making it profitable. This had been a dream of his ever since he was a boy, and he felt exhilarated by the fact that that dream was about to come true.

An encounter at Deauville with the aging but still hale

Charles Buchin had sparked the idea. "My boy Jim's taken a fool notion to run off to the tropics—bought himself a plantation in Martinique, place called Belle Fleur, for Christ's sake. If the fever or the clap doesn't ruin him, the rum will," Buchin had grumbled.

La Farge had condoled with his old acquaintance, but had inwardly taken fire. A plantation in Martinique—perfect! Leisure, sunshine, yet enough of a challenge to his managerial skills so that he would not vegetate. And above all, Martinique was French; La Farge's travels had firmly reinforced the standard French assumption that his country's ways and language were the only truly civilized ones.

He would inspect this Belle Fleur place, and, if it suited him, persuade young Buchin that it would be to his advantage to sell. If in realizing his plans he was able to oblige Charles Buchin by dislodging his son from his tropical languor, so much the better; it never hurt to do someone powerful a favor. He hinted at his plans and Buchin gratefully offered to write to young James and let him know when La Farge would arrive in Fort de France.

Now, after registering at the hotel desk, he decided to stop in at the cool, shadowed bar before going up to his room. It seemed to him that he could still feel the motion of the ship, and his brief walk through the port's streets had reminded him of the fierceness of the tropical sun; he could use a drink. He sat down on one of the stools and ordered a rum punch.

The swarthy man behind the bar wiped his sweaty face with his shirt sleeve.

"Some heat, right, monsieur?" He poured cane syrup into a small glass and then squeezed half a lime over it. He shoved the glass in front of La Farge, poured in a shot glass of white rum, and stirred. "There you are, monsieur. That's four francs."

La Farge surveyed the bar lounge. Three couples sat at two tables pushed together, talking and laughing, apparently drunk. A third table was occupied by an older man in a white uniform. A government official, La Farge guessed; from the width of the man's behind, doubtless a desk-bound one, costumed like an empire-builder. The small band in the far corner of the room was setting up its instruments for the cocktail hour. Two Créole waitresses, heads swathed in bright bandanas and dressed in white ruffled skirts and blouses, bustled about setting out ashtrays and table settings.

One of them bent down to pick up a dropped napkin; as she did so, her thighs were bared, the skin smooth and brown as chocolate pudding. She turned and looked up and her eyes caught his.

She is very pretty, La Farge thought. And ready for a white *métropolitain* with his pockets full of money.

She stood up slowly and pretended to have to fix her garter, exposing still more of her thigh, this time from a different angle. Her catlike eyes swept over him with such intensity that he seemed to feel their caress. He pretended not to notice, and turned his attention once again to his drink.

One must, after all, be serious, he reflected. I am here to embark on a new course of life; and, if things turn out so, to find a woman who'd satisfy me as a wife. No adventures just now; time enough for that later. . . .

"Do you mind if I join you?"

"*Pardon?*" La Farge looked around to see who it was. The man standing behind him, dressed in a light blue silk suit, had his hand out.

"Welcome to Martinique, monsieur. You must be Armand La Farge." He spoke again, slowly, so that La Farge could understand him.

His grammar was good, but his accent demeaned the French language. La Farge guessed he was an American.

"I am James Buchin," the newcomer said, smiling at La Farge, who, even seated, seemed much taller than the stranger. "My father is Charles Buchin of the Buchin Arms Company in Connecticut. He told me you would be staying here."

"Oh yes! How stupid of me not to have seen the resemblance. Your father and I ran into each other in Deauville, and he told me all about the Belle Fleur plantation. It is yours, is it not?"

"Yes, it is. A very foolish investment I made six years ago. It has cost me a mint so far."

La Farge waved a hand, motioning for him to sit down.

The man pointed to a small, red door behind the bar. "Will you join me at my table instead?"

La Farge shrugged. "Fine with me."

Buchin clapped his hands and hailed the young waiter across the room. "Marcel, would you have Antoine serve us our drinks in the back room?"

La Farge was surprised to find a cozy little room behind the bar, from where it was apparent Buchin had been observing him.

Two long, red leather booths took up most of the space in the tiny room. The narrow, white marble and wrought-iron table held a lavish display of hors d'oeuvres and tropical fruits.

La Farge sampled one of the smaller hors d'oeuvres as he sat down. The tiny shell-shaped fritter was filled with hot West Indian chicken peppers. He tried one of a different variety, as a chaser for the first, but that one was even hotter. Buchin, seeing his guest's discomfort, ordered a bottle of champagne.

"Dom Pérignon, please, Marcel." He tried one of the fritters himself. It did not seem to bother him.

This annoyed La Farge. Damned American, who does he think he is anyway, showing off like a child? So what! He can eat hot food. So much for Buchin. He noticed, however, a reddening of Buchin's earlobes, and the sudden moisture in his steel blue eyes. Hmm, La Farge told himself, either he's remembering a sad movie or else those chicken peppers are doing their work.

The two men were suffering, but gamely silent, by the time the waiter returned carrying the champagne in a large silver bucket, filled to the brim with cracked ice. The ice had a yellowish cast to it, and La Farge wondered if some cat had pissed into it. He had once owned a cat which every chance it got would piss into the champagne bucket and all over the ice. Finally, he had had to give the animal away because one day it pissed into Bishop Lernier's glass of champagne, which he had momentarily rested next to the champagne bucket. Lernier, for all his dainty mannerisms and politic suaveness, had expressed himself with a dock-worker's bluntness. That had been the end of poor Fido—a rotten joke, giving a cat a dog's name.

The waiter wiped the glasses and held them up to the light. "Would you like me to open the champagne now, monsieur?"

Buchin nodded.

"Say, waiter. You wouldn't happen to know if the owner has a cat named Fido, would you?"

The waiter and Buchin both gave La Farge a sharp look.

"No, monsieur. I do not think the proprietor even owns a cat."

La Farge dipped his finger into the cracked ice. He smelled the tip of his finger; the odor was pungent, but not like anything he had ever smelled before—not cat piss.

"Where do you get your ice, boy? In the sewers?"

The waiter looked offended. "No, monsieur."

He thumbed the toadstool-shaped cork from the bottle and La Farge ducked as it whizzed by his face. He could have sworn the man had aimed for him.

"We don't have any sewers in Martinique."

"Of course you don't have sewers in Martinique, you don't need them. You serve sewage in buckets around my fucking champagne." La Farge shoved the ice bucket into the waiter's hand. "Here, take it back and bring us some clean ice and another bottle of champagne. You can take this one to the manager and his cat."

The waiter rolled his eyes and hissed as he left the room.

La Farge turned to look at Buchin, who was by this time laughing helplessly.

La Farge nudged him with his elbow. "What do you think was in that bucket, my friend?"

"Martinique water, that's all," Buchin managed to gasp. "Depending on where it comes from, it can quench your thirst, cure you of malaria, feed you, or dissolve your guts. I think they figured that since you're not a barbarous American like me, you wouldn't be popping the ice into your wine, so it didn't matter where it had been before they froze it. What on earth made you wonder if there was cat piss in it?"

La Farge told him of Fido's indiscretion with the priest's champagne, and the waiter, returning with a new bottle—or possibly the same one, thriftily recorked—of Dom Pérignon, and a bucket of odorless, colorless ice, lifted his lip in a discreet sneer at the spectacle of the American patron whooping and pounding on the table.

In spite of the hilarity and the champagne, La Farge managed to get from James Buchin some of the basic facts about the Belle Fleur plantation before they parted. The diminutive American was no fool, and had done nothing obviously stupid, but La Farge sensed that the property held unexploited opportunities. Buchin undertook to show La Farge around Belle Fleur the next morning, and arranged to call for him at the hotel at ten.

Buchin poked his head around the doorway of La Farge's bathroom to observe the Frenchman supine in the tub with a cigar in his mouth and a glass of Dom Pérignon in his hand.

"I see that I find you exactly where we left off last night."

La Farge nodded and motioned for him to sit down. "I haven't slept all night, thinking. I have a feeling I'll like the Belle Fleur," he said, rubbing a little of the champagne on to his narrow mustache. "Hmm, I love that smell. I feel lucky today, as always," he added, smiling and rubbing his palms together. He pulled himself from the tub and toweled vigorously, then strode into the bedroom.

"Bring some extra clothes with you, Armand. We are invited later to the Férriers' for a beach picnic and then for dinner. I took it upon myself to accept for you."

"Well, now, that was quick. Do you mean *the* Férriers, the sugar people?"

"Correction, old man. Sugar and rum. More famous, though, for their daughter, Jacqueline—sweeter than sugar, more heady than rum; a real stunner, you'll see. They heard you had just arrived, and that you were taking an interest in Belle Fleur. And well, since their plantation is just a couple of miles away . . ." Buchin did not finish his sentence. La Farge had jammed some trunks and a suit into a bag, and was already heading for the door.

"Let's be on our way, then. I can hardly wait to see my new property."

At half past one that afternoon, the two closed the deal. La

Farge was now the new owner of the Belle Fleur plantation and a very happy man indeed.

They arrived half an hour later at the Férrier plantation, La Rose. As the car approached, massive wooden gates were swung wide by a young black wearing a wide-brimmed straw hat with a red band around it.

They drove slowly, admiring the lushness of the estate. Two rows of tall royal palms flanked the pebbled driveway; high, thick hedges of oleander, clipped back and trimmed in perfect sequence, lined the driveway. Their delicate pink and white blossoms struck a sharp contrast with the vivid yellows and reds of the hibiscus bushes behind them. An overwhelming smell of jasmine hung in the air, but they could not see the bushes, which were concealed behind the hedges. They came to a sharp turn in the road and into sight of the main house of La Rose plantation.

The white mansion sat on the top of a bluff, high and wide against the clear blue midsummer sky, with huge, curved terraces like parapets. Clumps of red and pink bougainvillea covered the balconies and arbors around the house, and a sea of buttercups along the cliffs brilliantly reflected the early afternoon sun.

The stone walls surrounding the property, built early in the last century by slaves, were now almost completely covered by masses of tiny corallita blossoms, and ferns grew from the crevices. La Farge's eyes fixed on the mansion with its magnificent filigreed balconies and carved pillars, and a feeling of anticipation came over him.

The beach that Jacqueline Férrier had chosen for her picnic was just below the bluff to the side of the house, gold-sanded, lined with coconut trees and red flamboyants, their bright foliage creating a natural umbrella for the festive gathering.

At once, La Farge saw the beautiful creature standing in the shade of the tall trees, lithe and brown-skinned. Her long, chestnut brown hair hung in thick coils down her back to her narrow waist, its rich glints complementing the pale primrose of her bathing costume.

Her slanted eyes roamed appraisingly over La Farge.

"Jacqueline, let me present Armand La Farge," Buchin said. "Armand, this is Jacqueline Férrier, our hostess."

Buchin kissed her affectionately on the cheek. "Well, Armand, what do you think? Isn't she quite as lovely as I said she was?"

La Farge looked directly into Jacqueline's eyes as he replied. "Old boy, you criminally understated the lady's beauty. But it is understandable that a man—any man—might have difficulty finding words to describe such rare exquisiteness."

She smiled, accepting the compliment, and offered him her hand to be kissed. He felt her staring at him and looked up. His eyes met hers and held boldly.

He was aware that his stature and coloring—the big-boned, fair-haired, ruddy-complexioned heritage of his Norman ancestors—made him as exotic to her as she was to him. And, his experience suggested, perhaps as attractive. . . .

Her father was by the buffet table. He had been one of the first to spot the new arrivals. He watched closely as the three strolled off together to the water's edge to join Madame Férrier, who was wading in the surf.

La Farge was introduced to the delicate, dark-skinned woman. Her tiny ankles and wrists, her firm rounded hips and dark skin suggested a romanticist's view of the ideal blend of African and European bloodlines—romance here made fact.

He recalled an article he had read about the Duc d'Artreuse, her father. The duke had married a black woman from Martinique, and they had had a daughter, Mélanie d'Artreuse, now Mélanie Férrier, wife of Henri Férrier, sugar and rum millionaire. She could well be proud of both heritages, La Farge considered, observing her.

The resemblance between mother and daughter was evident; though Jacqueline was considerably lighter in complexion, and her hair was straighter and finer in texture than her mother's.

Mélanie Férrier took Armand's big hand in her small one as she greeted him. "It is a great pleasure for us, Monsieur La Farge, that you accepted our invitation. Having you here is indeed an honor."

La Farge was well aware that the honor was not conferred by the presence of a successful and wealthy businessman but by the fact that, half a lifetime ago, he had managed to destroy six dozen—just half a gross, though the newspaper accounts had never put it in such a tradesmanlike way—German aircraft and a good number of their occupants. It was curious, he thought, that a man might spend almost twenty years amassing a fortune and enriching others in consequence—to say nothing of producing wines which added something enduring to civilized comfort—and still be remembered and respected primarily for his skill as a youthful killer. The times had made heroes of such as he; and there was a new generation waiting to be idolized in the murderous drama whose prologue was even now, on this pellucid day, being played bloodily in Spain and China. It came to him that his wish to make a success of the Belle Fleur property was a retreat from a world again spiraling into the madness which had inspired and infected him as a boy—his personal fortification, very like the line of concrete and cannon that idiot Maginot had caused to be dug along the borders of France. The Maginot Line was a perfect defense against the armies of the Kaiser or Frederick the Great; but the Kaiser was chopping wood in Holland, and Adolf Hitler might well be less obliging about his methods of *revanche*.

All the same, Voltaire had said it: cultivate your garden. To make Belle Fleur flourish, to take to himself a wife who could match his zest for life—that would be something that would last, and more than most men got out of their existence. He bowed to Jacqueline's mother and kissed her outstretched hand.

She went on, "I am very grateful to Monsieur Buchin for letting us know you were in Martinique. I'm glad you could come—and so, I am sure, is my husband." She turned to greet the man who now approached them.

Henri Férrier was considerably, though not at first sight obviously, older than his wife: tall, bearded, with a meticulously waxed mustache and deep-set green eyes. His chest and shoulders were wide, his belly flat and trim, his face chiseled and tanned. He welcomed La Farge with a strong handshake and a pat on the shoulder.

La Farge excused himself to his host, and went to change into his swimsuit and join the bathers.

The water was a pale turquoise, darkening gradually as it

stretched to the horizon; the sun bit into his back and shoulders. James Buchin was sporting in the placid surf with one of the younger female guests, whose lush figure appeared to be straining her rubberized swimsuit to its capacity. One more dive through the waves, La Farge thought, and she'll pop it like a balloon. How very American, to play sexual games when there wasn't a chance of collecting one's winnings on the spot.

He sat down on the sand and lazily stretched out, his hands behind his head. He could feel himself sinking, drowning in the peacefulness around him. He was about to doze off when he heard the sharp, snapping sound of a twig breaking. He heard Jacqueline's voice, clear and melodious.

"Do you always like to be by yourself?"

He opened one eye and squinted up at her. She was standing no further than three feet from him, dripping wet. He liked what he saw. He could almost taste her with his eyes. She was flushed from her swim, and fresh as a morning flower. Her long, wet hair lay smooth over her ears, curling in flat, snakelike coils along her neck and golden shoulders. Her cheeks were pink from the sun, her smooth skin shining as the tiny droplets of water made their way down her arms and legs.

He started to get to his feet.

"No, please don't. You look so comfortable lying there. I thought you could use some company."

He patted the ground next to him. "As a matter of fact, I was just about to fall asleep, so some company would be welcome."

She gave an exaggerated shrug, setting the splendid breasts, caressed rather than concealed by her bathing suit, quivering—intentionally, as he was suddenly and delightedly aware. "If *l'as des as de la guerre mondiale* is on the point of falling asleep, it will surely take more than the prattle of a provincial quadroon girl to rouse him. I prescribe, as any conscientious physician might, a regimen of ocean bathing."

La Farge followed her into the water; he relished its cool touch on his genitals, calming him yet at the same time exciting him with the realization that Jacqueline must be experiencing the same sensation as she gave herself to the embrace of the sea.

They swam away from the shore, separately at first, then closer, surface-diving like porpoises.

There was a sharp bite on his foot. It startled him.

"Aiee! What the . . . ?" At first he thought it was a fish; he had heard tales of man-eating sharks and barracuda in these waters, and was not eager to be today's menu. Then he noticed some bubbles rising between his legs; sharks, he knew, did not exhale. He dove and grabbed Jacqueline by the leg as she was about to swim away. She tried to pry it free, but he was stronger, and he pulled her hard against his body, crushing her against him.

He pressed his lips fiercely against hers, and forced them apart with his tongue. At first she offered some resistance and tried to free herself, but then relaxed slowly and first yielded, then wrapped her long legs around his and pressed herself to him. Slowly, silently, they floated to the top, mouths joined in a watery kiss. They surfaced gasping for breath, still holding on to each other, as though welded.

They did not speak, or need to. They knew that what they felt was not a passing attraction. Their hunger for each other had not yet been appeased; it would be, they knew, and soon.

Jacqueline gathered up her things from the beach without a word and ran up the sandy path to the bluff. La Farge watched her disappear over the top, then gathered up his towel and sandals and walked over to where his hosts were sitting under the flamboyant trees.

"I noticed you and my daughter together," Férrier said. "I am pleased that she finds you agreeable. I have read great things about you, monsieur, and I admire the man I've read about. Please feel that you are always welcome at our plantation."

La Farge extended his hand in response.

"I shall be pleased to accept your hospitality. Needless to say, you and Madame and Mademoiselle Férrier will always be equally welcome at Belle Fleur."

"Thank you. Young Buchin was just telling me you bought the place from him. Nice piece of property. I can't see why he sold it, though. I always told him that with the right architect to redesign the main house and a good overseer to run the place, he could have had himself the second-best plantation on the island. Second to mine." Férrier smiled proudly, waving a hand in the direction of the house.

"I hope I will make of Belle Fleur the best that it can be," La Farge said. "Whether that is second-best, who knows?"

Férrier smiled. "I suspect that it is not in your nature, my dear La Farge, to accept the second-best in anything." His eyes drifted toward the bluff over which his daughter had disappeared. "In any case, you are bound to do better with Belle Fleur than young Buchin has. A charming fellow, quite cultivated for an American, but not—at least about this—serious. For him it's a toy, a backdrop for a role he wishes to play for a while, and, I believe, is now tiring of."

La Farge was well aware of the undercurrents in his host's casual comments. "I don't tire easily," he said. "Or give up what's important to me." As had her father, he glanced deliberately toward where Jacqueline had last been seen.

Later, in the room in the main house that had been assigned to him, he stripped, showered, and prepared for a late-afternoon siesta. He opened the louvered windows overlooking the bay to let fresh air into the room, then lay on the canopied bed. After a while he got up and closed them again, sliding the backs of his fingers up along the wooden slats to shut out the light.

He thought of Jacqueline. What did she like best about him, he wondered? Would she return to Paris when she had had enough of West Indian life again? Would she prefer to live there where she had gone to school and made friends and had her place already as a society queen? Her parents' money could buy her anything she wanted, in Paris or anywhere else. She could have any man she wanted. No man could turn down such beauty. Could she love a man twenty years her senior, exactly twice her age? True, he did not look a day over thirty, and he was a wealthy man, but would she have him?

He arranged the mosquito net around him, feeling drowsy. He was about to doze off when he heard a light metallic clicking sound. He turned to look in the direction from where it came. The door handle slowly turned and Jacqueline stole in.

The room was quite dark. Already the sun had gone down

behind the bluff. She stood there for a moment peering through the darkened room, and then came to stand beside the bed where La Farge lay outstretched, pretending to be asleep.

She had on a white silk kimono with delicate pink embroidered blossoms scattered over it. Her thick hair flowed like a river from her head to the bed and flicked lightly across his lips as she bent over him, pushing back the bed hangings. He could smell the faint, pungent odor of the mixture of perfume and coconut oil she used on her skin. Her small, firm breasts plunged forward as she leaned over him. Her dark nipples showed through the transparency of her kimono.

Through tiny slits in his eyes, he was observing every movement Jacqueline made. Carefully, she untied the ribbons at her waist, letting the gown slide slowly off her shoulders and along her hips and thighs to the ground. It fell in a pile at her feet. Standing amidst the small pile of white silk, she had the symmetry and luster of a golden chalice. She stepped out of the tiny heap of fabric and climbed onto the bed beside him. She raised herself on her knees and straddled him. Her hair, falling along the sides of her cheeks, tumbled down to rest on his face and neck.

She reminded him of an extraordinary animal, a cross between a cat and a serpent. Gently, she moved her hands along his chest, then slowly downward toward his groin. La Farge could feel himself getting hard. It wouldn't be much longer before he would have to give up his pretense of being asleep. Her hands came to rest on his maleness and she stroked it gently, lovingly. He moaned and opened his eyes, pretending to have been awakened by her gentle massage.

She had not been fooled by his performance. "Have you been enjoying it, Monsieur La Farge?" she asked, looking boldly into his eyes.

Never before had he been seduced by anyone calling him "monsieur." As she moved, her breasts bounced softly in small, circular movements. His hands came up and cupped them, pulling her downward so that he could lick the erect nipples. His throat felt dry and his lips were parched.

"Kiss me," she whispered. "Kiss me and love me as you have never before loved a woman."

The urgency in her voice spurred him to an abandon he had not expected, and he moaned with pleasure as he lost himself in the raptures of her firm young flesh. When it was over, they lay still, side by side on the disheveled bed. She had indeed been like no woman he had had before. She had been wild, like a tigress at her prey. He rubbed his legs together, still feeling the shivers of wanton satisfaction and reveling in the memory of their lovemaking. She kissed him on the lips softly, and went over to sit in front of the dressing table.

"It was just as I thought it would be with you, La Farge. Perhaps even a little better." As she sat there naked, brushing out her tangled hair, he could see her from several angles in the three-sided mirror.

He was devouring her with his eyes, basking in her perfection, admiring each contour of her young body. She was bewitching from every angle.

"Well," he said, pausing, lightly stroking his chin, as if to think, "it was good, but I think I've had better."

Her mouth flew open, she grimaced and threw the hairbrush across the room at him.

He sprang to his feet and strode across the room to her. He grabbed her by her wrists. "Don't be so angry, little one. I was just kidding. You see, I find it hard to talk about what just happened. I have many mixed emotions about it. I did not plan for things to happen so fast."

She looked up at him and smiled. "That you did not *expect* things to happen this fast, I can believe. But that you didn't *plan* for them to happen, that's another story. I just thought I'd beat you to the punch, that's all." She smiled at him.

My God, he thought. He had finally met his match. He knew right then and there that *she* was going to be the woman for him. He knew she felt it too.

She began talking about the dinner party to be held that night. "It is already late. Elvire will be coming to my room soon to see which dress I'll want pressed. If I'm not there, she'll suspect something. She's an old busybody, always poking around where it doesn't concern her. She's been around for as long as I can remember. Sometimes I think she has eyes in the back of her head, the way she can always tell what's going on. The way she keeps after me, you'd think I was still a child."

La Farge chuckled at the way Jacqueline had wrinkled up her nose when she spoke of the old nanny. Right then she *did* resemble a child he thought, a mischievous imp.

She chattered on, talking about the people he would be meeting later on. "Just nod and say hello," she advised. "If you get into a conversation, I tell you it will be dawn before they'll let go of you." The expression on her face softened. "And we won't get to spend very much time together as a result."

La Farge nodded, amused. "Very well, I have it. Just nod and go my merry way to find my lovely lady and make love to her till dawn finds us and awakens us."

She blew him a kiss and slipped out the door and down the hallway to her room.

That night on the cliff overlooking the bay, he proposed to her. Their wedding a month later, lavish though it was, was a formality; their marriage had begun on the canopied bed in that darkened room.

A quarter of a century later, La Farge could recall vividly every sensation of taste, touch and smell that had marked that first union—and, with bone-deep bitterness and despair, recall also his conviction that what they had shared would be unending.

Chapter Four

Valence-Côte d'Azur, August 1962

It was dawn by the time Rosalie and Ahmed arrived in Valence. Ahmed had had to stop several times to ask the way to the inn. Finally, he pulled into the dirt road that led to it. It was as Rosalie had described it. Even in the dim light of the dawn Ahmed could see the great willows, their umbrella-shaped branches bending to touch the ground beneath them. He saw no swans or geese, and guessed them to be asleep among the reeds that grew along the banks.

Rosalie stirred as the car came to a stop in front of the scalloped awning. Ahmed felt as if he had not eaten in days and regretted not having stopped in Lyon. Rosalie was sleeping as they drove through that city, and he had not had the heart to wake her up.

Maybe he could bribe the desk manager into rustling up something for him to eat. He would have given anything right then for a good cheese sandwich—anything. He left Rosalie in the car, sleeping, and went inside. He checked in as "Prince et

Princess Ahmed Farahet." Usually Ahmed did not care for titles, but tonight he thought a bit of swank might get him the sandwich he craved, or at least some cold meat with a little Dijon mustard on the side.

In no time at all, the night manager was scurrying back to the kitchen in search of a feast for the "royal couple."

"Wake up, sleeping beauty. It is I, your prince." Ahmed kissed Rosalie gently on the lips.

She stirred and impulsively wrapped her arms around his neck. "Are we in Lyon yet?"

"We are in Valence, *chérie*. You know, at the cute little inn with the weeping willows and all those geese."

She opened her eyes and smiled up at him. "Not geese, silly, swans. There's a big difference, you know."

A sleepy porter came out to fetch their bags. "Follow me, m'sieur. We've put you and madame in Number 10. It is our very best. Balzac slept there, you know."

"No, really?" Ahmed said. "Are you sure he isn't still there?"

The boy gave him a sleepy look. "This way, Monsieur le Prince."

It was a lovely room, large and crisp-smelling with a tiny balcony and a breathtaking view of the Rhône. The big four-poster bed looked very inviting to Rosalie. She kicked off her shoes and threw herself across it.

Next came her dress.

She lay naked across the peach coverlet, looking like a rose petal cast in a pool of honey.

"Don't you ever wear underwear, you shameless wench?"

"No, not ever, and especially not when I'm with"—she switched to English in order to perpetrate a deliciously outrageous pun that had just come to her—"an Arabian knight!"

She arched her back, stretched herself wantonly across the bed, and moaned with pleasure.

"Oooh, after that matchbox car of yours, I feel like an animal set free from its cage. Ooooooh, my poor, aching back."

"Why don't you take a hot shower before bed? It'll perk you up a bit."

"Oh, stop it. You sound just like Papa: 'And how about a tall glass of Vittel to keep the bowels open?' "

They both burst out laughing at Rosalie's imitation of her father. They were still laughing when someone knocked at the door.

"Just a moment," Ahmed said.

"You answer it, Ahmed. I don't want anyone to see me with my shoes off. They might get the wrong impression."

He laughed, shaking his head from side to side as she darted across the lushly carpeted floor to the bathroom.

It was the night manager with a serving cart. "Monsieur le Prince, I regret that this is all I can bring you, but my cook does not live in, you see. Please accept my apologies, and I shall see to it that special care is given to your breakfast in the morning. *Bon soir.*"

Ahmed stood there looking down at the feast which the man had brought: *langouste froide à la mayonnaise,* served on a bed of fresh lettuce and trimmed with lemon slices and sprigs of parsley; a large helping of *jambon de parme* with melon and more lemon slices; an assortment of cheeses: *brie, chèvre, camembert, boursin, pont-l'évêque,* and . . . *Kraft?* What kind of cheese was that? Must be a mistake. And—he could not believe it! To top it all off, a *coupe melba* for dessert. "Ha!" He rubbed his hands together with glee. "A feast fit for a prince! For once the title paid off. This is one hell of a lot better than a *sandwich au jambon* in Lyon. Once again, that little witch has proved to be a genius."

Ahmed slipped off his clothes, glad to be out of the ridiculous tails. He had forgotten he was wearing them. He thought of the times he had stopped to ask directions along the way. What an asshole he must have seemed, freaked out of his mind on Aznavour and Mozart, racing through the streets in a wrinkled penguin suit. He could hear the shower running.

"Rosalie, make room, baby. I'm coming in with you."

The cool sting of the water was invigorating after the long drive. They dried themselves hurriedly and went back into the bedroom to begin their feast.

Rosalie dug out a pale blue dressing gown from her valise.

She held it up against her, twirling in front of the looking glass in front of the bed. She threw it across the room, and it landed in a small heap on the floor by the bathroom door.

"Blue is not my mood tonight, and neither is Dior," she said. "I want something more dramatic, more evil." She puckered up her lips and threw a kiss to Ahmed, who was having a hard time making up his mind whether he wanted to make love or eat.

He was not sure which looked better to him right then: a nip at Rosalie's round derriere or a bite of *melon glacé*. A lick of the rosebud nipples or a spoonful of the *coupe melba*. *Langouste froide* or Rosalie *chaude?*

Rosalie found a black silk negligee and draped herself in it. "There, that's more like it," she said, smiling approvingly at her reflection in the mirror. She turned to face Ahmed, hands on her hips, legs slightly apart, her pelvis stuck forward.

"I like it," he said simply. What else could he say? Didn't she see his tongue hanging out? Couldn't she see the cobra rising from between his legs?

She held out her arms to him enticingly.

He walked over to her and lifted her up into his arms, laid her on the rumpled bed. Her eyes were closed, the long lashes causing little shadows on her high cheekbones. He was remembering the first time. How shocked he had been to learn that he had taken a virgin. She had lied to him, telling him she was nineteen. He had assumed she had had some experience. It had certainly come as a surprise, later, when he learned from his father that Rosalie was not yet eighteen. Now, in the cloak of the warm room, age had no meaning. He kissed her flat belly, lovingy admiring its smoothness.

She moaned and turned to look at him. "What do you say we forget about St. Tropez?"

"Forget about St. Tropez? What do you mean?"

"I mean, why don't we stay here and eat and make love and eat and make love, until we both either get too fat or tired to move!"

She giggled, and Ahmed could feel his groin growing tense as he thought of her boldness. But it was what he loved about this woman-child: her openness, her unique ability to profess her emotions and desires without hesitation or inhibition. Such honesty! Such innocence!

She might have been not yet eighteen, but she was a woman, in ways most women twice her age never become. He paused for a moment in his thoughts, briefly remembering some of the women he had had. His eyes focused once again on his beautiful captive, the black negligee setting off her skin like a pearl in a velvet case.

He lightly stroked her partly exposed thighs with the back of his hands, then again with his forefingers, only slower, sliding them down around her knees and calves to the bottoms of her feet, over and over again.

Rosalie's huge eyes, green as the depths of the ocean on a stormy night, sparkled in the dark as they fixed on the flame of the lone candle on the mantel. Ahmed smiled. He knew she was falling in love with him, and he with her. There was no turning back now. He studied her face in the pale candlelight, her mouth so fresh and flowerlike, so tempting. Tiny streams of candlelight flickered across the tips of her breasts, exciting him while he flicked his tongue across their pink, hard nipples. Her youth, like forbidden fruit, drove him wild. Rosalie lay motionless, still staring into the light as if hypnotized.

Ahmed's kisses trailed up to her neck. His nostrils filled with the clinging smell of the gardenia she wore still pinned in her hair, slightly yellowed and wilted, but still smelling as strongly as it had. Its scent was maddening—like an aphrodisiac, he thought.

"Ahmed." Her voice interrupted his thoughts.

"Yes?"

"I am getting sleepy."

"Sleepy? Good God, not now, Rosalie. My God, you can sleep all day tomorrow if you like, but not now. What are you trying to do to me? You can't just go to sleep and leave me hanging here."

She gave him a grin. "From where I am, things don't look as though they're *hanging*." She giggled impishly. "Oh, Ahmed, you look so silly. I wish I had a derby hat so that I could hang it on—"

He didn't let her finish her sentence. He brought his lips down on hers hard, forcing her back on the pillow. He parted her legs gently and mounted her. Across the room he could see the food, untouched, wilting from the heat.

Before they left Valence, they took a walk along the right bank of the Rhône, throwing in bread crumbs for the swans. In the daylight, the willows had taken on an air of friendliness, and gently rocked their boughs in the breeze. The ground was covered by a thick coat of mint green grass, like a wide carpet unraveling itself along the slopes to the inn. The "ree-beep ree-beep" of a few hungry frogs could be heard clearly, even over the loud splashing of the swans, as they fought for the crumbs.

Rosalie and Ahmed stopped for lunch at the Café des Pompiers in the little town of Montélimar. In most aspects, it was a typical French town: narrow streets, ancient buildings and lampposts, comely fresh-faced matrons bustling along the narrow sidewalks carrying their bread, cheese, and other provisions. It was like any other little French town in the *midi* on a Saturday afternoon. Old men were grouped in the *place* across from the café playing *pétanque*. Each one brought his little bag of steel *boules*. Some were waiting patiently for the game to end so that they could join in the next one.

Rosalie sipped her *café noir* slowly, taking in the scene on the *place*. An old man with a white beard and mustache was wearing a shabby army jacket that dated back to World War I. The old relic engulfed his frail body as he bent to pick up his *boule*. One of his legs was missing. She shook her head in sadness and tried to catch a glimpse of the old man's face again. She could not. His black beret covered most of his forehead, and the heavy lapels of his jacket were turned upward, hiding most of his chin. A large black dog ran by, bumping into the man's crutch, almost knocking him over.

A *mutilé de guerre—mutilé*, she thought, in the same damn *guerre* that had made Armand La Farge a hero and started him on the road to success and wealth . . . and so, by a roundabout route indeed, had brought his daughter to sit in the sunshine and wait here for her lover, and pity a man the war had destroyed.

No, not destroyed, after all. He had survived, as ten million or so had not, he had the sunshine as much as did she, he had his *boules*, and—she grinned—he still had his temper and a sharp eye! The dog ran howling as the old man nimbly balanced himself on his one leg and caught it shrewdly in the ribs with the tip of his crutch.

One loses, one wins, she reflected. But if one survives, there's always something left to win—always. . . .

Ahmed reappeared. "Well, *chérie*, shall we get going?"

"Back so quickly?"

"It only takes a minute for a man to go, you know." He was still fumbling with his crotch, arranging himself comfortably. "There, that's better. Don't want to crease the damn things. There are enough eunuchs in my country already." He made a funny face at her. "Okay, let's go. It's getting late and your father will be worrying if he doesn't see us pull into that driveway before nightfall.

"I don't know why, but it's always the same story every time I drive down to the Côte. I do two thirds of the trip the first night, and then it takes me all the next day to get to wherever the hell I'm going."

Several hours later they arrived at La Farge's estate. Colombier was only a few miles outside of St. Tropez, with its own private road and beach. The property was on a slope, and the house itself was a good three miles from the road, completely hidden by pine woods.

They were met at the gates of the estate by Bertrand and two large, black Dobermans on leashes. Bertrand stood guard as always with his carbine and his two faithful companions, Igor and Samson, always ready for whatever situation might occur. He was one of La Farge's collection of devoted servants, men who, without hesitation, would gladly lay down their lives for their employer. La Farge had once got Bertrand out of a tight legal situation, a matter of a youthful smuggling escapade that would have earned him a long prison sentence without La Farge's intervention.

At a wave of the hand from Rosalie, Bertrand swung open the huge gates.

Berthe and Max, La Farge's German chauffeur, had both heard the car coming up the driveway, and together they had gone out into the courtyard to see who the visitors might be. Berthe leaned into the car as it came to a stop beside her; her face was anxious.

"Oh, Zalie, I've been so worried since your papa told me last night that you'd left with this—" She paused and glanced disapprovingly at Ahmed, her eyes taking in his tight-fitting blue jeans. "If I'd known, I would not have consented to this. Sometimes I wonder about your father's wits, the way he gives in to your every whim. Why, the very thought of it!" Once again her eyes shifted to Ahmed, glinting furiously.

Ahmed was enraged. "Now look here, you old crow, if you don't—" He did not finish. Rosalie's hand reached out and squeezed his, hard, stopping him. He threw up his free hand in dismay.

"*Aje Maniuke!*" The words were said in such frustration that Rosalie had to laugh. That expression always got to her; one really could not quite translate the Arabic phrase, especially when Ahmed said it.

"Come on, Ahmed, darling, don't be angry. Berthe is always a little overprotective with me, you know that. She is perhaps a bit forceful, but she means well. She's been almost like a mother to me all these years—you know how involved with society and such Maman is. Come on, *chéri*, let's go see Papa and then we'll go for a long swim, okay?"

Max, displaying his usual calm, said nothing. Only the slight smile on his lips showed his amusement at the whole affair.

Berthe led the way up the stairs to Rosalie's rooms, while Max took care of Ahmed and the bags. Armand La Farge was fishing, they were told. He had been out all day with several of his guests, including the Duc d'Artois, an avid sailor and fisherman, and the pale-faced Senator James Buchin from Connecticut. The sheikh had not been feeling well and was resting in his room. Some of the other guests were lounging about the wide terraces and verandas, soaking up the remaining sun, while others could be seen on the tennis courts in the distance, or walking along the beach.

Rosalie changed her clothes hurriedly and raced down the dozens of stone steps to the beach where Ahmed was already waiting for her. As she came up beside him, he reached out and pulled her to him. He was wet, his body glistening in the pale sunlight. It was already late; the sun was sliding toward the horizon.

"Is the water warm? Have you been waiting long?"

"Well, in answer to your first question, yes, the water is quite nice. And as for your second question, the answer is no, not exactly. Only I *feel* as though I've been waiting forever." He admired her suit. It was of a pearly beige color, its pale hue harmonizing with her tanned skin. He held her away from him, admiring her. Her hair was blowing softly in the breeze, like strands of gold outlined against the indigo blue background of the late afternoon sky. The sight left him speechless, his eyes dazed by the light of the setting sun.

"Ahmed." Rosalie's voice broke the spell.

He blinked his eyes, slightly blinded. "Yes, darling. What is it?"

She looked at him quizzically. "Ahmed, are you still with me? You look a little dazed. Are you feeling all right?"

He blinked his eyes once more and rubbed them with his fingertips. "Well, my love, I see you don't recognize true love when you see it, but that's what it is."

"Oh, I don't believe one word of it. I think it's all that sky-gazing you've been doing for the last fifteen minutes or so. Don't you know you shouldn't look into the sun? You'll burn your retinas."

"My what?"

She laughed. Every now and then Ahmed would fail to know the meaning of a word in French, and he hated to admit it. "Your retinas, silly; you know, in the center of your eyes."

"Those are not retinas. Those are called pupils or something."

"Oh, for God's sake, Ahmed. Your retinas are in *back* of your pupils which are in the center of your irises, which are the colored parts of your eyes, and they are surrounded by the whites of your eyes."

He reflected for a moment. "Yes, that's exactly what I said. The pupils are the little things in the irises."

"Oh, shit, Ahmed. I just wish you'd stick to Arabic. Maybe in Arabia people's eyes are slightly different."

They looked at each other and burst out laughing.

"I'll be sure to look up the word when we get back to the house, and if you are right, I'll be your slave for a whole day," said Ahmed.

She threw a handful of sand in his face. He ducked, avoiding it. "And why should I bother when I already have you as my slave? And furthermore, you didn't say what I would have to do if I were wrong. Not that I am, mind you, as you'll soon find out. It's just that I'd like to hear the rest of the bargain."

"Why, I thought you knew. If you are wrong, you'll have to marry me, of course, and accept me as your master forever."

Rosalie's face took on a more serious look. "Don't make fun, Ahmed, not about something like that." She could see him watching her, hanging on to every word she might say.

The loud chimes of a bell rang through the air and rescued her from the seriousness of the moment.

"Oh, there goes the bell. That means it's already past six and time to start thinking about getting ready for dinner tonight. I don't have a single thing I want to wear tonight. Damn, I knew I should have spent a little more time in Rome last week—I saw the loveliest gowns."

Ahmed could see that a sorrowful history of dresses not acquired would be forthcoming. "Hey, come on, Rosalie, we'll think about clothes later. It's already late, and you haven't even been in for a swim yet. Let's have a quick one before going up." He glanced up at the seawall and saw that it hid them from view of the house—and the beach was deserted. "Come on, take your suit off. It's more fun that way."

She nodded, smiling impishly at him. "Okay."

Together they walked down to the water's edge, their clothes left behind. Rosalie dunked the tip of her feet in first to test the temperature.

"Aiiii, it's too cold. It's bloody freezing, Ahmed. I thought you said it was warm."

He shook a finger at her and shook his head from side to side in protest. "Oh, no, I didn't say it was warm. I said it was nice. *Nice* is different from *warm.* You're always telling me every word has its specific meaning. Well, nice doesn't mean warm, and you can look that one up, too, while you're looking up *retina* and all the other words you don't understand." She ignored him and went and sat down on the sand. He came and sat beside her, studying the lines of her body.

He leaned over and took her in his arms gently, and he kissed her. She responded immediately, like a spark kindled by a gentle breeze. The flame seemed to rise in her as she returned his fiery kisses. He could feel her heart beating hard against his chest in rhythm with his own. She trembled slightly as he slid his hand over her shoulder. She seemed almost birdlike as she shivered, partly from his touch, partly from the cool *mistral* rising in the bay. Without a word, he laid her back gently on the sand, which was still warm from the day's sun. A growing urgency built in them as they stared into each other's eyes. She lay back, naked before him, her flesh soft and yielding. He moved closer to her.

She opened her mouth and whispered his name, "Ahmed . . ."

But his eager lips already were on hers, his tongue darting furiously, silencing her. His hands moved rapidly along the slopes and hollows of her body, exploring her secret places. He stroked her belly softly, trailing a finger downward, then in between her legs. He could feel her moistness, soft and palpitating beneath his fingertips. She moaned with pleasure, and reached out to touch him. She felt him, hard and throbbing with desire. He murmured her name softly, and darted his tongue along her closed eyelids. She held on to him, squeezing him gently, adoringly, massaging him with the instinctive expertise only a woman in love possesses. She felt him stiffen even more under her palm, rising into a position of readiness.

He lifted himself to rest on top of her, propping himself up on his left palm. He stroked her, sliding his fingers deeper inside her. Again, she felt that rush of helplessness, that feeling of drowning, that surging tide of rapture. She felt her heart racing, her mind skyrocketing, her body shivering and tingling all over as he plunged himself into her. He bent his head over hers and nibbled at her earlobe. She groaned, her stomach heaving in spasmodic convulsions, as he thrust himself again and again into the depths of her warm womanhood. They moved together in a love dance, their arms and legs wrapped tightly around each other, their hair blowing in the breeze, their bodies sprinkled with sand.

She cried out his name again, as he continued to thrust himself into her, panting with the fury of lust and complete abandonment. Her passion, heightened to meet his, reached its peak as he darted his tongue across her nipples again, gently sucking and licking them.

Beads of perspiration were rolling down his face and chest, falling on her and settling in a little pool between her breasts. Her hair was wet and clinging to her shoulders like a shroud. Her lips, bruised slightly by his kisses, were parted, exposing her teeth and the tip of her tongue. He was devouring her throat with his mouth. She felt ravaged, as if her body was being pilfered by an insatiable demon, yet she wanted more. She grabbed hold of his hair, pulling with all her might. She could feel her insides tightening, her loins exploding.

Ahmed stopped for a moment, raising his chest away from her to look into her eyes. He said her name in a whisper. With a groan he began to move again, slowly at first, then with a swift increasing intensity, faster and faster, his body glistening with perspiration, as he drove her with each thrust deeper and deeper into the sand. Her body overflowed, as with great, pulsating spurts he drained himself into her.

They had reached the *highest* mountain.

Ahmed rolled over, gasping, his head spinning giddily. "Good God," he said, when he could catch his breath. "That was unbelievable."

Rosalie, too weak to move, smiled and sighed.

He flipped himself over on his stomach, facing her once again. His lips were poised above hers, his eyes intent as he spoke. "Rosalie, will you marry me tonight?" His tone was completely serious.

Her green eyes widened. Her hand reached out and touched his cheek. She was both flattered and astounded by his proposal. "Oh, Ahmed, you know that's impossible."

"Impossible? Why?"

"People don't get married just like that. The license, all those documents, it takes time. And then there's Papa. Well, you know he'd never allow me to have anything but a big wedding. I'd hate to disappoint him."

"I know," he said. "I was just being a little foolish, I guess. One good lay and I want to marry the girl."

She bit him on the ear playfully. "If that's the way you feel about it, I'll just have to give you a replay."

"A replay? Now? Do you want to have to bury me in the morning?" He moaned in mock agony. "God help me."

She smiled, her face softening, the impishness disappearing. "Are you happy, Ahmed? I mean, do I satisfy you? Oh, damn it, Ahmed, you know what I'm trying to say. Well? Do I? Satisfy you, that is."

"Do you satisfy me? Good God! If I were any more satisfied, I'd be dead."

Rosalie's laughter rang out in the stillness. It was a sound of pure joy, the joy of knowing that Ahmed was content, replenished by their lovemaking. "Well," she said, getting to her feet, "I was just thinking, you see, that if it wasn't up to par, I might take a few brush-up courses, go to night school or something."

The lights from the terraces above shone down on the beach. Her body was covered with sand. Ahmed tried to grab her to kiss her, but she was too quick for him. Off she ran into the silvery water, her breasts bouncing freely as she plunged into the water. Ahmed could feel his groin tightening; he was getting hard again. By God, I will surely die young with her around! he thought, as he ran after her. They dove in and kissed beneath the water's surface, and swam back to the shore clean and refreshed.

The dinner that night was served on the main terrace

overlooking the sea. Everyone was gathered on the terrace under the overhanging pines planted along the edges. Drinks and hors d'oeuvres were being served. In the distance one could see the islands, L'Île du Levant and Porquerolles, which harbored two of the Riviera's most renowned nudist colonies. In the cove, the white yacht *Rosalie* rolled in time with the movements of the waves, serene and ghostlike on the shimmering sea. In the distance, directly behind her, La Farge's motor yacht, the *Créole*, sat majestically, her lights reflecting in the water. The doves had gone to sleep and the frogs and crickets were playing their symphony of the night. Only Diablo, the black leopard, roamed free, graceful and sleek, almost devillike with its green, flashing eyes and overhanging teeth.

D'Artois was leaning against a stone statue on the terrace sipping a glass of champagne. His eyes were fixed on the leopard.

Ahmed sat on the rail overhanging the cliff. He studied one, then the other. The leopard seemed bothered by d'Artois's presence. Ahmed noted the way it was watching d'Artois, the way the animal kept pounding its tail on the ground.

La Farge had brought the cat back from Kenya a year before, where he had been on safari. During the hunt for antelope there had been an accident. The cat's mother, while prowling in the area, had attacked one of the guides and La Farge had had to kill her. The cub was found nearby. Unlike its mother, with her spotted coat, it was black, a freak of nature. La Farge had fancied keeping it as a pet and had raised the cub himself. Now it followed him everywhere like a dog, licking his feet and begging for attention.

Ahmed thought for a moment, Isn't that just what everyone at this dinner table here tonight is doing? Begging and groping for La Farge's attention? Even he, tonight, needed it more than ever. He would have to find a way to get La Farge alone tonight, to ask him for Rosalie's hand in marriage.

Rosalie appeared from inside.

"Hello, everybody, I'm terribly sorry if I've kept you waiting. Papa." She went over and kissed her father on the cheek. "Ahmed," she said, moving near him. "I guess it took so long to get dressed because I'm still a little tired from that long drive from Paris." She winked at Ahmed. "You can't imagine," she went on as she placed her arms around Ahmed's neck and kissed him, "what a *terrible* time we had."

La Farge cleared his throat and suggested that now, since everyone was present and because he was starving, that it would be appropriate to sit down for dinner. He led the way.

The dinner was, as dinners usually were at Colombier, a true masterpiece. It was obvious that La Farge delighted in giving the best of everything he had to offer. There were twenty-two guests in all, besides La Farge and his wife and Rosalie and Ahmed.

The shrimp bisque was light and delicate. The fresh mérou, caught by La Farge that morning, was baked and stuffed with lobster and shrimp and served with a delicate wine and herb sauce. The fish was accompanied by trays of baked, stuffed Christophines, beds of fluffy wild rice and truffles.

And to top it all off, a true delight to *l'estomac*, a chocolate soufflé, so big that La Farge later told Rosalie that it reminded him of the *Hindenburg* dirigible. She reminded him that that had been a disaster, which was not the case with the enormous soufflé.

Throughout dinner, La Farge was in a pensive mood. He mostly listened to what his guests had to say and made a comment only when it was absolutely necessary. His interest was focused primarily on d'Artois.

In black gabardine trousers and white jacket over a black silk shirt, highly polished black shoes and a gold chain around his neck, d'Artois could pass for anyone from a banker to an Italian gigolo, La Farge thought.

La Farge sat sipping his coffee, anticipating d'Artois's response to a question put to him by one of the other guests.

"I heard, monsieur," said the man, "that you recently bought quite a lot of property in Germany and couldn't help being curious as to why you'd want to invest in any property in that country after what you have been through with the filthy *boches*."

The man was Jewish, born and raised in France. He had

spent time during the war in a German concentration camp and had later gone to America where he had made a fortune in textiles. He was embittered over the war, no matter how long ago it seemed that night.

"I have my reasons," d'Artois replied. "Business reasons, of course, and I wouldn't want to bore the ladies here tonight by discussing it."

The woman sitting on d'Artois's left commented that it was comforting to know that there were still men around who cared about the feelings of the opposite sex and immediately launched into a conversation with him. La Farge could tell d'Artois had no interest whatever in what the woman was saying. His eyes, La Farge noticed, kept shifting away from her toward the other end of the table where Ahmed and Rosalie were sitting. There was something about the way he looked at them that puzzled La Farge. The way his eyes would sweep over Rosalie's face and stare at her lips as she spoke. D'Artois would look at Ahmed, who was engrossed in Rosalie's story, and he would frown and look away again. Once, d'Artois's steely gray blue eyes caught his host's as he was looking away from Ahmed and Rosalie, and La Farge felt a shiver run down his back.

La Farge thought back on an incident which had taken place a few weeks earlier—a conversation he had overheard between d'Artois and a woman. They had been speaking in German. What he had heard had come as such a shock, he had barely been able to keep it to himself. It had caused him to reopen his investigation of d'Artois, initiated as a routine matter when they had first become associates, years ago. He was now no longer merely curious. It was now clear that d'Artois was hiding something from his past, something terribly important. He had to find out, now more than ever, no matter what the effort.

The sound of Rosalie's voice brought him back to the present. She was talking to d'Artois. La Farge glanced at d'Artois. D'Artois's eyes were fixed on Rosalie's face; he was smiling. La Farge had never seen d'Artois so attentive before. Rosalie was talking about fishing, one of d'Artois's favorite subjects.

I'm not about to sit here for an hour and listen to a blow-by-blow description of how d'Artois baits his hooks, La Farge decided. The last time someone mentioned fishing at the dinner table, it was three hours before anyone succeeded in changing the subject!

La Farge's thoughts once more became grave. What can the damn fellow be hiding!

La Farge folded his napkin and pushed back his chair from the long table. "Ladies and gentlemen, if you will excuse me, I am a little tired this evening, and I have some papers to go over. I shall see you all in the morning." With these words he turned on his heel and walked away, leaving his guests.

Ahmed watched La Farge's every move; he had style, style and compelling attractiveness. A magnetic personality. "Even his voice is big, big and commanding." Ahmed realized he was muttering aloud.

"What? What did you say?" Rosalie had overheard him. She shook her head disapprovingly, and he had to smile. The way she adored her father . . . he was sure she would adore him like that one day, and the thought gave him a secure feeling, a feeling of contentment.

Later that night Ahmed found La Farge alone in the game room. The others had either gone to bed or gone for a late swim, or were sitting on the terraces having brandy. Rosalie had taken on the challenge of a game of chess with one of the guests. La Farge had remained in the game room, working on some important papers. This was his favorite room.

Trophies from all over the world bedecked the walls of the large, green room—heads of rhinos and tigers and wild boars; elephant tusks; and skins on the floor. At his side as always was his trusted companion, Diablo. Ahmed wondered which one frightened him more, the man or the beast. He had worked up the courage, though, to invade the scene, and to his surprise had been welcomed with true fondness. The cat lay there motionless, watching, on guard. Choosing a seat, at an angle that would allow him not to look at the animal, Ahmed told La Farge of his wish to marry Rosalie. To his utter amazement, La Farge threw his arms around him in a pleased, fatherly way.

"Well, now, my boy, I was beginning to wonder about

you! About what was taking you so long, I mean. You see, years ago, before we met"—he pointed to Ahmed and then to himself—"your father and I made each other a promise that my daughter would one day marry his son. Yes, you, Ahmed, and that is why I allowed you and Rosalie to drive down together."

Ahmed gave him a surprised look. Not knowing quite what to say, he replied, "But I thought . . ."

La Farge interrupted him. "What did you think, man? That I would let my daughter, not yet eighteen, drive down in the middle of the night with a young stud like you without a damn good reason?"

Ahmed spoke, his tone sharp. "But then why did we have such a hard time persuading you to let Rosalie ride down with me?"

La Farge smiled wickedly. "Well, I had to protest a little. Otherwise it wouldn't have seemed right to you, you know that. Just think for a minute." He patted Ahmed on the arm. "I've seen you grow from a baby to a young boy, and then I've watched you mature and grow. I've loved you as a son, Ahmed, only I am not a very demonstrative man, so maybe you didn't know." He spread his arms apart. "Welcome, my son, now that you do know." They embraced. La Farge went over to stand by the wooden fireplace, his hand resting on the mantel. He gazed into the flames. Although it was August, he always had a fire in his den. He spoke slowly, his pupils reflecting the dancing flames. "Ever since Rosalie was born, I'd hoped that somehow you two would find each other one day and marry. That is why I was only too happy to let you alone last night."

Ahmed wondered what La Farge would do if he knew that he and Rosalie had been alone together long before then.

La Farge went on: "I can hardly wait to give the news to your father. He'll be joining me in here shortly, he and some others. I shall be glad to give him the happy news myself." He paused for a moment and turned to face Ahmed. "Unless you prefer to do it yourself?"

Ahmed nodded and waved a hand, indicating that it was all right for La Farge to do the telling.

La Farge squinted at Ahmed. "When is the wedding to be, my lad?"

Ahmed mumbled his words. "As soon as possible, sir."

"What's that, man? Speak up; I can't hear you."

"I said, just as soon as possible, sir," Ahmed repeated, this time more clearly.

"Well . . ." La Farge pondered for a moment, stroking his chin, the short bristles of his beard rustling softly. He had not shaved all day. He thought of Jacqueline's incredulous expression when he had come to dinner tonight with a day's stubble. "What do you think of an October wedding?" he asked.

"Sure, October is okay, but why not August or September?"

La Farge frowned a little. "Because, my impatient young friend, invitations have to be sent out and the wedding has to be planned. A trousseau has to be bought for Rosalie, all those kinds of details. Also," he added, "Rosalie will be eighteen in October, and I thought it might be nice to wait until then. In a sense you will be her birthday gift." He paused for a moment, then added slyly, "Naturally, the gift would come from you, not me."

"I have something much more subdued in mind." Ahmed rolled his eyes mockingly.

Seeing Ahmed's obvious displeasure at being compared to a birthday gift, as if he were a mere object, a toy offered to Rosalie for her birthday, La Farge laughed and apologized for his joking. He offered Ahmed a cigar and a glass of brandy. Ahmed declined the cigar, but welcomed the offer of the brandy gladly. La Farge poured him a glass and then poured one for himself. The two men sat down on the settee in front of the fireplace, resuming their conversation about the wedding and the plans which would have to be made.

At that moment, the sheikh, accompanied by Rosalie, walked in, the duke and Senator Buchin close behind. Rosalie came toward Ahmed.

"Ah, there you are, darling. I was looking all over for you, as you can see." She tiptoed and kissed the sheikh on the chin. "I found your father instead. A much more dependable man, I might add, than his very elusive son."

The sheikh laughed at her remark. "Well, Ahmed. What do you think? Do you think the young lady has a point?"

Rosalie came and sat on Ahmed's lap on the settee and the duke and the senator sat down side by side on the big divan. They talked for a while, mostly discussing the news of Rosalie's and Ahmed's wedding plans. La Farge had been the one to announce it first to the sheikh and to the others. The sheikh, like La Farge, was beside himself with joy. He, d'Artois, and the senator congratulated the couple over and over again, causing slight embarrassment to the two lovers. Ahmed managed, with a little help from Rosalie, to persuade La Farge to push up the wedding to September instead of October.

Rosalie and Ahmed excused themselves from the company of their elders and went for a walk in the garden behind the house. The garden was located on the north side of the main house, overlooking some of the vast vineyards and properties of the estate. The building itself had been a medieval monastery, which had been occupied by the Germans during World War II. They had ravaged its interior, leaving it in a pitiful condition. La Farge bought it soon after the war when the Church decided to dispose of it.

He had had to pay a considerable sum for it; it came, along with vast vineyards, with its own operating winery. It sat surrounded on one side by the sea and on the other sides by three hundred acres of rich, wine-producing land. To the right of it were tennis courts and an Olympic-sized swimming pool; to the left the stables and servants' quarters; and in the center of the circular cloister was a beautiful cobblestoned courtyard. In its center stood a fountain, which struck an impressive, though discordant, note: a tall, grotesque statue depicting a powerful, sinister figure, not quite human and not quite animal, down which water cascaded into a basin.

The fortune La Farge had spent remodeling and improving the place was evident. The vast grounds were immaculate and filled with rare plants and trees. The woods to the lower east side of the property were kept stocked with deer and pheasant. He had created for himself a paradise.

Ahmed and Rosalie took the pathway along the side of the

house. She wanted to show Ahmed Brouillard, her favorite horse.

At the stables, Ahmed and Rosalie stopped to pet the horses. Ahmed stole a kiss from Rosalie in the darkness. Brouillard joined in, pressing his wet nose up against Rosalie's cheek and neighing loudly.

"Let's get out of here before he brings the whole household out." Rosalie said. Brouillard neighed again, louder this time in protest, as they closed the stable door. They crossed back over to the house, walking slowly under the arbors covered by thick grape vines. They reached the house and passed through the gate into the courtyard. The August moon was bright through the branches of the trees, seeping through like golden strands of hair tumbling through the widespread fingers of a giant hand. They went over to stand beside the fountain in the center of the courtyard. The water trickled down the huge statue and splashed on the red and purple water lilies beneath.

Ahmed looked up at the statue. "Who is he? Some unforgettable boyfriend of yours? Gruesome fellow, isn't he?"

Rosalie poked him in the ribs. "Don't be funny. Don't you know? That's Mephistopheles, one of the seven chief devils in medieval demonology. I find him cute, in a way."

Ahmed stood back to get a better look. The statue seemed dreadfully out of place in such a peaceful spot. It seemed to leer down at him, pronouncing some dreadful incantation from the past. The aged stone, once white, was now gray except for green patches where moss had begun to grow. Ahmed's gaze held for a moment, and then he shuddered and lowered his eyes. He spoke finally. "You know, there's something about that hideous thing that reminds me of someone. Do you know who I mean?"

Rosalie studied it for a moment. "Hmmm, well, now, let me see. . . ."

"You see it or you don't."

"From behind he looks a little like you, and from the front, I'd say, maybe a little like the duke."

"That's it exactly! From the front, I mean. That's who it reminded me of, too, almost instantly."

"Oh, come on, Ahmed. That's not very fair. And besides, he's a very nice gentleman, and one of Papa's oldest and dearest friends, too." She paused momentarily, then went on. "It's funny, though, that you should say it reminds you of Jean, since he was the one who gave Papa the statue a long time ago, when Papa first bought this place." Rosalie's imagination ran wild as she seemed to see the statue come to life. She imagined its fiery eyes flashing and leering at her, its fangs gnashing and grinding together. She shuddered and with an effort shook the thought from her mind.

"Chérie."

Rosalie jumped.

"Aiii, *Aje Maniuke*, name of God, Ahmed! You scared me half to death. Shit!" She scraped mud off her foot with a twig. "You almost made me jump out of my skin. Dammit! And look at my shoe. It's ruined in the mud."

Ahmed could not help laughing. Rosalie's reaction to the sound of his voice had been so violent she had jumped into the pool with one foot and into the fern beds around it with the other.

She came over to him, barefoot. "Okay, you ghoul, now pick me up and take me inside. I'm soaking wet, and I'll surely catch my death of cold if I stay out here any longer like this." She pointed to her bare feet and to the wet hem of her dress.

Ahmed was still laughing.

Rosalie was a little angry at him for making fun of her, but she could not really blame him. She looked at him and broke out laughing herself.

Upstairs from a window overlooking the courtyard someone was watching. It was La Farge. He had just left his friends in the study and had gone upstairs to get ready for bed.

He heard Rosalie's shriek and came to the window to investigate. He could see her and Ahmed through the branches of the trees, in the shadows. They were clasped in a passionate kiss, and he smiled, watching them clinging to each other.

He closed the window, careful not to make a sound, and went to sit in the large red silk upholstered chair by his bed. He wondered what Jacqueline was doing, whether she was alone. He was tempted to find out, but what if she were not?

His eyes fixed on a photograph in a heavy silver frame on the Louis IV table by his bed. It was a picture of Rosalie with her mother, the only one they had taken together. Rosalie was nine when it had been taken. She was dressed in a beautiful pink organdy dress, with tiny satin bows and daisies in her hair.

Jacqueline was wearing a yellow, off the shoulder, *crêpe de chine* dress and a wide summer hat with a yellow ribbon and a white orchid pinned to the crown.

La Farge took the photograph from the table and traced a finger over his wife's beautiful image. He remembered well the afternoon he had taken it. Jacqueline and Rosalie had been picking flowers in the garden at Colombier. He had seen them from the terrace and had taken the snapshot.

Jacqueline hated it, said it "made her look too much like a mother."

La Farge smiled sadly to himself as he replaced the photograph on the table. Why had she been so against having children? They could have been so happy, he and Jacqueline and Rosalie, if only . . . But there were reasons, he thought, things that had happened.

He closed his eyes remembering how it was she came to be the way she was. . . .

Chapter Five

Martinique, January 1939

The restoration of the Belle Fleur plantation had taken more than a year, an undertaking started the day after his wedding to Jacqueline; and now, preparations were being made for a party in honor of its completion.

La Farge had decided to go visit James Buchin, who had just arrived back that morning from the United States; Jacqueline was vehement about not wanting him to go.

He tried to cajole her out of her bad mood, and promised to be back early to help her see to the last minute preparations for the affair. On his way out he bent to kiss her good-bye.

But she turned her face away like a spoiled child, and he left her finishing her breakfast on the veranda outside their bedroom. He took his horse, knowing the ride would relax him and make him forget their spat. He smiled and shrugged nonchalantly as she shouted down to him from the veranda.

"I hope you and your horse both break a leg!"

She'll calm down, he thought, the way she always does

whenever she gets into one of her moods. He couldn't help thinking, though, how she had changed since their marriage. She was becoming more and more demanding and almost childishly silly about things—trivial things, like insisting that he give up any social activities at all if she were not included. Only the day before they had had a spat over whether or not it was morally decent of him to play a game of cards with some of his old friends who had stopped by to say hello.

He smacked the horse's behind with his crop and galloped full speed downhill through the canefields, jumping fences and hedges, headed in the direction of the Buchins' house. It was a perfect morning for riding, a morning too precious to waste squabbling.

He arrived drenched with perspiration, dust clinging to his face and clothes. James was still having breakfast and invited La Farge to join him. La Farge gladly accepted a cup of coffee and asked for a damp towel to wipe the dust from his face and hands. He sat down in a rocking chair across from his friend and stretched his legs out onto the table right alongside Buchin's breakfast dishes. Buchin cast a glance at the dusty leather boots now resting inches away from his ham and eggs, but said nothing.

The look, however, did not go unnoticed. La Farge reached over and took Buchin's napkin from his lap and dusted off his boots, still lying out flat on the table.

"There! That's much better," he said, and replaced the napkin in his friend's lap.

Buchin looked helplessly at his dust-covered eggs and laid his fork down on his plate.

"Ah! What a day!" La Farge leaned back and contemplated the house and garden around him. "I like your new house," he said to Buchin. "It's not formal or pretentious, like you, my friend. Only a touch of Early American here and there."

His eyes scanned the big, overstuffed, leather pieces, much too heavy for the Caribbean, but very comfortable.

The two men spent much of the morning discussing James's recent engagement to Katherine Barnes, youngest daughter of Colonel Alfred Barnes of New York, a West Pointer. They were about to sit down to a lunch of cold lobster salad with green pawpaw and avocado, when a messenger came to the door. It was Félix, the overseer at the Férrier plantation. The man burst into the house, screaming in patois, repeating the same words over and over again. He looked as if he had come face to face with the devil. La Farge could not yet understand the local dialect, but he knew something was amiss, just by the look on the man's face.

"What is he saying, James? I can't make out his words."

James called for Camille, the cook, to come and translate. Her dark face turned gray as she listened to him, and she at once burst into tears.

"Ma'm'selle Jacqueline dead! Her father and mother, M'sieur and Madame Férrier, dead too, all dead in boat. Boat turn over. Them all drowned." She was in hysterics by the time she had got the last words out.

La Farge was stunned. He could not speak. Why? Why had Jacqueline gone to La Rose when she had so much to do at home? No, it could not be! There had to be some mistake; his darling Jacqueline could not be dead. He would not let her be!

James saw that Armand was becoming hysterical. He grabbed a bottle of brandy as the two of them simultaneously sprang to their feet, knocking over the table in their dash for the door.

The four-mile ride to La Rose took only ten minutes, but every inch seemed like a mile, every minute an hour. The car screeched to a halt in front of the gates, and La Farge did not wait for them to be opened. He climbed out of the car, jumped over the wall, and sprinted up the hill to the bluff. As he reached the top, he could see a small group of people standing together in a huddle, talking excitedly.

He yelled out to them as he came closer. "What happened? Where is my wife? Where is the boat?"

Félix, who by this time had caught up with him, pointed to the cluster of rocks about a mile out to sea.

"There! Over there, m'sieur. What's left of it. Only mast be seen. It wedged in rocks when broke off, just before boat went down. It so quick, m'sieur, so sudden. I just don't understand what happened." He wiped his grimy hands across his cheek to stop the tears from streaming down. "Me, I raking up leaves and stuff off beach, when they—m'sieur, madame, ma'm'selle—come down with Arnaud to go sail. Arnaud, he still diving for bodies, monsieur."

"Did you actually see my wife get on the boat with them? Are you positive it was she? Could it have been Mademoiselle Renée or one of Madame Férrier's friends?"

"No, m'sieur. It ma'm'selle Jacqueline. She even spoke to me just before Arnaud shoved off in boat. Ma'm'selle Renée went into town this morning. Oh m'sieur, it so horrible! I know it, that Belle Fleur place, that place full of Obéah. I know you and ma'm'selle should never gone to live in that place. I tell you it got a spell on it. Everybody die who live in it."

La Farge shook the man viciously. "Stop it, you fool. Stop talking nonsense about Obéah and magic. Get me the dinghy. Hurry! I'm going out there myself. *I'll* find her. I know I will." His voice softened as he let the trembling man go. "I—I have to. She is my whole life." His arms fell helplessly to his sides.

A small black boy came running up to him. "Is they all dead, M'sieur L'Farge? Is they all drowned?" he asked.

"I don't know, son. All we can do now is pray."

Félix was running down the beach to get the dinghy, while La Farge shed his clothes hurriedly, ready to swim out if he had to, to find Jacqueline.

"I see somebody," cried the little boy.

"It's a woman!" shouted someone from amidst the crowd.

"There she is! Right next to that reef over there behind those rocks."

La Farge squinted in the direction of the reefs. The sun was in his eyes. He saw nothing but the white of the surf breaking on the rocks. "Where'd she go, boy did you see? Did she dive in again?"

"Yes, sir, I see her go under just now. I just see Arnaud too, over there." He pointed to the reefs. "See, he just go under again."

Félix was back already, panting. "Dinghy ready, M'sieur L'Farge, but I tell you, you won't be able do much good.

Arnaud, he very good at this thing. He best diver in Fort de France. If anyone can find them, he sure can.''

By now the police were in a motorboat circling round the reefs where the boat had gone down. A couple of pelicans were flying overhead, flapping their wings and diving every now and then for fish.

''Where is Arnaud? I don't see him.''

''Where is the woman? Did anybody see her? She's been down there for three minutes already.''

''He'll never find them,'' came another voice. ''The woman is probably dead!''

''No!'' someone else shouted, ''there she is again. There's her head.''

La Farge bit his lip, trying to control the fear building up inside him. He jumped into the boat and started the motor.

''Reef runs out quite a way, m'sieur. You don't know waters round here. Please, you be careful,'' Félix said.

The pelicans hovered over La Farge, screaming and flapping their wings. More fishing boats appeared around the bluff, coming to lend a hand in the search for the bodies.

The water in the cove was glassy, like a mirror. La Farge wondered how anything that calm and beautiful could possibly be so treacherous. White clouds, fleecy as sheep, hovered directly over the scene. The sun had gone to hide behind them. As La Farge reached the reef, he cut the motor and threw the anchor overboard. As he was preparing to dive, Arnaud's head bobbed up. He was carrying someone.

He spat the water out of his mouth and screamed, ''I have somebody. Get a doctor, quick!''

La Farge could not believe his ears. He was afraid to look. ''Please, God, let it be Jacqueline. Just let it be her.'' He heard a shout. It was James Buchin. He had swum out and had climbed aboard the search boat.

''They've got her, Armand. They've found her. Thank God.''

Armand's heart was in his mouth. His prayers had been answered.

The big boat came closer, and two men grabbed the body from the diver's arms.

"Quick, doctor. Do something, please." It was La Farge, already aboard the other boat. "Quick! Somebody fetch a blanket to wrap her in."

Jacqueline's limp body was hoisted over the side of the boat and placed on a gray blanket someone had laid there just seconds before.

La Farge fell to his knees beside her. He wanted to hold her in his arms and will his own life into her. James held him back, pleading with him to get hold of himself. Already the doctor was at work, pumping the water out of her lungs. Every second that went by was like a lifetime of agony for Armand, as he watched for a sign of life.

Several other divers had by now joined Arnaud in search of the other two bodies. So far, there had been no sign of anything. La Farge sat staring back at the beach, remembering the day, only a year and a half ago, when he had seen Jacqueline for the first time. How beautiful she had looked, how full of life and laughter. Now she lay there stretched out on the deck, unmoving. Would she live? As he wept, a hand clasped his shoulder, and a voice filled with understanding spoke to him. It was the doctor.

"She will make it, Monsieur La Farge. She's alive."

"Alive? Did you say alive?" He could not believe it.

The man nodded. "Yes, monsieur, she is a fortunate young lady to survive such an ordeal, and strong too. Not many people could have taken such a blow on the head. But I'm afraid she'll have to be hospitalized for a week or so; she seems to have quite a bad concussion. We will need X-rays to confirm the gravity of her condition, but I think I can say she'll recover."

The boat was already on its way, speeding toward the town, where Jacqueline would be met by an ambulance and taken to the hospital.

Several days later, a specialist arrived from France and full-time nurses were hired to be at Jacqueline's bedside at all times.

She responded better than had been expected, and in no

time, she was sitting up in bed, feeding herself and primping for La Farge's frequent visits to the hospital.

The death of her parents had hit her hard. She had only learned the facts two weeks afterward. Her parents had already been found and buried by the time she had been informed. Her doctors had preferred to wait until she had recovered considerably before telling her. They had feared the shock might have been too much for her in her precarious condition.

After three weeks, Jacqueline was well enough to go home. Her body was healed, but her spirits were low. She could not get the accident out of her mind. Secretly she blamed herself for it, but outwardly she did not admit that. She said she had been bored at the plantation after Armand had left that morning. She had gone over to her mother's to have a chat. Her father had been puttering with his sailboat, and she had insisted that he take her sailing. Her father had given in, as always, to her whim, and had invited his wife to join them. They had been out only for a short while when a sudden wind from the east had risen. Henri Férrier, knowing that this type of squall lasted sometimes only minutes, but could be treacherous, had tried lowering the mainsail at once, but it had jammed halfway down the mast. As he had stood there trying to pull it free, a gust of wind had suddenly blown the boat against the reef, and the mast had cracked and fallen over, hitting him on the head.

The boat had begun to drift sideways, the keel scraping along the shoal. Jacqueline and her mother had tried to pull him out from under the mast, but the keel had suddenly hit a jagged rock, splitting the boat right across the middle. Jacqueline could remember seeing her mother being flung overboard, as the boat cracked open. She had tried to reach her father in one last attempt to free him, but the boat had given way just then, and she had been sucked under the surface along with its smashed hull. She had been knocked unconscious for several moments, then came to, washed up on the rocks behind the bend. When she had tried to swim for shore, she had passed out again.

The next thing she had been conscious of was the hospital room. Two weeks later she had been told of her parents' death.

She would always blame herself for the accident. If she had

stayed home, where she belonged, instead of running home to Mama and Papa the first time La Farge left her side, it might not have happened. But she blamed La Farge too. Why did he have to go over to be with James? Why couldn't he have been just as happy staying home with her until the party?

She put off visiting the graves of her parents, as if the whole tragedy would all just go away and she would wake one morning, the whole dream ended.

La Farge did not like the effect her parents' death was having on her. She did not cry or scream or yell. She just went around in a daze, not wanting to talk about it, avoiding the topic every time it came up, even viciously snapping at people when they offered sympathy and understanding. He decided it was time they paid a visit to the gravesites.

The Férriers had been buried on a slope of the bluff, overlooking the Bay of Petite Anse. La Farge remembered how Henri Férrier had once walked with him to that very spot and how they had stood together gazing out over the bay, talking about the days before La Rose had been bought and built. It had been clear that the site had been one of Férrier's most cherished parts of the property, and therefore La Farge had taken it upon himself to have him buried here, alongside his wife. He was sure Henri Férrier would have wanted it so.

They stood hand in hand, gazing down at the two fresh graves. The marble had been ordered for the headstones but it would be a while before it arrived from France. In the meantime, two wooden stakes and two red pine squares marked the graves: "Henri Férrier, born March 12, 1875, died January 3, 1939. Mélanie Férrier, born April 10, 1894, died January 3, 1939."

The wide, flounced skirt of Jacqueline's dress flapped loudly in the wind, in rhythm with the thundering waves below.

In the distance, the canefields with their spearlike leaves swayed gracefully in time with the gentle afternoon breeze. Bright buttercups of golden yellow lined the wall around the graves and a couple of large frangipani trees stood tall, bowing slightly in the breeze. Their pink, scented blossoms were falling softly from the trees, scattering over the two mounds of sand;

their sweet-smelling fragrance filled the air, mingling with the smell of the sea.

A small land crab bustled about from one grave to the other searching for the better site to dig his hole in. Jacqueline was looking at it, a strange expression on her face.

"Kill that thing!" she screamed. "Kill that ugly flesh-eating thing."

At first he did not know what she was referring to, but just then the small crab scurried across the space separating the two graves, and hid beneath a withered wreath.

"Why, it's only a harmless little sand—"

She turned and fled down the path to the house, crying and stumbling as she ran. It had been the first time she had cried since the accident. He ran after her to try to comfort her.

She stopped as she got to the front gate, sobbing and trying to catch her breath. The tears streaming down her wan cheeks were like the bursting of two dams; there seemed to be no end to them. Without a word, he handed her his handkerchief, not knowing what to do or say.

He placed his arms about her and pressed her to him gently, but she pushed him away.

"Get away from me! Take your filthy hands off me, you . . . you pig! I don't want you to come near me, now or ever."

Her words struck him like a blow on the head, but instead of complying with her demands, he grabbed hold of her again, this time with rage.

"What do you mean, you don't want me to touch you again?"

He released her and she turned and ran into the house.

He did not go home that night.

Several months passed, and outwardly things fell into a normal pattern. As far as everyone was concerned, all seemed well between the couple. But under that tightly buttoned cloak of perfection, hostile feelings and pent-up emotions continued to build. Jacqueline allowed Armand to "have her," as she referred to their lovemaking, on *her* terms only and always made it seem she was granting him a favor. For his part, Armand contented himself with whatever few liberties she allowed him and directed his excess energies to running the plantation. There were times, however, when Jacqueline would reject him for weeks at a time, and increasingly he needed someone to talk to.

Armand was beginning to rely more and more on James to fill the gap of loneliness in his life. James had married the West Point colonel's daughter Katherine, and she tried to befriend Jacqueline but she would have no part of it. James became a shadow in La Farge's footsteps. Hardly a day would go by without the two men getting together. Jacqueline withdrew more and more into herself. She demanded that Armand close up Belle Fleur, his beloved dwelling, and they moved into La Rose, the old Férrier plantation. She wanted to be close to her parents' graves, she said, and he gave in in the hope that this would appease her and that things would eventually straighten themselves out. They did not.

Then one day a blow came which was felt throughout the world.

On September 1, 1939, the mighty Wehrmacht of the German Third Reich smashed through the Polish borders. The bloodiest, most colossal war in history had begun.

On May 10, 1940, Germany launched an attack against the lowlands, and broke through the French border fortifications at Sedan four days later.

By June 17, France had lain down its arms; the catastrophe was felt immediately in every corner of the globe.

The Third Republic in France was abolished in favor of a totalitarian regime. Marshal Pétain was named Head of State, and established a government at Vichy. The swiftness with which France had fallen to the Germans had come as a shock to those in the islands. It was difficult for them to believe or accept what was happening. What would become of them under the Hitler regime?

At forty-two, La Farge was too old for the war, especially since the only thing he had been trained for was flying. He hesitated to return to France under the present conditions; for although the Vichy government's presence was strongly felt in Martinique, he knew that it would be a lot worse in Paris. He decided to remain in the islands for the time being and continue running the plantations as before.

In mid-November, 1942, German forces completed their domination of French territory by occupying Vichy. Almost everything he owned in Paris had been confiscated by the Germans. His home there had been requisitioned. He had heard that it had been taken over by one Lieutenant General von Witte as his personal headquarters.

One night after La Farge and Jacqueline had fought over whether La Farge had any "rights" to her body, he stormed out of the house and went into Fort de France, ending up drunk in some woman's bed. Jacqueline moved to a guest bedroom and would not let him near her. This drove him wild, since more than ever he wanted a child.

"I want a son," he would plead with her, "a son who one day can inherit what I have and carry on the name La Farge. And maybe a girl, too, to love and cherish in my old age."

Jacqueline would rant and rave and plead her case. "How can you ask me to bear you children, after what you did to me, after you humiliated me with that slut, whoever she was? After that, do you think I would want to have children by you?"

"Why don't you leave, then?"

"Because I want to make your life miserable! Why else? Why should I leave and make it easy for you when I can stay and have you crawl and beg every time you want me?"

Their fights would usually end with La Farge giving up and leaving the house, ending up in a bar in Fort de France with James. This went on for more than a year. Then one January morning, La Farge, beside himself with desire for Jacqueline, who seemed in spite of everything to grow more beautiful every day, took her by force.

Six weeks later, after fainting one morning in the garden, Jacqueline was informed by her doctor that she was going to have a child.

La Farge was beside himself with joy. His dream at last had

come true. He was about to become a father. He filled James's ear with his plans for his coming son. There was no doubt in La Farge's mind that the baby was a boy. He even had a name picked out for it. "Armand II, *not* Junior," he would say to Buchin. James would nod and congratulate him for the thousandth time, and they would then fall into conversation about where the baby should be born—Martinique, the United States, Puerto Rico? By the beginning of March 1944, La Farge had decided.

On March 18, 1944, the *Evening Star*, as Buchin's yacht was called, set sail for the United States. Their destination was Miami, Florida. From there they would fly to New York, and then drive to Connecticut, where a pregnant Jacqueline would remain with James and an even more pregnant Katherine, already seven months along with her second child. James's mother had died two weeks before, and James had finally decided to leave Martinique. He had persuaded La Farge to come with him.

Once in America, La Farge made arrangements for his wife's delivery, and for himself to be sent overseas to fight with General Charles de Gaulle.

La Farge had already communicated with General de Gaulle through the War Department in Washington, D.C., and had volunteered his services to him. He had relied greatly on the fact that he and the general had been acquaintances from World War I. The general's response had been affirmative. He informed La Farge that he would be pleased to receive him in London and that he was looking forward to utilizing his services as a former officer of the French Air Force.

La Farge had managed to be shipped out on the first scheduled troop transport, leaving New York for England in mid-April.

Three days before he left, he had a bitter and fateful quarrel with Jacqueline. He had found her with a bottle of harsh laxatives and immediately guessed her intentions. He took them and threw them into the toilet, slapping her face hard, in violent anger. Why? he thought—why was it so difficult for her to accept the fact that she was going to have a child? It was a result of his love for her, a symbol of their love for each other. And God knew he still loved her, more than his life.

She pleaded with him and begged him to understand. He yelled at her and called her a murderess. And then she collapsed on the bed in convulsions, retching violently. Suddenly sorry for her, he put his arms around her, but she pushed him away and kicked him in the shins viciously, calling him a sadist and a pig.

"Why? Just because I got you pregnant?"

"Yes!" she screamed. "Yes! Yes! Yes! I hate you for it, and as soon as you leave I'll get rid of it."

It was then the bargain was struck.

To be certain that Jacqueline would not attempt aborting the baby during his absence, La Farge made her a promise that he would never touch her again, as long as he lived, without her expressed desire for him to do so. She could see other men, or do as she pleased during his absence. But, in exchange, she would have the child, and she would remain married to him until the child was grown. He desperately wanted a child and he wanted that child to be raised by *both* its parents.

He persuaded Jacqueline to accept the proposition by promising her one third of his considerable income, and an additional third in trust for the child. By doing this, he said, she could indulge her tastes, no matter how expensive, while they brought up their child together. When the child reached maturity, she—and the child—would have the means to live as independently of him as either one would wish.

Jacqueline visualized herself as the queen of Paris with enormous sums of money to spend. And while she would not admit it to her husband, Jacqueline secretly wondered what it would be like to have a child, feeling that perhaps the bitterness she felt toward her life might thus be sweetened. She accepted her husband's offer, and he made the necessary legal arrangements before he left for England.

After signing the legal papers in New York, she stood up and smoothed out the wrinkles in her skirt, casually flashing him that beautiful smile which had captivated him from the beginning. "Who knows? Perhaps I'll like being a mother after all," and then she frowned like a little girl trying to make up her mind which sweet to choose. "There also is a chance I might not."

Now, eighteen years later and three thousand miles away, Jacqueline's words sounded over and over in La Farge's head. He shivered, the room was dark and cold. The wind had blown the window open, and from below came Rosalie's laughter. "They're still down there!" he exclaimed. "The girl must be freezing." He went to the window and threw back the shutter with a loud bang. "It's time you two got inside before you catch pneumonia, not to mention the fact that it is impossible for me to get any sleep with you making such a tohubohu there."

He chuckled to himself as Rosalie and Ahmed pulled away from each other and ran down the pathway to the house.

La Farge closed the window quietly and walked back to bed.

"Rosalie, my darling," he said to himself, "what will I do without you?"

Chapter Six

The following days were dazzling. Ahmed and Rosalie spent endless hours together on the beach, roasting themselves in the hot sun, gradually assuming a healthy, golden tan. Ahmed performed all sorts of complicated exercises to maintain his perfectly proportioned physique, while Rosalie, in an effort to overcome her amusement over the incredible expressions and contortions on his face, spent most of her time swimming or snorkeling along the cliffs nearby. There Ahmed would join her after he had exhausted himself exercising.

On the fifth day after their arrival in St. Tropez, La Farge announced to Ahmed and Rosalie that he would like to go to Nice that evening for dinner. He had made reservations for four at the Garoc. Rosalie was pleased that she and Ahmed would at last have some time alone with her parents. She hoped to discuss with her mother her plans for the wedding, and also welcomed the opportunity to have her father and Ahmed spend some time together. Ahmed too was delighted by the invitation.

They dressed with special care that evening. It was not often that Armand La Farge left his villa to go out for a night on the town. Tonight, La Farge felt, was a night to celebrate. He wanted everyone to know that Ahmed and his daughter were engaged.

Rosalie found it difficult to make up her mind which dress to wear. She eventually chose a Dior original—a beautiful, slinky number of fine turquoise silk, a dress she had put aside especially for such an occasion. The gown fit her like a glove, revealing the perfect body beneath. She wore nothing under the gown. Her nipples showed through the sleek halter top, and the plunging back exposed her smooth, tanned skin almost to the base of her spine. The dress was long but still allowed her matching turquoise evening sandals to be seen. Her cheeks were pink from the excitement of the night, highlighting her high cheekbones and setting off the even tan of the rest of her face and neck. Around her neck she wore a delicate necklace of fine coral beads and tiny white pearls, held together in the back by a diamond-and-coral clasp in the shape of a heart. Her hair was pinned back high at the temples with two small heart-shaped coral clips matching the necklace. The clips and necklace had been gifts from her father on her sixteenth birthday, almost two years before, but she had never worn them before tonight. Her mother had thought her too young at the time to wear such jewelry, and had made Rosalie promise to wait until she was a bit older. Tonight she felt she was old enough.

She stood in front of Ahmed, allowing him to admire her. She stood straight and tall, eyes softly shut, her mouth plump and full, glistening in the light from the fixture above. She waited to be kissed. He gazed down at her, admiring her lovely face. He reached out and touched her face softly, almost reverently, tracing his fingers along the lines of its delicate contours, starting from the temples and then trailing along the prominent cheekbones, down to her lips and chin. Her face bore no signs of makeup, except for the touch of soft brown mascara on her eyelashes and the tiny dab of cherry red lipstick. He leaned forward and kissed her lips softly, so as not to disturb their perfect redness. Her lips quivered lightly under his and she parted them enticingly as she received his tongue. He probed gently along her teeth and the roof of her mouth. He could feel his groin tightening; if he did not stop now, he would have her naked on the floor in a minute. He removed his tongue from her parted lips and trailed it softly along her neck to her earlobe. He could smell the faintest hint of her perfume, delicate, discreet—and overwhelming. Like Rosalie, he thought.

The sound of footsteps on the stairs startled them, and they both turned to look in the direction of the sound.

Handsome as the devil himself, in a pale blue dinner jacket, Armand La Farge descended the winding marble staircase to where the two were standing. Jacqueline was not with him. An hour before she had informed her husband that she could not join them because of a sudden severe headache, and she had gone to bed.

La Farge bent and kissed Rosalie on the cheek. "You are the best-looking couple I know." He beamed, putting his arms around both Ahmed and Rosalie affectionately.

"Except for you and Madame La Farge, of course," replied Ahmed almost instantly.

"Well now, that might once have been true. But," he went on, "seeing Rosalie tonight, I dare say her beauty surpasses her mother's by far. And you, Ahmed," he said. "Look at you; you're almost as irresistible to the ladies as I am." He turned to his daughter and winked. "Don't you think so too, *ma chérie?*" He threw back his head and laughed.

Rosalie laughed too, amused by her father's audacity.

"Since your mother isn't joining us, perhaps you two would enjoy the Hotel de Paris and the crowd there, more than the Garoc. Why don't we go to the restaurant at the hotel and to the casino afterward?" La Farge suggested.

Rosalie looked at Ahmed. "All right with you?"

As their car pulled up in front of the Hotel de Paris, another car was just pulling in ahead of them.

"Why, that's Jean— What's he doing here?" La Farge leaned over the seat and peered through the windshield. "I wonder why he changed his mind about staying home."

Rosalie wondered too. She had heard her father asking the

duke earlier that day about his plans for the evening, and d'Artois had made it quite clear that he intended to stay at the villa—with a good book, as he had put it.

"There is a woman in the car with him. I wonder who she is?" Rosalie's curiosity was piqued.

Ahmed chuckled. "Maybe he just has a little Mimi hidden away somewhere and doesn't want us to know about it."

"That is very unlikely," La Farge said. "He would have told me, I'm sure. I have known the man for nearly fifteen years, and in all that time, I have never known him to have a lady friend."

Ahmed raised his eyebrow. "Oh? What's wrong with him?"

La Farge gave him an exasperated look. "Nothing is wrong with him, at least to my knowledge. I guess some men never quite get over certain things."

"Like what?" Rosalie wanted to know.

"Like the war, torture. Things like that."

"Oh, Papa, something more must be wrong with him. No man can live without a woman unless . . ." She did not have to finish. Her tone made her meaning clear.

Ahmed chuckled. "I don't believe it. The duke a pansy? He's too masculine-looking for that."

"Don't judge a book by its cover, Ahmed. Sometimes people aren't always what they seem," Rosalie said.

La Farge quieted her. "Hush, Rosalie. I'm ashamed of the way you are talking about our guest, who, by the way, happens to be one of my closest friends."

Rosalie shrugged and dropped the subject.

Ahmed spoke again. "You know, I could have sworn I recognized that woman from somewhere." He thought for a moment, trying to remember. Then he shook his head. "I guess not."

"Maybe she reminds you of one of your old girl friends and you just don't want to say so in front of me, hm?"

La Farge burst out laughing. "That serves you right, Ahmed, for sticking your nose in places where it doesn't belong. Now let me see you get yourself out of this one. You know, though," he added, "I felt the same way myself. As if I recognized the woman, I mean." He laughed. "Good thing Jacqueline isn't here. She'd say she was a woman from *my* past, instead of *yours*, Ahmed."

Ahmed chuckled at the thought, for he knew Madame La Farge only too well as a woman of many whims and emotions. He wondered whether a headache had been the real reason she had not come tonight.

"Let's go into the restaurant," La Farge said. "I also have to see René, my friend at Harry Winston's. They're having a display at the hotel, and I have to pick up a bracelet I ordered for Rosalie. It's to be my wedding gift."

"But, isn't it a bit late?" Ahmed asked.

"It's never too late when you're ready to pay someone a million francs."

"A million francs for a bracelet? Oh, Papa, that's crazy! I have enough jewelry as it is, and I'm sure that with my dowry and Ahmed to take care of me, I'll be able to buy myself anything I want."

La Farge kissed the top of his daughter's head as he used to when she was a little girl. "It is a very special bracelet, Rosalie. It is made of the rarest collection of pearls and diamonds, and I want you to have it."

"But—"

"Hush, child, that's enough. I said I want you to have it, and damn it, you shall have it even if later you choose to give it away. It is the least I can do for my only daughter."

Rosalie knew it was useless to argue any further. Her father was too stubborn. Directly across the street, she could see the lights from the casino. A chill ran through her body as she thought of the excitement which awaited her that evening. Jules stood holding the car door open for La Farge, who in turn leaned to help Rosalie out of the back seat. Her eyes shone with anticipation and delight at the heads turning to admire her as she headed into the hotel. La Farge, of course, was recognized everywhere, but until now Rosalie had been a sheltered schoolgirl, kept hidden from the inquisitive eyes of the public and the press. Everyone knew of her, but until tonight she had rarely been seen in public. But from tonight on, she would be a center of attention, and newspapers in Europe and America would tell of her great beauty and poise and of her fairytale engagement to Prince Ahmed of Saudia Arabia, son of the wealthy Sheikh Farahet. It was an exciting prospect, and frightening; she wondered if she would handle it with the poise of her father. A crowd gathered to watch the trio as they ascended the steps to the hotel.

The terrace restaurant was crammed with diners, some already far along with their meals, some still waiting to be seated. The room was alive with the noise of conversation.

"Monsieur La Farge, it has been a while. Nice to see you again."

"Hello, Georges. We shall be a while before dinner, about half an hour."

"Your usual table, monsieur?"

"That's right, Georges, the one in the corner." La Farge pointed to a table which was occupied. He frowned.

"They are almost through, monsieur. I shall hurry them along; you shall have your table, I assure you. And you are how many?"

"Just the three of us tonight, Georges."

"But where is Madame La Farge? Not ill, I hope."

"Ah no, nothing serious, just a little headache. Too much sun, I guess." La Farge was about to turn and leave, when the man sitting at the table next to the one in the corner turned around and saw him.

He called out to La Farge: "Armand, over here."

La Farge turned to look in the direction of the voice. He saw the duke almost at once. He was accompanied by the woman observed earlier in the car and a man whom La Farge had never seen before. The duke got to his feet and called for the waiter. He hurried over to greet the trio. "*Mon vieux*, what a surprise to run into you here. I thought you were going to the Garoc in Nice. What made you change your mind? Don't tell me Pauline's bouillabaisse is slipping."

"No, not at all. We never got there," replied La Farge. "But it is I who am surprised to see you."

He could tell the duke was about to ask them to join his party. The duke did.

La Farge declined. "I'm sorry, but I have to refuse. You see, I have quite a lot to discuss with Rosalie and Ahmed, and I've promised myself entirely to them this evening. Perhaps another time?" He bowed politely to the raven-haired woman and her companion sitting at the duke's table. She was an interesting sort of woman, in a dark, almost mysterious way. She wore a black satin dress with a plunging neckline, exposing most of her tanned breasts. Around her neck she wore a diamond and emerald necklace. She was not beautiful, but sensuously chic.

She bowed her head slightly in response to La Farge's greeting and smiled up at him.

The duke made the introductions. "Monsieur La Farge, Mademoiselle La Farge, Prince Ahmed Farahet, may I present Fräulein Margot Koesler, my protégée, and Herr Schuster, my banker. He is from Zurich."

The banker, a fat, balding man, with a small patch of mustache seeming to be pasted over his upper lip, got to his feet and bowed.

"Monsieur La Farge," Schuster said unctuously, "my friend the duke has spoken to me many times of you and your lovely wife, but I must say, I am thunderstruck by your daughter's beauty. She is absolutely charming."

The duke had the air of approving of the banker's comment; Fräulein Koesler seemed less enthusiastic. The two young women nodded to each other and shook hands, then La Farge held his hand out to Fräulein Koesler. She extended hers and he noticed the long, delicate fingers and the expensive jewelry, especially a large ring. A strange piece for a woman to wear, he thought; a family crest ring?

Fräulein Koesler spoke. "Will you not join us, Monsieur La Farge? And your daughter and her fiancé, of course."

The dark young woman looked up at Ahmed longingly. "How did you ever escape me, Prince Charming? It seems that all the handsome ones get away."

Ahmed's ego did not mind the compliment, but his good sense told him to watch out for Rosalie's temper. He was about to respond when Rosalie cut in.

"For advice on fishing, I suggest you apply to the duke, mademoiselle; he is well known as an expert. It's a question of bait."

Ahmed suppressed a chuckle; La Farge just failed to; the duke's lips tightened. Fräulein Koesler kept her face carefully bland as she turned to La Farge.

"I've heard a lot about you, Monsieur La Farge. I hope that some evening you can join us for dinner." She lowered her eyes slightly and continued, "My villa is in Cap d'Antibes. I should like you to come to dinner there one evening."

La Farge flashed her a polite smile. "I can't promise you that, young lady, for I seldom leave St. Tropez. But if you are a protégée of my good friend Jean, you must accompany him one day for lunch at Colombier, or perhaps spend a weekend." He smiled wickedly and added, "That would give you and Rosalie"—he patted his daughter's arm—"a chance to know each other a little better."

Rosalie felt like kicking him in the shins. Instead, she rested her foot on her father's and tapped it lightly.

"Well, it's been nice talking to you," La Farge said, looking at the duke, "and nice meeting you both." He inclined his head to the two others at the table. "But we have to be going. I'm meeting someone in the lobby, and I'm already quite late." He placed his left arm around Rosalie's free one. Her other was already entwined with Ahmed's. As they entered the lobby, a man came rushing toward them.

"Monsieur La Farge." It was René Talbot, who had been patiently waiting for his client. "I have the merchandise you requested. It is in the hotel vault."

La Farge went off with Talbot to the hotel vault. "I'll join you later in the bar," he said to Ahmed and Rosalie as he went off in the opposite direction.

Together, Rosalie and Ahmed strolled into the elegant bar with its ornate *café intime* look.

At the table closest to the entrance a fat woman sat stuffing herself on hors d'oeuvres. She looked up as they passed by her table, her face lit up in recognition. She folded her glasses with a loud snap and leaned over to speak to the people at the neighboring table.

"It's Prince Ahmed, don't you recognize him? And he's with Rosalie La Farge." Her voice was hoarse with excitement. "Why, they say that Rosalie one day will come into more money than she'll know what to do with, and the prince must be at least that rich, with all that oil his father owns." She licked her lips and went on, "Those Arabs have got more money than they can count. He's a little old for her though, wouldn't you say?" She paused for a moment, still staring at the couple, and went on. "Well, if you can listen to what rumors say, if that girl is anything like her father she must be a fast one." The couple at the next table did not reply, but Ahmed and Rosalie overheard the woman's remarks.

Ahmed turned to look at the fat woman. "Why, if it isn't Lady Gertrude. Still getting wider, I see. I wish I could say it was a pleasure to see you again, but we sons of the desert are brought up to be truthful. It's no wonder your poor husband, rest his soul, shot himself to escape from you."

Lady Gertrude sputtered incoherently as she gathered up her belongings, fled from everyone's stares, and disappeared into the crowded hotel lobby.

"She deserved that, monsieur. Well done."

Rosalie turned to look and saw a handsome blond man, sitting by himself, sipping a brandy. For a moment their eyes locked, and a strange feeling swept over her, like a premonition—whether of good or evil, she could not tell.

Ahmed's voice broke the spell. "Merci, monsieur, and welcome to France. You are American, I would guess, from the accent."

The blond man laughed, flashing two rows of perfect white teeth. "I'm afraid so, and I guess, try as I might, I can't hide the fact." His voice was soft but strong—similar in some ways to Ahmed's, only much softer, like a caress, Rosalie thought.

The man stood up as Rosalie and Ahmed approached his table. Rosalie sized him up quickly. He was taller than Ahmed, his face more lined and rugged. His thin mustache arched perfectly over his lips. He reminded Rosalie of someone, but she could not think who.

Once again the man's lips parted into a friendly smile. "Would you care to sit down?" he asked, pulling out a chair for Rosalie. He had already scanned the room and knew there was no other table available. Ahmed glanced around the room.

"If you are sure we won't be imposing, monsieur."

The stranger gestured for them to sit down, and introduced himself.

"Jeffrey Allan Guthrow, at your service." His manner made Rosalie smile. She handed him her hand to be kissed. He bent and did so, his thin mustache flicking over her skin, sending a shiver through her arm. *That's* it, Rosalie thought. His resemblance to Clark Gable was astonishing, only he was blond and even better looking.

He looks so cosmopolitan, she thought, and yet there's also something so American about him. She couldn't put her finger on it. Perhaps it was his smile, so friendly and unguarded.

He pushed in her chair, and waited for Ahmed to be seated.

"What will you have, mademoiselle, monsieur?"

"Oh, I'm dreadfully sorry. I forgot to introduce us," exclaimed Ahmed. "This is Mademoiselle Rosalie La Farge, my fiancée, and I am Prince Ahmed Farahet. Do forgive my gaffe, monsieur."

The American nodded his forgiveness and signaled for the waiter. "Mademoiselle?"

"Martini, please."

"Monsieur?"

"Make that two."

"I'll have another Rémy Martin, please," the American said.

He turned to Ahmed. "I must say you really handled that old hag. I suppose she's Sir Cedric Taunton's widow? I read about his death last year when I was in London. The papers hinted pretty broadly that the poor man had taken his life to escape from his wife." A faint look of sadness crossed his face.

As he spoke Rosalie felt the American's eyes upon her,

bold and daring, making her very uncomfortable. She loved Ahmed, God knew she did, in every possible way. Then why did her heart beat so quickly in this man's presence? Why did her pulse quicken every time she looked at him?

A sudden lull in conversation throughout the restaurant caused the trio to look around. The cause was Armand La Farge, standing in the doorway, scanning the room. Ahmed got to his feet and in a few quick strides crossed the room to La Farge; Rosalie was left alone at the table with the American.

"I must be leaving soon," he said, "but I hope we'll meet again." His words were more a command than a wish.

Rosalie nodded yes, lowering her eyes to stare at the green olive in her martini. She could feel Jeffrey Guthrow's eyes on her. She nervously stirred her drink with her finger. As she did so, Jeffrey took her hand and, leaning forward, delicately licked the moisture from the finger. She was shocked. She could not believe the man's impudence. She felt like kicking him under the table, but she saw Ahmed and her father approaching and was afraid they would notice.

La Farge and the American exchanged words of greeting. Ahmed explained to La Farge how they had come to meet Guthrow.

"Good for you, Ahmed. I wish I'd been there."

"In that case, she probably would not have said anything, sir," said Guthrow.

Ahmed shot the American a disapproving look. He took the stranger's remark as a denigration of his own importance.

"No offense, Prince Ahmed," Guthrow said smoothly. "As I said, I thought you handled the whole thing beautifully."

Ahmed waved his hand to say that no offense was taken, but Rosalie could sense he was still angry

"Do you people ever get to Villefranche?"

"Why, certainly we do. Why?" Rosalie said.

"Well, I have a villa there, and I would be honored if you would stop by one evening for drinks and conversation."

"I'll bet," Rosalie couldn't help muttering.

"Did you say something, darling?" Ahmed said.

"Oh no, Ahmed, I'm sorry."

The American had heard her remark and could not keep from smiling. "Well, maybe you gentlemen would like to join me and Jean-Paul Gatz, who's my houseguest for the summer, for a little bridge? No doubt Mademoiselle Rosalie would be bored to death and has many more fascinating ways to occupy her evenings."

No one but Rosalie caught his sarcasm.

"Oh, it's a pity, monsieur," La Farge replied. "I have heard of Jean-Paul Gatz's skill at bridge and have always meant to meet him. It would have been a great pleasure." He straightened his tie and went on. "But I am leaving tomorrow for Paris for a few days, and I already have a fishing date in the morning with some of my guests. I would hate to disappoint them. Some other time, perhaps?"

La Farge frowned, thinking a moment. "Why don't you look me up when you get to Paris? Here, take my card." He handed Guthrow a crisp white card. "It might be interesting, one evening, for the two of us to have dinner at the Club d'Aviation on the Champs-Elysées and then play some bridge. I've seen Mousieur Gatz there on occasion."

Jeffrey Guthrow smiled his agreement and stood up. He glanced at his watch. "It has been a pleasure, messieurs, mademoiselle, but I am afraid I am already terribly late for a business appointment and shall miss it if I don't hurry."

Rosalie smiled to herself. A business appointment at this time of night? A likely story. She was sure that the only appointment this rogue was going to be late for was with some Côte d'Azur *poule*. Mechanically, Rosalie's hand stuck out to bid him good-bye, and as his lips touched her skin, he flicked his tongue across the back of her hand, ever so lightly.

With a sardonic undertone, he said, "I can assure you, mademoiselle, that only the most urgent appointment would draw me away from the pleasure of your company."

La Farge did not seem to notice anything unusual about the compliment. After all, this was France.

Guthrow placed a hundred-franc note under the ashtray to pay for the drinks and left without a backward glance. Rosalie's gaze followed the tall figure until he disappeared through the door. Rosalie felt as if she had been on a Ferris wheel. It was strange, the effect he had had on her. Slowly, she regained her calm, relaxing once again as Ahmed and her father seated themselves for the second time.

La Farge glanced at his watch. "My God, it's already nine-thirty, Ahmed. We'd best have some dinner."

"Any time you wish," Ahmed said.

La Farge signaled the waiter and paid him for the drinks, ignoring the perfectly visible note lying on the table. "Here, *garcon*. Keep the change. And, oh yes, here's an extra tip for you." He handed him the bill left by the American.

The boy stared at the crisp new note. "A tip? But, monsieur!"

"Hush, don't you have any sense? Not too much, I guess. At his age, Ahmed, I wouldn't have asked twice if some fool handed me such a gift." He laughed reminiscently.

The three of them stood up and walked out of the bar, through the lobby to their table on the terrace.

As they ate, a reporter approached and asked if he might take pictures for the morning paper. "May we have a statement, mademoiselle? Could you tell our readers who will be the lucky designer of your wedding gown and trousseau?"

"My God!" It dawned on Rosalie that she had not given the slightest thought to the task. "My good man, I really hate to talk with a mouth full of trout. All bones, you understand. And furthermore, I have not yet had the time to decide on these matters. When the time comes, I'm certain you will be the first to know." She swallowed her fish and washed it down with a sip of Bâtard-Montrachet. "In the meantime, you can tell your readers that the bride will not wear underwear, and that her dress might not be white."

Armand La Farge choked on his trout. He gulped down his wine, in effort to stop coughing.

Rosalie continued, "The Prince and I will be married in Paris and we shall then sail to the South Pacific on our honeymoon."

Now it was Ahmed's turn to choke. They had not discussed where they would be honeymooning, but apparently Rosalie had just made the decision.

The man took one last picture, thanked them and left in great haste to meet his deadline for the morning paper.

"It's a pity you won't recognize your statement in the morning. By the time the press gets through doctoring it up, it'll be a total misquote."

Rosalie shrugged at her father's words. "Well, I tried, anyway."

Chapter Seven

Paris, September 1962

The day on the rue Vieille du Temple was about to begin. The normal morning clatter of breakfast carts being wheeled to the bedrooms, and the soft pitter-patter of the maids hurrying back and forth with the usual armloads of fresh flowers for every room made the morning like any other at the La Farge mansion. Berthe went in to wake Rosalie.

"Breakfast in bed this morning for the bride-to-be." She beamed. "I just can't believe my little girl is grown up enough to get married."

"Oh, shut up, Berthe, you always bring me breakfast in bed, and I wish you wouldn't refer to me as your little girl. I'm not, you know."

"Hm, I can see you are in your usual mood after a few weeks in the sun. I don't know what it is, but I think you come back a little meaner each time you go away on holiday. It's that Prince Charming of yours, I'm sure. He's been putting ideas into your head."

"Are you crazy this morning, Berthe? What ideas can Ahmed be putting in my head that would have anything to do with you? Why, he doesn't even know you're alive. Now, shut up and get me my tea. Where's the croissant?"

"But I thought you wanted toast this morning. At least that's what you told me last night."

"True, but when do you ever do what I say, Berthe? I just assumed that if I said I wanted to have toast for breakfast that you would automatically make me toast *and* croissants. Well?"

"Some mornings I just can't win. You're getting more and more like your father every day." Berthe fluffed the lacy pillows behind her young mistress's back and set the breakfast tray across her lap. The small white rose nestled in the far right-hand corner of the tray was a new touch. Rosalie hurried to open the little card attached to it. It was from Ahmed. "Since I can't be with you this morning in your bed, I'm sending you this rose to keep you company. A." She read it aloud to Berthe, then rested it on the tray beside her toast. He wouldn't earn a living as a poet, she thought, but she was touched by his thoughtfulness. The beautiful china teapot sparkled in the morning's sun, reflecting glinting rays onto the bed. An ivory-colored telephone and her address book lay on the bed beside her, ready for a full day's work of phoning and planning.

The days were hectic as Rosalie streaked through Paris with her mother and Berthe, shopping for her trousseau. First she stopped in at Christian Dior's on avenue Montaigne and ordered several breathtaking dressing gowns with matching, frothy nightgowns, and dozens of scarves and accessories. Then it was Hermès on rue du Faubourg St.-Honoré for a wardrobe of elegant purses, belts, raincoats, cashmere sweaters, and jacket in case of a cold night en route to the South Pacific. She then came close to buying out Cardin, mostly things she thought might look good on Ahmed, except for a smashing, black evening cape, lined in red silk; though actually designed for a man, Rosalie fancied herself in it, bought it "just in case."

Choosing the designer for her wedding dress was proving to be difficult, for even Ungaro, one of her favorites, did not have what she wanted. She bought every other outfit he had to offer, but no wedding dress. Ted Lapidus, her old friend, designed for her a wardrobe of slacks and T-shirts fit for a true sailor, and by the time she finally decided on a wedding dress, she had bought so many clothes that Armand La Farge claimed to be considering buying another yacht to accompany the *Créole* just to accommodate his daughter's trousseau. Rosalie was practically in a state of collapse by the time she finally decided on a wedding dress. Henri La Tour, a young and upcoming French designer, came to see Rosalie with a design for a wedding gown that captured her heart instantly. It was a beautiful ivory silk gown with a low, swooping neckline. The long sleeves were to be fitted tightly around the arms to give support to the gown, since there were no shoulders or stays to otherwise hold it up. Small fresh pink-and-white cymbidium orchids were to be sewn on the dress just minutes before the actual ceremony, and the bridal bouquet would be made of matching baby orchids and sprigs of stephanotis and baby's breath, all displayed on a background of lemon leaves. The crinoline petticoat, trimmed with ivory lace and delicate pink satin ribbons, would emphasize the skirt's bouffant quality.

She was in a state of exalted near-mania about the gown. "Just think how Ahmed's eyes will pop out of his head when he sees me in it! He won't be able to keep his hands off me."

"That's news?" Berthe said tartly. "He can hardly keep his hands off you now. He probably won't even notice the dress, just what's inside it; that's all he's got on his mind, anyway."

The big day was upon them at last. Flowers ordered from Nice adorned the mantels, tables, and doorways of every room in the great house. A dozen chefs labored in the kitchen preparing the wedding feast. Presents sent from the sheikh were displayed in a pyramid on a huge table in Rosalie's sitting room. The smells of Eastern pastry filled the air as Hamdu and Jusif, Ahmed's servants, cooked and baked in preparation for the distinguished guests. Rosalie and Berthe ran around packing while Madame La Farge busily fluttered about from room to room, making sure that everything was just right. Even the normally imperturbable La Farge seemed a little nervous.

Precisely at four in the afternoon, the great chimes rang,

announcing the arrival of the first guests. The wedding was set for five o'ckock and Rosalie was already getting dressed in her boudoir next to her bedroom. Henri La Tour and two of his best seamstresses were putting the last-minute touches on the dress. Each tiny orchid had to be sewn on by hand, taking care not to damage the delicate petals of the beautiful flowers. Alexandre, the hairdresser, hovered over Rosalie, arranging and rearranging her long locks, painstakingly pinning and fastening each tiny flower in her hair. Rosalie would be his masterpiece. He and Henri had spent days deciding the right number and placement of each delicate flower in Mademoiselle La Farge's hair.

Jacqueline was dabbing a little powder on Rosalie's nose.

"I don't need any powder, Maman," Rosalie cried.

"*I* need it," Jacqueline replied, "and so do you. Every woman can stand a little powder on her nose."

"*I'm* one woman who doesn't want any. Perhaps when I'm your age, Maman, I'll think differently, and I'll need—ouch!" She looked down at Henri, who had jabbed her with the needle.

"I take your point," Rosalie muttered to the designer. Jacqueline La Farge was in her forties, and it was a known fact that she did not care to be reminded of it.

At exactly ten minutes past five, Rosalie entered the ballroom on her father's arm. A murmur could be heard from the crowd, whispering of the bride's beauty.

The organ began to play as Rosalie and her father walked toward the altar. Her silk gown swished softly with every step, the lace-trimmed crinoline brushing against her legs.

On her left arm she wore the bracelet her father had bought her in Monte Carlo; she wore no other jewelry. Instead of a veil, there were six white orchids in her hair, three at each temple. Her shoes were made of tiny white pearllike beads on a silk background. She had chosen not to perfume herself; the delicate scent of flowers was all she wanted. She looked straight ahead, not caring to see anyone but Ahmed. He was standing at the altar, dressed in a fine silk suit of a pale blue that was flattering to his dark complexion. He wore a white ascot at his neck; his dark beard was trimmed short. His dark eyes met Rosalie's and locked there.

As Archbishop Lernier, La Farge's longtime friend, conducted the wedding service—which, uniting a professing Muslim and a determinedly nonpracticing Roman Catholic, had been the subject of protracted negotiations from Rome to Paris to Mecca, arousing the delighted interest of the theological correspondents of *Le Matin, Time*, and *Der Stern*—certain of the secondary participants were indulging in their private considerations.

Armand La Farge: I wonder how it strikes Lernier, licensing a man and a woman to go to bed together? Must seem unnatural to him.

Jean, Duc d'Artois: A waste, a golden girl like that wedded to a boy, and a nigger at that. But it won't last—*abbia la santa pazienza,* as dear Benito used to say, unchurched though he was. I'll have this one, make no mistake.

Jacqueline La Farge: A wartime rape, even though the rapist was my own husband, and here's the result—my lovely daughter, a part of me. And lost now, gone to her own man; though she was never mine. I was *so* shrewd, *so* practical, holding her hostage in my womb, extorting ransom from my husband, punishing him for the crime of being a man. Now, no daughter, no husband, only me and my fortune. How he must hate me. . . .

She glanced toward La Farge, dreading what she knew she would be able to read beneath his public impassivity.

There were tears in his eyes. He reached for his wife's hand and squeezed it. "Thank you," he whispered. "Thank you for our beautiful daughter."

Thunderstruck with relief, delight, and a flood of revived love, she was about to speak, but Ahmed and Rosalie, now married, headed toward them. All around the guests were pressing to get closer, offering their congratulations. Members of the press began stampeding.

Their precious moment, Jacqueline knew, was lost—but only for the moment. . . .

Max was beckoning from the hallway, indicating that the

crowd outside was growing restless. "The people!" he shouted, his normal restraint abandoned. "They are still waiting outside to see the newlyweds." Ahmed and Rosalie led the way as two servants swung the heavy front door open. A roar went up as the two appeared in the doorway.

Ahmed waved to the crowd and Rosalie, laughing, swung her arm around and around, as if about to throw a baseball, then let go. Up went the bridal bouquet, green and pink and white. It seemed to defy gravity for a moment as it sailed over the crowd, then down it came, and arms waved wildly in the air reaching for it. A girl squealed excitedly as she caught it. She was a tall, redheaded girl, about the same age as Rosalie. She screamed as she clutched the bouquet and waved frantically at the bride.

La Farge came to stand beside his daughter and new son-in-law. "Champagne for everyone," he shouted out. "Let this night be as joyful for everyone as it is for me!"

The crowd cheered, and as the cases of champagne began to roll out, the three retreated behind the heavy doors of the mansion. It was time for celebrating, and as the band played, Ahmed swooped Rosalie into his arms and onto the dance floor. It was the same waltz that had been playing that night in this same ballroom when Rosalie and Ahmed had met "officially" for the first time. It was Rosalie's favorite, and Ahmed had requested it be played today just for the two of them. The guests stood and watched, dazzled by the handsome prince and his princess, as the couple twirled and twirled around the huge dance floor. At the end of the waltz, another one began, and this time everyone joined in.

Jean, Duc d'Artois, partnered with a Clermont-Ferrand mill owner's pudgy wife, stepped lithely around the floor. "What a marvelous room!" the woman gushed. "In the provinces, we don't go in much for such elegance, no matter how much money there is. In Paris, they know how to do things with style, that's clear! But you're a friend of the family, aren't you? So you must be used to all this—I suppose, when they're not holding a big affair, this room is just a drafty old barn of a place, with the furniture all in dust sheets, eh?"

D'Artois smiled thinly. "A room is a room, madame, an

enclosed space, that's all. It's the use that's made of it that counts.'' His mind drifted back twenty years to a time when the fortunes of war had prevented the room's owner from making use of it. In 1942, there were others who had known how to employ it. . . .

Lieutenant General Heinz von Witte understood well the administrative value of theatricality. Clerks and efficiency experts might cluck disapprovingly about the waste of space, but the sheer effrontery of using the ballroom of the La Farge mansion for one man's office had its effect. No one could enter through those massive doors and make his way across the unending stretch of gleaming parquet without being daunted by the time he approached the black-uniformed figure behind the desk. Let someone come bustling in from Berlin, swollen with the importance of a personal message from the reichsmarschall or the Führer himself, and the fellow would be pretty well wilted by the journey across the ballroom to von Witte's desk.

His personal aide, however, was hardened to the imposing atmosphere, and, on this spring afternoon, merely walked briskly to the general's desk and laid an envelope on it. ''Beg to report, sir, an urgent dispatch.''

Von Witte read the message impassively. ''This is a grave tragedy for the Reich,'' he said gravely. ''My old comrade and personal friend, Reinhard Heydrich, Protector of Bohemia, has succumbed to the wounds inflicted on him by the Czech bandits four days ago.''

''They won't be crowing much about that,'' the aide observed. ''Our chaps have rounded up a thousand or so of the locals in Prague, and from what I've heard, they've done 'em in already. And I doubt that's the end of it.''

It was not. Five days later, the village of Lidice in Czechoslovakia was destroyed, along with almost all of its inhabitants, in reprisal.

The death of his ''old comrade'' was not in fact a personal grief to von Witte. True, Heydrich had been the lover of von Witte's sister, Berta, and the father of her infant daughter; but any personal regret was overshadowed by several very good reasons—some fifty million reasons, that being the number of Swiss francs deposited in a secret Swiss account and jointly controlled by von Witte and Heydrich.

After the annexation of Austria in early 1938 by the Third Reich, Heydrich had set up an "Office for Jewish Emigration" in Vienna. Its chief was the Austrian, Karl Adolph Eichmann, but control remained under the SD, commanded by Heydrich. This "Jewish Office," as it came to be known, was the sole agency from which Austrian Jews could obtain exit permits. The price paid by Jews to leave their homeland was invariably all they possessed.

Von Witte, then an SD colonel on Heydrich's staff, was chosen by Heydrich as his sole accomplice in a scheme to obtain a handsome share of this Jewish treasure. Heydrich could trust von Witte not to betray him for a reason far more compelling than any personal loyalty: his sister, Berta, whom Heydrich had taken as his mistress. Heydrich was confident that von Witte was well aware of what would happen to Berta in the event of any treachery.

In order to obtain exit permits from Austria, Jews made payment in many forms; banknotes, of course, but also gold, precious gems, jewelry, silver, paintings, and other works of art. The Baron Louis de Rothschild won his freedom by "selling" his Austrian steel mills to the Reichsmarschall Herman Goering Steel Works.

The Office kept accurate records of the value of the received goods. Many items, however, were only approximated in value, purposely on the low side. Because the items were bulky and overwhelming in number, arrangements were made to sell a large number of the works of art outside Germany.

The official plan was to transport goods to Switzerland. There they would be sold through dummy Swiss corporations, or auctioned.

It was Heydrich's astute notion to put von Witte in charge of setting up several Swiss corporations which were to be kept separate from the official scheme.

At von Witte's direction, the secret dummy companies

"bought" works of art from the Nazi-controlled Swiss companies at artificially low prices. The proceeds of the sales would be credited to the Third Reich.

Heydrich and von Witte would then sell the works of art at great profit, and deposit the funds in secret Swiss accounts, the numbers of which they alone possessed.

Over fifty million Swiss francs had accumulated in the accounts. This fortune was now von Witte's, but he was concerned about his prospects of enjoying it. For von Witte, along with many other German officers, was by now certain that Germany would lose the war.

Half Alsatian in background, Heinz von Witte and his sister Berta had grown up with a near-native command of French; and Heinz's knowledge of the language and culture of Germany's once-and-future enemy had contributed to his rapid rise to a general's rank in his early thirites. It would now, he calculated, be his key to the new life he would have to lead in order to benefit from the immense fortune he controlled. Not for him the grubby business of haring off to South America, as some of his fellow officers were already furtively planning to do. Wealth, to be enjoyed, must be used openly and freely.

The first step was obviously to make sure of a base of operations near his money. He was able to pull enough strings to get Berta, still mourning Heydrich, permission to live in Switzerland with her infant daughter.

Next, what was needed was a man with whom he could exchange indentities—a Frenchman, since Germans of his age would be subject to a closer scrutiny than he would find convenient, once the war was over. Someone of his age and general appearance . . . perhaps a prisoner in one of the German camps.

He immediately set his plan into motion. He had been obtaining dossiers regularly from the Gestapo in order to keep informed about the prisoners in the camps. He now began to scan the dossiers in search of the man he needed.

He searched for almost two years. Then, one day in early 1944, he found his man. The name on the dossier read "Member of the Underground Resistance: Jean, Duc d'Artois." A duke, he thought; that's a bit of luck! He read the dossier carefully. *Age: 34. Height: 1.74 meters. Weight: 68 kg. Build: medium. Hair: light brown. Eyes: gray.*

He continued to scan the thick file on the Frenchman. There was much more in the dossier. Nothing of any great importance to the Gestapo, but to him the information was vital.

He read on. The Frenchman came from a very small village, Railleur-sur-Pelle. He had apparently not ventured much out of his village before the war, having been disfigured by a fire at the age of ten. His father had lost his life in the fire, and his mother, in her attempt to save her young son from the flames, had suffered grave injury. Both had had third-degree burns, mostly on the face and extremities, and had spent many months hospitalized. After that, mother and son had preferred to remain in their chateau at Railleur, rather than have people stare and point with pity. The young duke had lived, according to the dossier, the life of a recluse, alone with his invalid mother and a tutor.

Shortly after the occupation of France by Germany, the duke's mother died and Jean d'Artois joined the French Underground.

He had been apprehended by the Gestapo just outside his village and had been transported along with other prisoners to Lyon for interrogation. Everything fits perfectly, von Witte thought. A duke, a man of means, a recluse almost, with scars. His height, weight, general appearance, age—everything fit. No one would be able to tell. Von Witte left Paris for Lyon the next day. He wanted to get there before Artois had been tortured to death.

Jean d'Artois, weak and bleeding from wounds, was ushered into the room where von Witte was waiting. They had already begun the Frenchman's torture. The Gestapo wished to find out whether he knew the whereabouts of certain important members of the Maquis. A guard was posted outside the door.

Von Witte spoke in French: "A very clever scheme, my dear d'Artois. Your last attempted sabotage, I mean." He shook his head feigning regret. "A pity for you it did not work."

"You know what will happen to you now." It was more of

a statement than a question. Von Witte paused before continuing, his tone much softer than before. "I am half French myself, monsieur. On my mother's side."

D'Artois's expression changed slightly.

Watching d'Artois carefuly, von Witte went on after only the slightest pause. "I am prepared to offer you your life, if you will cooperate with me."

D'Artois's eyes squinted suspiciously.

Von Witte turned his back to the man, tapping a riding crop against the palm of his hand. "I have it in my power," he said, "to have you transferred away from here, to somewhere safe. I can even arrange for you to be smuggled out of France and across the Swiss border." He smiled thinly and snapped the leather crop hard against his palm. "But for this, I need a favor. I want you to tell me everything you know of the village where you were born. Everything—you hear?" He went on. "I have my reasons. They have nothing to do with the war." He waited a moment for the man to speak.

D'Artois finally spoke. His voice was dry. "I have nothing to tell you, you dirty *boche*. Nothing, do you hear?"

Jean, Duc d'Artois, had endured the torture of the flames that had scarred him and the drawn-out ordeal, even more painful, of recovery and surgery. He was no stranger to pain, and had learned to come to terms with it. He was therefore able to withstand Lieutenant General von Witte's ministrations for far longer than the general had expected. The beatings, the clubs, the careful mutilations, the hot irons, the charged electrodes, reduced the duke to a quivering, howling wreck, but they did not bring forth the capitulation that von Witte vitally needed.

At the last, a syringe of ether, squirted into the prisoner's eye, produced the desired result. Von Witte, fatigued and oppressed by the stench of d'Artois's scorched flesh and the involuntary voiding of his bladder and bowels—it was an oversight someone would regret, to have fed a subject before interrogation!—wished that the notion had occurred to him sooner.

Von Witte placed his hand under d'Artois's chin. "Are you ready now to talk?"

D'Artois nodded.

Von Witte strode across the room and sat down in the high-backed leather chair behind the desk. He began his questioning, slowly at first, taking time out to roll down his sleeves and button the cuffs once again.

"Who are your friends in the Underground? Who do you know outside of Railleur-sur-Pelle? Do you have any living relatives? Do you speak any other language besides French?"

D'Artois's responses were mostly a nod or a shake of the head, "yes" or "no." When it was absolutely necessary for him to speak, he would swallow first, the blood filling his mouth, and then he would slur out the answer with what was left of his tongue.

Then, suddenly, he fell over. He looked dead to von Witte, who rushed to his side to examine him. Von Witte tried to revive him, but could not. He had lost too much blood. Von Witte went to the door and called for the guards. They came and removed the limp body. He then called for the orderly to clean up the blood-spattered floor.

Von Witte had got most of what he wanted, but it had almost cost him his man.

After von Witte returned to Paris, d'Artois hovered between life and death for several days. After three weeks had passed, he had healed enough to convince von Witte he would live. Von Witte ordered he be kept in a cell by himself, separate from the other prisoners.

On June 6, 1944, the Allies landed in Normandy. The invasion that von Witte knew was coming had begun. On June 9, he ordered Colonel Friedrich Hernst to take a detachment to the village of Railleur-sur-Pelle. The colonel's instructions were to completely annihilate the village and all who lived there "in continuing vindication for the murder of our fallen comrade, Reinhard Heydrich."

Von Witte intended to destroy the town, and with it, every bit of information concerning d'Artois. There would be no one or nothing left to tell tales of the duke or anything concerning him.

On July 26, the Allies' breakout at St. Lô precipitated the rout of the Germans from France. Von Witte then knew for certain that Germany would be defeated, but he could not yet put the rest of his plan into motion. He would have to wait until the Allies reached Paris.

On August 15, Allied forces, including the Free French, landed on the Mediterranean coast and began pushing rapidly to the north, toward Paris.

For von Witte, the waiting was over. On August 17, he ordered d'Artois transported, in the custody of two Gestapo guards, to his headquarters in Paris, the former La Farge mansion. Von Witte's orders indicated that d'Artois would then be sent to Germany along with other prisoners held at the general's headquarters.

On the evening of August 19, the general walked briskly across the courtyard to the carriage house where d'Artois was being held prisoner.

A guard stood at attention outside the heavy door.

"*Achtung!* Take the prisoner immediately to my car outside. I have orders from Berlin to transport him to Metz myself."

The guard did as he was told. D'Artois, handcuffed, was put into the backseat, to the general's left. The guard sat in the front next to the driver. The car sped through the Paris streets, splashing through the tiny puddles of water left by heavy rain the night before.

They were headed northeast in the direction of Metz.

As their car approached Châlons-sur-Marne, von Witte, feigning a call of nature, ordered the driver to stop. As the car pulled off the road and came to a halt, von Witte, his Luger drawn, shot the Gestapo guard in the back of his head. The sound of the bullet shattering the man's skull was scarcely heard by the driver before he too was dead, shot between his eyes, wide with surprise. D'Artois met his end an instant later just as he was trying to open the door with his manacled hands. The bullet, as von Witte had planned, traveled upward from the back of his neck, shattering his face as it exploded through his head.

Working swiftly, von Witte exchanged clothing with d'Artois. Then, taking three grenades from his traveling bag, he taped one under each of his victims' chin. He replaced d'Artois's body in the car in the right rearseat, the one he himself had occupied. Standing back, he fired a round into the gasoline can strapped to the back of the car. The car burst into flames. The explosions of the three grenades followed shortly.

Von Witte turned, sticking the Luger into his waistband, and fled through the woods.

By dawn, he was a long way from Châlons, heading south toward the Swiss border. He planned to follow the Marne until Lons le Saunier. Then he would travel southeastward, cutting across to Geneva.

He had a long way to go. But he had outlined his route carefully and carried a map and forged papers in his breast pocket.

The papers belonging to d'Artois were carefully sewn inside the lining of his jacket. He could not risk having anyone connect him with the duke. The duke had scars that von Witte first had to acquire before he could claim his identity.

On September 5, von Witte successfully crossed the border into Switzerland. By early October he had, with Berta's help, found a plastic surgeon. Dr. Ernest Faust, a greedy and ambitious man, agreed to perform the surgery on von Witte for the price of half a million Swiss francs, with no questions asked. A photograph of d'Artois, which von Witte had removed from his files in Paris, served as the doctor's guide in performing the delicate surgery. The doctor was to make it look as if von Witte had had severe burns, the scars from which had been largely removed by elaborate skin-grafting. His nose was made to curve slightly downward and his cheeks were hollowed out, approximating the more bony appearance of the duke's face. His forehead was lifted to erase lines which the duke had not had.

On his hands and feet, scars were created. The doctor removed von Witte's fingerprints by cutting deeply into the fingertips and removing thick pieces of flesh which were then replaced by skin grafts.

Three months later, von Witte was admiring himself in the mirror. Strange, he thought, to look into a mirror and see my eyes looking back from another man's face.

He was completely healed from the surgery. He did not look offensive; scarred to be sure, but still handsome in a severe way.

He would be ready to be seen in public, however, only after having all his teeth removed and a false set obtained. He had taken care to blow up the duke's head, in order to wipe out any trace of the man's teeth. Now his own had to be replaced.

By April 1945, his transformation was complete.

A month later, the war in Europe was over.

Von Witte went to Geneva. There he bought a luxurious apartment on Quai des Berges. The papers were signed "Jean, Duc d'Artois."

Now d'Artois—he refused even to think of himself except under his new identity—needed a front, a business partner to launder his money. He needed someone respected and trusted by all those who knew him, someone whose reputation d'Artois could hide behind.

The man he decided on was Armand La Farge, owner of the mansion that had served as the late General von Witte's headquarters. La Farge suited his needs in every way: a hero of two wars, a rich and powerful man with fame and worldwide respect. He was perfect.

Through a banker in Geneva, a meeting was arranged, and d'Artois flew to Paris.

Seated in the study he had known so well in the past, d'Artois stifled a feeling of unholy glee as the rightful owner entered and greeted him.

D'Artois did not waste any time in coming to the point.

"I am here, Monsieur La Farge, to propose a partnership between us."

He reached into his briefcase and withdrew a leather-bound portfolio. He opened it to the first page. In large letters one word was written: ALUMINUM.

"I have succeeded, monsieur, in obtaining the mining concessions for the vast deposits of bauxite recently discovered in Jamaica!"

Indeed, when d'Artois had decided some months earlier that La Farge was his man, he had immediately traveled to Jamaica. He had heard of the initial discoveries and knew, of course, of the vast holdings that La Farge had in bauxite in France. Using over half of the funds in his Swiss accounts, d'Artois had systematically gone about buying out the existing concession holders, bribing government officials and local representatives of the mining and aluminum companies, until he controlled most of the ore discovered and virtually all of the prospective deposits. But d'Artois's greatest coup was in obtaining from the Government of Jamaica a ninety-nine year concession to mine the bauxite and export the ore to France. The concession and export permit were granted quite readily by the governor, an English aristocrat long on titles but short on money, when he was assured by his new Swiss banker that five million Swiss francs had indeed been deposited in his account.

D'Artois had then employed the best financial and legal talent he could find to prepare the plan now before La Farge. In short, d'Artois's proposal was to merge his ore interests with La Farge's if La Farge would build the aluminum mills to utilize them. The advantages for La Farge were enormous. He would be in a position to control the postwar aluminum industry in Europe.

La Farge studied the plans. He was impressed with the professional nature of the work, the reasoning behind the projections, and the staggering profit potential. He thought to himself that indeed this d'Artois was a clever man to have acted so decisively to obtain the ore deposits and to have been able to negotiate so successfully for the mining concessions and export rights. But he also knew that d'Artois was taking quite a gamble. Without plants to process the ore and access to the huge energy sources required to manufacture aluminum, his holdings would be worth far less. La Farge knew he was the perfect partner for d'Artois. He owned the leading aluminum company in France and had himself significant, although declining, reserves of bauxite ore in the Baux region. More importantly, his holdings in coal were large enough to support the power plants needed to enable much greater aluminum production than was presently possible for his company.

In short, La Farge knew that d'Artois was the perfect partner for *him*.

La Farge closed the portfolio and got up from his chair. He picked up his cigar humidor, opened it, and offered a cigar to d'Artois. Lighting one for himself, he said, "It is an interesting proposal, my dear duke, except for one aspect."

D'Artois said nothing.

"I do not like fifty-fifty partnerships. I grant that you propose to contribute half of the capital, including your ore reserves, but I insist upon owning fifty-one percent. Take it or leave it."

He waited for d'Artois to reply.

"I'll take it, monsieur. I might say, I came to you because you *are* a formidable businessman!"

La Farge was flushed with the success of his bluff. He pressed his advantage. "And for what other reasons did you come to me, monsieur?"

D'Artois's expression was modest. "I do not have your reputation, Monsieur La Farge, nor your standing in French industry"—he paused a second—"or French society."

La Farge smiled.

D'Artois went on. "You are a powerful man. This project needs a man like you, a man with your political contacts."

La Farge stood up. "Then it's a deal, man." He shook d'Artois's hand. "I will have my attorneys get in touch with you. And now, if you will permit me, I must excuse myself. I promised my daughter I would take her to the zoo this afternoon. I am thirty minutes late already."

Several weeks later their agreement was finalized and the project begun. La Farge gave a party to introduce d'Artois to his friends.

Their friendship grew as their business prospered. In time, d'Artois told La Farge about the fire which had disfigured him in his youth and his wartime capture by the Nazis after they had destroyed his town and its people. La Farge was touched by the duke's story. He felt sorry for the French nobleman, who had not been as lucky in his life as he himself had been. La Farge took d'Artois under his wing. He became part of La Farge's close circle of friends, and an investor in several other business ventures as La Farge's partner. Everything from a business standpoint seemed to click; however, as time went on, La Farge became more and more curious about his partner's lack of relatives and friends.

No one seemed to know anything of the duke's life from much before his first meeting with La Farge. The bank which had arranged their meeting had knowledge of d'Artois only for the period six months prior.

La Farge engaged a private detective to investigate the duke's background. There was a mystery about d'Artois's life, and he knew he would never trust his associate completely if he did not know all the pieces in the puzzle.

"I'm doing it for my peace of mind," he would say to himself when feelings of guilt over snooping into a friend's private affairs bothered him.

The private detective hired by La Farge confirmed that all d'Artois's relatives and friends had been wiped out when the Germans annihilated the town of Railleur-sur-Pelle. The detective also uncovered that the duke's family had been wealthy, but all the records had been destroyed along with the town. La Farge almost gave up the investigation when everything the duke had told him turned out to be fact, but decided nevertheless to have the duke watched, since he was still not entirely satisfied.

The duke, during this time, had found out that La Farge had hired the investigator. He also learned when La Farge had slacked off the investigation. D'Artois felt he needed to make sure that he always knew exactly what La Farge was doing. He decided to plant a spy in La Farge's household.

Berta was the key. She would be Rosalie La Farge's governess. La Farge had told d'Artois that he needed a governess for his two-year-old daughter.

D'Artois persuaded Berta to take the job and to give up her own daughter. He promised that he would be responsible for Margot's upbringing and education, not as her uncle, but as her guardian.

"Think of what her life would be like, if anyone ever discovered who her father was," he said to Berta. "And how, my dear Berta, will you take care of her and give her the things she will need in life? Do this thing for me and I will see to it that she has everything she ever wants in life. Refuse, and she will get *nothing*."

"I could expose you," Berta retorted.

He laughed. "Of course, you could, my dear sister, and people would think you had gone mad. Furthermore, don't you think you would be punished—along with me—as my accomplice? What about the dentist you helped me kill in Lausanne? They haven't found him in all these years, but I could arrange for it, if necessary. And think about the girl, what the publicity would do to her."

Berta could not refuse when d'Artois further proposed to make Margot his sole heir.

D'Artois contrived for Berta, as Berthe Giraud, to see La Farge for an interview, after arranging for fake references for the "bright Alsatian girl." Like her brother, Berta's French was fluent, her manners noticeably good, and her appearance clean and poised. She lied about her schooling, explaining that she had been brought up in Alsace and had begun studying for a teaching degree. She said she was an orphan and had no living relatives. Her references were checked and several days later, Berta was hired as governess for the La Farges' one child, the pretty little two-year-old Rosalie, a bundle of golden curls, green eyes, and peach skin.

Berthe would learn to care for this sweet child. She would see in her the child she had had to give up, her own four-year-old Margot.

She knew that Margot was lost to her forever; seeing her again could only bring disaster. Should anyone ever link the pieces of the puzzle together, the child, she knew, would suffer the gravest consequences of all. Berta knew she was bound to do her brother's bidding—bound by the secret they shared, and bound by the blood money she needed for her daughter's future.

"You're distracted, monsieur—I don't believe you've heard a word I've been saying!" the mill owner's wife complained archly.

"My regrets, madame," d'Artois said smoothly. "It's just that this house holds so many memories for me."

Across the floor, ranged with some of the servants who had been privileged to watch the dance, he saw Berthe, looking proudly and fondly at Rosalie. Take care, dear sister, he thought—remember where your true loyalties are. . . .

Chapter Eight

Paris, September 1962

It was ten o'clock, five hours had slipped by when La Farge called the music to a stop. "It is time that we leave for the airport if we're going to make it to the yacht tonight. If the ladies would care to freshen up before leaving, they may do so now. Max will see to it that the limousines are waiting out front. Now, if you will excuse me, everyone, Madame La Farge and I will go on ahead with Rosalie and Ahmed to Orly to see that the planes are ready to leave as soon as everyone gets there."

The music began again as soon as La Farge left the room. Two by two the guests lined up in the hallway to wait for their chauffeured limousines, and steeled themselves for the dash down the steps through the still-frantic crowd waiting outside.

Armand La Farge owned a fleet of airplanes, used exclusively for himself and his guests. Three Lockheed Jet Stars were lined up side-by-side in the private section of Orly airport, all fueled up and ready to leave the minute La Farge and the tower said so.

La Farge's pilots had been chosen from the finest available. He had hired them from a top airline. His secret was simple: he paid them double what they had been earning before. One of the three jets was plainly different from the other: it was painted black with a silver streak along the side, and on the door bore the image of a black leopard. This was La Farge's exclusively, his baby, and no one but La Farge flew it. His Air Force service had left him with a love of flying, and he was a skilled pilot. Rosalie had traveled many times in the unusual aircraft, and also knew how to fly it. Her father had taught her well, and sometimes she would serve as his co-pilot. Not this time, though; La Farge could play pilot if he wanted, but there were other games Rosalie preferred tonight, and La Farge for once had no part in them.

Ahmed congratulated his father-in-law as he looked around him in the plane. It was truly a masterpiece of elegant luxury and fantasy.

"Now, look at this, Ahmed. Isn't she a pretty bird, though?" La Farge said.

Ahmed glanced around for Rosalie. The only bird he felt like looking at right then was his wife.

"Come on, man, get your mind off the bedroom for a moment. It won't do you much good until the plane takes off anyway."

He could even read minds, the bastard, Ahmed thought. Damn La Farge and his airplane. But Ahmed had to admit that it was special. The walls were covered with oxblood leather, and the floors with deep green carpeting. The lavatory was luxurious in every detail with a marble sink and a *chaise percée* over the toilet, mirrored walls and ceiling, and chocolate brown carpeting. The plane had been decorated to order for La Farge in America. Ahmed laughed to himself and wondered whether he would see it one day in *House and Garden*. There was also a fully equipped kitchen which was used during long trips, when La Farge would always bring a chef along.

But the *pièce de résistance* was the small private cabin in the rear of the aircraft. Every inch of space was used to advantage. At the far end was a built-in bed with two small nightstands with drawers. Handsome brass sconces were on the walls; a Jean

Cocteau painting over the bed; in addition, there was a leather chair and ottoman, a full-length mirror on the back of the door, and a view of the skies from four portholes, two on either side of the cabin. Ahmed whistled out loud.

"Quite a *pied-à-terre—pied-à-l'air*, rather."

"Well, maybe I should have picked a French decorator, but your father gave me this company's address in New York, and this is what I got." La Farge spread his arms wide and smiled.

"Just what the sheikh ordered, hm?"

They both laughed.

"What does Madame La Farge think of it?"

"Oh, she thinks it's a copy of a harem."

Again they laughed.

The two men were interrupted by the co-pilot, Alain, who came to tell them it was time to take off.

Rosalie, Ahmed and Jacqueline seated themselves and strapped in for takeoff. La Farge disappeared into the cockpit with Alain.

Less than an hour later they landed in Nice, where La Farge's helicopter was waiting to take them to the *Créole*, which was docked in Monte Carlo, not far from the *Rosalie*. The other guests were to follow by car. The limousines were lined up waiting.

Several minutes later, the helicopter landed on board the *Créole*. La Farge screamed some orders to the pilot, and stepped out of the aircraft onto the gleaming deck of the *Créole*.

Yanni Corvès, the *Créole*'s captain, stood at the railing to greet La Farge. Beside him stood Helle and Carone, first and second mates. The captain saluted and extended his hand to La Farge.

La Farge headed straight for the galley to make sure the chefs had everything under control. Rosalie and Ahmed trailed after him.

"Two hundred guests will be arriving within the hour, and if they are anything like me, they will be starved," he shouted, then walked around checking and sampling the platters of hors d'oeuvres.

"Starved? Papa, how can you be starved? We just finished eating," Rosalie said, indignant at her father's behavior.

"Four hours ago, my child. That's a long time, and all that champagne has made me ravenous."

"Ah, what a beautiful night for a sea voyage. I wish I were coming along with you. Hey, that's an idea! *Me* on your honeymoon. How does that strike you?" La Farge tried to keep a serious face.

From the look he got from Rosalie, he could see that it was out of the question. He had to laugh. "I can see those *vahinés*—their long, dark hair glistening in the moonlight, smelling to high heaven of coconut oil and tiare blossoms." He made a face in mock disgust. "Bah! Who would want to get covered with oil, anyway? A man could slip and hurt himself seriously." La Farge smiled, amused by the thought.

"I tell you what, Armand," Ahmed said, smiling. "We'll mail you the first, nongreasy *vahiné* we find. Now let me see, a full-grown one should weigh about fifty, fifty-two kilos. I hope you won't mind if we send her collect."

Rosalie threw a cushion from the deck at Ahmed. "Just how do you two know so much about *vahinés*, eh?"

"You'd better watch out, Ahmed. One look at a *vahiné*, and you might find yourself minus a vital asset or so."

"Papa, if you and Ahmed don't stop this nonsense I'm going to throw you both overboard."

They were interrupted by the chef, who wanted to discuss the buffet with his employer.

"I'll leave you two to the stars. When our guests arrive, please let me know. I think I'll take a snooze in my cabin to be in shape for the party."

As La Farge disappeared below, Ahmed could see an impish look appearing on Rosalie's face. He knew she was concocting something good, whatever it was.

"Ahmed, I just had the craziest idea." It was difficult for Rosalie to talk, she was laughing so hard. She stood bent over, holding on to the railing, tears running down her cheeks.

"Come on, Zalie. Out with it, what's so funny?"

She motioned to him to wait, as she blew her nose. "Oh

God, that's funny. If only the great Armand La Farge could read my mind right now. Why, you know, I think he'd give me the spanking of my life. My first! And then throw me overboard."

"For God's sake, Rosalie. What's this crazy idea you have? I'm standing here like a fool while you're laughing your head off. What's so damn funny?"

She looked just then like Rosalie the child, not Rosalie, the woman, the wife, the heiress.

"Ahmed, what do you think Papa would do, if while he's taking his snooze down below in his soundproof cabin, we—that is, you and me—sent the crew off with him to St. Tropez, and the two of us took the *Rosalie* to Papeete?"

"What? I've never heard of anything so crazy. No, infantile! You want Armand La Farge to cut off my balls and use me as a spare eunuch to polish his shoes? If I ever went along with anything so preposterous, he'd have a right to have me quartered and sold for dog food."

"Cat food maybe, dog food never. Papa has too much respect for dogs. He'd never risk poisoning them with Arabian chicken meat."

"Damn it, Rosalie, you're being childish."

"Am I?"

"Come on, Ahmed, don't be chicken meat—be a devil! Let's do it."

"But *Rosalie* has never been that far out to sea before; she might not be seaworthy."

"Are you kidding, Ahmed? A four-year-old, million-dollar yacht not seaworthy? What do you need to sail to Tahiti in, the goddam *France?* Or maybe the *Titanic* is more your style."

"*Aje Maniuke!* Goddamit, you drive me crazy sometimes. Give me a minute. I've got to think." He rubbed his chin, his eyes squinting. "Okay. I'll do it, but the only thing I have to say is, if this is a taste of the half-baked ideas I'm going to be faced with . . ." He grabbed her, hard. "I'm going to show you some *chicken* meat, you little witch. I'll show you I have a few ideas of my own." They clung together on the deck, locked in a passionate kiss. Ahmed's dark hands trailed down her back.

Rip.

"Shit, Ahmed! What do you think you're doing? You've ruined my dress!"

"You put it on for me, didn't you? Well, now I'm just taking it off."

She bit his arm and kicked his shin. "You're being too rough, Ahmed. Stop it."

"Too late, mademoiselle. I want what I want when I want it, and I want it now."

Rosalie, like her father, always admired strength, and she was thrilled by this new surge of power from her usually gentle Ahmed. If this was what he was like when he was mad, then she would have to see to it that he was mad quite a lot.

Rosalie, adequately if sketchily redressed, went below and informed the crew that plans had been slightly changed. Instead of picking up the guests here in Monte Carlo, they would pick them up at St. Tropez. Her father wished the *Créole* to start at once for St. Tropez, so that the guests would not be kept waiting too long.

"But why St. Tropez?" the captain wanted to know. "It's more practical from here."

"*Because,*" Rosalie replied, using her father's authoritative manner, "we will be docking in front of Colombier, where some of the guests will be staying afterward. *Now* do you understand? Or do I have to go back downstairs and wake up my father, so that he can explain it himself?" She knew full well that there was no way the captain would have her wake up her father.

"Yes, mademoiselle, I see now," the captain said. "I'm sorry if I seemed impertinent." Rosalie waved her hand to show that it was of no importance, and went to join Ahmed on deck.

The captain proceeded at once, as ordered. He gave the orders to the crew to start the engines. Rosalie and Ahmed waited stealthily for the right moment to make their escape. As the loud roar of the engines rose from beneath them, they stripped, bundled their clothing under a bench, climbed down the ladder of the *Créole*, and dove into the dark water.

They were half frozen by the time they got on board the *Rosalie*. Naked and trembling, they crept around the deck so as not to be noticed by the crew of the *Créole* or by Raoul, the night watchman, on board below.

The moonlight shone down, lighting their way to the galley. They moved quietly down the steps and into the small cabin in the stern. There they found some clothes left aboard by Jacqueline and her friends. There were a few pairs of men's trunks and sweaters stacked on one of the shelves.

"Here, Ahmed, try these on. They belong to one of Mama's *protégés*. Nice size for an artist, wouldn't you say?" She giggled at her comments. "Well, at least you won't freeze to death now—I wouldn't want icicles to form around *them.*" She pointed to between his legs.

Ahmed grinned and pulled a brown cashmere sweater over his head. "Bah, I never did like brown. It just isn't a very good color for me. I guess your mother prefers blonds, eh?"

"Oh, and why's that?"

"Well, because blonds look better in brown, don't they?"

"I wouldn't know. Since my taste is more for darker types, the browner the better."

"Is that so? Then how is it you acted so fascinated by that blue-eyed American we met at the restaurant that night?"

"What night? And which blue-eyed American are you talking about?" She knew perfectly well what night and which American. She could not forget him.

"You know, the Californian. What was his name again?"

"Oh yes, Jeffrey Allan Guthrow. That's it."

He laughed in mock disgust. "Jeffrey Allan Guthrow. Quite a name, wouldn't you say? I must say, I liked the man though. Good manners and elegant, for an American."

"Do I detect a bit of sarcasm in that statement? It wouldn't be that the daredevil stud is a wee bit jealous?"

He threw a wet towel across the bed at her. "Well, shouldn't I be?"

"Well, yes, I like that—a little, as long as it doesn't get out of hand."

Ahmed grinned again. "Hey, if we're going to get moving, we'd better go wake Raoul up. I hope he knows how to handle this boat."

"Raoul doesn't navigate. He's just the mate. The skipper is ashore, so Raoul will have to fetch him."

They scared Raoul half to death as they flashed the bright light on his face.

"Mademoiselle Rosalie, Prince Ahmed! What the hell—excuse me—are you doing here? I could have shot you by mistake!"

Rosalie burst out laughing. "Oh, Raoul, that damn gun you carry around is never loaded—and, according to Papa, you wouldn't know how to aim, much less shoot anybody!"

"You can't always believe that father of yours. He was just saying that to make you laugh." Raoul clutched the pistol with an indignant glare.

Bang! The noise exploded in the cabin, and Ahmed and Rosalie jumped.

"*Aje maniuke!*" Ahmed's face was a fiery red. "What the shit do you think you're doing, Raoul? You almost blew off my nuts, man. I swear La Farge must have raided a goddamn asylum for some of the people he has working for him. I can't believe it. The *type* almost put me in the choir!"

Rosalie was holding her sides in uncontrollable laughter. "Raoul, what the hell came over you? Are you crazy?"

The gaunt little man just stood there holding the gun and staring at the hole in the desk behind Ahmed. "I—I—I don't know what happened. I guess I got excited and pulled the trigger by mistake. I—I didn't even know it was loaded. I could have killed you!"

Ahmed clutched his crotch protectively. "Well, my good man, killing me is one thing, but next time, aim a little higher up will you? More like two feet higher up." He pointed to his heart and sat down on the bunk tight-kneed.

Rosalie took the gun from Raoul and emptied it. "Let's put these bullets away before you kill somebody. We might need them for sharks later. Papa was always talking about how much fun it is to shoot the sharks that follow the boat. It might be exciting."

"Shark shooting? On our honeymoon? You know, Rosalie, I'm beginning to think it wouldn't have been such a bad idea to have invited your father along on our honeymoon." Ahmed lay back against the bunk. "I think I would feel a lot safer."

"Raoul, you damn fool! What's going on down there?" The voice came from above deck. It was the skipper. Henri Ganot was a strapping man almost two meters tall, looking more like his mother's Scandinavian ancestors than his French father—big and burly, with a shock of reddish blond hair, worn long.

He hurried down the narrow gangway and ran to the forward cabin. Rosalie met him at the door.

"It's all right, Henri. It was an accident. Raoul was a little nervous when we showed up in the dark in his cabin, and then by mistake he pulled the trigger of the old gun Papa lets him keep on board. There's no reason for alarm, though. We are all safe." She turned and pointed to Prince Ahmed and then to the desk. "Just a little hole in the desk over there, nothing to worry about."

Ganot scratched his head in confusion. "But what are you doing here aboard the *Rosalie?* I thought I read in the papers that you would be celebrating your wedding aboard *Créole*. What happened? And, for that matter, where's *Créole* heading? I was having a drink with an old chum when I noticed *Créole* leaving the harbor. I came out to see if the crew had said anything to Raoul, and the next thing you know, *bang!*—all hell breaks loose."

"We've decided to take the *Rosalie* instead of the *Créole* to Papeete. It'll be much more fun sailing, anyway. I prefer smaller boats, and the *Créole* is too big. I never understood why Papa spent so much money on that boat when we already had this one. I like the size of the *Rosalie* much more. It's more cozy." Rosalie might have been talking of a five-meter day sailer instead of a thirty-meter ketch. To the daughter of Armand La Farge, any vessel of less than fifty meters was a dinghy.

Ahmed glanced at his young wife, her hair still damp from

the swim to the boat, the long pink turtleneck sweater reaching to just above her hip bones, the tiny turquoise string bikini he had seen her mother wear once just covering the bare minimum of pubic hair. On her left arm was the bracelet her father had given her as a wedding gift. A gem on a gem, he thought. She was a handful, his Rosalie.

In the distance, they could hear car horns blowing; that would be the stranded guests, beginning to arrive at the dock. In a minute someone would come out to the *Rosalie* to check with Raoul.

"Let's get this scow sailing, man," Ahmed urged. "If we don't, we are going to be in for some pretty embarrassing explanations. Let's get moving."

Ganot was a man to heed a command almost as well as he gave one. At once he and Raoul were in motion, Ganot starting the motor, Raoul attending to the anchor.

Ahmed and Rosalie scampered up the gangway to the deck. In the distant glow of the streetlights, they could see their guests waiting at the dock for the *Créole*, now on its way to St. Tropez. Rosalie could make out a few of the people under the lights. Senator James Buchin of Connecticut was standing directly under a big lamppost, the light shining down on his crewcut making him look almost bald. She thought she recognized the brunette with the senator. Of course, Margot . . . Koesler, that was the name. The dark-haired girl who had been introduced to her that evening as the duke's *protégée*. But what was she doing now with the senator, Rosalie wondered? She had not been invited to the wedding or reception. Perhaps the duke brought her, Rosalie thought.

She looked for d'Artois in the crowd, and in a moment found him. She could barely make him out, but she knew she was not mistaken. She could not see his features, but she realized she could picture them more vividly than she would have expected—especially his eyes. There was something unique about them, so *intense*.

I wonder why *he* isn't with his protegée, she thought, looking once more over to Margot and the senator.

Buchin now had his arm around Margot's waist. I wonder

why d'Artois doesn't walk over and punch the idiot in the nose, she thought. I certainly would if I were he. Ahmed leaned over and poked Rosalie lightly.

"Say, isn't that Margot Koesler standing under the light, with the senator? I wonder what their connection is?"

"Isn't it obvious? The poor woman."

"The poor woman," Ahmed said. "I thought you said you didn't like her very much."

"Not her, silly. I was talking about the senator's wife. The poor woman is probably thinking the rat is attending the great La Farge affair alone. I wonder what excuse he gave her so she'd let him come solo." She raised a finger at Ahmed. "Let me warn you, husband, if you ever, *ever* cheat on me, you had better make damned sure that I never find out about it. Because I swear it, I'll leave you. But not intact." She made a sharp, twisting motion with her hands. "I hope you know what I mean."

"I have no idea."

She grinned at him wickedly. "Why don't you try it and find out?"

As the ketch tacked and turned about, the figures on the pier grew smaller in the distance. *Rosalie* was already heading for the open seas, and all that mattered right then were the stars and the moon and each other's warm bodies, pressed together, lying on the deck, wrapped in a soft blue blanket thrown to them by Raoul. The blanket smelled of *Calêche*, Jacqueline's favorite perfume. Rosalie wondered what glorious moments her mother had spent snuggled up with someone under this same soft blanket.

The flapping of the sails as the wind hit them was a comforting sound. A feeling of adventure came over Rosalie as she snuggled closer to Ahmed.

"Welcome aboard the *Rosalie*, darling," she said.

Ahmed kissed her nose gently and they made love once again under the stars.

Rosalie yawned and turned to look at Ahmed. "Darling?" He was already asleep. She covered him lovingly and tucked the blanket in under him, then snuggled closer, resting her head in the crook of his arm. He smelled good, a mixture of cologne and salt air. She yawned again and closed her eyes. Only the loud flapping of the sails could be heard. That and a tiny swishing sound made by the boat as the bow broke and cut the waves; and then the wind died down somewhat, and all was quiet but for the soft swish. She fell asleep.

Chapter Nine

Nice, September 1962

It was too early for the morning traffic. The coast seemed deserted and except for a few bread and vegetable trucks hurrying to get their goods to the hotels and restaurants, the Quai du Midi was almost abandoned.

A man sat reading that morning's *Nice Matin* at the Café St. Hélène, from time to time looking across the harbor to the anchored *Créole*.

A stir of motion on the yacht's deck drew his attention. A figure in white slacks and a blue blazer appeared, followed by a white-jacketed man carrying a bundle of papers. As he had for the previous three mornings following his daughter's wedding and abrupt departure on her honeymoon, Armand La Farge was following his set routine.

The man paid his bill and left the café, the newspaper tucked under his arm and cases containing binoculars and a camera slung from his left shoulder. Thus burdened, and in an undistinguished and unpressed suit, he was the very picture of a

Côte d'Azur tourist, hopeful of some unspecified enjoyment but no longer really expecting to find it. His dark features and hawk nose suggested an origin somewhere in the Levant, though his big-boned frame argued against that impression. Except that it was too improbable, a romantic passerby might have taken him for an American Indian.

This was, in fact, only half true. C.C. Youngblood's father, Yakita, had been a full-blooded Iroquois, one of the high-steel men who had carved out a specialty in construction work, nimbly threading their way along girders that left the round-eyes dizzy and scared; his mother an "American" schoolteacher. Since she had died at his birth, C.C. was Indian in upbringing if not wholly so by blood. Yakita Youngblood, though finding ample scope for his dexterity, daring and manhood in his dangerous work, had also given his son some of his people's traditional skills, teaching him on hunting trips in the Adirondacks to track the most elusive game on the most unpromisingly barren ground.

It had been a long time since C.C. had followed a beast's trail over rock and brush; but the sharp eyes, the understanding of what a quarry might or must do, and the habit of patience had stood him in good stead in his decade and a half of service with the CIA.

His abilities had won him a wartime commission in Intelligence at the age of twenty, but the postwar shrinkage of the Army had left him in a precarious position, barely managing to pull strings for a transfer to what was left of the OSS's operating division on the War Department. When, in 1947, Congress established the CIA—as a move to streamline and democratize the competing intelligence functions of Army, Navy and State Department—C.C. was among the first agents to be recruited. He was also the first, perhaps the only, agent to have his name legally changed in order to qualify for the job.

"I do not see myself," the man who interviewed him had said, "asking Harry Truman to place full trust and credence in somebody named Calvin Coolidge."

"My dad saw this newsreel of Coolidge wearing a war

bonnet when he was visiting some of the tribes out west, night before I was born,'' C.C. had said. ''So he figured the President was O.K. on the red-man stuff and stuck me with the name. I had to punch out thirty-seven guys in grade school before I got them to calling me C.C. and dropping the Calvin shit.''

''Well, if Harry can screw around with his name and give himself a middle initial with no by-God period after it, I guess we can strike Silent Cal from your record and leave you plain old C.C.'' The man had grinned. ''A C.C. for the C.-in-C., hah?''

Dead men on three continents had provided mute testimony to C.C.'s value to the ''Company''—whose initial establishment as a purely intelligence-gathering organization had not long outlasted the beginning of the Cold War. What he was here for now was a good deal less earthshaking than many of his assignments, but it was in his nature and his training not to give less than his best, whatever he might be tracking.

He had marked out the best location on the beach from which to observe *Créole* without attracting attention; now he made his way down the cobblestoned ramp to the beach and walked to it. A tall rock jutting from the pebbly ground cast a shadow from the still-low sun; in it, he would be less conspicuous and, more important, the lenses of his binoculars would be shaded, protected from the possibility of flashing betraying glints.

At the spot, he removed his jacket, folded it and sat on it. He leaned against a convenient projection of the rock, withdrew the ten-power binoculars from their case, and raised and focused them.

Armand La Farge sprang into sharp view, as though only a few yards away. He was seated in a deck chair, flipping threw a newspaper, and sipping a soup-bowl-sized cup of coffee. On a table beside him were the papers the servant had brought up, weighted down by an oblong rectangle of metal. To C.C. it had the look of a strongbox, and he felt a thread of excitement unwind in him. Ninety-nine percent of all surveillance was dull, hours of it producing no more than a grain of useful information, and he had over the years become inordinately sensitive to any change from expected routine which might signal something significant; the presence of the strongbox smelled of just such significance.

He sat patiently, unmoving, as La Farge finished the paper and then reached for the box. Using a small key, he opened the long lid and peered into it. With something unsure in his movements, he withdrew a small red book.

From its size and shape C.C. estimated that it might be an address book or a bankbook—impossible, at this distance, to be sure. From La Farge's intent study of it, from the notes he was making on a pad in his lap, it had to be important. Something flashed white; a page of the book was briefly visible. No hope of making out anything on it from here, but with the souped-up telephoto lens and the high-resolution film, the lab experts at Langley might be able to make out something useful.

He removed the camera from its case, snapped the long, heavy lens onto its front and brought it up, resting the barrel of the lens on his knee. He squinted into the viewfinder , . . at La Farge's broad back, the jacket pulled tight as he leaned over to replace the book in the box and lower the lid.

C.C. cursed under his breath. It was in the nature of long shots not to come off, but this could have been a real break. Though the camera was harder to keep steady, he kept up his observation of La Farge with it rather than the binoculars; no sense in missing another chance if one came along.

La Farge seemed to press a button, ringing for his servants, C.C. imagined. Within minutes, a dark figure appeared on the scene, wearing a white tuniclike outfit. He took the strong box from the table and left the scene as abruptly as he had appeared.

La Farge stretched himself lazily in the sun, getting up and going over to stand by the rail. In his left hand, he still held a small piece of paper, possibly a leaflet from the little red book. He looked at it for a moment, as if memorizing its contents. Then he crumpled it tightly in his fist and threw it overboard. C.C. knew it was no use trying to retrieve it. He swore under his breath in frustration, as he watched La Farge gather up his papers and disappear inside.

He stood up and looked about him. It was already ten

o'clock, and the beach was swarming with people, staking out their claim to their patch of sun and pebbles for the day.

C.C. considered them fools. He had been in enough sun, rain, snow, and every other kind of extreme weather to appreciate the comfort of moderation, especially air conditioning. Heat or cold was something to endure—and he was good enough at that—but not to seek out. The *Créole* could be observed well enough for the rest of the day from the *terrasse* of Chez Lolotte—not air-conditioned, but nonetheless sheltered by a colorful awning.

First, though, he'd better touch base with Harry Baines in Paris. That little red book had turned the tide, he sensed. It might mean nothing, or it could be the first real break. If Harry hadn't sniffed out something on Senator Buchin or the Duc d'Artois, it was C.C.'s hunch that he'd be better employed down here, giving double coverage to La Farge.

Not the usual kind of Company operation, for sure—but this one was special, and he enjoyed the unaccustomed freedom of action the assignment afforded him, as well as the chance to track the kind of big game he was after. A real bastard, a USDA Prime Bad Guy—unlike the usual victims of the removals or captures he'd been in on, mostly men pretty much like C.C. himself, only working the other side of the street—and a key piece in the U.S.-Soviet seesaw struggle. Not to mention all that money. The government—hell, be frank, the Company— would have it earmarked for its own uses, but you didn't do fifteen years in this trade without learning a few ways to let some of what passed through your hands stick to your fingers. C.C. didn't care for the idea of spending his old age getting by on a government pension, and a certain unnumbered account in Zurich already amounted to a pretty nice retirement fund. Von Witte's hoard might be in the same damn bank, for all C.C. knew; but if so, some of it would be discreetly transferred before the main haul went on to Washington, if he had anything to say about it. Blood money. But damn few dollars, marks or francs hadn't, somewhere along the way, picked up a whiff of death.

Of course, the murder of a whole town left a stronger stench than that, but eighteen years in a vault in Zurich could deodorize anything.

• • •

The records kept by the Gestapo of the investigation of the death of Lieutenant General Heinz von Witte on August 19, 1944, were among the mass of government documents captured by the Russians after the fall of Berlin in May 1945. These showed that the Gestapo and the *Wehrmacht* intelligence services had turned up no proof of the French Underground's involvement in the bombing of Von Witte's staff car outside Châlons-sur-Marne, although it had been assumed at the time that they were. Interrogations of Underground members captured after August 19 turned up no information of the bombing. A more extensive investigation into the death of von Witte had been planned, but the Allied advance had made this impossible. The three bodies found in the wreckage of the general's car were mutilated beyond recognition. Bones and teeth, as well as flesh, had disintegrated. No positive identification was possible, so that it was only assumed that they were von Witte, a guard from his headquarters, and his driver.

The files were examined by the Allied War Crimes Commission because the wanton destruction of Railleur-sur-Pelle had been ordered by von Witte. However, no action had been taken to obtain further confirmation of von Witte's death. The files were retained by the Russian military command after the Nuremberg trials and eventually found their way to Soviet Intelligence headquarters in Moscow.

It was not until 1961 that the files were again examined. The KGB had had in its employ for some time a former Gestapo agent who had settled in West Berlin after the war. His was a low-level job, acting as courier for Russian Intelligence Operations in Berlin. The German turned double agent in early 1961, offering to cooperate with the CIA in exchange for cash. The KGB quickly learned of his duplicity, however, and he was brought into East Berlin for "in depth" questioning. The man was frightened for his life and offered the KGB material that he hoped would secure his freedom. The information concerned General Heinz von Witte, and had not been included in the reports sent to Berlin when the man had been the investigating Gestapo agent on the von Witte case. In questioning, he admitted that, with the Allies swarming over France, he had not had time to deal with certain evidence and had destroyed it. He claimed it demonstrated that it was very unlikely von Witte was dead.

Thus it was the KGB learned that von Witte had made many trips to Switzerland between 1938 and 1942 as the envoy of Reinhard Heydrich, almost certainly to deposit funds obtained from Jews seeking exit visas from Austria. This information, combined with the inconclusive evidence of his death, seemed to indicate that as the Allies were chasing the Germans out of France, von Witte had escaped to Switzerland. The general would certainly have been convicted of extensive war crimes had he been captured. Proof that he was still alive, enjoying a fortune in Jewish blood money, would be very valuable to the KGB: such information could be traded to Israel, especially after the Eichmann capture, with all its attendant publicity. It could be offered in return for the release of Arab prisoners, thus greatly improving their influence in the Middle East. In October 1961, KGB agent Barkov was assigned the task of obtaining proof that von Witte was still alive.

In February 1962, Barkov defected and was sent to CIA headquarters in Langley, Virginia.

Soon thereafter, C.C. Youngblood was assigned to complete Barkov's assignment. It was six months before C.C. found something to go on. Not proof, but a very interesting coincidence. Von Witte had ordered the destruction of Railleur-sur-Pelle on June 10, 1944. On the night of his supposed assassination, August 19, 1944, a French prisoner escaped from his cell at von Witte's headquarters. This same prisoner, Jean, Duc d'Artois, was born and had lived his whole life in Railleur, until his capture and escape. Shortly after the war d'Artois had become the business partner and friend of one of France's foremost citizens, Armand La Farge, and appeared to be wealthy in his own right.

The connection between d'Artois and von Witte was there, but did it mean anything? There were an endless number of possibilities, but only a few hard facts: d'Artois had managed his escape from von Witte on the night that von Witte had supposedly died; d'Artois was associated with one of France's richest and most powerful men; both were connected with United States Senator James Buchin, industrialist and politician and longtime friend of La Farge. Would any of these men in any way—a victim of Nazi torture, a decorated war hero and respected businessman, a senator—in any way lend themselves to the concealment of one of the most wanted Nazi war criminals?

With a conservative estimate of the fortune von Witte had deposited running at fifty million Swiss francs, C.C. found that he did not find the proposition too hard to believe. If there was any point to all this, he had to assume that von Witte was alive. The d'Artois–La Farge–Buchin connection was all that there was to investigate; if that turned up nothing, then, like a hound finding a trail ending in running water, he would have to cast about again until he picked up a fresh scent.

C.C. had been partnered for the assignment with Harry Baines—typical CIA man, blandly blond, Ivy League in background and appearance. C.C. fondly referred to him as "my WASP buddy"—explaining once to Harry that the acronym stood for White Anglo-Saxon Prick. Harry had taken it as a compliment; in the Company, as in many trades, nice guys finished last—or at least were finished.

Rosalie La Farge's wedding had marked the opening of their hunt, bringing together the three targets of their mission. Knowing that Buchin and d'Artois were to return to Paris after the Côte d'Azur party and that La Farge would be remaining in the Midi aboard *Créole*, they had split. Baines was to watch the duke and the senator, remaining in Paris; C.C. headed south to cover La Farge.

Unless Baines was onto something hot, he might be needed here. That red book could mean nothing or everything. From the way La Farge had seemed, going over it, it hadn't been nothing.

A public phone in a bar was the best way to get in touch with Harry. Going through his hotel switchboard and its operator was asking for trouble. He found the right sort of place, a working-class establishment with a long zinc counter and a telephone far enough away from the midmorning drinkers so that he wouldn't be easily overheard, even if anyone in that crowd understood English. He checked his watch. Ten-fifteen, right on the button. Harry's orders were to be in his Paris hotel room between ten and ten-thirty each morning to await any call C.C. might feel necessary to make.

By the time he had fed a fistful of *jetons* into the phone, it was ten twenty-three.

"Hey, C.C."

"Any news from Arty and Buck, old buddy?"

"Both came back to town night before last, that's about it. No anomalies."

"Got any hunches you might come up with any?"

"Doesn't smell like that to me."

"I've got a sniff of something this end." C.C. gave a cryptic—but, to Harry, clear enough—account of what he had observed that morning. "Could be worthwhile," he went on. "Local informant I've been pumping tells me L.F. is planning on sticking around for a while. Also, she's given me a few lines on his people here so maybe you and me could divvy up checking out some leads. Anyhow, if there's nothing shaking up there, suggest you haul your white ass down here and link up with me."

"If I know you, *kemo sabe,*" Harry said sardonically, "I'll bet your local informant's been giving you some pumping herself, French style."

"Girl's got a tongue could strangle a snake to death," C.C. said cheerfully, then arranged a rendezvous with Harry for the next day. There were four brass *jetons* left out of the pile of tokens he had started the call with; he dropped them into his pocket.

Until dusk, he observed the *Créole* from a variety of vantage points along the quai, moving from one bar to another before his presence at any one of them might become conspicuous.

A wasted day, he reflected, except for that one flash of action this morning. But that was the way most days went, in this kind of work. The heat and the gallon or so of liquids, ranging from *pastis* to coffee to that mixer they called *Pschitt!*—no market for that in the States, for sure—to white wine that had passed through his system, leaving him feeling bloated and thicker-headed than he liked.

The streetlights winked on, and he decided to abandon his vigil. La Farge wouldn't be going anywhere, otherwise Michelle would have had wind of it and let him know. When Harry got here tomorrow, they could work out full-time surveillance, the way the book said; but for tonight, fuck the book.

And the same for Michelle, come to think of it. A little workout with that moist body would be just the thing to clear away the fog that seemed to be closing in on him. At thirty-eight, maybe he should be pacing himself a little better; time was, he could wait out a watch in the tropics or the Arctic and knock back a quart of booze or so, and not notice it. Could be the old organism was getting a little weathered; but what hadn't given out was the nose. Somewhere around here was what he was after, or something that would lead to it. And the day C.C. Youngblood couldn't follow a scent and pull his quarry down was the day he wouldn't be anything he'd want to live with.

Michelle was a bit of luck, no mistake. A waitress with her own apartment over the Café Ste.-Hélène, an easy and enthusiastic lay, and a damned good source of information on the doings of Armand La Farge and his friends d'Artois and Buchin. He'd been a little concerned that his interest in La Farge might turn her off, but, especially after the first night, she'd cooperated fully. Maybe, he speculated, she thinks I'm some big-time crook out to make a score, and that I'll split the take with her.

Whatever her motives, she was, as he had expected, waiting for him. Arms open, legs open, mouth open.

Sated physically, C.C. rolled away from the woman and zipped himself, still half-erect and moist, into his trousers. Some session that had been, fast and urgent, yet seeming to last forever. Brutal, maybe, on his part, but not much less so on hers.

He fished from his jacket pocket a crumpled pack of American filter-tip cigarettes, lit two and offered her one; they lay companionably side by side on her narrow bed, smoking.

"I was looking at that yacht, the *Créole,*" he said after a while. "Be something, wouldn't it, to have a cruise on that? Servants bringing you caviar and champagne and such, and when it rolls and pitches, why, it takes half the work out of fucking. That American senator, he must spend some time on that scow, I'll bet, and me spending my tax dollars so he can have a good time—enough to make you puke."

"Monsieur Buchin, I think he's here sometimes, sure," Michelle said. "A friend of Monsieur La Farge, why not?"

"And not only senators but damned *dukes,*" C.C. said, as though there were something dirty about the nobility. "We threw that kind out of my country close to a couple of hundred years ago, honey. Aside from freeloading on his buddy Armand's rowboat, does he do anything around here, this d'Artois guy? You know, get into business or politics?"

"Why do you want to know?" Michelle asked nervously. C.C. missed a sidewise flick of her eyes.

"A world traveler like me, I take an interest in a lot of things," C.C. said, stretching lazily on the rumpled, stained, and odorous bed. "Coming from America, I have this kind of curiosity about the Old World, noblemen and such. I could learn something about how folks like that—"

At the last moment, he sensed the displacement of the fetid, still air in the room and started a roll that would have brought him off the bed and into a fighting-stance crouch if he had been able to complete it.

The length of lead pipe took him neatly behind the ear, even as he launched himself into motion. He dropped to the floor with a boneless thud that made any consciousness out of the question.

The man holding the pipe laid several large-denomination notes on the bed beside Michelle. "Sensible of you to tell me about this *type,*" he said. "Even more sensible to let me hang behind those curtains while you serviced him. Questions about the *patron,* we can't have those without taking notice, can we?"

"You're going to kill him?" Michelle asked.

The man shook his head, stooping to lift the unconscious C.C. from the floor and sling him over his shoulder. "The *patron's* against promiscuous bloodshed. This one's to be taken off the board for a while, that's all. If he has good sense, he'll have learned that it doesn't pay to poke your nose into an electric fence. If he doesn't, next time he's roast meat."

He closed the door behind him and headed for the stairs. There was no need for him to sneak out the back. People would just think he was taking home a drunken pal. The concierge, Mémé, was just locking up as he reached the ground floor.

Mémé glanced suspiciously at the man, and then at C.C.'s body dangling over his shoulder. The man pressed a bill into her hand and informed her that it was La Farge's bidding. She nodded her approval. The name La Farge immediately made everything legal. She cackled loudly and stuffed the bill in her brassiere. She looked like an old crone with her messy gray hair sticking to her face in the heat of the late summer night. Cigot made a face as he passed her.

One thing good about Mémé though, she could be trusted. Her son Bertrand was the guardian at Colombier, the trusted and loyal servant of Armand La Farge, and the apple of his mother's eye. Bertrand, as a young man, had got himself into serious trouble smuggling arms and liquor across the Italian border, and La Farge, in search of people to work for him, had interviewed Bertrand and saved his neck from the law. Since then, Bertrand, as well as his mother, had been eternally grateful to La Farge, and Cigot knew they would stop at nothing to protect their benefactor.

A man came out of a nearby doorway as Cigot passed by, and fell in step. Cigot let C.C. slide off his back and together they propped him up between them, putting C.C.'s arms around their necks.

"There's the car, over there." It was the voice of the second man. He pointed straight ahead to a black Citroën parked alongside the curb in front of the Café Hélène. There was a man in the seat behind the wheel. He was smoking a cigarette, his face barely lit by the small light. As they approached, the man in the car leaned over the seat and opened up the rear door closest to the curb. The two men hoisted C.C. off the ground and dumped him into the backseat. Cigot got in beside

C.C., and the other man, a massive black with a deep scar on his cheek, went around and got in on the other side.

The man behind the wheel turned to look at C.C. It was Fritz, d'Artois's chauffeur.

"Hope you didn't kill him. We don't want any unnecessary blood on our hands. You know the *patron* is strict about that," Fritz said.

"No. He's still alive, but he's not kicking." The black was West Indian, from Martinique. He had worked on La Farge's plantation for many years, before La Farge decided to bring him back with him to France. A year later, La Farge had fired him for raping a teenage daughter of one of the maids. La Farge had not nicknamed the man "Goliath" for nothing. The girl had been hospitalized in critical condition. La Farge had arranged for him not to be imprisoned and had seen to the girl's hospital bills, but he had fired him and given him a ticket to return to Martinique.

The old concierge, peering out into the street, thought it strange that the black man and Cigot, a well-known wharf rat whose services were available to anyone for the right price, would be doing La Farge's bidding, but Cigot had done odd jobs for La Farge, such as helping with the cleaning of his yachts. She dismissed the whole thing with a shrug. She would find out more in detail from Bertrand when she next saw him.

Fritz stubbed out his Gitane on C.C.'s cheek. The smell of burnt flesh filled the car. C.C. did not flinch, and Fritz was satisfied. He rolled down the window to let some fresh air in and threw the butt out onto the sidewalk.

The car drove off, turning into a side street, and then headed back onto the Quai du Midi, in the direction of St. Tropez. Fritz checked his watch as they drove past a streetlamp. It was already almost one, a perfect time to dispose of a body, he thought.

The car drove swiftly down the coast, turning and weaving dangerously around every curve. No one spoke. One hour later, they pulled onto a dirt road and drove down to Pompelone Beach. In the distance they could see a boat. As the car came to a stop, Fritz doused the lights, waited for a minute or two, then he flicked them on once more, then off, then on again. Again he doused the lights and waited. This time the boat signaled back, flicking a huge light on and off, then on and off again.

"They're coming in to get him. Take the man to the shore," Fritz said, motioning to Goliath and Cigot. "They'll be out with the dingy in a few minutes."

In the distance the men could hear the sound of a motor starting up. They began to drag C.C. to the water, holding on to his feet, his head digging a trench in the sand as it bobbed across the deserted beach.

Fritz puffed on a Gitane as the launch approached the shore. An odd job, this one. Two days before, as he was driving d'Artois to the airport to catch the Paris plane, the duke had nudged him sharply. "That dark man at the café table there, see him? It comes to me that I saw him in the crowd outside Mademoiselle Rosalie's wedding—and even then I had the feeling I'd seen him near the La Farge place once or twice before. I doubt, my dear Fritz, that he's a wedding guest, down here for the party, eh? Perhaps a journalist, but . . ."

He had instructed Fritz to stay in Nice and discover what he could of the dark man. On his instructions, and for a good sum, Michelle had made herself available to the stranger, discovering on the first night that he claimed to be an American tourist called Wilson Browning, visiting in Nice for the past week—and that, for a foreigner, he seemed to have an inordinate interest in the doings of Armand La Farge and La Farge's associates, particularly Senator James Buchin and Jean, Duc d'Artois.

"He has certainly not been in Nice for a week," d'Artois had said when Fritz reported to him by telephone the next morning. "And therefore he is certainly not a tourist or a journalist. Journalists do not, my dear Fritz, assume other identities when they're after a story; rather, they proclaim their occupation in the hope that the newspaper-mad public will rush to inform them of what they wish to know. Let the girl answer whatever questions he asks, and give me a full report tomorrow. And meanwhile make sure that Cigot and that black giant are in readiness."

The next day's account emphasized the fact that "Browning" retained his curiosity about La Farge, Buchin and d'Artois.

"Whether this man is an actual danger, I can't say," d'Artois had muttered. "I'll take it for granted that, whatever his plans, they are not in my interests. It will be best to discourage him."

"Permanently, *patron?*"

"I think not. A discreet removal to the *Zodiac*, then a quiet sail some distance down the coast to that place we've used near Saintes Maries de la Mer, and, say, a week's vacation under sedation. Waking up some hundreds of miles and seven days away from his last recollection should suggest to him that he's involved in something he'd do well to drop. If he doesn't take the suggestion, I'll know that it's time for more serious measures."

The *Zodiac*'s lights twinkled offshore as the yacht's launch grated on the stony beach. Fritz threw his cigarette into the sea and stooped to help lift C.C.'s limp body into the craft.

Chapter Ten

Casablanca, September 1962

About five miles off the shore of Morocco, the *Rosalie* tacked, getting into position to head into the port of Casablanca. The food supply was running low and Rosalie needed to wire her father to send Ahmed's and her clothes on to the next port. She also needed to ask for money, since they had left without a sou, leaving everything aboard the *Crêole*.

Rosalie and Ahmed could see the harbor of Casablanca in the distance. They had never been this way before. The only place in North Africa either of them had ever been was Tunisia, and they were looking forward to the experience.

The *Rosalie* anchored in the harbor at three in the afternoon. It was exactly four days since they had left Monaco.

"I wish I'd brought some clothes along. I must look awful in these slacks of Maman's. She's a little taller than I am, you know." Rosalie pulled the slacks up high, practically to her breasts, and pulled the blue T-shirt down over them. "There!

What do you think, Ahmed? Do you still find me attractive enough or should I just disembark in the nude?''

Ahmed studied Rosalie's reflection in the mirror on the door behind her, and pensively stroked his chin. ''Well, frankly, I think I'd prefer you naked. But wait! I have an idea.'' He pulled the sheet off the bunk and draped it loosely about her, leaving a small slit for her to look through. ''There, that's more like it. This is more what's 'in' in Casablanca.'' He twirled her around to let her look at herself in the mirror. ''Well, what do you think?'' Before she could answer, he grabbed the sheet off the other bunk and wrapped it around himself. ''There, now what do you say?''

His boyishness made Rosalie laugh and she threw herself on top of him, covering up his face with her sheet. ''I'll tell you what I think, *salaud*. This is how I like you best. When I can't see your evil face!''

Ahmed threw himself across the bunk and pulled her down on top of him, pinning her arms behind her back. Rosalie lapsed into uncontrollable laughter as Ahmed tickled her feet. Her shrieks brought Ganot and Raoul running to her aid. They thought the prince might be exercising his ''Arab rights'' by beating her. Ahmed acted a little embarrassed when he saw the two men and released his victim, who immediately pounced on him and bit his calf, drawing a yelped curse of pain. The two men shook their heads as they left the pair alone to their games.

''The way those two make love and fight, I doubt we'll make it to Papeete in one piece,'' said Raoul.

From the Hotel Grand Atlas in Casablanca Rosalie placed a call to her father aboard the *Créole*. She was pleasantly surprised by his obvious amusement at the whole escapade. It was not as if she had expected him to disown her, but she had not expected such a warm greeting. She had to admit that her father was a man with a sense of humor equal to his greatness. He promised to wire her the money at once and gave her a few names to contact in Casablanca if she should need anything. He also promised to send their luggage on to Martinique, where they would be met by the overseer of the La Rose plantation. They exchanged a few remarks, his about the guests and what had happened the night of the wedding, hers about the voyage and how happy she was. The connection was bad and they had trouble understanding each other, so after Rosalie promised to call as soon as she arrived in Martinique, they exchanged good-byes and hung up. By this time, Ahmed had found himself some sandals which he paid for with money he borrowed from Ganot. He proudly showed them off to Rosalie, who in turn wrinkled up her nose.

Very . . . Moroccan, wouldn't you say?"

Ahmed threw up his arms. "Well, you wouldn't expect them to look Chinese, would you? After all, we do happen to be in Morocco, or didn't you notice?" He kissed the upturned face lightly on the cheek. "I tell you what. Let's go get you a pair."

"But where did you get the money?"

"Oh, just a little magic. The old one-two, you know. A talent only Arabs have."

"*Thieving* Arabs, you mean. Did you take poor Ganot's money, or was it Raoul's?"

"Take? Now there's a word that doesn't exist in the Arabic dictionary. Borrow, yes; take, never."

Together they crossed the street and headed for the shop where earlier Ahmed had bought his sandals. A wad of Moroccan francs was clutched in his left hand, his right around Rosalie's waist.

Casablanca was not as big as Rosalie had imagined. It was a busy place, though, with people of all types bustling back and forth. The stalls were filled with greedy vendors, pulling, tugging at them, offering their wares for sale.

They spent three glorious days in Casablanca and even found time to take a train trip to Marrakech, where they spent two more days. On the sixth day, their arms laden with souvenirs and pockets heavy with the money Papa La Farge had wired them, the two newlyweds boarded the *Rosalie* ready to set sail for Martinique, where they would spend two weeks before continuing to Tahiti.

Chapter Eleven

Martinique, October 1962

Gaston Rouvier, the overseer at La Rose, closed the door as Rosalie sat down beside Ahmed in the backseat of the white Rolls Royce. He walked around the car and got in behind the steering wheel. Rosalie tapped him on his shoulder. "Gaston, drive slowly so my husband can see the island will you?"

"Oui, madame, I will take . . ." His voice was drowned out by the loud blowing of the *Rosalie*'s horn. Ahmed and Rosalie waved at Ganot standing on the deck, and the car pulled out of the parking space onto the busy street.

The white Rolls sped through the crowded streets of Fort de France swiftly heading for the outskirts of the city. It had just rained and everything looked washed and clean. Even the gray asphalt roads glistened in the sunlight, as the car sped along, from time to time splashing a passerby. As they left the city behind, the ride became more interesting. The smell of earth and sea was everywhere, refreshed by the occasional smells of tropical flowers and the ripened, fallen mangos along the way.

For Rosalie, the island was a second home. The smells and the breathtaking views were all very familiar. She had spent many vacations here with her mother and father. She had learned to love the island and its people as her father did. She had even learned to speak Créole and patois fluently, and felt at ease among the West Indian people. Ahmed had never been in this part of the world before, preferring the Greek islands and the East Indies. He had always thought that the West Indies, whether French, English, or Dutch, were where American tourists went. Now he was delightfully surprised by the island's charm. No wonder La Farge had thought it fit to settle on, he mused to himself.

They drove on, passing through dense, leafy groves where banana bunches hung heavily from the trees, protected by blue plastic bags to shield them from the birds and the insects. They passed a beautiful old manor and the ruins of a sugar mill, overgrown by vines and wild flowers. "Must have been quite a place at one time," Ahmed remarked as they passed by.

"Yes, according to Papa, it was. When he first came to Martinique, he met the owners—they are dead now, have been for some time. I heard some people recently bought it to make into a restaurant."

"What a pity, I hate to see something as beautiful spoiled." He sighed.

"We're almost there now, Ahmed," Rosalie whispered excitedly, as if it were a secret. "There—see over that hill?" They could see the Belle Fleur plantation now in the distance, with its bright red roof and the stately pillars of the front terraces.

He whistled loudly. "What a place! Is that it?" Ahmed leaned over the front seat to get a better view.

Rosalie nodded. "That's it, all right, but that's not where we're going. We're going on to La Rose. Papa had things set up there for us."

Ahmed looked a little disappointed. "Oh, I guess we're going to the beach cottage, eh?"

Rosalie smiled, amused. "Well, yes. Maybe 'cottage,'

isn't exactly the right word; but yes, we're going to the beach house."

As they drove by the gates of Belle Fleur, a group of children, playing in the meadow directly across the road from it, hailed out and waved to them. Rosalie had the driver slow down, and the car came to a stop alongside the stone wall, covered with green and yellow coralita vines and their frothy pink blossoms.

Two little boys skipped through the tall grass and scampered over the stone wall to where the car had now just about come to a full stop. The little girls in the group stood together in a huddle, giggling and then stooped to hide behind the tall grass.

"Hey, messieurs! Hey, Mademoiselle Rosalie!" the boys hailed. "Want a mango?" The bigger of the two offered a mango to Rosalie, and then one to Ahmed.

"Thank you, Claudie. Thank you very much. Is that your little brother Michou with you?"

The boy nodded, pleased that Rosalie had remembered them. "Ya sum, that's Michou all right. He growed an awful lot since you last come, no?"

Rosalie laughed. She held out her hands to the boys, who pumped them eagerly up and down.

Michou grimaced and stuck out his tongue at Ahmed. His older brother placed a grimy hand over the boy's mouth, and grinned apologetically. "Oh, don't mind him, Monsieur. He just mad cause I gave you the biggest mango. See?" He pointed joyfully at the large, fleshy fruit Ahmed was holding. "That's the biggest one I see yet all year, and, Michou, he wanted it."

Ahmed looked down at the fruit. It had a little hole and was badly bruised on two sides where little hands had squeezed too tightly. Some of the thick, orange, yellow pulp was oozing through the hole. It vividly brought back his days in medical training, when, for a whole year, he had thought he wanted to become a doctor. He felt his stomach churning inside.

"Eh, why don't I give it back to Michou, and I can share Mademoiselle Rosalie's, hm?"

Michou's face lit up like a Christmas tree. "Yeah. Yeah.

Gimme. Gimme." His eager little hands were grabbing into the car for the mango. "Gimme here."

The older boy shrugged. "Okay, if that's what you want, but I tell you, m'sieur, you would like that one. Is a *really* big one."

Everyone laughed at the expression on the boy's face as he spoke. Even Rouvier, who until now had sat silently, hands on the wheel, staring ahead of him, joined in.

Michou grabbed the mango and sank his teeth into it! The skin broke and sent a spray of mango juice and pulp flying through the air to land on Ahmed's face and neck. The little boy grinned apologetically and ran off to join his sisters, still hiding in the grass.

Rouvier started the car up again and continued on slowly down the twisting, winding road. Rosalie looked at Ahmed and broke into a fit of giggles.

The phone was ringing as they came through the front door of the rambling mansion.

"Who could it be?" Rosalie wondered. She looked at Ahmed, and they both shrugged.

Somehow a telephone sounded out of place here, not like Paris or Rome or even St. Tropez, where you *had* to have a phone to keep in touch with the rest of the world. Here you did not want to. Her father had had the phone put in only a few years earlier, and she had argued the point for weeks with him. But she had finally had to accede to her mother's wishes, for heaven forbid that Jacqueline did not have a phone to keep in touch with the rest of the world during her vacations here. Rosalie's thoughts of her mother were interrupted by Ahmed's voice.

"Aren't you going to answer it?"

At that moment, a large, fat, black woman entered, her portly stomach rolling as she walked. She picked up the phone. "Allô? Eh? Allô?" A smile lit up her face suddenly as she recognized the voice on the other end. "Ah, Monsieur La Farge. How are you? Eh? Ah, yes, monsieur. They just come. I heard the car. Eh? Ah, yes, monsieur. I go get them. Good-bye, monsieur." She rested the receiver on the table and clapped her hands together loudly at the two children, Claudie and Michou, who had run all the way back to the house to be on hand for any excitement which might take place.

"Go on, scat, shoo, out of here! You boys going track mud on my clean floors. Out of here or I take a tamarind whip to your bottoms."

The boys scampered out, eating their buttered bread and sugar, which they had grabbed from the kitchen on their way in. The comely woman's face lit up with joy as she saw Rosalie. She had heard the car drive up, but had not noticed them come in.

"Oh, Ma'm'selle Rosalie! How nice have you home again. Is a real pleasure. My! Oh my! I do declare. Married and all."

She held her arms out to the young woman. "Oh, baby. Is so good to have you with me again. I so powerfully happy."

She wrapped her plump arms about Rosalie, and enveloped her in a warm embrace.

"Where that man of yours, ma'm'selle? Don't tell me your temper drove him away already!" She pursed her lips and rolled her eyes at Rosalie in mock despair. "Oh! Oh! Don't tell me," she said. "I guess. You had fight and put him out and made him walk, eh?" She heard giggles behind the front door and snapped her head in its direction. Two little black heads ducked behind the front door.

Rosalie spoke in Crêole. "Maman Rose, I see you still having trouble with them boys yours, eh?"

The woman chuckled behind her hand. "Oh, Ma'm'selle Rosalie, I can see you never forget Créole. No sure you too much like you father for you own good." She kissed Rosalie on the cheek. "You papa right when he say you should been boy instead. I agree, but then," she added, pursing her lips and raising her brows once more, "you wouldn't have married no prince, eh?"

At that moment Ahmed returned from answering the telephone. "It was your father," he said. "He sounded a little under the weather. The connection was bad, and he'll have to call us back. He said to give you a kiss till then though, and I promised I would." Ahmed grabbed Rosalie to do so, his embrace causing her short skirt to ride up, exposing the swells of two round buttocks. She was wearing no underwear,

Maman Rose looked at her. "Rosalie, you half naked in that thing. You mean to tell me, you come all the way from France, where is all them clothes and things, in that? Good thing you two married, or I pack you off back to you father, dressed like that, I tell you. What the world is coming to lately, I just don't know." She shook her head and gave Ahmed an apologetic look. "She ought to be shamed of herself, but she not. I know she not. Come on, you two. I'll show you to you rooms."

"What? Show me to my rooms? After all these years? Come on, Maman Rose, this is Rosalie. Remember me?"

"Oh, you never mind, Ma'm'selle Rosalie. You papa tell me what to do, and he say you two have his and Ma'ame Jacqueline's rooms this time, seeing you married and all. Now come on."

"But where's Emile? He knows you shouldn't go up and down the steps too much with your heart condition and all."

"Heart condition? I got no heart condition. Just plain old fat from eating too much good food."

Ahmed asked, "Who is Emile?"

"Oh, he's butler, but I bet he's out in canefields chasing women. I tell you, that man has too much of a good thing." Maman Rose turned and threw Ahmed a knowing look. "If you know what I mean."

Ahmed nodded and fought to keep his composure. He was madly in love with this woman already. It was no wonder, he thought, that Rosalie was so fond of her. Maman Rose had helped take care of Rosalie since Rosalie was three and had first come to Martinique. Berthe in those days had seen mostly to Rosalie's manners and tutoring, but Maman Rose had been hired to play mother where Jacqueline and Berthe left off. She must have had a lot to do with the forming of Rosalie's character, Ahmed thought, especially that sense of humor and bubbly personality.

The phone began to ring again as they got to the landing of the second floor.

"Oh, that must be Papa again." Rosalie ran down the hall and flung open the large mahogany door to the bedroom suite. She grabbed the receiver off the hook.

"Hello! Papa?"

"Rosalie? Hello, darling. What's new?"

"I should ask you that, don't you think?"

"Oh? How so?"

"Well, I mean, has anybody played any pranks on you lately, since I left?"

"Nope."

"Not even James?"

"James? Why James? Why would he play any pranks on me?"

"Oh, I don't know. I just thought that maybe he might have bought you a few pairs of pajama bottoms—just to amuse himself."

She heard a gulping sound on the other end as he paused. "Papa, are you there?"

"Uh huh, still here."

"What was that sound I just heard?"

"Just me taking a pill."

"A pill? What in hell for, or isn't it any of my business?"

"Just an aspirin. I have a terrible headache."

"Oh. Who gave it to you, James or Maman?"

"Your mother. She dragged me to this god-awful party last night, and I think their caviar must have been refried or something. I've been sick all day, if you get the picture."

She giggled over the phone. "Sure do. Guess you won't need your Vittel then tonight, hm?"

"That's right. Say, how is that husband of yours? Did you get him safely there?"

"Yes, he's right here beside me. Want to talk to him?"

"Yes I do, but first I want to wish you both lots of happiness, and I want you to relax and enjoy the house by yourselves during the next few days." La Farge chuckled softly into the receiver and lowered his tone to a near whisper as if someone else might be listening. "I had a fight with your mother after you left." He made a growling sound.

"Oh, really? Knowing Maman, it must have been a good one."

He laughed and continued. "She had this crazy idea about

coming down to Martinique to stay during the time you and Ahmed were there, and . . ."

Rosalie did not let her father finish his sentence. "Maman coming here? Why would she want to do something like that? Doesn't she know three on a honeymoon is a crowd?"

La Farge exploded into loud laughter on the other end. "I got that idea loud and clear after that stunt you two pulled on me, and I must say, I had to laugh at your audacity. But your mother . . . well, you know your mother. She didn't take too kindly to what you did. But don't worry, I managed to talk her out of it. I only wish she wasn't still so upset with you. She doesn't even want to talk to you."

"I see. Now I get the picture. She wanted to come down and spoil my honeymoon. To punish me for what I did, hm?"

"It's not so much what you did to *her*, as much as what you did to her friends."

"I can just bet." An amused tone came into Rosalie's voice once more as she spoke. "Imagine all those ladies all gussied up for the soirée of the year aboard the *Créole*, and then pouf!—nothing. I wish I could have seen their faces. When I get home, Papa—and that won't be for a long time, by the time we get to Papeete and back, with all the stops we're planning in between—but as soon as we're back, you must tell me more about what happened that evening. Promise?"

"Promise. Oh, don't forget to check with Emile or Gaston about the package I sent you."

"A package for me?"

"Well, yes, there's one for you and one for Ahmed. I hope you like them."

"Them? What's them?"

"Oh, come, Rosalie. You're too old for shaking and smelling boxes. It's a surprise, so you'll just have to wait till you open it. Ahhh . . . youth!" He laughed and blew her a kiss into the receiver. " 'Bye now, pet. I'm going to let you get back to Ahmed. I'll call again before you leave."

She blew him a kiss into the receiver. "Okay, 'bye, Papa. Hey, Papa?"

"Yes?"

"I love you."

"I love you, too, darling, and so does your mother. Maybe you can write her a little note or something special—to cheer her up and make her forget, eh?"

"Sure, Papa. Will do. I love you. Here's Ahmed."

She handed the receiver to Ahmed and ran out of the room calling for Maman Rose.

That night, dinner for two was served on the veranda in back of the mansion. The round glass and wrought-iron table was pushed close to the low stone wall near the edge of the bluff, overlooking the cove. The sea was calm in the bay, almost motionless, like a great shoreless lake of shimmering glass. Not the slightest ripple or spot of foam could be seen. Rosalie sat dressed in a pink and gray silk pareu, her legs crossed casually, her elbows resting on the arms of the large rattan chair. She was looking down at the sea. The light fabric of her pareu fluttered gently from time to time in the softest of evening breezes. She wore it wrapped snugly around her body, the ends tucked into the hollow between her breasts. She inhaled and exhaled rapidly, drinking in the fresh night air. Her breasts rose and fell in rhythm with her breathing. Ahmed could see her nipples through the sheer fabric, like pink rosebuds, small and pointed. Ahmed admired his wife's incredible beauty, her gracefulness and soft femininity. He studied her profile and tried to guess her thoughts. She seemed far away just then, as if in another time, as she sat silently looking out over the shining sea. He wanted to reach out and touch her, to be even closer to her, but he dared not break the spell of her magical thoughts, whatever they might be.

Rosalie felt Ahmed's eyes on her, and suddenly realized she had been sitting totally quiet, engrossed in her thoughts of herself and her surroundings, without sharing them with her husband. She smiled at him and blew him a kiss across the table.

"I was thousands of miles away," she admitted, "somewhere between Afghanistan and Zaire."

Ahmed picked a small, pink oleander blossom from the centerpiece and leaned over to arrange it in her hair.

"There. Now you not only look and smell like a queen, but I hereby crown you Queen of the Flowers."

She touched her fingers to his and stroked his hand softly.

"Ahmed, darling, do you know something?"

"No. What?"

"I was just thinking what it would be like to have a baby by you. Would he look like you or me?" She raised her eyes to gaze up at the sky and crossed her hands under her chin, her elbows resting on the table. "Maybe it would be a little girl—or twins, even."

Ahmed sputtered and choked on his martini. "Twins? God, Rosalie! Why not do things the normal way? Like one at a time?" He pretended to scoff. "And furthermore, I don't think you should rush into pregnancy. You're still young and have lots of time ahead of you."

She eyed him closely, a wicked grin on her face, her eyes sparkling. "Well, I know *I* have a lot of time, but do *you?*"

He raised his eyebrows. "And what do you mean by that?"

"Well, you know, I hear stories all the time about men suddenly not being able to . . . you know . . . anymore." She finished her sentence with a soft chortle and hid her face behind her hands.

He shrugged. "It's possible. Probable, even. I figure that if we were married for let's say sixty years . . ."

"Sixty years, why sixty? Why not fifty or seventy or even eighty?"

"Now wait a minute; let me finish. If we were married for sixty years, that would mean, let me see . . . sixty years at three hundred sixty-five and one-quarter days a year . . ." He did some quick mathematics in his head. "That would be twenty-one thousand, nine hundred and fifteen days, which would mean, at our rate of three times a day, that would be sixty-five thousand seven hundred and forty-five lays." The words came out like a yell in the still night.

"Sh!" She placed a finger on her lips and frowned. "They'll hear you!"

"Who?"

"The servants, silly. You want everyone to hear what we're talking about?"

"Not especially, but do you think it would really matter?"

"What do you mean?"

"What I mean, Miss Fake Prude, is what do you think everyone thought we were doing all afternoon up in our room, licking stamps or coloring pictures?"

She gave him an exasperated look. "No, but—"

"But nothing, they all heard you moaning and carrying on." He was on the verge of bursting into laughter at the expression on her face.

"Me? Me moaning and carrying on? Listen to me, you barbaric piss-in-the-mud, I'll have you know that I don't make sounds when I'm making love, but *you* do." She shook a menacing fist at him. "If you weren't so big, I, I'd . . ."

"Yes?"

"Oh, never mind."

"And what's that you called me?"

"A piss-in-the-mud."

Ahmed broke out laughing as she said it again.

"Ah, my Rosalie. Soft as a petal in honey you look, but you're as funny as a dildo in a convent!"

Rosalie collapsed in giggles. "Ooooh, stop it. You're killing me. God, that's funny!"

"But wait. I wasn't finished with what I was saying. I had begun to tell you how to avoid being cheated of sex in your old age," Ahmed said.

Rosalie pointed a finger at herself, her sharp fingernail making a tiny crescent-shaped mark on the upper slope of her breast. "*My* old age? You've got to be kidding. Look who's talking. Now, you listen here."

He placed his hand over her open mouth before she could speak again. "I said I wasn't finished. Damn, you're a talkative wench tonight."

She stuck her tongue out at him, between his fingers.

He ignored her and went on. "As I was saying, if we started right this minute, do you see, we could speed up our rate from three times a day to six. Let's see. Ah, yes, by the time I'm sixty-one and you're forty-eight, we'd have our quota, and it wouldn't matter after that if I couldn't get it up."

"Oh, Christ! You know, sometimes I think you'd have been better off as a bachelor all your life."

"Hm, think so? I don't know. I mean, why go out to a smorgasbord when you have filet mignon at home?"

"Ah, bah. At least, you didn't compare me to a horse steak."

"The only reason I didn't was because you're too *tender.*" He reached over and pinched her thigh playfully.

"Ouch. Stop that!"

"See? That's what I mean. If you pinched a horse, it wouldn't scream."

"Oh no? But it might kick."

He caught her foot as she brought it up between his legs.

"Now none of that wild stuff, you crazy filly."

"Ah ha! See? I knew it."

"Knew what?"

"That sooner or later you'd compare me to horsemeat."

She was barefoot, and her tanned toes looked very inviting. He bit them playfully, tickling the bottom of her foot with his finger at the same time.

At that moment, the door to the veranda opened, and Emile and Henriette came outside, he carrying a large silver bucket with ice and two bottles of champagne and she carrying a large tray laden with steaming platters of food. Maman Rose followed close behind.

"You two so hungry you can't wait, or what?" She waved a disapproving hand in the direction of Rosalie's foot lying on Ahmed's lap. He was still bending over it. "You a cannibal or something? You know, long time ago, the Carib Indians who lived in these parts used to be cannibals. You not one of them people, I hope, me."

"I don't think so, Maman Rose, but I am *starved.*"

"What are we having tonight, Maman Rose?" Rosalie asked.

"You mean you can't smell, child? We having stuffed crab backs, and pawpaw, and sautéed shrimps for starters, caught fresh in bay this morning. Bico caught them 'specially for you and your handsome husband." She flashed Ahmed a toothy smile.

"Then," Maman Rose continued, "we having game hens done in honey and herbs with grapes and wild rice, you father favorite; yours too, Ma'm'selle Rosalie." She turned to look at Ahmed. "I hope you like it, me. Cocotte has her faults and nips the bottle a little from time to time, but she can cook up a storm. Hmm, smell them crab backs."

Ahmed's mouth was watering as he savored the food. "Ahhh, that smells good."

The rest of the evening was spent quietly. The two lovers ate slowly, enjoying their meal and each other's company. It was warm and relaxing, sitting there under the half shade of the big old tamarind tree. The starlit sky shone through the wide-stretched branches. The long, cylindrical-shaped fruit dangled and clicked softly in the breeze.

Ahmed swirled his wine in his glass. He raised it to his nose and sniffed the bouquet. "Ah, Mouton-Rothschild, '49, the best. Though the '47 was—"

"My grandfather planted it, you know?"

"What? The Mouton-Rothschild?"

"No, silly. The tree."

"What tree?"

"The one you're sitting under, idiot. What other tree do you think I'd be talking about? One on the Champs-Elysées or in New Guinea, perhaps?"

"So, your grandfather planted it."

"Yes, he did. Tamarind trees are supposed to bring good luck, according to the old wives' tales. Didn't you know that?"

"I thought tamarind trees were some sort of sex symbol in India."

"Sex symbol? In India?"

"Well, I don't know, but I always read about tamarind trees in East Indian books. Must be the phallic shape of the fruit that stimulates the authors or something."

"You're hopeless," she said, getting up and walking over to lean against the large reddish brown trunk. A spotlight from the second floor shone down on it, highlighting the gnarled, knotty bark. Rosalie stood there for a moment and then walked over and sat on the low stone wall overlooking the cliff. She straddled it.

"You want to commit suicide or something? Get down from there before you fall. Now!" His tone was angry.

"Oh, pfui. Don't be ridiculous, Ahmed. It's quite safe, actually. Come on, sit next to me." She patted the wall behind her. "Come on!" She pursed her lips and batted her eyelashes at him. "Please?"

He did.

They sat together looking down at the jagged rocks and shoals below.

"Isn't it beautiful, Ahmed?"

"Magnificent."

"Let's go for a walk on the beach? It's such a beautiful night tonight."

Hand in hand they descended the tree-lined gravel and dirt path. They came upon a second gate on the left of the pathway and stopped to look at the view beyond it. The moon was hiding now, partly behind a thick cloud. Only the faintest of light shone through.

"What's that over there?" Ahmed asked.

"What? Where?"

"There, behind the hanky-panky trees."

She burst out laughing. "God, you're funny, man. They're not hanky-panky trees. They're frangipani trees."

"Yeah, that's what I said."

Rosaline threw herself on the mossy edge of the path. "Ooooh, my stomach. I can't stand it."

"What's the matter? You ate too much or something?"

She was in stitches and couldn't stop. "No, it's just you."

The thick gray cloud drifted by, allowing the full moon to light up the garden path once again.

"See. Over there. What are those two white pillars for?"

She stood up and dusted herself off. "Oh, those white things. They're not pillars, silly. They're crosses."

"Crosses? On the beach?"

"Sure, why not?"

"I don't know. I just never saw crosses on the beach before."

"They're grave markers; my grandparents are buried there."

"You mean you just dig a hole and bury your grandparents in your backyard here?"

"Well, not exactly. You have to own a certain amount of land and have a lot of influence to do so, but what's so strange about it? In your country, you go around cutting off people's balls—so?"

"I don't go around cutting off anybody's balls, and furthermore, I don't see the similarity."

"I didn't accuse you personally, silly. I meant your country. I can't see how you can find burying somebody 'in their backyard,' as you put it, stranger than gelding a man. Shit!"

"Well," he laughed, "you have a point, but think about it in this way: they at least never have to worry about getting pinched when they sit down."

She shrugged. "Tell *them* that."

She lifted the chain up over the gatepost. "Come on, let's go see."

"Go see what? A pair of graves, at this hour?"

"Don't be so damn blasé, Ahmed. They're not just *any* graves, they're special."

"I see, special. All right, but only for you would I go look at a pair of graves at"—he looked at his watch and squinted to see what time it was—"twelve-thirty. Just past the witching hour, too."

They stumbled through the flower pots and conch shells lining the path.

"Man, this gives me the creeps."

"Oh come on, the dead can't bite."

"You sure your grandparents weren't vampires?"

"Say, did I marry a man or—"

"I know, or a mouse. Well, young lady, what you married is a horny Arab, and, I tell you, the last thing I had in mind tonight was skipping through the ferns in a graveyard with a half-naked woman. Brrrrr." He wrapped his arms about himself and rubbed his palms quickly up and down the sides of his back. "It's colder here than up there." He pointed with his chin to the veranda above. "Unnaturally cold."

"You're just making it up, trying to scare me. I've been coming here ever since I was a little girl. Even got my first kiss right behind that 'hanky-panky' tree." Rosalie giggled and turned to look at Ahmed. "You know, for once, I think you were right. It was a hanky-panky tree during those days."

"*Those* days?"

"Yeah, the days when Philip used to meet me here." She sounded almost like a little girl. "That was a long time ago, long before I knew *you* even existed."

"Hm, and all along I thought I'd been your first affair. Shows you how a man can never be too sure."

"Well, you were my first lover, but not my first affair."

"Oh? Tell me about it."

"There's nothing really to tell. Philip is Senator Buchin's second son. He's a few months older than I am, and as I told you before, the Buchins also spent a lot of time here."

"I thought you didn't know the senator very well."

"I didn't and I still don't really, but Philip and his older brother were here one summer with their governess." She giggled wickedly. "We were eleven then."

"Eleven? That's jail-bait age!"

"Oh, but we didn't think so at the time. We vowed to marry when we grew up and sealed the pact with a passionate kiss. I thought it was the hottest love affair of the century."

Ahmed's thoughts were full of imaginary visions of Rosalie as a little girl kissing a boy behind the graves.

Ahmed jumped. "Shit! What was that?"

"What was what?"

"You heard?"

"Mr-r-r-r-auw." The gray kitten slid down the trunk of the tree and fell with a soft thud on the grave nearest Rosalie.

"Shit, that cat scared me half to death."

"You're right. Let's get out of here." She turned and looked wide-eyed around her, as if she expected to see something or someone.

"You looking for somebody, Rosalie? Perhaps the headless horseman or a grave robber?"

"Oh, cut that out, Ahmed. Let's go, okay? You know me, once I get jumpy, that's the end."

"Want to walk down on the beach still?"

"We'll do that some other time." She picked up the kitten in her arms, and snuggled close to Ahmed. "Let's go back to the house."

The next morning, Ahmed was awakened by the loud call of a male peacock, strutting proudly about in the garden below. He rubbed his eyes and glanced at the clock on the night table beside him.

"Six-thirty! Christ! What the hell is that, anyway? A damn mongoose?"

He listened; it came again, a loud cawing sound.

Sounds more like a man hung up on a barbed-wire fence, he thought. He did not feel like getting out of bed to go see what it was. He was still languid from lovemaking the night before. He rolled on his side and propped himself up on one elbow. He peered down at Rosalie lying next to him. She was sound asleep, her knees drawn up, almost touching her chin, her hands clasped over her breasts. He raised himself slightly to get a better look at her.

God, she looks sexy like that, he thought.

Her hair was spread loosely and abundantly about her pillow. The sheets were pulled back slightly, away from her shoulders and breasts. A pink nipple peeped out at him, from between her open fingers. He felt himself a lucky man to have this next to him each morning.

"To have and to hold, until death do us part," he whispered.

Rosalie stirred just then and stretched herself lazily across the bed. The sheets dropped even lower across her sleeping body. Ahmed bent over and kissed her neck and sucked a tiny bit of flesh in between his lips.

"Hmmmm." She wriggled a little and smiled sleepily. "Hmmmm."

He took her in his arms and entered her fiercely, forcing her to awaken and respond.

Breakfast consisted of piping hot, fried goat-fish and chilled Dom Pérignon, then some fresh guavas and dates. It was a morning to remember. Sunlight was streaming in everywhere, and outside were a flawless sky and a dazzling blue ocean with only the tiniest ripples of waves.

The bold peacock still strutted back and forth on the lawns below, making his loud, shrieking announcements. His dowdy, plain brown hen companions waddled slowly behind in total awe of his handsome plumage. Ahmed watched and smiled. That cock knew his stuff. He wondered why in only the human species the male was not the most resplendent. He was certain that the beautiful creature who sat munching a date beside him was far more beauteous than he with his hairy chest and legs and stubbly beginnings of a beard. He glanced at his watch and then back at Rosalie.

"Well, what shall we do with this fabulous day, my princess?"

Rosalie sank her teeth into a ripe, yellow guava and pretended to swoon from its nectar. The pungent perfume filled his nostrils as she came toward him.

"How about a little horseback riding this morning and then, later, a trip into town, and then, afterward, if we're not too pooped from all the heat, a little water skiing, perhaps?"

"Hey, I asked one little question. So how come I get an endless answer?"

They went for a quick swim in the cove and raced each other back up to the bedroom suite. Sand and dirt were tracked all over Maman Rose's gleaming parquet floors and spotless white carpeting. Once at the top of the stairs, Rosalie raced Ahmed down the banister and then again to the bathroom. A hot tub with scented oils and pungent spices grown on the plantation was already drawn and waiting for them. They removed their swimsuits and lowered themselves gingerly into the warm water. A thick, rich foam covered the top, like the head on a beer. They sank slowly beneath the bubbles, enjoying each moment of their descent. Pieces of vanilla and cinnamon floated among the bubbles on the surface.

Ahmed broke a stick of cinnamon and smelled it.

"Hmmm." A little round ball rolled under him and came to lie between his legs. What's that, Ahmed thought, marbles in a tub? He felt for it, getting his chin and cheek wet, as he scrounged around the bottom of the big tub. "There." He had it, whatever it was. He withdrew a small, reddish brown nut and held it up for Rosalie to look at. "What's this," he asked, "a bathtime snack?"

"Don't be silly. It's a nutmeg."

"A nutmeg in the bathtub? What in hell for? Are we making a cake for somebody's birthday?"

"They're for refreshing your skin, stupid. I like spices in the tub much better than flowers or perfume."

He placed the nut between his teeth and bit down hard on it. "*Peste!* It's hard."

"Of course, silly. It's not a nut to eat, but one you grate. Oh, what's the use. Don't you know anything about anything?"

"I know a lot about lots of things. Come here. I'll show you." He grabbed her and kissed her and passed her the nutmeg, which he still had clenched between his teeth.

A rapping on the door just then broke the spell of the moment.

"Me, Maman Rose. André want to know if you taking mare and stallion, or the two mares, and when exactly you both going riding."

Ahmed called out that they would be taking the two mares.

Maman Rose left without further ado and went to tell André.

Rosalie and Ahmed took their time dressing, and then went down to the stables where the mares were saddled up, waiting. They rode through the canefields along the bluff and on the beach, and then they galloped off together over the top of the peak to the Belle Fleur plantation, jumping hedges and walls, cantering down the dusty road. They dismounted and opened the wrought-iron gates.

They closed the gates behind them and walked up the driveway through a tunnel of green and yellow flamboyant branches and blossoms, entwined across the driveway.

"God! This is beautiful!" Ahmed exclaimed. "What are these trees called? They are beautiful!"

"They are flamboyants, or *immortelles* if you prefer. These are a yellow variety. Papa planted them here, long before I was born, or even a gleam in his eye."

She reached up on tiptoe and kissed Ahmed's cheek. He grinned wickedly at her.

"I think you were a gleam in your father's eye from the moment he first laid eyes on your mother. I just think you took a long time being born, that's all."

She rolled her eyes in mock disgust. "We came to see the house, *not* to discuss my father's gleams or his sexual drives. Now come on."

The huge entrance hall looked somewhat forbidding as they walked in, glancing at themselves in the mirrored walls along the sides. Massive Louis XIV and Louis XV consoles lined the way. Paintings by West Indian artists stood stacked in rows along the walls, still waiting to be hung. At the far end, a bust of Jacqueline La Farge stood, dominating the long foyer, white and ghostlike in the semidarkness of the huge room. Rosalie walked up to the statue and pulled the drapes open behind it. At once the room was filled with sunlight, and everything seemed to come to life. The parquet floors shone, and the dark green runner felt like a grassy pathway as they walked over it. They roamed about, inspecting this and that. Much of the furniture was covered with dust sheets, but it was plain to see that the pieces hidden underneath were massive pieces.

Ahmed marveled at the beauty of the dining room, the huge Venetian mirrors and the elegant chandeliers. The master bathroom, however, was the *pièce de résistance*, created as an oasis for Jacqueline.

La Farge had had it modeled after his own design strictly for his wife; his own bath was separate and much less spectacular. He had taken two large bedrooms, removed the wall between them, and created for his beloved Jacqueline a masterpiece of elegance and serenity. Exquisite peach-and-white mosaic walls formed a backdrop behind the sink and tub. There were mirrored sidewalls and ceiling. The glistening floor was of tiny green-and-white mosaic tiles, laid to depict the flying horse Pegasus. Stacks of towels, peach and soft green and white, lay stacked in perfect rows atop the shelves of a large wrought-iron and brass rack. The towels all bore the initials "J.L.F." in black, and in the corners, the head of a black leopard. The tub, a solid piece of ivory-colored marble, sat smooth and sparkling clean against the peach-and-white mosaic wall. La Farge had picked it up in Rome, along with the beautiful antique *lavabo*, from a friend whose villa was being demolished. He had paid a pretty penny for them, but, to him, the mere fact that Jacqueline would adore them made them worth it.

They went from room to room admiring the huge antique mahogany bedsteads and the many family portraits. François and Elvire, the old black couple who had been in the La Farge's employ since well before the war, went about opening room after room for Rosalie and Ahmed to see; then locking each one again, with great care, as they went on.

Ahmed was astonished that La Farge had decided to keep the mansion locked up all year round, except for very rare occasions when he brought the *Créole* to Martinique and had his guests stay there. It was fully staffed, with a butler, two maids, two laundresses, a cook, a chambermaid, and three gardeners. Boisy, the stableboy, still took care of the three mares and two stallions kept in the nearby stables, and Shu-Shu, the chauffeur, continued to polish up the old yellow roadster, day after day, in the hope that some day La Farge would come back, and it would be ready for him.

"Why doesn't anyone ever use it anymore?" Ahmed asked as they were leaving the house.

"Oh, I don't really know. I guess it's just that ever since Maman's parents died, she has preferred to stay at La Rose." She shrugged. "I guess it's because my grandparents are buried there. She was very close to them."

He shook his head. "Well, it's a shame, though."

"What is?"

"To let this beautiful place just go to waste like this. Why doesn't your father sell it, then?"

"Sell it? Are you crazy? Why, that would be like cutting off his right arm." She smiled wanly. "As a matter of fact, I think he'd rather do that than to ever get rid of this place. It's like Maman," she sighed. "A beautiful possession of Papa's, but only outwardly." There was remorse in her tone as she said it. "You know, I never really can figure out why, with all Papa's drive and love of life, he and Maman never got a divorce. They have had separate bedrooms and interests for as long as I can remember. He could have been so much happier. I'm sure you're right; he *would* be better off if he sold it, but then he wouldn't have it to remind him of the 'good old days' when . . ." Her voice trailed off. She did not finish her sentence.

"Hey, let's get going if we're going to go into town."

They mounted and rode off into the wind. They jumped the old stone wall separating the boundaries of the two plantations and galloped off across the fields, zigzagging through the tall cedar trees laden with their tiny purple flowers. The cashews were in season, the red and yellow fleshy fruit hanging heavily from the branches, the oily cashew nuts dripping gum under the hot sun. The horses galloped through the orchard, trampling the fallen fruit, scenting the air around them. Flocks of fat turtle-doves rose off the ground and flew away as they passed by. A yellowish brown mongoose scooted out from the bushes and darted across the path to hide himself in a hollowed-out log by the trench along the side.

Chapter Twelve

Paris, October 1962

In Paris, the time was twelve noon. La Farge sat drinking coffee in his study with a certain M. Piétz. The mood was serious, no smiles or pleasantries.

La Farge sat in his dark green leather chair, a pile of papers on the desk before him, a cigar in his left hand, the other hand supporting his chin. He was addressing the aged gentleman sitting in the tan chair across from him.

"I see, Maître." La Farge employed the term out of recognition of the old man's past academic standing. "Then if I understand you correctly, you knew the duke personally, when he was a boy, you say. How long ago would you say that was, thirty-five, forty years ago?"

"Well, to be exact, monsieur, I was employed by the family right after the fire, which was in 1920. The boy was only a little over ten years old at the time." Piétz leaned back in the chair and puffed on the cigar La Farge had offered him. "I went to work for them that following winter and stayed until the fall of 1931. He was already grown by then."

"Then he would have been about twenty years old when you last saw him, am I right?"

"Yes, sir; that's correct."

"Why did you leave the d'Artois's employ?"

"Well, the boy's education was completed. After all, I had been hired as his tutor because of his disfigurement, you know, from the fire. His mother could not bear the thought of people looking at him or her and pitying them. He was a good, respectful sort, that young man. He knew how much the poor woman suffered. Her burns had been even worse than his, and she spent the rest of her days confined to a wheelchair. A good boy, he was. I loved him as my own son." A tear rolled down his wrinkled cheek as he spoke.

"It's been a long time, monsieur, since those days,' and I have suffered much. I lost an eye in the concentration camp at Le Vernet, and I can't see too well out of the other one. My hair is all gone, and my body is weak from what I went through, but most of all, it's my mind that fails me."

"Oh, how so, Maître?"

"Well, sometimes when I think of all the people I knew and saw put to death, I wonder why I survived. I mean, why me? I'm nobody special, just an old Jew tired and worn out from a hard life, and a little addled, perhaps, from all the blood and suffering I've witnessed. By the way, you still have not told me how you found me, nor why it is that you seek this information from an old man who might not be telling the truth because he is forgetful and somewhat senile. Isn't the duke your friend? It does not seem right that a man should be prying into another man's life without a very good reason, especially a man he calls a friend. But more important to me, monsieur, is how did you find me?"

"Through an employee of mine, a certain Clérot, former Inspector of Police Jean-Jacques Clérot. Do you know him?"

"No, monsieur. I do not. Should I?"

"No reason for you to. You see, my dear friend, M. Clérot, who has been retired from the Sûreté for many years, has been working for me ever since my last private investigator was found dead in Dieppe two years ago. And before him, another man also working for me died mysteriously in Geneva. He was found knifed to death in an alley. No clues were ever uncovered. After his death and the death of his successor, I became even more curious. Someone was killing off these people to cover up something, but the question was who and why? I had been curious about d'Artois's past ever since we became partners after the war. I needed to know whatever I could of his background to reassure me of the type of man I had let into my business and, most of all, into my home." He paused for a moment and lit up another cigar. "I didn't find anything to go on at all. His town was annihilated by Hitler's scum. His family and friends were killed among the ruins of his birthplace. I could find no one outside Railleur-sur-Pelle who had known him, only a few who had *heard* of him in Lyon because of the dreadful fire which had taken place at the Chateau d'Artois in 1920. But no one knew him. Then Clérot got lucky. Someone remembered that the family had engaged a tutor from Paris for the boy after the accident, but they could not remember the tutor's name. A week ago, I received word from Clérot that he had located you, Maître Piétz. It was not easy since hardly anyone calls you by your name."

"Ah, yes." The old man nodded and smiled. "Everyone calls me Maître. I don't know why; I guess it sounds friendlier than Léon or plain Monsieur Piétz." He broke a piece of cake from the thick slice on the plate before him, dunked it into his coffee, and placed the soggy lump into his mouth. "Ah, that is good, monsieur. You must have an excellent cook. I can tell that this is not store-bought cake. More like my mother used to make in the days before Hitler."

"I know it has been hard for you, monsieur. I have investigated you too, you see: born in St. Germain in 1887 to Yvonne and Solomon Piétz; your father was a shopkeeper, your mother a seamstress. You had a younger brother, Alphonse, who was killed at Le Vernet. You have no living relatives; no wife or dog or cat, and you live alone on your small pension for the disabled."

La Farge stood up and walked over to the window. He opened it and threw back the shutters, letting the cold late October air in.

"Ah! That's better. I was beginning to stifle in here with the fire blazing." He turned around and leaned his back against the windowsill. "I'm sorry, monsieur, that you have had such a hard life. I respect you tremendously for having kept your dignity and your concern for mankind. God knows, if it had been me, I doubt I would have survived. Anger and disgust would have strangled me, for I would not have been able to live with my hardships the way you did. Allow me, Maître, to help you know a little comfort in your old age."

He walked over to the desk and studied a piece of paper with some notes on it. "Seventy-five—a great age, as my grandfather used to say. An age for savoring the many other aged things the world had to offer. Such as good wines, good brandy, old friends, and an old wife, who by this time should be as gentle as a lamb and as quiet as a churchmouse for lack of vigor or things to say. 'Ah, what a time to enjoy!' he used to say. But the old goat did have a wife to cherish and good wines to relish in his old age. You, my friend, have neither." La Farge smiled sympathetically.

"I cannot recommend a wife, Maître, but trust me. I can provide you with all the rest. And if you should at times grow lonely, in need of someone to talk to, I shall be glad to offer my ear and open my home to you." He handed the man an envelope. "You do not carry a sack or briefcase in which I could discreetly place this, so I shall have to be blunt and come right to the point. Take this and buy the things you need. I only wish I could take away your pain and ugly memories, but we both know that *that* I cannot do. Only accept my friendship and my hospitality please, and don't say no because of pride or lack of reasons to say yes. Accept it as a gift of friendship from me, a Frenchman, to you, another Frenchman in need."

The old man looked up into the warm gaze of his elegant host and saw him reaching out, one man to another. "Thank you, monsieur. May God bless you for your help. I shall never forget."

La Farge glanced at his watch. "*Merde!* It is already twelve-thirty, almost lunchtime, and I am starved. Will you join me, Maître?"

The old man nodded his acceptance.

La Farge smiled approvingly and rang for the butler. Instead, Berthe arrived, carrying a fresh pot of coffee and some mints on a tray.

"You called, monsieur?"

"Yes, Berthe, but where is Max?"

"Today is his day off; only James and I are here and Marie-José, the upstairs maid. Hamdu and Jusif are in the kitchen preparing for the dinner party tomorrow night. They wished to know exactly how many guests we can expect."

"You can tell those two harem-keepers in the kitchen that they'd better learn to read French as well as they speak it. I left clear instructions for them for the party, and I specifically wrote down thirty-six for dinner. Now, go back and find out if they understood the rest of my instructions!"

He threw up his arms in frustration and turned to Maître Piétz. "My two cooks are a present from my son-in-law while he's on his honeymoon."

He glared at Berthe and spoke with his cigar clenched between his teeth. "Where's André and Simone for that matter? Why aren't *they* in the kitchen preparing for tomorrow night?"

"But, monsieur, today is the day their niece is getting married. They asked you for the day off over a month ago, and you said it was all right."

"Oh, damn. That's right."

La Farge ordered a copious lunch for them both and excused himself momentarily from the room.

Berthe followed him out.

La Farge returned promptly with a large manila envelope bound with a thick red rubber band. He pulled up a chair next to the old man and pulled out a bundle of photographs. He arranged the prints on the desk and stood up again to fetch something from the bookshelves. He touched what appeared to be a book, then stood back as the bookcase slid to one side, exposing a safe hidden behind it. He fiddled momentarily with the handle and almost instantly it swung open. It contained some papers and a reel of film. He removed the reel of film and strode over to the Louis XVI bureau against the wall in back of Maître Piétz and plugged in a waiting projector.

"Have you looked at the pictures yet, Maître?"

The old man nodded.

"Did you notice anything strange about your pupil, any changes, perhaps?"

The old man shook his head. "He's just bigger, and more imposing, somehow. But," he added quickly, "my memories are thirty-one years old. A man can change a lot during that time."

"Yes, I guess he ean at that. Here. I would like you to keep one of these photographs. Take it home with you. Study it. If you think of anything, call me. Now, I'd like to show you a piece of film taken during my daughter's wedding this fall."

"Oh yes, I heard of it and saw a newscast on television. Who would have thought then that I would be here in your library, invited to stay for lunch? I won't tell anyone," he sighed and shook his head. "They wouldn't believe me, anyway. Me a guest here! Would anyone believe it?"

James came in and set up the card table for two. "Commandant, I will be leaving shortly to go to André's. His niece was married today, you know, and I'm invited to the reception this afternoon."

La Farge squinted his eyes and frowned at the impeccably clad James. "Did I give you the day off, too?"

"No, Commandant, just the afternoon. You said I could go after I had laid out your things for tonight, and it's done. So may I leave now?"

Armand La Farge was a big man; his presence filled the room as he spoke. "I guess every man has his touch of madness. Mine is that I let you get off at the drop of a hat half the time. I'm paying twelve servants to take care of things, but I end up having to fend for myself in this big house. I tell you, James, things will have to change around here. Go on, get out, James, before I change my mind about giving you the afternoon off." He smiled and winked at him. "Don't get into any trouble now; the bride is married."

James laughed and excused himself, taking with him the dirty ashtrays to be cleaned.

La Farge turned to Piétz. "I know, Maître, that you must be wondering why, if I haven't found anything incriminating about the duke, would I want to continue an investigation? And why would I go about it so secretly? Right?"

The old man nodded affirmatively.

"Well, for one thing, I did find something. I found that both times, when my private investigators were murdered, the duke was in the general vicinity. For instance, when Cirac was found dead, shoved off a cliff in Dieppe, d'Artois, according to someone living nearby, had been in that general vicinity the night before. When I later asked him about it, however, he said the person had been mistaken. The police never came across this person; my man did. Then, Delacroix, my second man, was found murdered in an alley in Geneva. He had called me three days before with some information. He was trying to find the doctor who might have performed the corrective surgery on d'Artois. D'Artois never wished to discuss his operation. No one knew the doctor who supposedly operated on him. Apparently, somehow Delacroix had found a clue, and then he was murdered. By whom, do you think? Sure enough, Artois was in Geneva at that very time. Yet, only one day before Delacroix was murdered, d'Artois was in Paris, and said nothing to me of his plans to leave for Geneva the next day. Now you can say it's a coincidence. Especially since Clérot was unable to find any clue pointing to whatever Delacroix had found." La Farge smashed his fist loudly in the palm of his hand. "But, why then would he have lied about the fact that he was in Dieppe the day before Cirac's mysterious death? If he knew nothing of it, why not come right out and say he was there?" La Farge slammed his fist into his palm again. "I keep hoping that Clérot will turn up something. Maybe there's an innocent explanation for all this." He pulled up the straight-backed chair next to the tan leather one in which his guest sat and straddled it. "Now, Maître Piétz, that's where you come in.

You can either prove I'm right, or better yet, convince me that d'Artois *is* d'Artois, and that I've been a fool for pursuing this investigation. But the clincher to this whole affair is a conversation I accidentally overheard about three months ago.

"I had been staying with d'Artois for two days in Geneva while my own apartment, in the same building, was being redecorated. Some painting was being done, and I couldn't stand the smell, so he suggested I stay with him. On this day, I had been out of the city visiting friends and was not expected back until the following afternoon. But something came up, the way things almost always do whenever you try to take some time off somewhere, and I had to return to Geneva for a very early meeting the following morning.

"Well, it was very late when I arrived at d'Artois's apartment. Everything was dark, except for a tiny light coming from his bedroom. I assumed he had fallen asleep reading and had left the light on. I didn't feel like disturbing him at such an ungodly hour. I believe it was about two-thirty or three in the morning. As I was coming up the stairs—the duke has a duplex—I heard his voice."

Maître Piétz's quizzical look was almost comical as he cocked his head and scratched behind his ear. He was about to say something, but La Farge resumed his story.

"You see, what startled me at first was the fact that he was yelling at the top of his voice at someone. A woman. I could hear her muffled voice, coming from behind the closed door."

"Could you tell who she was?"

"No, but that's not all. The second and *most* startling factor was that he was yelling in German."

"German, did you say?"

"That's right. Now, it's true d'Artois did tell me that he spoke a little German. He said he learned it from a Swiss girl he used to know, when he lived in Geneva after the war. However, my dear man, the German he spoke that night was not the German you casually pick up with a girl friend, but more like a language he had spoken all his life. You see, I myself speak German. I have studied it along with English and several other languages, and, I can assure you, it is not an easy language to pick up and speak with an impeccable accent.'' He cocked an eyebrow at Maître Piétz and squinted the other eye inquisitively at him. ''Did you teach him German?'' he asked.

''No. I do not speak German myself,'' the old man replied.

''Then where could d'Artois have learned it?''

''He never studied any other language except French and Latin, and he was already a full-grown man when I left Railleur-sur-Pelle. I agree with you, monsieur. He could not have mastered the language in the short time you say he spent in Geneva.'' He frowned and pursed his thin lips in thought. ''The reason I say this is that the boy was not particularly bright in any way, just average, and certainly not very good with languages. As it was, he had a difficult time with French, but he did have a head for music. Now there was his strong point.''

''Oh? Did you teach him music?''

''Yes, monsieur. And so did his invalid mother. She was quite a pianist herself. Before the accident the boy had been taught music by none other than Raoul Finetti, himself. You have heard of him, no doubt.''

La Farge nodded, and the old man went on.

''A great man, he was, but he was destroyed along with all the others when the Germans annihilated the town and every one in it. Even after the fire, the boy showed great promise and responded more to music than to anything else. It was what kept his mother alive. She would sit, horribly scarred and crippled as she was, and she would instruct him, and then she would sit back and listen to him play. With the right training he could have been great.'' His thoughts left the past and returned to the present. ''But doesn't he play now? I mean, with all his money, I should think that he would find all the time in the world to play and further improve his talent.''

''I'm afraid d'Artois does not play the piano, nor any other instrument for that matter. The man is tone-deaf, as far as I can tell, but that does not prove anything. No, what clinched it for me was that morning when I heard him say to the woman, whoever she was, 'I did not get this far to have everything I've worked for and planned for all these years washed down the drain by you.' " La Farge took a puff on his cigar and continued. "'He said the woman's name, but I didn't get it. He also said that he knew I was investigating him, but that he knew me well enough to know that all I was doing was investigating the money he had put into my various companies, and that sooner or later I would come to my senses and find out that there was nothing to be gained by it all. As he ended the conversation, he said, 'If La Farge wants to spend his time and money investigating me, fine; but he will come up with nothing. Everything has been taken care of too well and you'—meaning the woman—'have nothing to worry about.' Then in a threatening tone he told her never again to come there, nor ever to contract him again. It was too dangerous, he said. He would take care of her and the girl as he had promised he would. There was some more, but he had lowered his tone considerably after the outburst, and I could hear no more. Only a word here and there, but nothing which made any sense.

"I left the apartment shortly afterward and spent thirty minutes, at least, waiting for the woman to come out. She finally did, but she was wearing a cape and a scarf and dark glasses.

"The next morning, d'Artois acted surprised to see that I was at breakfast. He remarked upon my early return. He made no comment about the night before, however, and I did likewise. There was no point in saying anything. I could not take the chance, not after Cirac and Delacroix. But it was then that I became suspicious that d'Artois might not *be* d'Artois, but someone else with a lot to hide—enough, perhaps, to kill for it."

Piétz removed his glasses and wiped them clean with the corner of his handkerchief. He had been startled by La Farge's last remark. "You mean, Monsieur, that you suspect d'Artios is somebody *posing* as d'Artois, an imposter?" His eyes were wide with disbelief. "I cannot believe that, monsieur. How? It would be impossible. I mean one reads of such things in novels, but they don't really happen. Do they?" He shook his head at his own question. "No, I can't believe that. It is he, all right. I know the boy." He pointed to the photograph on the desk. "I can't forget that face—and the scars. I tell you, it's him. I'm sure.''

La Farge did not say anything. He stood up, walked around his desk, and pulled down the movie screen concealed in the ceiling above. He then strode across the room to the desk behind Maître Piétz and turned on the projector. He motioned to Piétz to observe the screen. The film was a series of separate shots spliced together, showing the duke walking, sitting, standing, or talking to other guests at the ball. In his tuxedo, he looked trim and dashing.

Maître Piétz raised his hand to make a comment, but La Farge motioned to him that the film was just about over. The final picture was a close-up of d'Artois, showing in detail his scars, and catching him for the first time in the film with a smile. The film ran out, and La Farge switched off the projector. He returned to sit beside Maître Piétz in the straight-backed chair, and offered him another cigar. Piétz declined this time, but said he would like to take it home to smoke later. La Farge pointed to a large box of Havanas on his desk and reminded the old man that they were meant for him.

Maître Piétz smiled his thanks and took the Churchill out of the open humidor. ''Thank you again, monsieur.''

''It is a pleasure to find a man who enjoys cigars as much as I do, Maître. Such men are few, believe me. They do not know the difference between a Havana and a Tampa. It is like drinking Asti Spumanti, if you know what I mean. Well, anyway, to get back to more serious matters. Do you still say he is your man? And forgive me for having asked you to wait. You seemed to have a comment?''

''Ah, yes, I did. It is unbelievable what they can do today. Doctors, I mean. That plastic surgery, it was an unbelievable job.''

''How do you mean?''

''Well, it's just incredible to me how much better he looks since he has had it done. He is lucky.'' He continued, ''It must have been a great surgeon, indeed, who performed such a miracle; and his hands too, they look so much better.''

''Well, that's exactly the point, though. Someone who was

burned so badly as you say he was, and who was later operated on so successfully, would be telling the world about his wonderful doctor—it would seem only natural, wouldn't you say? But the two times I brought it up, he simply declined to comment, and I have had no openings since to discuss it. His whole attitude has only added to my suspicions. I mean, what if—Ssst! Did you hear that?"

"No, what?"

"A sound like someone outside the door."

La Farge tiptoed across the carpeted floor and pushed open the door. The two sides were flung back against the outside wall with a loud thud.

"Who's there?" La Farge looked out and saw no one. The hall was empty. An uneasy feeling crept over him. Why had he thought he had heard someone outside if he had not? He ran down the wide hall and out into the round foyer and up the curving staircase. He stopped as he got halfway. There, lying on his belly, was Diablo, half on the steps, half on the landing above.

"Mr-r-rrauw . . . prr."

"Oh, damn it, Diablo. Was it you scratching behind the door?"

The black beast slithered down the steps on his belly to meet his master. He rubbed up against La Farge's legs and purred loudly.

"Oh all right. You can come down with me; only you have to wait outside until Maître Piétz leaves. He's a frail old man, and I wouldn't want him to die of a heart attack."

He patted the animal on the head and snapped a finger in command for it to follow him. As he came to the study, he thought he heard the door at the end of the hall slam, but could not be sure. He motioned to Diablo to wait outside the door, and the animal squatted down, plunking his head on his forepaws like a kitten. La Farge rubbed his shoe against the beast's neck playfully and reentered the study, closing the doors once more behind him.

"Did you see who it was?" Maître Piétz wanted to know.

"Yes, unless there is a ghost in this house."

"Who was it?"

"Just my pet cat."

"A cat?"

"Yes, a leopard I have as my watch dog. He is completely harmless," he hurried to add, seeing Maître Piétz's horrified expression.

"Leopard, did you say? A real one?"

"Yes, a real one. Only he doesn't have spots as most leopards do. He is black, a freak of nature. But he is a beautiful and very reliable animal. He makes a wonderful pet."

Piétz glanced worriedly over his shoulder at the closed door. "Is he still out there?"

"Yes, but he won't bother us. He's as gentle as a lamb, really, once you get to know him."

The old man swallowed a mouthful of wine. "If you will excuse me for saying so, monsieur, I would rather not—know him, that is, personally. I'm allergic to cat's fur, you see."

La Farge threw back his head and laughed. Maître Piétz joined in.

"That's the best one I've heard yet! The last time Diablo came in unannounced, during a meeting I was having with some Japanese businessmen, one of the men got up on the conference table and announced he was about to make a speech."

Maître Piétz and La Farge looked at each other and exploded into laughter. Their amusement was interrupted by the shrill sound of the telephone. La Farge strode over to the desk and picked up the receiver.

"Hello?" There was a pause as he listened. "Ah yes, Clérot. I've been trying to get in touch with you since right after you left last night. I want you to come to my office this evening. I have some information for you." He paused again, listening attentively. "Very well, if you say so. You are the detective. See you at six then. What? Oh, for sure. I'll be in my office on rue Marbeuf, not at home. I believe Jacqueline is having a bridge party here tonight." He paused again and listened. "Right, see you then. 'Bye."

He hung up and glanced at his watch. "Oh, my God, it's three-thirty already, and I have to be at l'Elysée by four-thirty, and I still have to shower and dress for the affair. I forgot what it's all about, even." He strode quickly over to the bookcase and pressed the button of the intercom on the wall next to it. "James? James? Oh shit! I forgot he isn't here. Well, Maître, that means I'll have to leave you in a hurry. But I do hope you'll forgive me. Maybe," he added, "we can do this again sometime soon. Get together for a nice chat, I mean."

La Farge reminded Maître Piétz to take the box of Havanas and bade him good-bye. He rang for Max, but instead, Hervé, Max's stand-in on his days off, entered, carrying his chauffeur's hat in his right hand.

"You rang, Commandant?"

"Yes, I rang. Max is off, right?"

"That's right; I'm here one day a week."

"I know that, man. I pay the bills around here, and I should know who the hell I'm paying and why. Now, will you please drive Monsieur Piétz here"—he nodded his head in the direction of the old gentleman—"to his home. And please find Berthe, wherever *she* is, and have her give you the parcel I had made up for Monsieur Piétz. Where is she, by the way?"

"Who, monsieur?"

"Berthe, of course. Who else have we been talking about, Hervé? I've been ringing for her for the last ten minutes or so without success. Will you go and see where she is please? And, oh, Hervé?"

"Yes, Commandant?"

"Have a cup of coffee before you take Monsieur Piétz home will you?"

Hervé looked baffled. "A cup of coffee, sir?"

"Yes, damn it; maybe it will wake you up. God, I wish Max didn't have to take a day off." He sighed and motioned with his index finger for the chauffeur to leave. "Go on, man, move—move."

La Farge placed the box of cigars under his arm and led Maître Piétz out the door to the foyer. As they passed through the hallway, the old man caught a glimpse of Diablo and quickened his steps considerably. La Farge smiled but said nothing. He opened the side door off the ballroom to the garden, and helped his feeble guest down the wide steps.

Hervé was just coming out the pantry, carrying a large box tied with some string. He hurried to open the gate for the two men and ran around the car parked in front to deposit the parcel in the trunk. He held the door for Maître Piétz, and La Farge helped him in.

"Remember now, Hervé, when you get there, help Monsieur Piétz upstairs to his apartment, and"—he raised a warning finger—"don't forget to carry his parcel upstairs for him." La Farge slammed the car door and then leaned through the backseat window. He extended an immaculately manicured hand to the old man, who was reclining against the black leather seat of the Rolls.

A gnarled, wrinkled hand reached out and took La Farge's.

"Good-bye, Maître. It was a pleasure. I hope to see you again, soon."

"Thank you, monsieur. I shall never forget today. I enjoyed myself more than I have in a long time." The old man's eyes misted and his pale hands shook with emotion as he pumped La Farge's tanned one up and down. "I am sorry that I could not be of more help to you, but," he whispered, tapping his fingers on the manila envelope in his lap, "I will study these photographs some more, and if I think of anything—anything at all—I shall give you a call. You can count on that."

La Farge smiled and nodded, and he backed away from the car. He stood for a moment and waved, as the Rolls pulled out from the curb and drove away. Then he turned and went back into the house, hurrying now to make up for his tardiness, and hoping to make it in time to the meeting at l'Elysée.

Chapter Thirteen

Paris, October 1962

Guests began to arrive at the La Farge mansion in le Marais at eight o'clock. Armand La Farge was not yet home. He was still at his office in conference with Clérot. At eight-twenty he called to say that he was on his way, and that Jacqueline should wait dinner until he arrived. At ten to nine he drove up and stole through the side entrance and up the back stairs to his rooms. He showered, dressed, and came downstairs just in time to welcome the last arriving guests. Jacqueline looked radiant that evening, like a new bride, all smiles and blushes and soft doe-eyes for La Farge. Their guests could not help noticing that she and Armand were holding hands as they greeted them. Armand spent most of the evening holding Jacqueline's hand, nuzzling her neck, and devouring her with his eyes; she in turn held on to his arm as if she were afraid to let go. Once, during the latter part of the evening, she even sat on his lap. It was obvious to their guests, as well as to the servants, that Armand and Jacqueline were "back together," so to speak. La Farge knew that it would only be a matter of time before the press got hold of the news, and for the next several months it would be in every newspaper, until someone else did something more scandalous than take his own wife to bed. He had to admit though, that nineteen years was one hell of a long time between lays; with one's own wife, that is. He had, of course, bedded other women; there had been Micheline, his Swiss banker's daughter, and Natalie, the lovely little actress he had met on the Côte only a year ago, and before them, there had been Brigitte, the young poet from Montmartre, and Judith, the divorcée from New York. . . . He had cared for some more than for others surely, but in the back of his mind and in his heart, there had never really been anyone but Jacqueline. He had managed to keep his extramarital relationships totally to himself, and, although he assumed that Jacqueline must have suspected that he had women on the side, she could not have been sure, and it was probably better so. In any case, it had been her idea to live apart and do as they both pleased. He had gone for two whole years without a woman, until he had met Chantal, and then, after her, one had just led to another. But that was all in the past now, for he had Jacqueline back. It was not the same as what they had had once when they were young—it was even better. Maybe, like good wines, some people just got better with age.

La Farge's mind was filled with memories of the night just after their return from the Côte. Jacqueline had stormed into his bedroom, screaming about what a pig he was for having excused himself early from her guests to go to bed. He had embarrassed her, she had said, in front of her friends, and she demanded an apology then and there. She had been wearing a crimson jersey robe with a neckline that would have made a dead horse get up and whinny, and he was certainly not dead. There he had stood, naked and unashamed, watching her scream at him, and then, suddenly, he had felt himself grow hard, hard for her, a woman with whom he had not slept in so long that he could not even remember what she looked like naked. He had reached out and slapped her, and he had grown harder; and his desire swelled full as she slapped him back. He remembered, relishing the rapture, still fresh in his mind, of that night as he had grabbed her and thrown her across his bed and mounted her like an animal. She had put up a strong fight and had even given him a nasty bite on the shoulder, but he had promised himself that he was going to do it one day, and that night was as good a time as any he could think of.

The next morning when James came in as usual to take care of the Commandant's needs, he had been surprised, almost shocked, to find monsieur and madame, of all people, sound asleep, completely uncovered and still tightly clenched together. James had scurried out like a streak of lightning, and in minutes the news had spread throughout the household.

Monsieur and madame had fucked last night. The marriage was on again; no news could have been more agreeable. That would surely mean a lot of grand parties in the ballroom, and new room arrangements, and madame would certainly be in a better mood now that she was "getting it again" from the master.

La Farge looked around the dinner table at his guests and smiled across the table at Jacqueline. Yes, he would call Rosalie and Ahmed tomorrow and tell them the good news, and he would perhaps mention something to Ahmed about his suspicions concerning the duke. He would have to think about it some more. In the morning he would decide.

Max entered the dining room, approached La Farge, bent over and whispered something in his ear.

"Did you tell him I had guests?"

"Yes, monsieur, but he says it's urgent and insisted that I disturb you."

"Very well, Max, tell him I'll be right with him. I'll take it in the study."

La Farge excused himself from the table and hurried to the study to take the call. He dismissed Max with a wave of his hand and picked up the receiver from his desk. "Hello, Maître Piétz? What can I do for you?"

The old man's voice came haltingly over the phone. "I'm sorry, Monsieur La Farge, that I had to disturb you at such a late hour, and when you have guests, but I thought you would want to know this right away."

"Yes?"

"You see, after I came home last night, I rested for a while; then I made myself some soup and after eating it, turned on the telé to relax with my coffee and one of those wonderful cigars you so kindly gave me. Oh, by the way, thanks for the package, but you didn't have to. Anyway, I appreciate it. So thanks, and God bless you again. . . ."

La Farge said with forced patience, "Yes, Maître. You were saying?"

"Ah, yes. That after my soup, I turned on the telé to relax with my coffee, and something kept nagging at me, bothering me. I didn't know what to make of it, but then I got up and took out that picture you gave me and studied it." He gasped a little over the phone in his excitement. "I spent almost five hours staring at that picture. I even used a magnifying glass." He paused again.

"Yes, and then what?" prodded La Farge once again.

"Well," gasped Maître Piétz, "you're not going to believe this, but there I was staring and thinking, and all of a sudden, like a blow on the head, it came to me." He paused again.

La Farge gritted his teeth. "Yes, what came to you, Maître? Did you remember something specific?"

"You can say that again, my friend. You were right all along. This man, whoever he is, is *not* the Duc d'Artois."

La Farge could not contain himself. "I knew it, damn it. I just knew it. But then who the hell is he? Do you know?"

"That I don't know. But what I *can* tell you is that I am positive that he is not the real Duc d'Artois."

"But how can you be sure? I mean, you saw all the pictures and the film and went over every detail with me, and you were sure then that it was him. What makes you so sure *now* that it isn't him?"

"It's really a very small thing, but vital. Something so small that even I, who have known the boy as long as I have, could have overlooked it."

"What, Maître—*tell* me."

"His eyes, monsieur."

"Yes?"

"Well, the real duke, that is, the boy I knew, had a small birthmark."

"Yes? Where?"

"In his eye."

"*In* his eye? But that is impossible."

"No, monsieur. I tell you, he had a birthmark in his eye, in the iris, a small brown fleck. I believe it was in his right eye, but it could have been his left, I'm not sure which; but the man in the picture you gave me, he does not have it. The fleck, I mean. His eyes are as clear as a bell. And one thing is certain, monsieur. He could not have had it removed by surgery, not even by a plastic surgeon."

"Good God! Are you sure, man? I mean, do you know what this means?"

"Not exactly, but I have my ideas."

"Hold on a minute, Maître. I think I hear someone coming." There was a sharp rap on the door. "Yes, who is it?"

"It is Max, Commandant. Madame is becoming impatient. She asks that you return as soon as possible. Some of the guests are about to leave."

"Very well, Max. Tell her I will be but a moment. And tell her that I love her."

Max raised his thick eyebrows and rolled his eyeballs. "Very well, monsieur. I will tell her that you won't be but a moment, but, sir, couldn't you—eh—wouldn't it be better if *you* told her the other part yourself? I think I would feel silly."

"Silly or not Max, that's what I want you to tell her. And by the way, why are you filling in for Alphonse tonight? You are my chauffeur, not my butler, or my messenger boy either."

"That's what I was trying to tell you, monsieur, but it is much better that you said it."

"Where is Alphonse tonight? Why isn't he bringing me these messages?"

"I don't know, sir. He did not show up this afternoon, and so I filled in for him." He clicked his heels and bowed graciously.

La Farge flinched at the sound of the clicking. "Must you do that?"

"No, monsieur."

"Then, why the hell do you do it? I know you are a German, and I can overlook that, but God damn it, don't act like a damn Nazi. I hate it."

"Yes, sir."

"And as for Alphonse, when he does show up, you can have him come to see me. He'd better have a damn good excuse, or I'll fire him on the spot, and you can tell him that."

"Yes, sir." Max turned on his heel and left, taking care to close the door softly behind him.

"Maître Piétz?"

"Yes?"

"I'm sorry I kept you waiting, but you don't know what I go through sometimes with the help."

"No, sir. I wouldn't know, since I don't have that problem myself."

"I don't know what to say at this moment, except that I am flabbergasted by this news. Not that I can't believe it, but after your visit yesterday and my talk last night with Clérot, I was almost convinced that I might be on a wild-goose chase after all. And now you tell me this—I'm dumbfounded! I would like to talk to you again. Could you come to my office tomorrow afternoon, or would you prefer for me to come to you?"

"I'll come to your place, monsieur. I'm afraid you wouldn't appreciate my modest room."

"Oh, nonsense, man! It's much easier for me to come to you, and it'll give me a chance to drop off the new walking stick I got you this morning. I noticed when you were here that yours was quite worn. I hope you'll like it."

"Well," said the old man, "I won't say you shouldn't have, because I dearly need a new one, but, what I will say is, I hope you don't feel you owe me anything for whatever little help I've been to you."

"Nonsense. I don't feel I owe you anything except respect. I must leave you now, though. My wife is getting impatient, and my guests are getting ready to leave. Good-bye and thank you for calling. I'll see you tomorrow at, let's say three o'clock? Will that be all right?"

"Fine. Three then."

All that night La Farge struggled with his conscience. What should he do? Go to the police? Confront d'Artois himself? Say nothing? If he went to the police, what would he say? "This man is not d'Artois, because some old man who claims he used to work for the d'Artois family swears that the *real* d'Artois had a brown speck in his eye?" And who would back up the story? Nobody! Everybody who knew the duke had been slaughtered in that village. And d'Artois, the man posing as d'Artois, that is, would he just stand there, let himself be accused, and then admit everything? Of course not! He would just deny the whole story and charge La Farge with slander and defamation of character; he would be the laughingstock of Paris. No, he could not take the chance. He would confront d'Artois. He would force the man somehow to reveal himself, his true self, but how? He was seeing Clérot in the morning. Maybe the detective would have some idea.

Chapter Fourteen

Martinique, October 1962

As Ahmed was about to step out the front door, the telephone rang. He paused, then reached for the doorknob once more. The car was waiting, Rosalie was already in it; Maman Rose, Emile and the rest of the staff were bustling around outside in preparation for their departure. Let it ring.

But he found he could not ignore its summons. It would certainly turn out to be something trivial—most calls, in his experience, were—but the very noise was an infallible creator of curiosity. He turned back and lifted the receiver.

It was the overseas operator, with a call for him. In a moment, he was speaking to Armand La Farge.

"Ahmed, my boy! I'm surprised to find you up so early—it's only eight o'clock there, surely? I'd counted on having to send Maman Rose to shake you awake."

Ahmed shifted uneasily as he stood holding the phone. It seemed to him that his father-in-law's tone was strained, that his joviality was forced.

"I've been up two hours and breakfasted already," he said. "You see, we—"

"In any case, my apologies for disturbing you at this hour. I'm tied up the rest of the day—I have to see the President in half an hour, and then there's a very knotty tax situation—and I particularly wanted to speak to you about something."

La Farge fell silent, and Armand, wondering at this evidence of an unusual indecisiveness, finally asked, "About what?"

"It's a problem," La Farge said slowly. "I mean, it's a problem what to say. It's something to be discussed. But is it at a discussable stage, that's the question. I must learn more, I must decide what to do, and then . . ."

"Look here, old man, you can't just bring up something odd and leave me dangling," Ahmed protested. "Has this problem anything to do with Rosalie and me?"

"Somewhat, yes, as it concerns . . . ah . . . d'Artois."

"Monsieur le Duc?"

La Farge's reply was interrupted by the sound of a door opening and closing in distant Paris and the unintelligible murmur of a new voice.

"I'll be right with you," La Farge said, evidently talking to the arrival. "I have my son-in-law on the other end, Clérot. Hello, Ahmed?"

"Yes?"

"I think I'd better call you back later. I expect to learn something soon, and by some time this evening I should be able to settle on a decision that we can discuss. Where can I reach you at, say four or four-thirty, your time?"

"You can't."

"Excuse me?"

"Rosalie took a notion to spend our last four or five days in the West Indies in Guadaloupe, before we go on to Panama, and we're on the point of sailing there right now. In fact, Rosalie's waiting for me in the car. Ganot's figuring on getting to Guadeloupe about dawn tomorrow. If it's important, though, I could delay—"

"No, no, you might as well get on with it. Put through a call to me when you can tomorrow, though, eh? If I'm not here, I'll leave word where I can be reached."

"Of course," Ahmed said. "I don't know what this is all about, whatever this is with the duke, but take care. I don't trust that man, I don't know why; but I've always had an uneasy feeling about him."

La Farge grunted sourly. "It's funny you should say that now. A couple of months ago, I'd probably have resented it, but as it is . . . Look, we'll keep this between us, eh? No need to worry Rosalie."

After their farewells, Ahmed replaced the receiver and turned once more to the door. On its polished surface he seemed to see for a moment the face of d'Artois . . . or, no, the face of the Mephistopheles statue at Colombier.

The Hotel Caravelle in Guadeloupe was situated in a little town called St. Anne. It had been built only a year or so before, and was the best on the island. It had two private beaches, stables, good food and all possible water sports and nighttime activities. Behind it, lushly green hills rose to the skies. The hotel rooms were large and impressive, the furniture ultramodern. There was an open dining room with a view of the ocean, and at night while couples sat in twilight, holding hands and kissing, a band would play the beguine, a lively island rhythm, while young mulatto dancers would perform.

Ahmed sat alone at the bar, sipping a planter's punch, waiting for Rosalie. She was off trying to place a call to La Farge, whom they had not been able to reach since his call to Ahmed four days before. A storm had broken off overseas telephone service, and there was no indication of when it might be resumed.

He could see Rosalie in the mirrored wall behind the bar, and hoped that this time she would get through. He stirred his drink and stabbed the cherry with his stirrer.

What was it that La Farge had called to tell him. Why didn't he want Rosalie to know?

The bartender poured the rest of Ahmed's drink into his glass. "Hope you like it," he said. "I'm new here and I'm a little nervous. Tonight's my first night."

Just my luck, Ahmed thought, a talkative bartender.

He glanced in the mirror and saw Rosalie coming toward him. From the look on her face he could tell she hadn't got through to her father. He stood up and held the barstool for her as she sat down.

"What will you have, mademoiselle?" the bartender asked, flashing Rosalie a smile.

"It's madame, and she'll have what I'm having," Ahmed replied.

When her drink came, Rosalie sipped it appreciatively. "Papa always says that if anything justified the French Empire, it was the fact that it made the West Indies French, and so made it respectable for Frenchmen to drink planter's punches."

There was a wistful look on her face and Ahmed said, "You couldn't get through to him, then?"

She shook her head. "It doesn't matter. He knows we're all right; if there were anything urgent, we could sent him a cable."

Ahmed stirred on his barstool. Might it not be a good idea to cable La Farge? But then, what about? *Sorry can't phone you?* But La Farge would know about the phone problems. *Tell me all re d'Artois?* La Farge would thank him for that, surely, on a matter of this discretion!

And tomorrow they would be off for Panama, then the Pacific and Tahiti. At the Canal Zone they should be able to get a phone connection to La Farge—or maybe it would be worthwhile taking a detour and making a landfall in the States, to get the call through earlier.

In the morning they were awakened in their room by the maid pounding on the door. "Your breakfast. You ordered it for nine."

Ahmed groaned and squinted at his watch on the night table. "I'm coming, I'm coming, don't break the door down," he called. Rosalie, awakening, turned to look at him. He was about to open the door.

"Ahmed, what are you doing?"

"Opening the door for the maid. She has our breakfast." His hands clasped over the doorknob and began to turn.

"Wait!" Rosalie screamed as she threw the covers back and leaped out of bed. "You can't let the maid in like that, stark naked." But it was too late, the maid had pushed the door open before he could stop her. Rosalie dove under the covers and pulled the sheet up under her chin. The maid's eyes popped as she entered with the breakfast tray. She blushed and turned her head away.

"Where shall I put the tray, monsieur?" she asked Ahmed, standing directly beside her.

"I'll take it," he said, quickly removing it from the girl's shaking hands.

She did not wait for him to sign the check. She turned and ran out the door. Ahmed locked the door behind her and carried the tray over to Rosalie.

"Now, my pet, we can have breakfast in peace, and I'll bet a million francs that we will be undisturbed for the rest of the morning."

Rosalie burst out laughing, and they fell into each other's arms. Some *confiture* got on Rosalie's right breast and Ahmed licked it off.

"Think we have time for a quickie before we get dressed?"

The phone on the night table was ringing. It was Ganot.

"Don't forget, sir, we are setting sail this afternoon at four. I just thought I'd call and remind you."

Ahmed slammed down the phone. "Let's eat, girl, then it's time to pack up and head into town. We have a lot of shopping to do for the trip, and you wanted to send some flowers to your mother, so I guess I'll just have to wait."

He bit into a hot brioche oozing with butter and jam. "Come on, Bébé, you shower, I'll eat. You don't need breakfast anyway. Seems to me you've put on a little weight since this trip started." He pinched her bottom as she got up.

They spent the morning in Pointe à Pitre in the marketplace buying all kinds of things for their trip. Rosalie found some pink anthuriums and insisted on driving out to the airport with Ahmed to see if a stewardess from Air France would deliver them to her mother in Paris. They found a girl who, for a not unreasonable fee, promised to deliver the flowers in person, and then they stayed and watched the plane as it took off. As they were climbing into the car to return to the boat, Rosalie turned to Ahmed and asked; "Do you think Maman will like them, Ahmed? Do you think she will forgive me?"

"I'm sure she will, Zalie. At least, I'm sure she'll like the flowers. As for your second question . . ." He shrugged. He had never experienced Jacqueline La Farge as a forgiving sort of woman.

Ganot was standing on the bow waiting for them; it was slightly after four. They climbed aboard and went and sat down in the bow, waiting for Ganot and Raoul to shove off.

A speeding jeep rounded the bend of the bay and pulled up in a cloud of dust, almost going over the edge in front of their anchorage.

"The fool! What the hell does he think he's doing?"

A man jumped out of the jeep and came running up the ramp.

"What does he want, the damn fool?" Ganot growled, spitting into the water.

"Maybe we forgot to pay for something at the market?" Rosalie asked.

"Don't be silly, *Chérie*. You think some man is going to come driving up here like all hell has broken loose, just to collect a few francs? It has to be something else, something serious," Ahmed said, troubled.

The man was boarding the boat and was coming toward them, waving an envelope.

"Monsieur Farahet, I have a telegram for you. This is the *Rosalie*, is it not?"

"My good man, can't you read? Of course it's the *Rosalie*. What can we do for you? We were just about to sail."

"In that case, I'm glad I caught you. I have a telegram for you from Paris, most urgent. I'm afraid it's bad news, monsieur."

The old "fear of the telegram," Ahmed thought, as he ripped the envelope open. Rosalie looked up at Ahmed, intensely watching his eyes as they slid across the paper.

Ahmed's face turned pale and his expression changed from

curious to the stiffness of shock. He read the printed words before him once more, unbelieving yet sickly accepting their meaning.

> Farahet, on board ship *Rosalie,* Pointe à Pitre, Guadeloupe, FW1 27 October 1962. Madame La Farge dead. Monsieur critical in hospital. Please come at once. Wire time of your arrival. Will meet you at Orly Airport. Regretfully, James.

Chapter Fifteen

Paris, October 26, 1962

At his apartment at 10 Avenue Foch, Jean, Duc d'Artois, sat in his favorite gray velvet chair by the fireplace, dressed in a maroon velvet smoking jacket and black trousers, his feet propped up on the matching ottoman. Opposite him in a similar but smaller gray velvet chair sat Margot Koesler. She was wearing a short, red jersey dress and silk stockings. Her red-and-black patent-leather pumps were neatly tucked under the frill of her chair. She was holding a martini in her right hand and twining a lock of her hair around the forefinger of the other.

She had arrived that afternoon by car from Geneva at the invitation of the duke, and was exhausted from the trip.

"Why did you invite me so suddenly, Jean? I thought you didn't like having me in your hair when you are in Paris."

D'Artois puffed on his cigarette and exhaled, making rings with the smoke. "I've been feeling a little lonely lately, I guess. I needed some company for a while. Why? Didn't you want to come?"

He tapped his cigarette on the crystal ashtray on the small oval table beside him and glanced at his watch. The time was ten minutes to seven. According to his calculations, he had ten minutes in which to get dressed and leave, and one hour and fifteen minutes after that to carry out his plan.

He looked at the ornate clock on the mantel. To his dismay, it showed the same time as his watch—unlike all the other clocks in the apartment, which claimed that it was now thirty-five minutes past seven. He must have overlooked this one, damn it, when he'd changed the rest of them. No harm done—Margot didn't register details unless they were called to her attention, otherwise this scheme of advancing the clocks wouldn't have been feasible—but it was disquieting that he'd made even so trivial a slip. And in any case, it must be rectified—now.

"Would you do me a favor, Margot, my dear?"

"What?"

"Would you bring me a glass of water and some aspirins? My head is splitting since this morning."

"Of course. Where are they? In your bathroom?"

"No, in the drawer of my night table on the left side of my bed."

"Do you want two or three?"

"Two will do. I hope I get some relief before I get to Armand's tonight. They're having that dinner party I told you about, remember?"

"Yes, I remember. I also remember you said I couldn't go. I don't know why you never want me to go anywhere with you! Ever since that night I dropped in on you in Monte Carlo and you had to take me out, you've been acting as if I had two heads or a beard."

"It's just that I don't think these are your kind of people, that's all. La Farge is my partner. I have to attend his parties. You don't."

"But the fact is, I'd like to. That's what I can't seem to make you understand. I liked him when I met him that time, and I'm sure I'd like his parties. Who wouldn't? I read about them all the time in every newspaper."

"Go on, Margot, get me my aspirin, will you? My head is

ready to burst, and I don't want to argue with you right now."

"Oh, all right. Screw it!" She got up and flounced out of the room.

D'Artois rose immediately and moved the long hand of the clock forward to seven thirty-five—forty-five minutes fast. He stubbed out his cigarette in the ashtray and followed Margot.

"Margot?" He could hear her returning from the bedroom.

"Yes? What now?"

"Come and talk to me while I get ready, will you? Maybe your chatter will put me in a better mood."

"Oh? I didn't notice you were in a bad mood. You sure you want me hanging around while you get dressed? I won't get in your way?"

"Of course not. Come, I'm late; I don't want to arrive when everyone is having their dessert."

"Oh! Is it that late already?"

"Yes. It's after seven-thirty."

He dressed in a dinner suit, white kid gloves, patent leather shoes with a black bow tie and a gold watch. He rubbed the insignia ring he always wore on his left hand with his handkerchief, blew on it and rubbed it again.

"I notice you always wear that ring, Jean. Is it something special?"

"Special? No, I just saw it in the window of an antique shop in London and bought it."

"Does the design mean anything?"

"Doubtless; all designs mean something. Come on, girl, I have to go. I don't have any more time to waste. I'll see you tonight when I get home, or, if you're already asleep, I'll see you in the morning at breakfast. Don't forget, leave a note in the kitchen for Mathilde, so she knows what to fix you for breakfast when she comes in the morning."

Margot came over to where he was standing, brushing his hair in the mirror.

"You know, Jean, sometimes I can't stand you, and then there are times like right now when I feel I can't stay away from you." She ran her finger up along the middle of his back. "Are you sure I can't come along?"

"I'm sure." He pushed her aside gently. "Come on, walk me to the door."

As they passed through the hallway he stopped in front of the doorway to the sitting room. "Your eyes are better than mine, can you see what time that clock says? My watch seems to have stopped."

She craned her neck into the room. "It's a quarter to eight, Sixteen minutes to eight, to be exact."

D'Artois feigned winding and resetting his watch.

"How long will it take you to get there?"

"Oh, about twenty-five or thirty minutes. Why?"

"Didn't you tell me it was for eight?"

"That's all right. I'll just be a polite fifteen minutes or so late. That's customary."

Fritz, his chauffeur, was waiting out front by the car. D'Artois got in and waved good-bye to Margot, who waved back from the window upstairs.

The day was finally here, the day d'Artois had planned and waited for. It was all perfect. As soon as he had got the invitation to the La Farges' dinner party, two weeks ago, he had immediately set his plan in motion. He had invited Margot to spend a week with him. He had notified Cigot and Goliath, imported to Paris, after their capable work with the interfering "tourist," to be ready and waiting for his signal; and the household staff, except for Fritz, from whom he had hardly any secrets, had been given the day off.

With the clocks altered, Margot would be able to swear, if necessary, that they had been together until twelve minutes to eight, when he left with Fritz for the party.

At the La Farge mansion, everyone was preparing for the soirée. The mood was festive. Max was dressed in his chauffeur's finery, standing outside the front door, ready to park the guests' cars. Inside, just beneath the wide, curved staircase, Alphonse stood in butler's tails and spotless white gloves. In the men's room around the stairwell and down the hall, sat James, dressed in his gray valet's uniform with his hair wetted down and slicked back, smelling strongly of La Farge's eau de cologne.

Simone and Clotilde, the two upstairs maids, sat huddled together in the rose-marble ladies' room across the hall from the men's room. Hamdu and Jusif, still on loan from Ahmed, and the La Farge kitchen staff busied themselves in the kitchen, setting out the hors d'oeuvres on filigreed antique silver trays. Berthe was in the dining room with Madame La Farge, taking a last-minute inventory of the lavishly decorated table.

Madame La Farge was arranging bright yellow daffodils in tiny crystal vases alongside each of the pale blue place cards. There were thirty of them in her favorite color of lavender blue. Thirty arrangements to do, and there was little time left. At any moment now, the guests would be arriving, and she was still in her dressing gown. The pale blue satin wraparound robe hugged her body, revealing the ripeness of her curves as she moved about arranging and rearranging the flowers. Berthe reminded her of her tardiness, but Jacqueline continued without a word. She merely smiled sweetly at the governess and placed a young blossom behind her ear.

"Don't worry," Jacqueline said. "I'll be ready on time, all I have to do is slip on my dress, and it's done." She stood back, admiring the bouquets. "What do you think, Berthe? Will they appreciate all this hard work, or do you think they won't even notice?"

At that moment, before Berthe could speak, the loud chimes at the front door rang out throughout the house. The first guests had arrived. Jacqueline ran out of the dining room, down the hallway and up the back stairs. She had to pass Armand's room to get to her own and noticed his door was open. She went in.

"Armand? *Chéri?* Are you there?"

"Yes, darling, I'm here. What can I do for you, my pet?"

"Oh, nothing much; just give me a kiss. That'll be enough to keep me till after dinner, I hope."

La Farge could hardly believe the change in his wife. She had blossomed forth these last weeks since he had taken her to his bed again. She was changed, somehow, completely. The bubbly sound of her voice was young, almost girlish, and the sparkle in her eyes was one of a woman in love. He wondered briefly what Paul would do now without the rich Madame La

Farge to support and pamper him—but hell, why did he have to worry about poor Paul right then, when he didn't care about anything except Jacqueline and making love to her? She had ignited his passion for her once again. He was like a man who had lost his sight and then regained it. He could now appreciate what he had, perhaps more than he had before.

He came out from his dressing room into the bedroom where she was waiting. She was lying back on the bed, one leg bent, the other crossed over it. Her blue peignoir, which had fallen open on one side, revealed her naked thighs and hips.

"What are you trying to do to me, Jacqueline? Seduce me?"

"Oh, I don't know; that all depends on you. Can I still seduce you, do you think, after all these years?"

"If you make me take you now, you'll be sorry," he said. "You'll have to start all over again with your hair. Are you ready for that?"

"I'm ready if you are. Well, what are you waiting for, a written invitation?"

The buzzer on the night table interrupted him as he was about to speak. "I wonder who that is now." He picked up the receiver to the intercom. "Yes? Who is it?"

The voice came loudly through the grate in the wall. "It is I, Alphonse, monsieur. Some of the guests have already arrived and are asking for you and madame. When shall I say you'll be down?"

"Oh, shit. Is it that late already?" He checked the clock on his night table. It was his old Air Force alarm clock. "Why, it's only seven thirty-five!" He turned to Jacqueline, still lying on the bed. "Didn't the invitations say eight?"

She nodded her head affirmatively. "Yes, they did, but I'll bet it's the Du Plésises, Francine and Georges. She mentioned to me the other day that Georges wanted to talk to you about something."

"Something tedious, if it's Georges," La Farge muttered. He spoke into the intercom once again: "Alphonse, it's M. and Mme Du Plésis, *hein?* I thought so. Ah, well, you and Berthe hold the fort till we get down, please. We'll only be a minute."

He hung up and turned to Jacqueline. "Only a minute, Armand?" she said in mock reproach. "Aren't I worth more than that?"

"To dress, I meant," he said.

"You'll spoil the fit of your trousers if you try to step into them in that state," she said, pointing. "You'd scandalize poor Francine—or else she'd enjoy the sight too much, and I don't know which I'd like least. If thinking about what dullness Georges is about to inflict on you doesn't depress your ardors, you need more drastic treatment; fortunately, I happen to have with me just the instrument for that." She undid the belt of her peignoir and let it slide away as she lifted her arms to receive him.

Downstairs, Berthe was hurrying down the hallway past the powder rooms, her arms laden with open boxes of flowers. She dropped off a box of lavender blue and white orchids at the ladies' room; corsages for the guests who would come in to freshen up later. She handed James a box of pink and white carnations for the men's boutonnieres, and continued on down the hallway to La Farge's main study. Berthe was going there supposedly to place a dozen long-stemmed roses in the Ming vase under the portrait of Jacqueline and Rosalie, a vase so valuable that only Berthe was allowed to handle it. She locked the doors behind her as she entered and placed the twelve perfect roses in the antique vase. Next she walked over to the bookshelves and pushed a chair up in front of them. She climbed onto the cane-backed chair and pressed the red book in the center of the top shelf. The shelves slid to one side, revealing the vault. She leaned closer and turned the dial: forward two, back four, then forward one, then forward three. There was a faint clicking sound as the vault opened.

She looked around nervously. She had locked the doors carefully but still felt frightened. What if, she thought fearfully, this once La Farge changed his habits and came in here before greeting his guests? What if . . . But she couldn't back out now, not when Heinz was counting on her. Too much was at stake, their lives for one thing, and Margot. Oh Margot, if only . . .

She checked her watch. God, already seven-forty! Heinz would be waiting for her upstairs! She was supposed to have done this at least fifteen minutes ago and be waiting in her room for him. Her fingers clutched the reel of film marked "X," and she stood on tiptoe, reaching further into the deep vault for the manila envelope in the back. There were also several keys on a brass key chain. She slipped them into the envelope and closed the vault. She pressed the book again, and everything returned to its place. She put the chair back where she had found it and went through the drawers of the big desk. There were nothing but checkbooks and tax statements and a few postcards from Rosalie and Ahmed from Casablanca. She flicked through every item quickly, and replaced them exactly as she had found them. She slipped into the bathroom next to the study and removed one of the clean face towels from the shelf. She wrapped the reel of film and the manila envelope in it and crept out the door to the hallway. She had to pass the men's and ladies' rooms on her way back, but no one saw her. James was busy brushing off one of the men's jackets; his back was turned, and Simone and Clotilde were busy sprinkling the ladies' room with lilac water.

Berthe glanced at her watch as she hurried to get to her quarters unnoticed. Unlike the other servants' rooms, hers was upstairs, the first room at the top of the stairs. She glanced at her watch as she unlocked her door.

My God, Heinz will be furious—I'm so late.

He was sitting on her single bed, clenching his fists nervously, an angry frown on his face.

"I'm sorry I'm late, Heinz, but she wouldn't let me out of her sight tonight. If the doorbell hadn't rung, I would still be down there, helping her arrange flowers."

"Don't call me *Heinz*, Berta! I've told you a thousand times before; you might forget yourself one day and call me that in front of others. Don't *ever* do it again. And as for being late, these extra fifteen minutes you've cost me could make all the difference. I got here, as I said I would, at seven-thirty on the dot. I only hope La Farge hasn't gone down yet. I see you have the papers. Hurry and burn them. What you can't burn, tear up and flush down the toilet. As for the film, take it out the back way to Fritz. He's waiting at the end of the street, out of sight. He knows what to do with it. Now hurry, he'll be waiting for you."

D'Artois eased himself out into the hallway, checking first to see that no one was around. He tiptoed past the linen room, past La Farge's bathroom to La Farge's bedroom door. He checked around him once more and pressed his cheek up against the door. He could hear voices. Damn, someone was in there with La Farge. Who was it? James? No, it was a woman's voice, coming from the bedroom.

"Oh, Armand, so what? The guests will have to wait awhile. It won't kill them. Come on, don't stop now."

"Oh, no, it won't do; twice in a row is too much for me at my age. You want to kill me?"

The phone in the bedroom was ringing. It drowned out Jacqueline's answer. Someone was coming toward the door.

D'Artois ducked down the hall and into La Farge's unlocked study. The door to the bedroom opened and Jacqueline came out. D'Artois heard her go into her own room across the hall and close the door behind her.

The coast was clear.

D'Artois wiped his brow with his handkerchief and picked up the phone to eavesdrop. It was seven-fifty; there were only ten or fifteen minutes at the most left to do what he had come to do.

It was Clérot on the phone. He recognized the voice from tapes Berthe had made of conversations between the detective and La Farge.

Clérot's tone was serious. "I think I'm on to something. I'm not a hundred percent sure yet, but I'm supposed to meet a woman tonight. I got a call this morning. She was very mysterious about it, but said she knew what I was looking for and had the information I needed. I don't know what it is about the call that makes me feel the way I do, but something tells me this is it."

"Be careful, Clérot. You never can tell, if you know what I mean. Be very careful *where* you meet with this person. I have a strange feeling that d'Artois suspects someone is after him. You don't want to get caught in a trap, but he'll be here tonight, so I guess that takes care of him. I had to invite him as usual, or he might have guessed something was up."

"Don't worry." The voice sounded sincere. "Somehow I know my rendezvous tonight will be of great importance."

D'Artois had to smile to himself. The man doesn't know how right he is!

Michelle had certainly done a good job, calling Clérot up, pretending to be a rejected love of the duke's, with a lot to tell. She had said that a friend of hers, whose name she did not care to mention, but someone Clérot knew quite well, had put her in touch with him.

Clérot had been too eager to please La Farge, too eager to learn the truth. He had blindly agreed to meet Michelle at the gypsy camp outside the entrance of the Marché aux Puces and had agreed not to bring anyone with him, since she had said she was a married woman with a child and could not risk her reputation being ruined. He had taken the bait, and an hour from now he would arrive, only to find Cigot and Samson waiting instead.

Clérot's voice interrupted d'Artois's thoughts.

"I'll see you in the morning when I come by and pick up those papers you have for me, the statement from Maître Piétz. I'll need them. You're sure he's telling the truth, now. I mean, remembering that spot in d'Artois's eye. He's old; he could be confusing d'Artois with someone else."

"No, I tell you I'm sure. I've spent a lot of time with the old man. I'm convinced he's telling the truth. This man who calls himself the duke is *not* d'Artois, and I won't rest until I find out who he is."

"I don't know. I still say you are making a mistake. You should go to the police; expose him. What if he ever finds out you're on his trail? A man like that would stop at nothing."

"We've been through this before, Clérot. I say we wait until we are *sure*. There is still a chance, no matter how far-fetched, that d'Artois, or whoever he is, has a good reason for whatever he's done."

"Very well. I hope my meeting tonight will put an end to this. I worry about you, La Farge. He would kill you if he knew what you were up to. I have to leave you now. I'll see you first thing in the morning. Will eight be a good time?"

"Eight will be fine. I'll see you then, and do be careful, will you? This is a dangerous game, and it follows that the players are also."

Clérot bade his employer good-night and hung up. As La Farge was about to replace the receiver, he thought he heard a noise.

"Yes? Who is it?" La Farge turned to look at the doorway. Must be Diablo going out, he thought.

He went to get the papers Clérot would come by for in the morning. They were in the desk in his study. He trudged barefoot across the blue carpet, his toes curled in the air as if he were afraid to touch the floor with them. He went into his private study off his bedroom. As he entered, he heard a sound. He couldn't quite define it.

"Jacqueline, is that you?" There was no answer. "James? Goddamit, who's playing tricks on me, then? Speak up, whoever you are."

As La Farge reached for the light switch, a hand shot out from behind him and clasped itself tightly over his mouth. A split second later, he felt the muzzle of a gun pushed up against his back. The hand pulled him backward toward the door.

La Farge had not seen anything, but he knew who it was. He had recognized almost at once that faint smell of Jean Patou eau de cologne that d'Artois wore. It came to him from the hand clasped over his mouth.

His attacker spoke finally. "I am sorry, Armand, that it has to end this way between you and me." He paused, as if choosing his words before a jury. "You should have minded your own business. Even when you found out I wasn't d'Artois, you should have trusted me. You were supposed to be my friend."

La Farge tried to speak, but d'Artois would not let him.

"You'll speak when I am finished with what I have to say. First I want to tell you who I am. After all, that's what you want to know, isn't it?"

La Farge struggled against d'Artois's grip, but the duke jammed the gun up hard between La Farge's shoulder blades.

"It won't do you any good to struggle. Before you could get two feet away, I would blow your head off. I know that you know I'm not d'Artois, and that it would be only a matter of days, weeks perhaps, before you either found out *who* I am or turned me in to the authorities. I can't allow that, you'll understand." He removed his hand from La Farge's mouth and ordered him to sit down, still pointing the gun at him.

"Sit down and listen to me, Armand. If you move or try to call out I'll have to shoot you."

"You'll have to shoot me in any case, won't you?"

"To my regret, yes. Maybe, if things were different, I could trade your life for your promise to keep my secret, especially since I have known you to be a man of your word; but it's too late for bargains."

La Farge was inching his knee up under the desk to ring the buzzer, but d'Artois saw this and kicked the swivel chair backward, sending it flying across the floor on its wheels.

"If you try anything like that again, Armand, I'll put a bullet in your head right now."

There was a soft rapping on the door. It was coming from La Farge's bedroom. D'Artois rushed over to La Farge and clamped his hand back over his captive's mouth. He jabbed the gun up against his left temple. He raised his foot and kicked the light switch, turning off the light.

"Don't make a move or a sound," d'Artois whispered, "or I'll let you and whoever it is have it right between the eyes."

"Armand? Are you in there?" The door pushed open, and Jacqueline walked in. She flicked on the light. She was fully dressed for the party. She saw d'Artois with the gun pointed at her husband's head. She froze, screaming in her mind, but not able to let it out.

"Jean? What are you doing? Are you mad?"

"I'm extremely sorry you had to come in just now, Jacqueline. I hadn't planned for you to get involved. Now I can't let you go."

She watched his eyes for the sign that he was joking. They were fierce. She could tell he was dead serious. "B-B-But why,

Jean? What did Armand do to you? I thought you were friends."

"Don't ask me; ask him. I trusted him, and he betrayed me."

"Betrayed you? But how, Jean?"

The duke smiled coldly at her. "Tell her, Armand; tell her what a good friend you've been. How you've been spying on me all these years and what you found out." He pushed the gun's muzzle up against La Farge's cheekbone. "*Tell* her," he commanded. "I haven't got all night. Any minute now one of those cretins you have in your employ will come upstairs to find out what's keeping you both, and I don't want to be here when they do."

La Farge spoke for the first time since Jacqueline had entered the room. He spoke haltingly, as if in a daze. He could not believe this was really happening to them. Jacqueline stood glued to the spot, listening. Her eyes grew wider by the moment as La Farge related to her the incredible story.

"Our friend, here, is indeed a prize chameleon," La Farge said, "only he dares not change back into his true skin, not even for a second. He is too afraid. Even though he points the gun at us, he is still afraid to tell us who he really is, but I know who he is. He *has* to be who I think he is; a dirty, stinking Nazi, that's our friend. It's the only explanation I've been able to come up with. After all, if a French nobleman and a Nazi general drop from sight about the same place and the same time, and the nobleman reappears—and is *not* the nobleman . . . one must draw one's conclusions, isn't it so?"

"You have a Frenchman's logic, my friend," d'Artois said. "And, I fear, a Frenchman's luck, of the kind that your race experienced in forty. But you're mistaken in one thing: I was never a Nazi. I worked with them, why not? They provided the only opportunity there was, and I can assure you that most people of my class despised Corporal Adi and his thugs and their lower-class hobbies such as Jew-killing. But there was a lot of good business to be done out of it, and we made the most of it. Goebbels now, he was a proper Nazi, poisoned himself and his family once his Führer had taken that way out. Me, I've had the best of both ways—died, with a body to prove it, and still kept my life, my health, and a very handsome portion of the Reich's money."

La Farge thought of a moment forty-six years before, when he had seen three neatly spaced holes blossom in the fabric of the upper wing of his Spad, made by slugs from the Spandau firing from the Fokker diving on him. The fourth, he had calculated in that eerily prolonged instant, would take him neatly between the eyes. But it hadn't come. Perhaps the enemy gun had jammed, perhaps its ammunition had been exhausted. In any case, the instant had passed, and he had lived. Until now.

"I should have known, Armand, when I saw that portrait of you hanging in my study downstairs, when I had my headquarters here. It's a good study of you, it shows your character, your tenacity. I knew that with your drive and ambition, you were the one to pick for my cover, to establish my position, to make me so many times richer than I already was. But I didn't take into account that the same qualities would lead you, even after all these years, to find me out. A mistake, I must admit it. But"—his voice which had been gently mocking, almost friendly, took on a steely tone—"in *my* case, not a fatal one."

He looked at Jacqueline, who was numb with shock and fear, and then back to La Farge. "I congratulate you on your thoroughness, my friend. You have made my task—my lifetime task—of concealment the easier by your meddling. The old Jew Piétz would have been a time bomb. It never occurred to me that someone like him, with his inconvenient memory, existed."

La Farge's mouth dropped open at the mention of Maître Piétz.

"Ah, you didn't know I knew about him, did you? You kept him well hidden, just like those clippings and the reel of film you had of me. I say *had*. Twenty minutes ago, I had them removed from your safe downstairs and burned."

La Farge said hoarsely, "How? How did you find out about all this?"

"How? It's very simple, my dear La Farge. Berthe has served me well all these years. I couldn't have done it without her."

"Berthe? You mean *our* Berthe? It can't be, I don't believe you, you're mad," said Jacqueline.

"Your Berthe, as you call her, has been my spy all these years. She was the one who tipped me off about Cirac. I took care of him and Delacroix and now Clérot. All along, I knew everything, every step and every phone call you made. I kept hoping you would give up, but you chose not to. Now I have to kill you both. I'm sorry about you, Jacqueline; I've always had a soft spot for you."

"You won't get away with it," said La Farge. "The authorities will get you. Clérot will tell them."

"No, Armand, you're wrong. I shall kill you both, and then I'll go out and come in again, as if I were just arriving, and I'll be as shocked as anyone else when the servants find you up here dead, murdered, as it will appear even to the police, by a burglar; that will not be hard to arrange."

"Clérot will tell the police what we know about you, and Maître Piétz, too. And then the guillotine, no question."

D'Artois grinned. "I'm afraid Maître Piétz and Inspector Clérot won't be around for anything except their own funerals. He won't be missed for a few days, an unwanted old man like that, and when he's found rotting in his apartment, it'll clearly be a question of natural causes. A heart attack, to be exact. As for your man Clérot, about now, one of my men is scheduled to be seeing to him. It's a pity you won't be around to see the headlines. 'Former inspector victim of murderous violence. When will the police awake?' "

D'Artois threw back his head and laughed. La Farge saw his one slim chance and jumped the duke from the side.

For a moment d'Artois lost control, but then Jacqueline screamed, and he fired at her. La Farge was stunned as he watched his wife fall. He lunged at d'Artois and hit him hard in the temple. D'Artois stumbled backward, hitting his head on the sharp edge of the desk. La Farge leapt forward, throwing himself on him. d'Artois was younger and quicker; he rolled to one side as La Farge lunged forward, and he fired. The shot did not ring out; only a "feup" sound was heard as the bullet left the silencer-equipped gun. The bullet hit La Farge in the neck, passing through the left side of his throat up through his jaw and out the right side of his head, just under the temple. He fell, his head jerking to the right side and onto the floor, partly under the swivel chair.

"Jacqueliiiiiine!" La Farge yelled as he fell.

D'Artois crouched near Jacqueline, examining the bullet wound in her chest. It had passed through her heart. "She can't hear you anymore. She's dead."

A wail came from La Farge's throat like the cry of an enraged beast. *"Oh, God!"*

D'Artois stood up, walked over to La Farge, and aimed the gun at his forehead. The injured man's eyes opened wide to stare at the weapon for a second, then rolled upward to fix d'Artois's icy gaze.

"It's true, then," La Farge said thickly, his voice choked by the blood welling in his throat. "You're really . . ."

D'Artois straightened and made a mocking present-arms gesture with the pistol. "Lieutenant General Heinz von Witte, reporting for duty. Poor d'Artois has been reposing under that name and rank in a military cemetery these eighteen years; and as I lent him my honors, it's only fair that I should have his, don't you agree? He was convenient, that was his main virtue—otherwise, a weakling. That's bothered me all these years, that he wasn't a stronger man, someone I could truly identify with. Someone like yourself, my dear Armand—that would have been a good game, to become Armand La Farge. But then . . . there would have been no Rosalie."

A horror beyond that of approaching death flickered in La Farge's eyes as he understood d'Artois's intonation—and, in his fading consciousness, linked together incidents and impressions over the years, meaningless then but dreadfully significant in these last moments.

La Farge's eyes twitched wildly in their sockets, and his lips moved, but only the gurgling sound of blood forcing itself through the holes in his throat could be heard; and then his eyes softened into a pleading expression, as he shook his blood-drenched head. His lips formed words: "No . . . please . ... not Rosalie . . . spare her . . . and . . ."

La Farge's right hand moved slowly up along his chest, and with the last strength left in him, he raised his right hand and dropped it to his breast. His lips formed a word, as he was about to slip his fingers under the lapel of his dressing gown.

D'Artois thought La Farge was reaching for a concealed weapon.

He yanked the dressing gown away from La Farge's chest. La Farge's index finger pointed to the gold key on a chain around his neck. Once again his lips formed a word. D'Artois leaned closer, trying to read his lips. "Rosalie . . . spare her . . . for this."

D'Artois yanked the key and chain from around La Farge's neck, breaking the clasp as he did so. "What is this?" he asked. "La Farge, what is this a key to?"

La Farge's lips moved once more, and then he was unconscious. The word he had formed with his lips, D'Artois was sure, was "Colombier." Some secret had been kept at Colombier.

D'Artois's face resembled that of the statue he had bestowed on La Farge. "I must make sure you are dead, my friend, although I would like to spare you to find out what you have hidden at Colombier." He checked his watch. "I don't have the time. I'll have to find out for myself."

He pointed the gun at La Farge. "Perhaps you have screwed me after all, my friend. Perhaps you will have the last laugh. We shall see."

His right forefinger squeezed the trigger slowly for the third time that night. La Farge's head jerked forward from the impact of the bullet and slammed down hard against the wooden floor, inches away from the upturned rug. Then it rolled to one side and was still.

D'Artois unscrewed the silencer from the gun and shoved the two pieces into the breast pocket of his dinner jacket. He checked quickly to make sure that there were no bloodstains on his clothes, and proceeded to ransack the room to make it look as if it had been burglarized.

He picked up a key off the ground which had fallen out of La Farge's hand. He opened the lower left-hand drawer of the desk. It was the only drawer that was locked. He knew the papers Clérot had mentioned over the phone had to be inside. He found them in a dark green folder under some other papers. D'Artois replaced the empty green folder and jammed the papers down inside his waistband.

He threw open the back door of the tiny study, which opened out onto a narrow balcony overlooking part of the gardens. Across the courtyard was the old carriage house. He remembered the day he had left here more than eighteen years before with Jean d'Artois as his prisoner.

He felt as if he were living the same scene over once again; fleeing once again for his life with everything he lived for riding on the outcome of the next few hours. He climbed down the balcony onto the wooden arbor, which joined the house to the garage, and climbed over the garage down into the alley. No one had seen him, he was certain. He walked quickly, taking great strides as he hurried along the side walk. A light blue Mercedes-Benz pulled up alongside him as he reached the corner where the alley came out onto the street. The door was flung open by the driver, and he got in.

D'Artois slid into the backseat and leaned back against the soft gray leather.

"It's done, boss. Clérot has been taken care of." Fritz spoke in German.

D'Artois consulted his watch. It was eight-fifteen, five minutes later than he had planned, but still perfect in every detail. He straightened his bow tie and leaned over the seat to check his hair in the mirror over the dashboard.

"Did you get the film from Berthe?"

"Yes, I did, but she was very late. I was beginning to worry if something had gone wrong."

"No, nothing went wrong. She was just late, that's all. Did you do with it what I told you to?"

"Yes, boss. I took care of it like you said."

He removed a comb from his inner breast pocket and passed it through his hair. He replaced the comb and handed Fritz the gun and the silencer.

"Here, as soon as you drop me off at the La Farges', take these and dump them. I saw they were repairing the street just off rue St. Denis. Take them and bury them in the wet cement."

D'Artois handed Fritz the papers he had removed from La Farge's desk.

"Here, take these too and burn them. You hear? Burn them! After that, go home and turn back the clocks to the right time. I'm sure by now Mademoiselle Margot is sound asleep. I drugged her martini, so she won't hear you come in. Come, now, let's hurry. I wouldn't want to keep my hosts waiting, eh?"

It was thirty-seven minutes past eight by the time James decided to go upstairs to see what was keeping the master and mistress of the house.

The guests had all arrived, and were becoming impatient.

James climbed the back stairs off the pantry to the second floor and went straight to La Farge's bedroom. He knocked on the door and waited. There was no answer. He knocked again, louder this time, and called out to his employer.

Still getting no reply, he pushed open the door, which was slightly ajar, and went in. The light was on, and he could see the rumpled bed where Jacqueline had lain, hardly more than an hour ago.

Her perfume still lingered faintly in the room, and the belt of her peignoir was strung across the dark Louis XV headboard. At first glance, James assumed that monsieur and madame had been "at it" again and had forgotten entirely about their guests below. He assumed that they were now probably bathing together in madame's Roman bathtub, and he wondered how he would go about breaking it up. If there was one thing La Farge hated more than pajama bottoms, it was being interrupted in the act. He remembered only too well the couple of occasions on which that had occurred. La Farge had been so enraged that James wondered still how he had managed to keep his position.

He was about to leave when he heard a noise: the flapping of a door in the wind. The sound was coming from the study. James walked through the dark bedroom to the study entrance and flicked on the light.

The room was lit at once, like a theater set. On the floor, the two actors lay, each in a puddle of blood. James's hand flew to his mouth, bile rising in his throat, as he took in the horror of the scene before him.

He rushed to Jacqueline's side first, for she was closest to him. He felt for a pulse, then knelt down and placed his head against her chest. She was still, he knew at once that she was dead. He crawled on his hands and knees over to where La Farge lay, blood pulsing from the wreckage of his head. The fact that La Farge was bleeding, James knew, meant that the man was still alive. James ran to the door, out into the hallway, and down the front stairs. As he ran, he yelled for help, tears streaming down his face and stumbling in his haste.

"Monsieur and madame have been shot."

A loud gasp rose from the crowd, and then a roar, as people began screaming and running upstairs.

"Hurry, call an ambulance. Get Dr. Labans at his home, at once." James screamed the orders to Alphonse, who was standing glued to his spot. "Hurry, man!"

Alphonse, like a toy wound up and then released, raced across the room's circular floor, across the winged Pegasus design, and into the living room to the phone.

People were standing around crying and sobbing. Most of them were in the bedroom or the hallway. James ran back upstairs. He saw that someone had closed Jacqueline's eyes.

He sank down on his knees, Tears streaming down his face, as he prayed for his *patron*'s life.

The duke stood nearby, clicking his tongue and shaking his head. "Who could have done such a thing?" he said.

"There are crazy people in this world," came a woman's voice. She was sitting on the foor next to Jacqueline's body. "Maniacs."

Berthe stood outside the room, hanging over the staircase railing, a sick gray look on her face.

When the police arrived, the guests and staff alike ran at them, screaming, crying, babbling incoherently.

The ambulance came and took the bodies to the hospital.

La Farge was still alive, but there was little hope he would survive.

The house and the grounds were searched from top to bottom and photographed. The servants were allowed to retire, and the guests permitted to go home.

The police concluded that it had to have been a burglar, someone very experienced, perhaps someone who at one time or another had been in the La Farges' employ. One thing was sure—the person or persons knew the layout of the house very well.

Rosalie and Ahmed arrived at Orly Airport the following day and went directly to the hospital. Rosalie's eyes were red and puffy, her face totally void of makeup. Ahmed helped her out of the car and up the hospital stairs. Nurses and doctors recognized her as she entered and gave her looks of sympathy.

Rosalie and Ahmed had to wait a long time for the elevator, and she leaned up against him, her eyes looking down at the floor. The elevator finally arrived.

They were met on the third floor by Dr. Daniel Labans, the family physician. Ahmed had called from the airport to find out if La Farge was still alive and to let the doctor know that they were on their way. The long, antiseptic corridor from the elevator to La Farge's room seemed endless, like a tunnel in a terrifying dream. To Rosalie, everything was spinning; the doctor seemed upside down as did everyone else in the narrow corridor.

It must be the tranquilizers the doctor in Guadeloupe gave me, Rosalie thought. She had never felt so strange.

La Farge was propped up slightly in bed, and to Ahmed, looked shrunken. Ahmed was alarmed when he saw the large bottle of blood and the long needle attached to La Farge's arm. Most of La Farge's head and face and neck were bandaged. Ahmed's eyes studied the wan figure on the bed. His gaze came to rest on La Farge's nails and fingertips; they were blue and shriveled.

In spite of the clear signs, Ahmed tried not to think that La

Farge was going to die. He knew he had to be strong for Rosalie's sake. If he cracked now, she would be lost. Already he could imagine how difficult it would be for her, not to have her father around, not to ever see him again. But he fought with himself, driving the thoughts out of his mind.

The surgeon, Dr. Branget, came in just then with a nurse following in step and Dr. Labans directly behind. He motioned to Ahmed to keep Rosalie away from her father. They could not risk the slightest movement, for it might be fatal. She was not allowed to touch him, only to watch.

"Oh, Papa! Papa! Why? Why you?" Rosalie cried out.

Dr. Branget looked into La Farge's eyeball with a little flashlight. He closed the lid gently, and proceeded to check the other.

"How bad is it, doctor? I have to know," asked Rosalie.

The doctor looked at Rosalie, a helpless expression on his face. Ahmed placed his arm around her and pulled her tightly against him.

"You can tell us, doctor. We must know. My wife can take it."

The doctor explained the circumstances to them bluntly. La Farge had one chance in a million of surviving, and even then he would be "a vegetable." Too much of his brain had been damaged. As the doctor spoke, his words took on solidity, like daggers of ice, piercing Rosalie's and Ahmed's hearts.

"You mean to say, doctor, that there's nothing at all that can be done?"

"That's right. We're doing all that we can for him. We've called in the best in the field of brain surgery, but we can do nothing more than what we have already done. All we can do now is wait and pray."

All that night Rosalie and Ahmed stayed up with La Farge, and most of the next day. Finally, Ahmed and the doctors had to drag Rosalie home for a few hours' sleep. Even then, they had to knock her out with an injection of tranquilizers.

That afternoon at four, after she had awakened from a three-hour nap, Rosalie tried to insist on returning to the hospital. Ahmed talked her out of it, reassuring her that the doctor would call if there were any change. She had given in in the end, only because she was still heavily under sedation and could hardly stand up. At five-thirty they were preparing to return to the hospital when the phone rang. Its shrillness was like a knife cutting the silence. The news was bad. La Farge was failing; he would not last much longer. They would have to hurry.

They arrived fifteen minutes later at the hospital. Both were out of breath.

A nurse sat outside the door, waiting. From the woman's face, Rosalie knew at once. She felt as if a cold hand had clasped her fast-beating heart. The white figure stood up.

"I'm sorry, madame, but you're too late. Your father just passed away."

A cry escaped Rosalie's parched lips as she flung her weight against the door and then ran across the white room to her father's bed. She threw herself on top of him and wept.

"Oh, Papa! Papa! Why? Why you too? Oh, God, why?"

Ahmed came and stood beside her, feeling her anguish, but not knowing quite what to do. He placed his arm gently about her shoulders and pried her away from her father's limp, lifeless body. His hand touched the dead man's cheek, ever so lightly as he pulled Rosalie away, and a chill ran through his own warm body, making him cold. The finality of death had always scared him, and he had never been this close to it before.

Ahmed tried to avoid looking at La Farge's face, but something compelled him to look. In death as in life, La Farge commanded attention.

The lips were relaxed, but slightly blue. The eyelids, purplish blue, seemed taut over the eyeballs, which looked sunken into the skull. The layers of white bandages made the dead man's head and throat seem eerily detached from the rest of his body.

Rosalie broke down and had to be sedated again before she would leave the hospital. Ahmed was finally able to take her home, assisted by Dr. Labans, whose services were now no longer needed by Armand La Farge.

Chapter Sixteen

Paris, October 31, 1962

For most people it was a morning like any other October morning in Paris. The weather was a trifle cool and the skies a dusty blue with a golden yellow sun rising over the steeples and chimneys of the beautiful old buildings. It should have been a day for singing and rejoicing, a good day to be alive. But for Rosalie and Ahmed, on rue Vieille du Temple in le Marais, it was a bleak day. It was the morning of the funeral. The sound of an old church bell not far away could be heard, tolling its sad, slow good-byes; it came from the church where La Farge had baptized his daughter and had gone to Mass the first Sunday of every month. Archbishop Lernier was saluting the morning of his friend's burial. Rosalie and Ahmed, dressing for the services, heard the haunting "bong, bong-g-g, bong-g-g" of the big bells, as they got ready for the services.

A tear rolled down Ahmed's cheek as he watched his lovely Rosalie moving about the bedroom like a ghost. There was no expression on her face. It was pale and drawn-looking.

He watched her as she dressed, solemnly, slowly, as if every move she made was caused by someone pushing a button. She stood up and walked past the floor-length mirror without glancing in it.

"I'm ready," she said, almost too brightly for this day. "Are you?"

He nodded and handed her the small, black silk gloves and her purse, which were on the bed. "Let's go."

"Yes, let's, or we'll be late for the services."

"You don't have to hurry, Rosalie. Archbishop Lernier would never begin without you."

"I think he might. After all, the principal parties are already there and have been for some time."

"What do you mean?"

"What I mean is, the dead are already there. The services are being held for them, not for me. *I'm* still alive."

They descended the winding stairs to the round entrance hall and were heading for the front door when suddenly, without warning, Rosalie turned around and headed in the opposite direction. She crossed the marble floor with the winged Pegasus, the insignia of her father, and pushed open the large, double doors to the ballroom.

Ahmed stood rigid on the spot, watching his wife as she stood there in the doorway of the bright, sunlight room, her arms spread-eagled as she held on to the open halves of the door. She pushed forward, hard, and the doors opened, slamming with a loud boom against the massive inside walls of the ballroom. She went in. He followed. She did not say a word, and neither did he. Then she walked over to the wall on the left and stood in front of a portrait of her grandfather, Henri Férrier. She stood silently and stared at it for a moment or two; then she walked a few steps further and stopped and looked up at the portrait of her grandmother; then of her mother. She continued to walk around the circular room and stopped in turn in front of the portraits of both her grandparents on her father's side and, finally, in front of her father's. He was standing tall and handsome against a clouded sky background, his blond hair sleeked back behind his ears, his face smooth, as in the days before he started wearing a beard. His eyes were bluer than the sky behind him. He looked a dashing figure of a man in his white planter's suit, hat and cigar in hand.

Ahmed searched Rosalie's face for something, anything: grief, anger. He saw only admiration for the handsome man in the portrait. Rosalie turned around then and pointed to the portrait above the mantle. It was of her at about fifteen, ravishing in her innocence and dazzling in her purity.

"See?" she said. "The Sole Survivor."

Her hand dropped to her side, and she gazed up at the portrait in its gilded frame.

"Papa had it made for me for my sixteenth birthday. I had by then outgrown the other."

She was referring to the other portrait of herself, at the age of four, which hung in her father's upstairs study, the one with curls and ribbons in her hair and all the charm in the world in her big, green eyes.

"Do you like it?"

"Yes, I like it. Very much. It's—it's so much you; it's as if the artist captured your very soul on his canvas. No wonder your father kept it in the place of honor."

"You mean over the mantel? A mirror used to hang there, but when we got married, he put the portrait there instead. I don't think I like it there, myself, but . . . What time is it? Late?"

"Yes, it's quite late. We must be going."

Ahmed took Rosalie's arm, and together they walked out through the double doors, without a glance backward, and out of the house.

Max was waiting at the car. The short drive to the church was spent in silence. They arrived ten minutes later and parked behind the shining black hearse, in the space reserved for them in front of the massive doorway of the church.

A flock of people had gathered outside the church. Weeping mourners in purples and blacks were craning their necks to see inside the church. As Max and Ahmed helped Rosalie up the stone steps of the church, the people, in silent respect, made way for her to pass. Many of them had worked at one time or another in La Farge's many factories and vineyards and had come to pay their last respects to a decent *patron,* a man who had heart as well as money and power. Others were just people off the street, curious people, sympathetic people, who had come to say good-bye to the dead man, another human being.

Members of the press stood across the street from the church, waiting and watching. Out of respect, they stopped taking pictures as Rosalie ascended the steps.

The church was packed with friends and relatives.

Ahmed could feel Rosalie tense as she beheld the two bronze caskets at the end of the runner and started to make her way toward them. People lifted their heads from prayer and gazed solemnly as she passed by. Her face was hidden, for the most part, by her veil. Her slender figure seemed too thin in the plain black dress.

Archibishop Lernier came toward her, his small blue eyes sunken in his head, his round face pink and puffy. There was great sadness in his face. He had cared for La Farge deeply. He held his arms out to Rosalie.

"Come, my child, we have been waiting. I was worried."

He looked up at Ahmed, who was considerably taller.

"Come, my son."

He placed his arms around them both and ushered them to the pew near the sealed twin coffins.

Archbishop Lernier returned to stand before the altar. The services were to begin.

As Ahmed knelt down beside Rosalie on the hard boards, his thoughts raced back to the night before. People had come from all over to pay their last respects to the couple. Two by two, they had filed by, shaking hands, saying words of peace, and love, and sorrow, weeping as they did for the loss of two dear friends, and stopping a moment, each one in turn, to gaze down at the shells of what once had been a great couple. Ahmed saw himself coming up to the coffins, first of Jacqueline, dressed in a pearl gray silk gown with her hair combed down over her shoulders, her arms folded across her breast, like a sleeping beauty, waiting to be awakened. The creamy camellia in her hair had been placed there by Rosalie. All the rest had been taken care of by Berthe. He would never forget Jacqueline's beautiful face, pink with rouge, lips glistening with a touch of gloss.

He bowed his head lower as fresh tears welled in his eyes and rolled down his cheeks. "Oh, God, why? Why do you work in such strange ways?"

He would never forget the face of the man who had so openly proclaimed his fatherly love to him so many times. A man so special, he would mourn him as much as a son would.

How proud La Farge looked on his silk pillow. James had insisted that *no* satin be put in the coffin and had described the little episode about the satin sheets to get his way. The new gray suit, which La Farge had planned to wear on the tragic night, was chosen to bury him in. James had taken delicate care in brushing and grooming the dead man's hair and had touched his cheeks with a burnished color to give the face the look of health and peaceful sleep.

The crew from the hospital had taken great pains to minimize the bandages necessary to hide the ugly wounds in his head and cheek. His suit and tie hid the neck wound. His nails had been brushed and buffed and his hands placed, folded, on his chest.

A heartbreaking scene kept returning to Ahmed's mind. Earlier that morning, when they had come to take the bodies to the church, Rosalie had thrown herself on top of her father's coffin and had screamed at the hospital crew to leave her father alone and not to touch her mother, or she would kill them. She had gnashed her teeth and spit angry words at them and had finally collapsed in a spasm of anguish, thrashing and throwing herself about, until Ahmed had slapped her and carried her upstairs.

Dr. Labans had been there and had administered a sedative, and it had calmed her; but in a way Ahmed was glad Rosalie had let some of her anguish out.

His thoughts kept sailing back in time to the first time he had met La Farge, and then later Rosalie; to his immediate infatuation with her; their marriage, the trip; the phone call he had received from La Farge about d'Artois, just days before that fateful night.

Ahmed looked up, slightly ashamed of himself for letting his thoughts stray during the services. He could not believe they were over.

People were beginning to leave the church and, in the family pews behind him, others were beckoning to him. Rosalie was still kneeling, her head bowed on her folded hands. Through the tears welling up in his eyes, Ahmed saw his father, Senator Buchin, d'Artois and the President, followed closely by Max, Alphonse, James and Dr. Labans.

Ahmed watched as the eight men took their positions, four alongside each of the two caskets. His arm tightened around Rosalie's shoulders, bracing her trembling body.

Two at the head, two at the foot, the four men closest to La Farge during his life stood by his coffin, their arms rigid against their sides, their faces grave and twisted with agony—all, that is, but one. Ahmed's eyes focused on d'Artois. His black suit made him look thinner, but his face, Ahmed noticed, was, as usual, calm and composed.

Ahmed compared him to the others.

James was sobbing uncontrollably. Buchin's face was pale and bloated, his eyes red and swollen. The sheikh's head was bent over in an effort to control a new rush of tears.

The four men hoisted the coffin and placed it on their shoulders.

Rosalie stood motionless, watching in silence, as her mother's gleaming casket was next hoisted into the air.

Ahmed took Rosalie's hand in his and squeezed it. He felt his heart about to explode with grief as the eight men began to move toward them.

The organist was playing the funeral march, soft and haunting, and from the innermost depths of the church, the lone bell tolled its final good-bye.

"Ashes to ashes, dust to dust; the Lord giveth, and the Lord taketh away."

At the gravesite, Archbishop Lernier was passing incense over the open graves, in the sign of the cross, now over one and then the other.

"Ashes to ashes, dust to dust; the Lord giveth, and the Lord taketh away."

People pressed toward the graves, sobbing and leaning on each other for support. President de Gaulle, tall and solemn in his general's uniform, stood at attention. He saluted, then bent to throw a handful of dirt on the graves, first Jacqueline's, then Armand's; his wary eyes misted and his voice croaked as he said, "Amen."

Tears were streaming down Rosalie's face, coming to rest on her breast and soaking the front of her dress. As she stooped to pick up a wreath, a bouquet at the foot of her mother's open grave caught her eye. It had a card dangling from it, a small card of lavender blue, her mother's favorite color. A sob escaped Rosalie's lips as she turned her veil up over the brim of her hat and fell to her knees to grasp the bouquet. It was the one she had sent from Guadeloupe, her peace offering.

She read the handwriting on the little card: "Maman. A bunch of flowers for the prettiest flower of all. I am sorry I did what I did. I am sorry I was so childish. Please forgive me, Maman, and know that I love you, perhaps differently from the way I love Papa, but just as much."

The bouquet fell from her hands and bounced into the grave, falling on her mother's casket.

"Oh, Maman, Maman," she wept, trying to climb down into the grave. "Did you forgive me?" Ahmed and his father pulled her back.

"Come, Rosalie. Come, my darling, it's over. There's nothing more you can do."

As people began throwing dirt on the coffins, Rosalie lost control of herself completely. The drumming sound of the dirt clumps hitting the coffins beat against her eardrums.

"Papa-a-a-a! Mama-a-an!"

Ahmed fought to control her. Dr. Labans hurried to his side.

"Here, someone hold her," the doctor called out, as he

rubbed the cotton swab on Rosalie's arm and injected the clear fluid into her veins. "Take her, while I help her husband; he's almost as badly off. I'll have to give him something, too."

D'Artois stepped forward and clasped Rosalie to him. "It's all right, my dear. Everything is going to be all right. *I'm* here," he said. "*I'm* here."

Chapter Seventeen

Paris, November 3, 1962

Rosalie sat in a corner of the room on the floor, clasping her knees with her hands, staring down at her arched feet. A lone pink flower lay half wilted, not far from her feet. It was an anthurium, from the bunch she had sent her mother from Guadeloupe, only days before. Bits of the glossy, waxlike blossom lay scattered around her. Its white phallic center lay smashed flat underneath her toes, where she had crushed it in her anguish. Why should a flower live on and continue to be beautiful, when all that was beautiful and worth living for had been taken away from her, had died and gone beneath the cold, black dirt to decompose and rot? Her left foot shot out once more and crushed the remaining part of the petal.

"*Why*, Ahmed? Why Papa and Maman? Why them?" she sobbed.

Ahmed stood looking out the window nearby. "I don't know, Rosalie. I guess no one understands life."

"Do you understand death, Ahmed?"

"No, I don't, but I don't think of it very much."

"You are wrong not to. You should think of nothing else; for it waits and hides behind every corner and snatches you up without the slightest warning. I hate death. It is cruel. What kind of god is a god who can be so cruel? What kind of god is it, who preaches love and kindness, and yet abuses and destroys his own creations?"

Ahmed did not know what to say to her. He stooped down to her level and took her face between his hands. He looked into her eyes. There were dark shadows and deep lines under them. Her face was wan and drawn, her eyes red and swollen from crying. She had lost almost ten pounds since the funeral. Sitting there in her slip, which was sodden at the hem where she had blown her nose on it as she sat and cried, she reminded him of a charity-appeal poster had once seen of an orphan waif.

"Oh, Rosalie, darling, I love you so much. I wish I could make your hurt go away. I would give my life to bring your father back and your mother too, but it doesn't happen that way. You can't exchange one life for another. God does not bargain that way. He gives and takes when he pleases, and we must learn to bear it. Somehow, to go on, you must accept that."

Rosalie stared blankly up at him, and turned her head and spat on the floor on the remnants of the pink flower beside her.

"God! I won't accept a brutal god."

James came to the door just then. They were in the upstairs study, in the room where it had all happened.

"Madame, monsieur, the movers are leaving. Are you sure there's nothing else you wish packed?"

"No, James, just our clothes and personal belongings. Anything we forget, you can bring over later when we are settled."

James nodded. "Yes, monsieur." He backed out of the room, closing the door softly behind him.

"I hate to leave James behind, but I understand why you

want him to stay on here and take care of things. A house like this would suffer greatly if it were left without the care of someone who loves and appreciates it." Ahmed put his arms around Rosalie.

"Do you understand why I cannot stay in this house any longer?" Rosalie said.

"Yes, I do. There are too many memories here, too many joys, and too many sorrows. You'll be better off away from it all. Come, get dressed. The car is ready. Everything is packed and on its way to the apartment, and James will cover everything and close up after we have gone."

Rosalie donned the black pantsuit she had worn on the plane from Guadeloupe and the same silk shirt, and threw her soiled slip into the wastebasket across the room. She whirled around once to take one last look at the room where her father had spent so much of his life. Everything was in perfect order. A dozen white lilies stood magnificently in the tall, dark green vase under her mother's portrait, a seminude her father had always liked but had kept hidden up here in his private den away from the eyes of the unprivileged. Next to it hung a portrait of her father, gleaming in the sunlight. On the commode under it, a lone red rose stood in a matching green vase. Rosalie had put it there that morning when she had placed the lilies for her mother. On the desk, now in perfect order and wiped clean of all traces of the hideous night, was the small portrait of Rosalie as a child, propped up on a stand. Beside it was a lone, white rose in a bud vase. Ahmed had put the flower there for her to find. She looked up at him and smiled a tiny smile, mostly with her eyes, and she went over and took it.

The servants all stood at the foot of the stairs in dress uniform: the chef, the maids, Alphonse, Oscar, James. With tears in their eyes, they bade their young mistress good-bye, and wished the couple happiness in the future.

As she descended the front steps, one step ahead of Ahmed, Rosalie waved to James, now standing alone on the wide step just outside the door. Max hurried to open the door of the old Rolls for them. It was the only thing of her father's she was taking with her; that and Diablo, the leopard, already ensconced in the backseat, his green eyes flashing with anticipation. The car door closed, and Rosalie took one last lingering look as Max turned the car around and they slowly disappeared.

Chapter Eighteen

Paris, February 1963

C.C. Youngblood settled his large frame in the small cane-back chair in the tiny cubicle he called his suite at the Hotel Florentin in Passy. He leaned back, cocking the chair on its two back legs. He had a chewed-up pencil in his hand and a piece of yellow notepaper on the desk in front of him.

Before him he had spread out a pile of newspaper clippings, which he had been accumulating since he had read of the deaths of Monsieur and Madame Armand La Farge on the evening of October 26, 1962. He leafed through them with one hand, while he scraped a match on the wall behind him and lit a cigarette with the other.

Ten major European newspapers bore headlines of the October murders at the La Farge mansion in le Marais. *Soir* and *Figaro* featured special articles on the daughter, Rosalie La Farge Farahet, her fairy-tale life, and conveyed the news that she had closed down the family mansion and had moved to a new residence with her wealthy husband, an oil billionaire in his own right and sole heir to his father's colossal fortune.

C.C. picked up the November copy of *Femme* magazine, which had a photograph on its cover of Rosalie La Farge at the double funeral. He turned to the article and stretched himself out on the bed to read. His eyes scanned the article. He had read it before many times, but he was still hoping to find a clue, any clue, something to lead him to who was behind the mysterious double slaying. He had no particular interest in the murders of a French bigwig and his wife as such—but this had the smell of something connected to General von Witte.

The burglary explanation was weak on the face of it—a burglar skilled enough to make his way in and out unnoticed, and nothing taken? The papers had said that the police had come to the conclusion that something must have scared the burglar away before he had had the time to get into the wife's bedroom. C.C. was not convinced.

His attention focused once again on the clippings before him. He arranged them in a line, side by side: Armand and Jacqueline La Farge murdered October 26th. Retired Inspector Clérot found dead the morning of October 27th. Marcel Belmont, handyman, knockabout, known better as 'Cigot,' and Félicien Saint-Ange Raphael, Negro, found in the Bois de Vincennes, their throats slashed, only feet away from each other. The girl, Michelle Pichon, who had picked C.C. up in Nice, found in her one-room apartment, rotting, seven days after the La Farge slayings. According to the papers, she had been strangled sometime between the morning and afternoon of October 26th. Was this all coincidence?

He picked up another clipping. A short article was circled in red:

OLD MAN DIES ALONE

> The body of a man identified as Léon Piétz, age estimated at 80, was found decomposing in his rooms on October 31. He was discovered by a neighbor, who had reported to the concierge that a horrible odor was coming from the old man's apartment, and

that Piétz had not been seen for days. The concierge used his passkey to enter and discovered the corpse. According to the police report, the old man died of a heart attack sometime late on the evening of 20 October or early dawn of 27 October.

Police reported that the man, until recent years, had earned his livelihood as a tutor. He obviously lived in near-poverty, but they were puzzled upon finding a partially used box of very expensive cigars and half a bottle of hundred-year-old Napoleon brandy.

C.C. glared at the clippings before him. His job now was to find out the connection, if any, between La Farge and Clérot; the connection, if any, between La Farge and Cigot; *and* the connection, if any, between La Farge and the old man. But did all this connect to the duke? Did La Farge, and perhaps the duke, know where von Witte was? Did von Witte kill La Farge? Were La Farge and d'Artois perhaps being used by von Witte to cover up his disappearing act? The duke was La Farge's partner in many ventures, but La Farge had always been the boss.

C.C. picked up a picture accompanying one of the articles in *Femme* magazine, taken at the cemetery, showing d'Artois's arms wrapped around Rosalie La Farge at the gravesite.

Yes, La Farge had been the boss. The one who knew the most, and perhaps had gotten too greedy? Did von Witte have La Farge killed? Was the La Farge fortune based on blackmail? And the daughter Rosalie? Was she in on it too? Or could it have been the duke who killed La Farge in order to take over his place as blackmailer of von Witte?

Then he thought of the CIA. C.C. was being pressured to deliver. The last time he had had contact with the Company he had been told:

"Youngblood, either you break this soon, or consider yourself removed from it. Let the fellows from the KGB take over."

C.C. grinned wolfishly. You want a dog you can call off, Buster, get yourself one of those satchel-assed Harvard pinstripers that JFK likes. But don't give C.C. Youngblood a scent and then try to whistle him away. I'm gonna pull that sucker down at the end of the trail, and that's for sure. And if I feather my nest a little, while I'm doing it, what's wrong with that? One way or another, old von Witte's going to feel these old fangs locking in his throat.

He resumed his study of the clippings.

Chapter Nineteen

Paris, February 26, 1963

Rosalie was at the cemetery with Berthe. At their avenue Montaigne penthouse, in his sumptuous beige-and-blue office, Ahmed sat tensely, chain-smoking and tapping his sleek gold pen on the desk. The door to his office was locked, but the doors to the terrace, overlooking avenue Montaigne, were open. On the desk before him were spread out dozens of newspaper clippings and magazines.

He was wearing a tan camel's-hair sport jacket with leather elbow patches, a light blue sport shirt, and immaculately tailored chocolate brown trousers. He was in his socks, his brown Gucci loafers arranged neatly beside his briefcase under his desk.

Ahmed stood up and went outside to the terrace in his stocking feet. He looked down over the edge as if expecting to see someone. He stood there for a while, contemplating the gray February sky, puffing on a Gitane. Then inside, the phone rang, and he hurried to pick it up; but Hamdu got there first and handed it to him as he approached.

It was the security man downstairs.

"There is a Monsieur Cazelli down here to see you, monsieur. He says you are expecting him."

"Yes, of course I'm expecting him. Isn't Gaston with him?"

"No, monsieur. He's alone. That's why I thought it necessary to call up. From the looks of him, I wasn't sure he was telling the truth. I'm sorry to have disturbed you for nothing, monsieur. I shall send him up directly."

Ahmed rang the buzzer on his desk; the door to the hallway opened almost instantly.

"Hamdu, bring in some refreshments for Monsieur Cazelli, will you? He's on his way up. Oh, Hamdu?"

"Yes, effendi?"

"When my wife gets in will you tell her I will be busy for a while but will be free for the rest of the afternoon, in case she wants to do something later?"

"Very well, effendi. I shall tell her."

"And, oh, Hamdu, don't mention who my visitor is, will you? If she knew, she would wonder, and what I'm after is still too premature to mention."

"I'll take care not to, effendi, but if she asks, who shall I say it is?"

"Business. You know women; mention the word, and they're suddenly not interested."

The servant smiled and nodded and left.

Two or three minutes later, there was a knock on the door. Ahmed slid his feet into his shoes.

"Come in."

The door opened, and Cazelli entered, carrying a battered overnight valise and an even worse-looking gray Samsonite attaché case.

"Ah, Bertrand. Come in, my dear fellow, sit down. I've been waiting for you. It appears Gaston missed you at the Gare St. Lazare, eh? I sent him out to pick you up, but somehow you must have passed him by."

Bertrand looked surprised. "Oh, I'm sorry, monsieur. I didn't know you would send a chauffeur to meet me. I wish I had known. I had a hard time getting a cab, and I thought I'd never get there, the way the driver kept circling the area. I think he was trying to run up his meter. I guess I can't blame him. I must look like an out-of-towner."

Ahmed's eyes narrowed as he contemplated the man before him. It would take a blind man not to figure out right away that Cazelli was Niçois through and through.

"You've been to Paris before, Bertrand, haven't you?"

"Certainly, but just for a day or so at a time, and then I never have come to avenue Montaigne. I mean, what would I be doing here?"

Ahmed nodded. "You have a point, but this time, perhaps I can arrange for you to have a suite across the street at the Georges Cinq, and I'll see to it that Gaston takes you wherever you want to go. Before you leave, check with my man, Hamdu. He'll have made all the arrangements. How does that sound to you?"

"You're too generous, monsieur. I can see why Mademoiselle Rosal—I mean, why Madame Farahet was attracted to you. You must remind her a lot of her father. Although," he laughed, "you *look* different. I never saw two more opposite-looking men."

Ahmed smiled. "I take that as a compliment, Bertrand. I admired my father-in-law tremendously; he was a great man."

"That he was, monsieur. You know my story, how I came to work for him. I—"

A sharp knock on the door interrupted him.

"*Come in,*" Ahmed boomed.

The door opened and a smiling Hamdu entered, pushing a brass cart laden with cheeses and breads and wine and fruit.

"You must be tired, Bertrand, and hungry after your trip." Ahmed's eyes shifted to the man's hands. "There's a lavatory in there." He pointed toward a dark blue door directly across from his desk. "You can wash up a little and join me for lunch," he suggested.

"Oh, certainly, monsieur."

Hamdu ushered Cazelli to the washroom. Ahmed began organizing the clippings on his desk, moving them like game pieces until they assumed a significant order.

"Ah, I feel much better," Bertrand informed Ahmed. "That hot washcloth your man brought me certainly helped. I thought only the Japanese did that. I didn't know your people did it too."

Ahmed ignored the comment and motioned for Cazelli to sit down in the chair in front of his desk. He then stood up, walked over to the door, and locked it.

"I don't want my wife walking in here and finding you," he explained to Cazelli. "She would want to know why we were having this chat."

"And you don't want her to know?"

"No, not yet. You see, I only suspect there is more to La Farge's murder than a simple burglary. I have no proof, and until I do—*if* I do, that is—I don't want to put her through any more grief. You understand?"

"Yes, monsieur. I certainly do, and I give you my word, no one will know I came here, if that's what you want."

"For now, yes, that's what I want. It's safest for you, too."

"I take your meaning. This whole business is beginning to give me chills."

Ahmed looked at his watch. "I don't have much time. My wife will be home soon, and I have promised to spend the afternoon with her. As you know, she has not been feeling too well, ever since . . ." His voice trailed off.

He changed the subject. "So, what is it that you have to tell me? It was important enough to make you come all this way. Your telegram didn't even hint at what it might be, but I know it has to do with the murders."

"That's right. It's something that's been bothering me. After you called a month ago asking about Cigot and Goliath— Don't get me wrong," he said, stopping. "I told you everything I knew *then*. But a week ago, I was visiting with my mother— she's the concierge of a little hotel just off the Quai du Midi.

Well, there we were, the two of us, sitting and talking about Monsieur La Farge, and I mentioned also reading about the murders of Cigot and Goliath. She began to tell me about the night she saw an American go upstairs to one of the rooms, where a waitress named Michelle was staying; how later that night, she had seen Cigot coming downstairs with the American strung over his shoulder. The American was out like a light."

"But how did she know he was an American?"

"Because he had spoken to her in American on his way up earlier. Mémé was sure he was an American, and, believe me, that old woman might not look like much, but she's very astute. If she says he was an American, he was an American."

"I believe you; go on."

"Well, as I was saying, he, that is, Cigot, came downstairs with this man over his shoulder; and when Mémé asked him what was going on, he told her he was doing La Farge's business. What she didn't know was that months before, La Farge had fired Cigot. I mean, I knew, of course, but I rarely discussed the *patron's* doings with her, you know."

Ahmed nodded and motioned with his hand for Cazelli to go on. "Well, when I told her that it couldn't have been Monsieur La Farge's work because he had fired Cigot for stealing, she went wild and started to blame herself for abetting a criminal. Finally, when I got her calmed down, she started remembering things. She had gone upstairs and had looked outside from her window after Cigot had left and had seen another man join him. She said he had looked like a black man, and from the way she described him to me, I'm convinced it was Goliath."

Ahmed's eyes opened wide. "You mean the fellow La Farge let go for beating up that servant girl?"

"That's him! He swore he would get even with La Farge, and he and Cigot used to be thick as thieves when they worked for Monsieur La Farge. But still it doesn't mean they killed him, and in any case, who killed *them?*"

Ahmed stood up and walked over to the door leading to the terrace. He turned suddenly to face Cazelli.

"Any chance of us finding out who the American is, or was? He might be dead. Could your mother describe him, you think?"

"Oh, I can, monsieur! As a matter of fact, that's the real reason I thought it was vital that I see you. You see, I saw this man, exactly the way mother described him, at the cemetery."

"What cemetery?"

"At the *patron*'s funeral. He was there. As you remember, I had come up from Nice for the funeral, and I saw him. I didn't know who he was then, but after Mémé described him to me, I am sure it was him. She said he looked like an Indian, a redskin, and that he wore a baggy brown suit and wore his hair in a cowlick in the front. She said he had a large nose and the blackest eyes you ever saw. I tell you, when she had finished describing him to me, I had the feeling that I knew the guy. And then it came to me later, days later: I remembered that I had seen precisely such a man among the mourners. I remember him because he was the only one present who didn't seem to give a damn about what was going on around him. There was just something strange in the way he kept moving around, shifting from one spot to another, studying everybody's face."

"Couldn't he have been a member of the press?"

"No, the reporters were all long-faced and sad."

Ahmed sighed and ran his fingers through his hair. He went back to his desk and settled himself into the elegant swivel chair.

"Then this man *is* alive, and you may be right. Somehow he may be behind this all. It doesn't make sense, but neither does life. And yet—"

Hamdu interrupted on the intercom to tell him that Rosalie and Berthe had just returned with Max.

Ahmed resumed speaking in a much lower tone.

"I guess, Bertrand, this is our next step: I'm going to get in touch with my private investigator and have him contact you, perhaps tonight or tomorrow. In the meantime, I would like you to check into the Georges Cinq. Call me and let me know if you have any problems, but don't worry, I'm sure the hotel will accommodate you comfortably. I'll have my man contact you as soon as possible, and you can rack your brain some more for any detail you may have forgotten about our man. A mole, a beard—anything might help to trace him. I'm sorry to rush you, but I must not keep my wife waiting—not after her visit to the cemetery. I'm sure she is distraught and needs me."

He stood up and so did Cazelli. Ahmed extended his hand.

"Well, Bertrand, I thank you for coming forward as you have. I am most grateful and shall see to it that you are handsomely rewarded."

Cazelli shook his head and raised his hand in protest. "I couldn't accept anything, monsieur. I'm merely returning a favor to the *patron*."

Ahmed nodded and summoned Hamdu.

"Is everything all set at the Georges Cinq?"

The servant nodded.

"Very well, then, show Monsieur Cazelli down the service elevator, will you?"

The two men shook hands, and Cazelli disappeared down the carpeted hallway with Hamdu. Ahmed put his shoes back on, gathered up the papers from his desk, locked them in his safe, and went to join Rosalie in the sitting room.

"You got something?" C.C. said as Harry Baines walked into the hotel room.

"*There's* a greeting and a half," Harry said, peeling off his raincoat and dropping it with a squelching sound to the floor. "I mean, 'How you doing, old buddy?' or 'Did you get soaked in that lousy rain?'—that's what's usual when one gentleman pays a call on another."

"You got something?" C.C. repeated.

Harry shrugged. "Something, yeah. Whether it's a *something* something, I can't figure yet."

He handed C.C. a crumpled piece of paper. C.C. gave his complete attention to the scribbled words. "Cigot and Goliath had been working for someone *other* than La Farge, huh? Clérot had been working for La Farge. Maître Piétz was a Jew; he had been in a concentration camp, at Camp du Vernet in le Vernet." There were other names scribbled at the bottom of the sheet of paper.

"Son of a bitch!" C.C. exclaimed as he handed the paper back to Harry. "I was right, but why was Clérot working for La Farge? What did he do for him? And who the hell are Cirac and Delacroix? Where do *they* come in?"

Harry cleared his throat. "They were also working for La Farge, and zapped by parties unknown. The fuzz don't know that."

"You mean they were La Farge's spies?" C.C. could see the pieces fitting together. "But who were they supposed to have been spying on? Do you have that?"

Harry shook his head. "No. If we knew that, I have a feeling we would know everything."

C.C. said, scratching his head, "Maybe the old man can lead us to the answer. We have three facts: One: he was a Jew and did time in a concentration camp. That immediately associates him in my mind with Nazism, so maybe von Witte. Two: he spent some time in Railleur-sur-Pelle, and, so could have known the duke. And three: he was found in his apartment, dead-broke by all accounts, but with a partially used box of very expensive Havana cigars and a half-empty bottle of rare Napolean brandy. Each of those two items would have cost the old man most of what he lived on for a month."

"So?"

"So he had to get them from somebody. Somebody rich—and generous; it isn't every rich man who gives away his best brandy and cigars. Now who does that lead us to? La Farge? The duke? La Farge was famous for his cigars and for his booze, but the duke smokes too, and could afford brandy like that."

C.C. and Harry looked at each other.

"You know, C.C.? This is the first time since this damn chase began that I feel we are on to something. We can rule out the senator, for sure, now. He isn't even in the ball park anymore.

C.C. shook his head. "He was always your pigeon. I never thought he was smart enough to play ball in the same court with La Farge and d'Artois."

Harry chuckled. "Well, the Company wanted him investigated. They're convinced now, though, that he was side issue."

"Do you think he's alive?" C.C. asked.

"Who?"

"Von Witte, you asshole. Who do you think, Hitler?"

"Well, I don't know. Sometimes I do; but then again, sometimes I don't. If you ask me, I think he's dead, and either La Farge or the duke did it, and kept his money—all those Nazi bastards had bundles stashed away. D'Artois probably killed him, took what he had, and then La Farge probably found out somehow and went into the blackmail business. He got too demanding, and the duke put him away. The duke has an airtight alibi though, and as a friend of the family for so long, no one suspects him. I mean, even when *I* think about it that way, it's hard to believe. What do you think?"

"Maybe it's my Indian mind but I have a gut feeling that that bastard von Witte is alive and hiding out somewhere. I agree with you on some points, though. For instance, I do feel that d'Artois is the one who holds the key to the whereabouts of the general. The two men disappeared on the same night, one as mysteriously as the other, and I don't buy the story that d'Artois escaped. Also, the fact that the La Farge house in le Marais was the place where they were both seen last makes me believe that La Farge was in on it with them. Perhaps not from the start, but he could have found out somehow and then blackmailed d'Artois or the both of them—and I do mean the *both* of them, since I have this gut feeling that von Witte is alive, maybe holed up in South America like some of the others. La Farge probably got too greedy. Either that or he decided to repent and confess all he knew."

"And von Witte killed him?"

"Yes, he knew that damn house better than anybody else besides the immediate family. Perhaps there's a secret passage to the upstairs which he discovered while he was staying there during the war. It has to be him, but, Goddam it, where the hell is von Witte, and how do we find him?" C.C. Sighed. "I guess from now on we'll just have to watch every move d'Artois makes, even more than before. He has to lead us to the general sooner or later."

"It better be sooner," Harry said. "We're about at the end

of the line on this unless we start hitting pay dirt. Control made that pretty clear."

C.C. looked dourly at the drift of papers on the table in front of him. "Comes a point, maybe," he said after a while, "where Control don't control worth spit any longer, if you take my meaning. I am after this fucker, and I'm going to get him. And if the Crappy Idiot Assholes don't feel like budgeting the project, then it could maybe be private enterprise time."

Chapter Twenty

Paris, February 20, 1963

"What sort of business were you tied up with just now?" Rosalie asked, stirring her long-handled spoon in her *glâce pralinée*. She and Ahmed were seated at the crowded counter at Le Drugstore on the Champs-Elysées.

"Oh . . . business business," Ahmed said vaguely.

Rosalie studied him for a moment. "You know, monsieur," she said, "you may as well start letting me learn something about 'business business.' It's all very well being a princess, but I don't want to spend my life dressing up and being seen at all the best places—at least not only that. I'm Armand La Farge's daughter, after all, and it's in my blood. I don't intend to become a tycoon, don't worry; but I do think I ought to know something about where all the money comes from."

"Fair enough," Ahmed said. "I feel silly sometimes, having to look wise and nod judiciously when some manager or banker goes over a report with me, and then wind up approving it without much of an idea of what's in it. I'm catching on as I go along, but it'll be a help to be able to discuss things with you." There was one piece of business he would not be discussing with Rosalie, though, he told himself—not until it was a good deal more advanced, if ever. If Cazelli and the investigator, Bonnabelle, turned up anything shedding light on the murder of her parents, it would have to be handled very carefully indeed, to avoid bringing back the full intensity of that horror.

"We'll get at it Monday morning," he said. "Meanwhile, we've got all Paris to enjoy for the weekend. What'll we do?"

"A *rainy* weekend," Rosalie said glumly, looking out Le Drugstore's window to where the open-air stamp sellers who congregated at that end of the park were hastily shutting up their booths and protecting their precious collections from a sudden downpour.

"Paris in the rain. No, that doesn't have much of a festive sound to it," Ahmed agreed.

"Let's get away, then," Rosalie urged. "Some place completely unlike Paris."

"Where?"

"Oh . . . Deauville."

"Why Deauville?"

"Can you think of anything less like Paris?"

Ahmed, laughing, went off to telephone Max, instructing him to pack, with Berthe's help, enough things for the weekend, and bring them to Le Drugstore.

The rain had increased in intensity by the time Max appeared in the Rolls, followed by Gaston in Ahmed's Porsche. The luggage was transferred from one car to the other, and Gaston, relieved because he hated to drive sports cars, got into the Rolls with Max, and went home, having first been granted the weekend off by Ahmed and Rosalie.

Through the slippery streets the silver Porsche sped, splashing pedestrians from time to time as it tried to avoid others hurrying to get out of the cold March rain. Ahmed smiled fondly at Rosalie, glancing at her from time to time as he concentrated on getting through the weekend traffic jam.

He was wondering how long it would take for her to come

out of her mourning. God knew *he* was not over it yet, and he would not be until he had exposed the murderer.

"What are you thinking about, Ahmed?" Her voice had startled him, not because of its tone in any way, but because she was asking a question he could not truthfully answer.

"Oh, nothing much. I guess I was just wondering whether you wouldn't have preferred staying home with a good book or the télé. It could be god-awful in Deauville. The rain probably won't let up at all."

"That won't matter; after all, I can hardly remember a time we've gone there when it hasn't rained, or at the very least, threatened to rain. We can always find a book there, if *reading* is what you want to do."

Ahmed's eyes widened, and a faint smile appeared on his lips. "You mean you . . ." He hesitated, "you . . ."

"If it isn't too much to hope for. I've been so terrible to you, so utterly selfish and uncaring. I'm so sorry."

"Oh, *bébé,* don't." He pulled the car over to the side of the road. "Come here, let me hold you." He put his arms around her and kissed her on the tip of her nose.

"Oh, Rosalie, darling, if only you knew how much I've been waiting for this, for you to tell me you needed me and wanted me to make love to you again."

She moaned softly and wrapped her arms around his neck. "Oh, Ahmed." She began to cry, softly. "I've missed you. I've missed the love we shared."

Cars were passing them by, and a man pulled up alongside them to see if they needed help.

"No, monsieur, we are merely lost. Could you tell us where we might find a nice little inn around here?"

The man pursed his lips and removed his cap when he saw Rosalie. "Ah, let me see. Yes, as a matter of fact, there's a little place just outside Mantes, about fifteen kilometers or so from here. I am a salesman. I know the place quite well. I have stayed there many times."

The man leaned out of his car slightly, trying to get a better look at Rosalie in the Porsche. From the amused look on the man's face, Ahmed could tell the man did not buy his story about being lost, nor did he think they were married.

They thanked the man and without a word to each other they turned off the main road, taking the small side road the man had recommended. Deauville would have to wait for another weekend.

Two days later, late on Sunday evening, they returned to the penthouse, Ahmed relaxed and happy, Rosalie radiant and smiling. The household staff did not have to be told the weekend had been a booming success; they did not know, however, that monsieur and madame had never got to Deauville. The following day, when Max inquired about the mileage on the car, Ahmed winked and said, "We took the train. It was more romantic."

Max shrugged his shoulders and shook his head in disbelief. Romantic? The train, which both madame and monsieur had often said was the worst means of transportation, vowing never to set foot in the damn things? Max decided he would never understand the rich.

Somewhat to Ahmed's relief, Rosalie did not insist on starting her tutoring in "business business" on Monday. Cazelli or Bonnabelle would surely be calling in, and it would be awkward discussing things with them with Rosalie in the room. If she were to take an active part in the running of the La Farge empire, he would have to devise a clandestine way of communicating with his agents.

On entering the office, he stopped short. It looked much the same as when he had left it Friday afternoon . . . but not completely so. Surely the pile of papers had been on the left side of the desk; not the right? And the portrait of Rosalie that hung concealing the wall safe—he remembered that it had been slightly askew and had made a mental note to straighten it. He had not done so Friday; yet it was perfectly straight now. He opened the desk drawers and inspected them, detecting subtle signs of disarrangement.

He sat in the chair and stared thoughtfully out the window. Someone had been searching the office during his absence; that was almost certain. But who and why?

No one but Hamdu was ever allowed in the office when he

was not there; only Hamdu and, of course, Rosalie, knew the combination of the safe. Hamdu belonged to him and had been with him since he was a boy. A Sudanese, he was utterly loyal, hardly ever leaving the establishment and certainly not driven by any craving for wealth. Ahmed knew it was not Hamdu who had gone through his desk. Nevertheless, he checked with the servant to find out if, perhaps while dusting, he had disarranged the portrait. Hamdu told him that he had not dusted the painting, but did say that he had misplaced the key to the office and had not found it until Sunday night. He could not understand how he had come to misplace it, since, along with all the other keys to the house, he had had it on the master key ring on his belt. Ahmed pretended to dismiss the whole thing and reassured Hamdu that everything was all right, but in reality was not at all satisfied. He decided to lay a trap for the culprit. Yusif? Berthe? Gaston? Max? Emilienne, the maid? He decided to activate the alarm connected to the safe and wait until someone unsuspectingly tried it again.

Across the street from the penthouse, at the café on the corner of avenue Montaigne and rue François Premier, C.C. was staking out the penthouse. He sipped his coffee and watched the building. A few tables away a small man with a gray suit and horned-rimmed glasses was sitting with another man, an awkwardly dressed, big, burly type, who looked like an out-of-towner. They were watching C.C. After a while, C.C. got up and went to the pay phone. He called Harry and told him he had a feeling he was being tailed and described the two men to him. C.C. paid for his drinks and left, heading toward the Champs-Elysées. The two men came out of the café; one headed in the opposite direction, toward the Seine, and the other crossed over to the other sidewalk, following C.C.

Moments later, Ahmed, in his office, got a call from Cazelli: "We have spotted the man in the café, and Bonnabelle is following him."

Ahmed had no choice but to wait for Bonnabelle to contact him. Who is this American? he wondered. What does he have to do with all of this?

C.C. turned right onto rue Balzac and hurried up the street, hugging the buildings with his body. He could still see the man following him. He continued on, coming to the rue Lord Byron and then to rue Chateaubriand. Harry's hotel was there, but he did not want the man to see him go in. He came upon some iron gates on the right and quickly ducked through, ran down the steps and through the long courtyard which separated two large old buildings. He hugged the trunks of the old trees planted every eight feet or so and dashed down the steps at the other end onto rue Washington and around the corner into a café. He bought a cup of coffee, drank it down, and hurried back to Harry's hotel.

Harry was waiting for him when he got there.

"Who the hell do you think is after me? The same guys who kidnapped me that time in Nice?"

"You know, C.C., I still haven't been able to figure out the *why* much less the who."

"Goddamit, Harry, sometimes you talk like an old woman. The why and the who; I don't know why, or who is after me, but the biggest mystery of all is why once they had me—and they *had* me—they didn't kill me. If somebody thought I was onto them and somehow, let's say, by some fluke of fate, they found out who I was, and what I was after, then why didn't they kill me?"

"I don't know. You said you were drugged. Maybe whoever set it up felt safe enough to let you go. Maybe he was hoping you would for some reason kill La Farge, or that he could arrange it to look like you did. Hell, I don't know, C.C. I can't figure it out."

"You know, you got a point. Those two creeps following me today were probably the same guys who beat me up on the beach. I remember when I was coming to, I heard voices. I got a faint glimpse of the man in the chauffeur's uniform, and then I saw a fuzzy outline of two other men. One was big and burly, the other slighter. I don't know. Could be."

The shrill ringing of the beige telephone on the desk startled Ahmed, and he jumped to his feet and rushed to pick it up.

"Allô?"

It was Bonnabelle. "I think I have found where the American is staying, monsieur. He gave me the slip, but I tracked him down. I saw him go into a hotel on rue Chateaubriand, and he has been there for nearly two hours now. What should I do now, monsieur?"

"Find out his name, and whatever else you can about him, but don't let anyone suspect you are snooping. We don't want to tip him off. Hello? Hamdu?"

"Yes, monsieur?"

"Bonnabelle, is that you?"

"Yes, monsieur."

"Hm, that's funny. I heard a strange clicking sound on the phone. Where are you calling from?"

"From down the street, monsieur. From a pay phone in a café."

"It must have been the operator. Very well, find out the man's name, and report back to me later with whatever you have."

Ahmed locked up his office and trudged down the carpeted hallway past the living room and library, past the dining room and study, to Rosalie's studio. He peeked around the corner at her. She was seated on a high stool, working on a canvas: a basket of flowers.

"Hey, that's pretty good for a beginner." He leaned down and kissed her neck affectionately.

"Pretty damn good, you mean."

Ahmed laughed, and Rosalie joined in. It was the first time she had laughed out loud since . . . She stopped almost at once, a look of guilt in her eyes, as if laughing were a mortal sin. He understood and said nothing.

"Do you think it will ever stop raining, Ahmed? It's such a bleak day; one minute it's pouring, and the next it's cold and windy."

He walked over to the huge glass doors leading to the terrace. It was only five o'clock, and yet it looked almost like nighttime. Evening had come suddenly, prematurely, with heavy dew and dark gray clouds.

A flash of lightning lit up the sky, and Ahmed backed away from the glass doors. The small trees on the terrace outside were swaying madly as the wind rose. A sudden gust of wind forced the doors open and knocked over a small plant on the terrace. Ahmed wrapped his smoking jacket tightly around him and pulled the doors shut.

The buildings across the street were already lit for the night, their lights not seeming bright enough in the half-light of the late afternoon.

"Are you almost finished?" Ahmed asked.

Rosalie nodded. "For now." She removed her blue smock and rested the palette on the table beside her. "Just let me clean my brushes, and I'll be with you."

"Here let me." He dipped the brushes, one by one, into the yellowish turpentine. "Pfui! I hate that smell. I could never become an artist, just because of that."

"Tsk. Tsk. The talent the world is missing. What a pity. You also don't like the smell of oil or gasoline for that matter; but that doesn't stop you from getting rich on it and putting it in your sports car."

"Hm, I never thought of it that way. You have a point there."

"I always do."

"Have a point?"

"Sure."

"You know, you're right. You have more than one point at that." He playfully nibbled at her nipples, showing through the crepe blouse. "I can plainly see *two* points you have right now."

She hit him playfully with a thick new brush. "Oh, you—you—"

"Horny bastard?"

She collapsed laughing in his arms, and her legs gave way beneath her as she sighed his name. "Not here. I—someone might . . ." But she did not resist.

As he lowered her to the floor, he whispered her name and fumbled for the knot at the front of her blouse. He could feel her body trembling, her breasts quivering beneath his touch. A flash of lightning lit up the room and illuminated the rosy tips of her breasts, hard and pointed. She clung wildly to him, her body rising and falling on the soft carpet beneath them. His hands untied the laces of her black pants and slid them down along her arching hips and thighs. He threw them across the room, and they landed on some canvases stacked in a pile by her easel.

Rosalie's honey blond hair was spread wildly in silken disarray over her breasts and shoulders and part of her stomach. Like a sea nymph, she lay before Ahmed, causing him to harden even more at the sight. He caressed her thighs, her hips. He cupped her breasts in his palms, hot and moist from excitement, and pressed them gently together, flicking his tongue from one pointed nipple to the other. He pulled them closer together and took them both in his mouth at once. He bit gently, running his teeth up and down the tiny points.

Rosalie moaned, "Oh God, Ahmed, stop it. I can't stand it any longer. I want you *now*."

"Yes. Now."

He knelt beside her, ripping off his clothes, then stood up to let his trousers slide down to his feet. He stood tall and big, bursting with sensuality, like a dragon about to devour what was his. He lowered himself on top of her and took her, while outside the thunder roared and the lightning flashed, illuminating their writhing bodies against the backdrop of the carpeted floor, a painting come alive in the studio.

"*Chambre numero quinze, s'il vous plaît,*" C.C. said into the phone.

"Hold on, monsieur, I will ring Monsieur Block's room."

Block was the name under which Harry Baines was registered.

"Allô? Monsieur?" It was the concierge.

"Yes?"

"There is no reply, monsieur. Monsieur Block must have gone out."

"Did he leave a message for Monsieur Barnes?"

"Non, monsieur. There is nothing in his mailbox, either, and his key is gone, so he must have gone out without anybody noticing."

C.C. did not like the sound of it. It wasn't like Harry to go out without calling when they were supposed to meet.

C.C. took the Métro to the Champs-Elysées and walked the rest of the way in the rain. It was still pouring. As he approached the hotel, he saw a figure in a navy blue trench coat dart through the iron gates, and down the same alleyway C.C. had ducked into earlier that afternoon. Guy's in a real hurry, he thought, as he watched the tall, cloaked figure disappear down the steps and out the gate onto the other street.

Something told C.C. to hurry, that old gut feeling he always had whenever something was wrong. He kept thinking of the two men who had been following him earlier; but he had lost them both, he was sure. Nevertheless, the fact that Harry went out without calling him worried him. Harry could have gone out for cigarettes, but that was only a hope.

C.C. was dripping wet by the time he ducked into the hotel lobby. There was no one in sight. A sign next to the bell on the counter read SONNEZ POUR LE CONCIERGE.

He did not waste any time; he rushed up the stairs to room fifteen, picked the lock and went in. The room was dark. He groped for the light switch on the wall by the door. At once the room was filled with light. The room was empty. He opened the closets and headed for the bathroom.

There was a terrible odor in the room.

"Damn bastard didn't flush his toilet."

He turned on the bathroom light, and his mouth dropped open. Behind the separation wall between the sink and the water closet, he could see Harry, sitting on the toilet, hunched over, naked, with a knife in his back. The stench coming from the toilet, a mixture of blood and excrement, was nauseating. He plucked a couple of sheets of the brown paper from the box on the toilet tank and, using it to cover his fingerprints, he pulled the chain. The rush of water startled him in the otherwise still room. He went to the front door and locked it, then returned to the bathroom.

Harry's throat had been slashed, and the knife stuck in his back. A pool of dark, brownish red blood lay at his feet.

Looking at the full tub, C.C. guessed that Harry was about to take a bath when he got the urge and, with the water running, had not heard anyone come in.

The man he had seen running outside came to his mind. It was probably the killer. The water was still very warm in the tub. The faucet was dripping.

C.C. surveyed the room once more and left, quietly locking the door behind him.

The hallway lights were dim; the hall was empty as he made his way down the stairs. He checked around the corner as he got to the foot of the stairs and saw that the concierge still had not reappeared. He tiptoed across the carpeted lobby. He opened the door and slipped out into the dark cloak of the Paris night.

He walked down the street, hugging the buildings and doorways with his body for shelter from the pounding rain, then turned onto the Champs-Elysées. He stopped in at a café and went to the pay phone. He dropped a jeton into the phone and dialed. The phone buzzed on the other end, and then was picked up.

"Hello? Removals? C.C. Youngblood here. It's Harry Baines. He's at the Mayflower Hotel, rue Chateaubriand, room fifteen. It's messy." He hung up the receiver and slipped out of the café into the rain. He took the Métro headed for avenue Montaigne, planning to stake out the penthouse.

> In the doorway of a small grocery store, closed for the night, the body of a private investigator, Marcel Bonnabelle, was found on rue Washington in the VIIIth Arrondissement. Police report Bonnabelle was stabbed in the brain with a fine-pointed needle of some kind sometime between the hours of 7 and 8 last night. No clues to the culprit are reported, but an investigation is being made to find out who, if anyone, the victim might have been working for when the murder took place.

• • •

Cazelli almost choked on his brioche as he read the words. A small photograph of Bonnabelle was in the upper right-hand corner of the page, at the head of the article.

"My God!"

His mind raced to the night before, when he and Bonnabelle had parted ways in front of the café and he had gone back to his hotel to wait further instructions from Monsieur Ahmed.

He had been instructed not to call at the penthouse unless absolutely necessary, but this news certainly seemed to make it necessary! Cazelli pushed his breakfast aside and hurried to get dressed.

Something was going on. From the look of things, his own life might be in danger at this point. Who was behind all these murders? Why didn't Monsieur Ahmed go to the police? Why did he want to handle it himself?

Cazelli was dressed and out of the hotel in no time. It was nine-thirty, according to his watch, and he hoped everyone at the penthouse would be awake by now.

He nodded to Néstor, the security man, who recognized him from before, and the two men took the service elevator to the penthouse.

"Are you sure you are expected this early? I was not informed by monsieur that he was expecting any company this morning."

Cazelli gave him an exasperated look. "I'm expected."

The elevator came to a stop with a sudden jerk, and the door slid back.

Néstor rang the doorbell and stood waiting with Cazelli. After a few moments, the door opened, and Hamdu appeared, fresh as a clean-scrubbed apple, dressed in a crisp white uniform and smelling of hair pomade and after-shave lotion. His face was composed as always.

"Yes?" He recognized Cazelli at once. "Ah, Monsieur Cazelli. Come in. What can I do for you?"

Cazelli spoke casually. "I have to speak to Monsieur Farahet. I must talk to him about something. About the estate.

There's something he should know that I forgot to mention the last time I was here. It's important."

Néstor shifted his weight from one leg to the other and addressed Hamdu. "Do I wait?"

Hamdu shook his head. He motioned for Cazelli to follow him. He led the way to the servants' sitting room and handed Cazelli some magazines.

"The prince is not yet awake. He and madame had a late night and asked not to be disturbed before ten. You may wait here. When he rings for his breakfast, I will give him your message."

Cazelli nodded and picked up a magazine.

"Can I bring you some coffee or tea?"

Cazelli shook his head. "I've already had breakfast, thanks."

Hamdu left and went back into the kitchen, where he had been setting up the breakfast cart for Rosalie and Ahmed.

The little gold *réveil* on Ahmed's night table was ringing. He turned over drowsily and plunked a hand down on the small clock.

"Aa-a-ah, time to get up already?"

He pushed the little button in back of the clock and rolled over to snuggle closer to Rosalie.

The gentle morning light seeping through tiny gaps between the draperies bathed her nude shoulders. She lay on her side, sound asleep, undisturbed by the loud ringing of the alarm. Her knees were pulled up to her breasts, and her hands were tucked under her pillow. Her hair was tousled and tangled from their wild lovemaking the night before. Her breathing was relaxed and even, like a sleeping baby's. Ahmed smiled to himself, remembering the heights of their passion the night before. Rosalie was back. She had suffered and grieved and sobbed out her soul; she had cursed and screamed and sometimes even blasphemed; and she had been unable to love or be loved. But she was back now to stay, and he would heal her wounds with his love, and one day she would forget the anger and the hurt.

She turned over in her sleep and snuggled up closer to him. Her breasts, damp and dewy from the warmth of their two bodies clamped so closely together, pressed lightly against his chest. Her rosebud nipples fluttered softly over his skin.

He nibbled her ear playfully and stuck the tip of his tongue in it. "Wake up, sleepyhead. It's time to get up. You've had enough beauty sleep for one night."

She made a little whimpering sound and stretched herself out against his own outstretched body.

"Wake up. I'm starved after last night."

She opened one eye and looked up at him. "Huh? What did you say?"

"I said I'm starved, and I'd like you to get up and put on some clothes and join me for breakfast."

She smiled up at him, her green eyes slanting in a feline manner.

"Hm, sounds good. Especially since we skipped dinner last night. The way you picked me up and carried me off to bed last night, stark naked, I thought you had gone raving mad. We can't just prance around in the hallways without a stitch on. I mean, what will the servants think?"

"Only what they already know—that I'm crazy about my wife, stark naked crazy."

Rosalie laughed and stuffed her pillow in Ahmed's face.

He retaliated by getting up to pull back the drapes. He stretched himself before the door and opened back both halves. It was a beautiful sunny morning. He stepped out onto the terrace and did a few knee bends and one-handed push-ups for Rosalie's benefit.

She came to the door, wrapped in the sheet. "Come on back inside, you idiot, before somebody sees you and calls the police."

He made a face at her and flipped over to stand on his hands. "Make way, I'm coming in."

The sight of her naked husband walking on his hands was hilarious. "You need a nose lift," she laughed pointing to his groin.

He somersaulted upright, grabbed Rosalie, and ran into the shower with her in his arms.

They showered together—and dried each other with a giant

yellow bath towel with a map of Martinique on it. She had bought it for him as a joke, but he insisted he liked it better than all the other towels in the house. When they had finished pampering themselves, they adjourned to the small sitting room off their bedroom where they normally had breakfast together every morning.

Ahmed rang for Hamdu, and like a genie, Hamdu appeared, pushing his cart laden with fresh coconuts cut in half, croissants, fresh orange marmalade prepared by himself, butter pats in the shape of seashells displayed in a silver bowl with ice, and a silver pot of steaming black coffee.

"Good morning, madame, monsieur. It is a beautiful morning this morning. The first signs of spring are outside."

"Good morning, Hamdu."

"Coconuts! My God, where did you get fresh coconuts this time of year?"

"Chez Fauchon, madame."

Ahmed laughed. "I'll bet that for the price of those two coconuts we could get on a plane and go to Guadeloupe or Martinique and pick our own."

The mention of Guadeloupe upset Rosalie. Ahmed noted at once her changed expression. But sooner or later the name had to come up. She could not hide forever from everything which might cause her to remember.

Rosalie took the small white rose from the bud vase on the breakfast cart and brought it to her lips. She sniffed it delicately and replaced it.

Ahmed held her chair for her and sent Hamdu away. He sat down across from her and took her hands in his. He bent and kissed her fingertips. "You know, I'm the luckiest man in the world, having you."

He lifted her chin with his hand and looked searchingly into her sea green eyes. He could almost feel himself drowning in their depths.

"You have always been beautiful to me," he said, "every night and every day since I first set eyes on you. But sometimes you seem to radiate life and love and everything beautiful, and at those times I look at you and capture you in my mind—how you look, how you are dressed—so that even when I'm old and gray, I can look into your eyes and see you as I see you now."

Rosalie's lips quivered, and she smiled. Her eyes brimmed over with tears, tears of happiness, and they streamed down her cheeks and fell on her yellow robe.

The buzzer by the bed interrupted them. Ahmed excused himself to pick it up.

It was Hamdu. "Monsieur Cazelli has been waiting for half an hour in the servants' sitting room, monsieur. I tried to motion to you when I brought your breakfast, but monsieur's mind was elsewhere."

"What?" Ahmed laughed. "You are observant, my dear fellow, aren't you? Well, I will be another twenty minutes or so. I have to leave shortly for Versailles. Tell the gentleman to wait for me downstairs. I'll be down shortly. Oh, Hamdu? Tell Max, no need to bring out the Rolls; I'll take the Porsche. It's already parked out front."

"Who was it, anyone I know?" Rosalie asked.

"Sure, it was Hamdu."

"Not him, you goof. I mean, the man you asked to wait."

"Oh, just someone who has an old gull-wing Mercedes I want to buy. I'm going to go and have a look at it. It's in the suburbs."

He kissed her on the top of her head and pulled out the long hairpin she had holding up her hair. It tumbled down, covering her back and shoulders like a cape.

"Hm, you look wilder this way, less innocent," Ahmed said.

Rosalie raised her lips to meet his.

"I must hurry," he said, "I can't keep the poor fellow waiting much longer. He's been here since nine-thirty, according to Hamdu."

Rosalie poured herself another cup of coffee and reached for the folded newspaper on the far end of the cart.

"Aren't you going to even glance at your paper?"

"Don't have the time. I'll glance through it when I get back." He was heading for the dressing room. "Say! Why don't we meet for lunch? I'll be busy most of the morning, but then I can meet you someplace casual. I don't feel like getting particularly dressed up today."

"Okay. Where is your meeting after you get back from looking at the car?"

"St. Germain."

"Great. Then I'll meet you at the Brasserie Lipp. It's been a while since we've been there."

"Good idea. I'll meet you there, say at one-thirty? I won't be late, I promise."

Ahmed rang Hamdu to ask him to bring him his briefcase from his office. He blew Rosalie a kiss and disappeared into the hallway.

Rosalie stretched herself happily in her chair and picked up the folded newspaper. Hamdu came in and removed the cart, leaving the coffeepot and her cup and saucer behind. She scanned the headlines and clucked her tongue as she came upon the story of the murdered private detective. Downstairs Ahmed was getting into his car. Cazelli was talking to him rapidly, his hands flailing wildly in his excitement.

"I tell you, it's all over the papers. Bonnabelle's been murdered. I'm probably next. Who is behind this, Monsieur Ahmed? Why don't we go to the police?"

"Get in, Cazelli; we'll stop at a newsstand and pick up a paper. After that, we'll see; perhaps you're right. We should inform the police about this American."

Ahmed's slender fingers inserted the key and turned the ignition.

There was a shocking, ear-shattering blast, as the car exploded and burst immediately into flames.

Upstairs, a cup shattered on the floor, and coffee splashed in a sudden stain on the rug as Rosalie jumped to her feet and ran out onto the terrace.

She looked out over the edge and saw her husband's car in flames and people running toward it.

"No-o-o-o-o-o! No-o-o-o-o-o-o-o!"

There were footsteps running toward her, hands holding her back, as she tried to throw herself onto the flaming wreckage below. Her scream ripped through the morning, and people below looked up and gasped as they beheld the struggle above them.

The screeching of the sirens pierced her eardrums, as the *tan-teen-tan-teen* sound grew closer and closer to avenue Montaigne. The fire department came and put the fire out, and amidst the choking clouds of smoke, the remains of two charred bodies could be seen: one ripped to pieces, with arms and legs strewn upon the sidewalk; the other, welded to the steering wheel, headless.

A curious crowd looked on as police and ambulance attendants worked rapidly to remove the mutilated remnants of the two victims from the debris of the car.

Then the fire trucks were preparing to leave. It was over: swift, complete, final. Amidst the mass of squirming, retching people, C.C. Youngblood slapped his fist down into the palm of his other hand and kicked the sidewalk violently.

"Shit!"

Chapter Twenty-one

New York, February 1965

Rosalie made her way through the tight knot of men and women hovering between the entrance and the rear dining room of P.J. Clarke's. The night was young, the crowd at the bar thick and rowdy. The crowd was mostly men, all on the prowl. The women are attractive enough, Rosalie thought, except for a shriveled apple here and there, and a prune or two. Rosalie gave a brief, bitter smile; she wished she could be more generous in the way she looked at people these days. She glanced quickly around her, taking in the crowd, recognizing many familiar faces. Phillippe Marchand, the curly-haired French film producer, was there. He recognized her and beckoned wildly for her to join him. The stringy-haired blond with him looked ill at ease. Rosalie had no intention of joining them. The girl would be put off, she could tell. She smiled reassuringly at the young woman. Poor fresh-faced child, she thought. I wonder what Phillippe promised her to merit the puppy devotion shining in her eyes? Probably a small part in his latest movie, *A Forever*

Affair. She waved and blew Phillippe a kiss as she passed by. She was stopped by Terence Garner, London's number-one playboy, and his girl, Julie, another stringy-haired blond with a chest like a boy's. A real fun couple, those two, she thought. The B. and B. couple, Ahmed used to call them—Bitch and Booze.

Memories of Ahmed came pouring into Rosalie's head. Ahmed, my darling, how I still miss you! It's maddening, after all this time, almost two years. But sometimes it feels like only yesterday that you died and left me. Oh God, why did you do it?

A tear rolled down her cheek. She caught a quick glimpse of herself in the mirror, and the wide brim of her brown felt hat reminded her of the one she wore that horrible March day when Ahmed's charred remains were laid to rest beneath the hard, cold earth.

Somehow, she managed to escape the strange duo and was shown to her usual table in the back room. Frankie murmured his pleasure at seeing her again.

It had been nearly six months since she had last been to New York, and she felt ill at ease among all these smiling, plastic faces.

My God, she thought, why did I come?

Solange, an old school friend, had given a party for Rosalie in her father's suite at the Pierre and had tried, for what seemed like the hundredth time since Ahmed's death, to pair her off. Martin Finkelstop or Finklestern or was it Finkeldorf was a nice fellow, but she just did not go for Ringo Starr look-alikes with gangster connections. Nor had she felt any better the previous week in Los Angeles when Solange, dear Solange, had tried to get her interested in "Mr. Surf and Turf of Malibu Beach."

That one had so much yellow hair down his back, she thought, it would be like going out with an afghan. He had muscles, God knows, from the surf, but on the turf, he had nothing between the ears.

Frankie pulled out Rosalie's chair for her and helped her with her coat. "What can I bring you to drink?"

"A vodka on the rocks, please."

"Certainly, Mrs. Farahet." He hesitated for a moment.

"Will you be dining alone?" He pointed to he empty chair across from her.

She nodded her head yes, and he departed at once to order her drink.

Rosalie lit a long, thin Cuban cigar, and leaned back, folding her arms on her lap, puffing on the cigar, intent on her thoughts.

Frankie brought her her drink, and she ordered dinner.

"Steak Diane, spinach salad, and espresso . . . and the pepper mill, Frankie. You know I like a lot of pepper on my steak Diane.".

"Of course." Frankie wrote it all down and gave the order slip to the waiter serving that table.

Rosalie sipped the ice-cold Smirnoff and relished the velvety smoothness as it went down her throat. There were two women seated at a small table directly across the room from her. She noticed them because she had felt their eyes fix on her from the moment she had sat down. She had even glared in their direction in the hope that this would discourage their ardent curiosity.

One was dressed in a gray pinstripe suit, the other in skin-tight jeans and a light blue cashmere sweater. The pinstriper's hair was bobbed short and parted on the left like a man's. Her face was void of makeup, and her hands and nails bore little resemblance to those of a woman's.

Transvestite? Bulldyke? Whichever it is, Rosalie told herself sourly, it's certainly a persistent bitch. The way its eyes rove, and the way it licks its fat lips as if about to pounce.

Charles Mansfield of Mansfield Productions came in with a small, rowdy group. He spotted Rosalie and sauntered over to her table. "Are you alone?" he asked.

"Are *you*, Charles?" Rosalie's tone was almost rough.

He grinned sheepishly. "Naw, I'm with a few of the guys." He leaned forward and whispered, "You know how it is, baby. Wine them, dine them, make them enjoy; then, wup, bag them into the tightest little contract you've ever seen." He winked knowingly at her. "Know what I mean? Say, how about joining us for a drink? It's been a long time."

She threw him a cold look. ''Charles, why don't you be a good boy and go on back to your reporter friends? You didn't think I'd fall for that 'taking out the members of the cast' line, did you? I can spot a reporter ten miles off, even *under* his rock.''

He threw up his arms in dismay and opened his mouth to speak.

Rosalie forestalked him. ''Tell me, Mansfield, how much did those buzzards offer you for a private interview with the poor little rich widow? A rock for your wife's eleventh finger, or the money to produce that new play I heard you bought the rights to?''

Mansfield looked dumbfounded. Even after all the years he had known her father, he had still not learned to handle the La Farge straightforwardness.

He shrugged and forced a tiny smile. ''I'm sorry, Rosalie. I should've known better. I won't bother you again, and I *was* sorry to hear about Ahmed's death, believe me.''

''I believe you, Charles; only I wish you and your reporter friends would drop the subject once and for all. I will *not* give anyone an interview; for I have nothing to say to the public. Ahmed was *my* husband, and only I grieve for him.'' She added solemnly, ''He was no damn playboy Arab, Charles. He was just a man. A very private man.''

Mansfield nodded, and took her hand in his. He shook it clumsily. ''I understand. I think it finally just sank in, and I promise I won't bother you anymore, Rosalie.''

''Thanks, Charles. Lots of luck from here on, you deserve it. You know something, Mansfield? I think your tailor should be shot for malpractice, and I think your shaving lotion smells like skunk spray, but''—she squeezed his hand and patted the top of it with her other one—''you have one good quality. You are a fairly decent human being; and it doesn't take Scotland Yard to tell that you're in a spot. Tell you what, you come to my place in Malibu next week and bring the script with you. If I like it, I'll put up the money. Fifty-fifty, all the way, okay?''

The man could hardly believe his ears. ''But I thought you—''

"I know, Charles. Your problem is that you think too much at the wrong times and about the wrong things. Let's just say I'll never forget how you tried to help me survive after Ahmed's death. The day you offered me the starring role in that silly film of yours. I still can't believe it was a success. More power to you. That you could take somebody's mistake, or insanity, for that matter, and turn it into a box-office smash—"

"But, you turned me down cold."

"Yes, I did. I'm not interested in a career, Charles. You knew that, but I appreciated your offering me the part. You *tried*, and that's what counts."

He held the lighter for her as she lit another cigar.

"I feel I owe you something, Charles. I want to help you if I . . . can."

Rosalie's voice had cracked, and her fingers trembled as they brought the slender cigar to her lips.

Across the room a young couple were gazing tenderly into each other's eyes. The scene evoked memories.

"Do me a favor, Charles, will you? Tell Frankie I had to leave. I . . ." She jammed the cigar case and lighter into her purse and stood up.

The waiter arrived just then with her steak Diane and a huge wooden pepper mill. She laid a fifty-dollar bill on the table and left by the side entrance, leaving a misty-eyed Charles to explain to the baffled waiter.

She walked the few steps to the corner of Fifty-fifth Street and Third Avenue and hailed a cab. The driver of a Checker saw her, cut across the avenue in front of two other cars and pulled up in front of her. His maneuver caused a red Chevrolet almost to collide with a gray Mercedes. The avenue came alive as enraged drivers yelled and screamed and honked at the cab.

She gave the driver her address: "Sixty-third and Fifth, please, and go the long way, will you? Go to Sixth Avenue and take the Park Drive to Seventy-second Street and then down Fifth. You can drop me off on the south corner."

The cab driver checked her out in his rearview mirror as she got in; her yellow sweater and brown leather slacks fit like a second skin.

"Whatever you say, lady. It's your dough."

He kept looking at her slyly in the mirror, pretending to be observing the traffic behind. He was young, in his late twenties, with long blond hair and more than a trace of city dirt on his rugged face.

Fresh kid, Rosalie thought, as she leaned back against the ragged black imitation-leather seat. She fumbled in her purse and withdrew her cigar case and lighter. There was a small sign taped on the back of the front seat: "Please don't smoke cigarettes, they burn me." She smiled a sly little smile as she prepared to light up.

"Mind if I smoke a cigar? I noticed your sign doesn't say anything about pipes or cigars."

She could see the surprised look on his face in the mirror and could hardly keep from laughing at his wide-eyed reflection.

"Cigars? Hey, no, miss. I don't mind, but do you *always* smoke cigars?"

"No. I took them up six months ago. Before that I smoked a pipe." She was joking.

For the second time he looked aghast. The light turned green and they sped across Third Avenue and headed toward Lexington. Rosalie continued to puff away on her cigar. She rolled down the window. The cold Manhattan air stung her face like a jet of cold water. They stopped for a light and waited, as people hurried across the street, some fighting for cabs to get out of the rain.

It had just begun to drizzle, and Rosalie chuckled at the scene taking place ahead of them. Two couples had seen and hailed the same cab. Suddenly, a very chic, innocuous umbrella had turned into a lance, and some poor *type* from Keokuk, Iowa, or God knew where, was getting stabbed by some black dude, holding the arm of his mama, who was bedecked in tight rhinestone pants and a hot pink rabbit fur jacket. The other woman just stood and watched. Rosalie's cabby turned to look at her.

"I'm betting on the spade," he said. "What do you think?"

"I don't know. The other one looks pretty mad to me."

The light changed again, and the frustrated cabby drove off, leaving the enraged foursome to continue their fight on their own.

"The fella was right," the cabby commented. "I woulda done the same thing. I tell ya, miss, people are crazy in Manhattan. They go wild at the drop of a hat."

"Oh? Is it the weather, or the food they eat?"

He looked at her questioningly in the mirror. "You're not from here, are you?"

"No, I'm not."

"Where you from? I detect a slight accent."

"Slight? You're being kind. Either that, or deaf, my friend. I'm French, but you can say I'm from everywhere, really, or nowhere, depending on how you look at things in life. You know? Do you see a glass half full or half empty? A person half alive or half dead?" The word *dead* shot into the night like a bullet. "I," she continued, "see the glass half full, but on the other hand I see myself as half dead. I guess that's because I *am* half dead, and *he* is all dead."

"I beg your pardon, miss. Who's dead?"

"My husband. Killed, murdered, burned to death in an explosion in the prime of his life." Her eyes misted and filled with hot, angry tears.

They were still in the park, nearing the Seventy-second Street exit onto Fifth Avenue.

"Let me off here, my friend. I feel like walking the rest. The fresh air will do me good."

"But you could get yourself mugged, maybe even killed, alone in the park at this hour. Let me take you home, lady. Believe me, this ain't the Champs-Elysées."

She shook her head. "No! Let me off right *here*, please."

The taxicab lurched a little as the driver stepped on the brakes and pulled up alongside the curb.

"Okay, lady, but I sure hope you were born lucky."

Rosalie gathered up her coat and purse and handed him a ten-dollar bill.

"Keep the change," she said as she got out of the cab.

He reached over and closed the car door. "It was nice talking to you," he said, looking after her as she walked away.

Later, after a warm bath, and a cup of coffee, Rosalie relaxed in her living room in front of the fireplace on the white, silk-upholstered sofa, with her feet stretched out on the red, antique Chinese coffee table in front of her. She lit another cigar and took a long, languid puff. She felt nervous, almost like a cat before a storm. Thoughts of her father and mother and especially of Ahmed filled her mind and dragged her down into a dark pit of grief. She kept twitching her toes and biting the inside of her lower lip until it bled. She could not sit still; the apartment was too quiet. Elvira, the housekeeper, was asleep; and Tomó, her Japanese houseboy, was out on a date with Maude, the new American maid she had hired only eight days ago. Tomó and Maude had hit it off right away, and she hoped she would not have to replace them soon because of wedding plans. Rosalie smiled to herself as she thought of the two servants. Tomó was a jewel, bright and ambitious, with the personality of a star. Maude, small and freckle-faced, a New Englander from Maine, was shy and reserved, with an authentic fresh-faced look and fair, fair skin.

What a match, she thought, but, then, were not Ahmed and I exact opposites? Why could she not stop thinking of him tonight, as if he were trying to reach her? She was letting things get out of hand. She did not believe in ghosts or communication with the dead. She thought of waking up Madeleine, her secretary, for company, but she changed her mind.

She had to go out again. Walking was the only thing that helped when she felt like this. She had come to New York to stay awhile in the apartment her father kept there, because she had thought that, since he had hardly ever stayed in it and since Ahmed never had—he had preferred to stay at the Plaza—she had hoped she could get away from their faces. But she could never forget that charred, scorched blackness where Ahmed's handsome face had once been. She would never sleep again without dreaming of it; and awake, she would remember again and again, always haunted by the memory.

"Oh God, where were you? You sadistic God, I hate you for doing this to me, for doing what you did to my father and mother, and for letting Ahmed die so horribly. I damn you, and I will live on to damn you for the pain I suffer every day. And when I die, I will feel no remorse, only pleasure, for you will not have broken my spirit. Meanwhile, I will find out who is responsible, and when I do, I shall avenge myself. I shall destroy whoever is your messenger of evil. I will pluck out his soul, and gladly give up my own life, if need be, to accomplish what I have sworn to do."

She got up and walked across the living room to stand in front of the window. She looked out over the park. The rain was falling hard now, no longer a drizzle, but more like sleet. The weather reports that day had promised snow. She wished it would fall and never stop until the whole world was buried under its purity. She pressed her face against the cold windowpane and looked down at the park.

"Come, snow. Come and cover up the evil which surrounds me."

As she chanted the words softly to herself, the glass pane clouded over from the heat of her breath. She thought of her home in le Marais, of the apartment she and Ahmed had shared together, of Colombier, of Belle Fleur and La Rose. Normally on nights like this, when she was feeling particularly blue, she would sit on the wide marble windowsill, with her knees drawn up, and gaze down at Central Park and at the busy Avenue. Other times she would spend the evening curled up on the couch in front of the fireplace with a drink and a smoke and sometimes a book, enjoying Manhattan from her own private domain. Tonight her "theater of the park" was rained out, but instead of curling up with a smoke and a drink on the sofa, she decided to go out again for a walk in the rain. She put on a long black trench coat and tucked her hair up under a khaki-colored rain hat.

She liked walking in the rain. Often, in Paris on nights like this, she found it invigorating, and very private, since hardly a soul ventured out into the cold, sleety rain and muddy slush. She walked along, taking long strides, jumping over puddles. The icy February wind was fierce, blowing down Fifth Avenue like a tornado caught in a tunnel. Her black trench coat flapped loudly in the keening of the wind. She threw her weight against its force, hands jammed down into her pockets, head bowed to protect her face from its sting.

She reached the entrance to the park and decided to walk on the grass under the trees. She walked slowly, heading for the lake, her footsteps making soft, sucking sounds in the slush. She kept a steady pace. Two mounted policemen passed by. They waved to her and went on their way.

It was a dark night. The moon was faint in the sky, appearing and disappearing as thick clouds sailed by. The sky reminded her of an angry ocean; she imagined that the rain was ocean spray, as it splattered on her face and hands. A loud clap of thunder exploded, and a fierce flash of lightning lit up the sky, for an instant. She walked until she came to the statue of Hans Christian Andersen, and sat beside it. The wet bronze glistened softly in the light of the nearby lamp. The tiny plaza was momentarily flooded with light as another streak of lightning flashed through the black sky. It made the statue seem almost alive, and Rosalie jumped back, startled. She got up and walked over to the edge of the lake; the water was high, almost to the brim. Pieces of paper and a plastic cup floated on the top. A large black rat darted past her into the lake. She flinched.

"God, I'd better be getting back. I'm as jumpy as a cat," she said out loud.

"Ahem." The voice came from behind her. She reeled around, startled.

A man was sitting next to the statue where she had sat only moments before. She stared at the man, trying to make out his face in the dim lamp light.

"I've been watching you for a while. Don't you think it's dangerous for a woman to be walking in the park this late?"

A chill ran through her, as she remembered the taxi driver's warnings earlier that night. She glanced in the direction the two mounted police had taken. They were nowhere to be seen.

"I . . . I'm not alone," she said.

"Oh? And where is your bodyguard, pray tell?" His tone was sarcastic, but nevertheless soft.

She looked around her to see if they were alone. No one else was in sight. She began inching her way along the edge of the lake, one step to the right and then another. She saw the man move. He got up and came toward her. There was something about him which intimidated her. Maybe it was the way his broad shoulders were packed into his trench coat. Maybe it was his black hair. It reminded her of Ahmed.

But Ahmed is dead. Oh God, I'm going mad.

Rosalie turned and bolted. In her panic she headed in the wrong direction. She did not care, as long as she got to Fifth Avenue. She ran wildly, slipping and stumbling on the frozen ground. She reached the steps of the Alice statue and raced up them, calling for help. Her throat was dry. Her cries were mere whispers in the night. She could not yell. A baby squirrel scampered out into her path from behind the bronze figures. She lurched backward and began to fall. A pair of strong arms reached out from behind and grabbed her. A stifled scream escaped her lips. He spun her around and lifted her face to the light. Hardly an inch separated them. She looked up at the big, dark man, and his eyes held hers like a trap. He reminded her of a storybook beast. He was strong and overpowering, somehow magnetic.

Subdued, she waited for whatever was to come. Her eyes searched his face. His dark, curly hair covered his ears and curled over the collar of his shabby tan trench coat. His hair glistened in the light, as drops of rain rolled down it and clung to the tips like crystal droplets. His jet black eyes were compelling, his wide mouth opened a slit. He had the coloring of Ahmed, but the stature of her father. She looked into his eyes, a prisoner in their stormy depths.

"Who are you?" he asked. "And what are you doing alone in the park at this hour in the rain?"

"I . . ." She started to speak, but his grasp was hurting her. "You're hurting me, let me go," she pleaded. It was almost a whisper.

"Not before you answer me. Who are you, and why are you out this late?"

"I . . . my name is of no importance to you. I live down the Avenue a way. I was just out for a walk."

"A walk? In the rain? At one-thirty in the morning? You must be crazy. Don't you know you could get mugged—raped, even?"

The way he said it frightened her even more. His hands, like steel bands, still held her. The light was dim. Some vandal had smashed the light bulbs in the lampposts nearby, and except for the faint light coming from Fifth Avenue, it was dark. Only the whites of the man's eyes were clearly visible as he scowled down at her. He wrapped his fingers tighter around her arms and lowered his face to meet hers.

"You're pretty," he mumbled, clamping his mouth down over hers. "Very pretty."

Rosalie squirmed and fought to free herself, but his hands were like traps and his mouth a vacuum. She could feel the big man beneath the trench coat. She could feel his body tensing, the muscles in his arms and chest rippling as he pressed himself up against her.

The sleet was falling harder. Her hat had fallen off, and her hair was wet and sticking to her face and neck, like half-cooked spaghetti.

He released her from the kiss and looked into her eyes.

"I could rape you here and now, and it wouldn't be anybody's business. In this weather, no one would be passing by, outside of a squirrel or two."

His lips broadened into a grin, showing a little gap between his two front teeth. It added to his charm.

"But I won't," he added. "I'd hate not to make friends with you first."

Her shocked expression caused him to laugh. For the first time since he had jumped out at her from his dark hiding place, she had the feeling he was harmless and that he might be just pretending to scare her. He was young, too, much younger than she had judged at first glance.

"I'm twenty-three," he said, almost as if he had read her

mind. "Twenty-three, single, and an artist, and—" he stuck his hands inside his trousers pockets and pulled them inside out—"broke. That's why I'm walking tonight."

She looked at him suspiciously. "May I go now?"

"Go? You mean, you just met me, and already you want to walk off and leave me standing here all by myself? In this weather?"

She gave him a long, hard, exasperated look. "Look, Mr. Whatever-your-name-is, if you don't get out of my way, and let me pass, I'll call the cops." She took a deep breath and opened her mouth.

"Go on, call the blasted cops if you feel like it. I don't care. I'll say I never touched you. Or then again, maybe I'll just barely have the time to rape you for real before they get here. Because, let me tell you something, Miss Whoever-*you*-are, if I'm going to get blamed, you can bet your pretty little ass I'm going to play the game all the way."

She screamed once, then a second time.

He grabbed her and placed his hands over her mouth.

"Shut up, you little fool. I warned you what I'd do if you screamed, and I wasn't bullshitting." His tone softened. "This time I'll let you go, but if some other guy catches you alone in the park like this, you better do like he says. Now come on, let's get out of here before the cops come running. Where do you live?"

She would not answer.

He shook her violently. "Where do you *live?*"

"C-Corner of Sixty-third and Fifth."

"Now that's better. I'll walk you home. You're soaking wet, and your teeth are chattering. If I don't get you home soon, you're gonna be in the hospital with pneumonia."

He removed his rain coat and placed it over her shoulders.

"Here, wear this, and maybe you'll only come down with a cold."

She nodded her thanks and smiled wanly at the stranger, who, after all, was turning out to be at least considerate. Her eyes roamed approvingly over his massive frame. She admired his broad chest and shoulders. His thin gray turtleneck sweater clung to him like a second skin. At the sight of his long, muscular legs and the bulge of his maleness between them, outlined by his faded blue jeans, she trembled, her yearning reawakening after almost two years.

Her wide-eyed stare had not gone unnoticed. He chuckled, and pulled his sweater down.

"My mother didn't call me 'Peter' for nothing, you know."

She blushed and turned her head away.

He burst out laughing. "There's just a lot of me all over," he teased. "Nothing to be scared or embarrassed about."

She turned to look at him. "Scared? I'm not scared, not anymore, just . . ."

He lifted her chin with his fingertips and quieted her with his lips on hers. "I knew one day I'd meet a blond with great big slanting green eyes and a sexy mouth. You know something else?"

She shook her head slightly from side to side.

"I knew I'd find her in the rain. That's why I always walk in the rain. When I'm broke," he added. His lips widened once more in a wide, boyish grin. "Merry Christmas."

"Christmas?" Her voice was amused. "It's February."

"I know, but since I wasn't around to wish it to you then, I'm doing it now. Happy birthday, too. When were you born?"

She giggled, charmed by his boyishness. "I was born on October eighth, nineteen—" She paused. "Oh, no, I won't tell you my age. It's a woman's privilege, you know, to keep that a secret."

"Okay." He placed a strong arm about her shoulders and pressed her against him. "Let's go. I'm getting drowned, and I don't know how to swim."

The sucking sound of their boots in the mud and slush was the only sound they could hear as they walked, closely pressed together to keep each other warm.

And so it was that Peter Brian, poet, artist, athlete, came to meet a lonely Rosalie in the park in the rain. She moved out of her apartment on Fifth Avenue and Sixty-third Street, closing it up, and moved to Morton Street in Greenwich Village to live with her new lover.

From time to time, Jean, Duc d'Artois, visited the couple and brought news of the world Rosalie had left behind.

He would never let a visit go by without remarking on how he thought Rosalie was throwing her life away. At times, he would even go so far as to refer to Peter as "that hippie artist."

"How can you do this?" he would ask in exasperation. "Waiting on him hand and foot, while he locks himself up for hours in his studio, pretending to paint."

She would defend Peter: "He doesn't *pretend* to paint, he's a good artist. He has a chance of becoming great one day. I feel I can help him, Jean, and if you're my friend, you'll understand and try to like Peter."

Peter did not like d'Artois either. He thought him a bad influence on Rosalie, always bringing memories of the past which left her sad and aching inside.

Rosalie hoped that in time the two would learn at least to accept each other, and understand that she needed them both.

One afternoon Rosalie knocked on Peter's studio door, and announced, "I've been sitting out here, thinking about you, wondering if you'd get uspet if I interrupted you." It was her opinion that what she had been thinking would be well worth an interruption. Even a clerk was entitled to a coffee break; a Rosalie break ought to be welcome indeed.

Peter wiped the brush he was holding on his jeans and dipped it into a blob of chartreuse paint on the palette in his other hand.

"Uhuh?" he said, still concentrating on the canvas before him. "And?"

"Well? Are you?" Rosalie asked sharply, irritated at his refusal to look up from what he was doing. "Do you want to know what I've been thinking? Or is that . . . that . . ." She pointed to the canvas.

"Piece of shit, why don't you call it?" Peter exclaimed, jumping up from his stool and charging toward her.

She turned and retreated into the living room. He ran after her.

"I didn't mean to get you upset—all I—"

"I know. All you had in mind was cock. So I'm going to give it to you—"

He caught her skirt and yanked it off her. She jumped on the sofa and covered herself with the cushions.

"Stop it, Peter—you're being too rough!"

In a minute he had his clothes off, and had pulled off the rest of hers.

"Come here, you little shit. Who do you think you are, criticizing my work?"

His right hand reached out and grabbed her by the buttocks.

"Let's hear what you have to say about *this*." He sank down on top of her, his hands squeezing and guiding her hips. His lips found her throat. "Is *this* what you were thinking about?"

At that moment, the shrill sound of the phone ringing filled the room.

"Let's ignore it," he whispered in her ear.

It kept on ringing.

Peter looked at Rosalie, exasperated.

"It never fails, does it? Every time we're making love, some asshole decides to call."

He groped for the phone, but it was out of his reach. He sighed; untangled himself from Rosalie, stood up, and walked over to the phone.

"Hello?" he bellowed. "Who is it?" He paused. "Oh, it's *you*." His tone was hostile. "Yes, she's here, hold on." He turned and threw the phone onto the sofa next to Rosalie. "It's for you—it's d'Artois."

"Jean? Funny he should call at this moment." She took the receiver from him.

"Jean? Where are you? Really? Of course. Come on over. Peter and I are alone. What? No, we don't have any plans."

After she hung up, she followed Peter into the studio.

"Peter? Are you angry?"

"Yes."

"He's at the airport. He just came in from L.A. He won't stay too long. I'll tell him we're tired and have to get up early, okay?"

"Why didn't you tell him we were busy?"

"But we aren't. Not really." She caught the look on his face. "Well, I mean—oh, for God's sake, Peter, what the hell did you expect me to say? 'You can't come over, Jean, because we're in the middle of fucking.'"

Peter stood up in a huff. "I'm going out. I don't want to be here when he arrives. I'm sick of him."

His tone was so fierce that she stepped backward as if expecting a blow. She had lived with Peter long enough to know that when he lost his temper he was dangerous. Although he had never hit her, there were several dents in the bedroom door where he had punched it in a fit of anger.

Peter shrugged. "Have it your way. God knows, I love you, Rosalie, but I can't bear to see you duped by that man. He's tormenting you." Peter glared at her. "Don't you see it? He's in love with you. I can see it every time he looks at you, I can read it in his eyes. He hates me. He hates the fact that we're living together. Please listen to me, Rosalie. That man is evil. I don't know why, but he is. There's something in his eyes that makes me uncomfortable every time I look at him."

"Then it must be *you*, Peter. It's foolish to feel this way about Jean. He has been a friend of my family ever since I can remember. I didn't really get to know him well until I was seventeen or so, because I was in boarding schools all the time, but he and Papa were always very, very close friends. That's why it's so hard for me to give in to you, and say I won't see him anymore. I can't do that. It would be like severing a limb. He is all that is left of my past. He and Berthe, of course. Silly as it may seem to you, I can't let go of the past. I find comfort in being with those who were close to those I loved. Jean was close to my father. And Berthe, well, she is as much my mother perhaps as my real mother was."

"I think you should give up the past and think of the future, *our* future. Forget Jean. He can only bring you grief. He has a hold on you. Shake him loose. Tell him you won't see him again."

"I'm sorry, Peter, I can't do that. You're asking me to cut out my heart and throw it away to satisfy you! I love you, but I love Jean too, in a different way. Without him these past two years, I don't know what I would have done. He has helped me a great deal. Perhaps I've come to depend on him too much, but time will take care of that. One day I hope, I won't need to cling to the past anymore. And, as for Jean's being in love with me, that's silly. Why, he's more than twice my age."

Sometimes, remembering the pain in Rosalie's past, Peter felt guilty about his vehemence against d'Artois. He knew that d'Artois was her link with the past, with her father, but now, thinking of the duke's voice moments ago over the phone, he could not control his anger.

"I hope I'm not disturbing you children," d'Artois had said, with false solicitude. "I'm in town only for a short while and thought I'd stop by and pay Rosalie a visit. Is she in?"

He always makes that jab, Peter thought to himself. He never misses saying it's *Rosalie* he wants to see.

Rosalie was calling to him. "You'd better get some clothes on, darling, and help me tidy up this place."

She giggled as she pointed to Peter's trousers hanging overhead from the light fixture where he had ripped them off and thrown them just before pouncing on her. Clothes were strewn all over the room.

"For all I care, everything can stay just the way it is, or you can get d'Artois to clean it up when he gets here."

"Oh, Peter, must you be so pigheaded about Jean? Can't you just accept the facts as they are and try to see him in a different light?"

Peter's eyes narrowed. "Yes, I'd like to see him in the middle of a bonfire. That a different enough light?"

He grabbed his brown leather jacket from the hat rack and left.

Rosalie tidied up and dressed and set out some hors d'oeuvres. D'Artois arrived a little over an hour and a half later. She thought he looked younger than the last time she had seen him, only three weeks before. He was wearing a light gray wool suit with a pale blue shirt, open at the neck, and a navy blue ascot. On the middle finger of his right hand was the ring he always wore, with the *scarabaeus* beetle carved into the stone.

He had brought her a gift, a little charm for the charm bracelet he had given her right after Ahmed's death.

"I saw this in the window of a little store in Beverly Hills. I thought it looked like you." He handed her the tiny package and waited for her to open it.

She untied the narrow pink ribbon and unwrapped the little box. She hesitated a moment.

"Go on, open it. It won't bite." He laughed as he said it, and she smiled back.

She opened the black velvet case and her face lit up with pleasure.

"Oh, Jean, it's beautiful. I've never seen anything like it."

She lifted the small charm from the velvet casing and held it up to the light admiringly. It was a tiny orchid made from a piece of black coral, set in gold with two miniature gold leaves.

"It's a find, Jean—I don't know what to say!"

"Do you like it?"

"Of course I do. It's unique."

"Like you."

She blushed. "Oh, Jean, I wish you wouldn't always make me feel so young and silly."

"Me? Make you feel silly? How?"

"Oh, never mind. I'm just being silly on my own." She laughed. "Now I'll have to find the right place to put it." She raised her left hand with the charm bracelet dangling from it. "I think I'll put it in between my jade shamrock and my ivory lily. Then I'll really have all the charms my bracelet can stand."

She tiptoed and kissed him lightly on the cheek. With her hair in a ponytail and no makeup, she looked far younger than her twenty-one years.

"You keep getting prettier every day, Rosalie. Each time I see you you look more beautiful than the time before. Although," he added quickly, "it's hard to believe you could be any prettier."

"I think *you* look younger. What did you do to yourself since I last saw you?"

"I had a face-lift. I thought I needed one."

She backed away from him, stifling a giggle. "I don't believe it. A face-lift? You, Jean?"

"Oh, I knew I shouldn't have told you. Now you will always see me as a sewn-up old tapestry."

Though fifty-five, he now looked no more than forty-five.

She giggled. "No, I won't. I won't think any such thing. I just didn't think you needed it, that's all. But you look good with it, I have to admit. Not that you didn't look good before. It just makes you look a lot younger."

"I hope you won't disclose my secret to anyone?"

"I won't. I promise."

They went over and sat down together side by side on the sofa. He unbuttoned his jacket and reached in his breast pocket. He pulled out a sleek gold cigarette case and flipped it open. She looked surprised. "Are you smoking cigarettes now?"

"Yes, I thought I'd give up cigars for a while. What I'd really like to do, though, is give up smoking all together. Are you still smoking cigars?"

"Yes, sometimes."

He sank back against the green and white cushion. "When will Peter be back?"

"I don't know. He just went out for a walk. He'll be back in time for dinner."

"Did he leave because of me?" His tone showed amusement.

"No, he was just feeling a little restless, that's all."

"You don't have to cover up for him, you know. I know he doesn't think very highly of me. He's young and he's possessive of you, but that's understandable. I would be too, if I were in his shoes."

She cocked an eyebrow. "It's funny you should say that. Peter thinks you're in love with me." She giggled girlishly. "Isn't it silly? *You* and me?"

A deep frown appeared on d'Artois's brow. "Yes, it's silly," he said finally. "Are *you* in love with Peter?"

"We're living together, aren't we?"

"That doesn't mean you love him. Lots of people live together for convenience."

She laughed. "Well, perhaps I'm one of those people who live with a handsome desirable man for *in*convenience's sake. I mean, honestly, Jean, do you think I would choose to live here in this small, cramped apartment, instead of in my own ten rooms if I didn't love Peter? I love him, really love him. I don't know what would have happened to me if I hadn't met him when I did." She passed d'Artois a dish of olives and pickles.

He uncrossed his legs and tapped out his cigarette lightly on the ashtray on the table beside him. He sucked in his cheeks; the pickle was overly sour.

"I just don't think he's mature enough for you," he said. "I wouldn't want to see you hurt by him."

"Hurt? By Peter? He would never hurt me. He's too decent, too good."

D'Artois shrugged. "It's your life, Rosalie, but as a friend of your dear father, rest his soul, I thought I should offer some advice. I won't come again, if that's what Peter wants. I wouldn't want to cause more problems than I've already caused between you two."

She leaned over to kiss his cheek. "Don't be silly. Peter will come around, but I want you to try and like him, too. Okay? For me?"

D'Artois took advantage of her closeness, and wrapped his arm around her shoulders."

"Okay. For you."

He lifted her chin and was about to kiss her, when the door opened, and Peter walked in.

He was misled by the scene before him. "Take your fucking hands off my woman, you pig."

The look on his face was violent. He slammed the door, and came towards d'Artois. His eyes were filled with rage.

D'Artois rose to his feet and faced him. "I think you are jumping to conclusions, my dear fellow. I think you owe me an apology, and to Rosalie as well."

Peter swore under his breath and lunged, his fist flying through the air. D'Artois ducked, avoiding the oncoming blow by a hair. Peter fell forward, his fist cracking against the wall behind the sofa. He swore again and pulled himself up. Like lightning, his right foot shot upward, slamming into d'Artois's face and sending him flying across the room. D'Artois's arms flailed wildly as he fell backward, but Peter was upon him and landed another kick in his stomach. With blood oozing from his face, d'Artois fell, hitting his head on the edge of a glass-topped table. He slumped to the floor.

"God, Peter! You've killed him!"

It had all happened so fast that Rosalie was still standing with her hands clamped over her mouth in bewilderment. She screamed when she saw d'Artois fall and heard the snapping sound of bones breaking. Peter was on top of him, pounding his head against the floorboards.

Rosalie lunged forward, grabbing Peter from behind. "No, Peter! Stop! Stop it! You'll kill him. Stop!"

He stopped suddenly, as if a button had been pushed, and released d'Artois.

"Filthy pig. I hope he's dead."

She threw herself on top of d'Artois, shielding him with her body. "No, Peter, you don't mean that. Call a doctor, quickly. He's bleeding badly."

In a daze, Peter walked over to the telephone. He picked it up off the floor where it had fallen during the commotion. He dialed a number written on the small green pad on the telephone stand.

"Hello, is this Doc Forley?"

The answer came loudly on the other end. "Yes, this is Doctor Forley."

"Good. This is Peter Brian, your neighbor. There's been an accident in my apartment."

Rosalie bent over the duke, looking to see how badly he was injured. He was lying in an awkward position, with his head twisted and his arm under him. She didn't want to move him, for fear his spine might be broken. She sat silently beside him on the floor, tears streaming down her face, praying that he would be all right.

Peter sat straight-backed on the sofa, his hands on his knees, his eyes lowered to the ground. He muttered, "I never meant to hit him that hard, but when I walked in and saw him holding you like that, something went wild inside me. I felt like killing him."

Rosalie shook her head from side to side and looked up at him. "Oh, Peter, Peter, I wish you had given him time to explain. It wasn't what you thought. He was just—"

The shrill blast from the doorbell made them jump, and she did not finish her sentence. "It's the doctor."

Peter stood up and walked over to the door. He opened it. A tall, slender man with graying hair and thick, horn-rimmed glasses stood in the hallway. He was not the type you would expect to find in the Village. Peter motioned for him to come in.

"Where's the patient?" he asked, looking over Peter's shoulder.

"Over there, on the floor. I hit him, and he fell. It was an accident."

The doctor's eyes widened. "An accident? You know, if it's serious, I'll have to report it."

Peter nodded. He went and sat down once again on the sofa. He lay back and crossed his legs on the coffee table.

The doctor pushed Rosalie aside gently. "Let's have a look at him."

He opened his little black bag and pulled out a stethoscope and a small flashlight. He fixed the stethoscope in place and listened for d'Artois's heartbeat.

"Is he alive?" Rosalie asked, frightened by what his answer could be.

"Yes, he's alive." He opened one of d'Artois's eyelids with his thumb and shone the tiny flashlight into the eyeball; then he did the same thing to the other.

"Is he all right, doctor? Is he going to be all right?"

"I think so," he said, running his hands along d'Artois's collarbone. "But he's got a busted collarbone and a nasty blow on his head. He may have a concussion. I'll have to call an ambulance, and then you can tell me what happened. I'll need it for my report, just in case."

"Just in case of what?" Peter yelled out from across the room. "In case he sues?"

"No. In case he dies. A concussion can be very serious. You never can tell."

Peter shrugged and stood up.

"He won't die. I bet you anything he won't die; he's too despicable to die. Look," he said, pointing to the ring on d'Artois's right hand with the *scarabaeus* carved on it. "He even wears the symbol of immortality. He'll live because he's evil. Only the good and the decent die."

Peter turned and walked away into the bedroom.

The ambulance came, and Rosalie lied to the doctor to cover for Peter. They were having an argument, she said. The duke hit Peter; Peter hit him back. The duke fell and hit his head on the table. His collarbone broke as he fell to the floor.

The doctor took down the information and left with the ambulance and d'Artois.

D'Artois recovered quickly. A plastic surgeon patched up his face where the stitches from his face-lift had come apart, and his collarbone was knitting nicely according to his doctor. He did not press charges.

Rosalie went to see him every day in the hospital. Peter stayed home and grumbled.

D'Artois was allowed to go home after seven days in the hospital. He told Rosalie he was going to Aspen to recuperate.

Chapter Twenty-two

New York, November 1965

Two weeks later, Rosalie and Peter had another blowup. A large bouquet of white sweetheart roses, Rosalie's favorite kind, and a pound of Beluga caviar had just been delivered to their apartment. Inside the box of roses there was a small package wrapped in silvery paper and tied with a pink ribbon. It was another charm for Rosalie. Attached to the ribbon was a card from d'Artois which read: "I saw this in a window in Denver before I left for Aspen. It looked like you so it's for your birthday. I hope you like it. You can wear it around your neck if there's no more room on your bracelet. With all my love, Jean."

Peter had a fit when he read the card. He threw the roses into the crackling flames in the fireplace and threw the jade cloverleaf charm out into the street.

Rosalie was furious. "What's wrong with you, Peter? Do you have to be so insanely jealous? It's stupid! I love you, but I can't stand your jealous fits anymore."

Instantly Peter's hand shot out, slapping her hard on the

cheek. She ran crying to the fire to try to rescue the wilting roses from the flames, but she was too late, and she dropped to the floor on her knees and watched through tears of frustration as the flames devoured the flowers.

Peter came over and stood directly behind her.

"This is the last time that man is going to come between us. It's him or me, Rosalie. Make up your mind now. If it's me, call him up and tell him you don't ever want him to call you or bother you again. If it's him you want, then go to him. Make up your mind. *Now!*"

The *now* made her jump. She got to her feet and turned to face him.

"All right, Peter, if that's the way you want it, I'll leave. I've told you a hundred times already that I love you and that I only love Jean as a friend, but if you intend to carry on like this every time his name is mentioned or he sends me some flowers, then I guess I don't have any choice but to leave. I can assure you, Peter, I'm not the type who turns her back on her friends because her lover commands her to do so. I don't tell you who your friends should be. You have no right telling me to get rid of mine. I'm leaving."

She flounced off into the bedroom and locked the door. She threw her things into her suitcases and dressed in a hurry. She came out, calm and serene-looking, her hair sleeked back in a neat chignon, wearing a black tailored suit. The contrast of her elegant attire against the simple, inexpensive furnishings emphasized her intent. She looked considerably older than when she had left the room earlier in her blue jeans and yellow halter. She looked like Rosalie La Farge Farahet, breathtakingly beautiful and imperial. Peter stared at her as though he were seeing her for the first time. He had become used to her in blue jeans and T-shirts and Indian caftans. She had changed her mode of dress as well as her way of life for him, and he had taken it for granted. He had been blinded by his jealousy and his possessiveness, and now she was leaving. His arms shot out and he came toward her.

"Don't go, Rosalie. I'm sorry. I've been a monster. Please

forgive me. I promise nothing like this will ever happen again. I'm sorry I slapped you."

Rosalie could feel herself weakening. Her knees were shaking as she looked up into his sorrowful eyes.

"I don't know, Peter. Right now I can't think straight. I think it would be best if I left now. It'll give us both time to calm down and think things over. I will be at my apartment for the next few days. I'll call you when I've been able to straighten things out in my own mind. Now will you call me a cab, please?"

"I'll drive you."

"You don't have to do that, a cab is easier."

He shook his head. "No, I'll drive you."

His arms fell to his sides, and he turned and went into the bedroom for her bags. "You wait here," he said softly. His tone was sad. "I'll have to make three trips at least." He stopped as he was about to go out the door. "You're sure you don't want to leave some of your things here until you make up your mind?"

She shook her head. "No. You can have the paintings and knickknacks and my guitar if I don't come back."

He nodded and closed the door behind him softly.

Half an hour later, they pulled up in front of her building at the corner of Sixty-third Street and Fifth Avenue. Peter's yellow Morgan looked as if it would collapse under the weight of Rosalie's luggage. He helped the doorman unload the car and went to help her out.

She took his hand, climbed out onto the sidewalk and said, "Thank you, Peter, for driving me. Good night."

He barred her path as she tried to go into the building. The doorman and elevator man were discreetly busying themselves with loading the luggage into the elevator.

"Let me pass, Peter. I can't take any more roughing up tonight."

"I'm not going to rough you up. I just want to say something before you leave."

He spoke with difficulty. She could tell he was as shaken up as she was. She listened, quietly aching inside.

"Whatever happens," he said, "never forget that I love you. Never forget this." He drew her hard against him and lowered his lips to meet hers. He stopped to gaze into her slanting green eyes, half closed and misty, and at the gentle curve of her lips, and for a moment his breath caught in his throat. His mouth went down on hers with a desperate moan, and he wrapped his arms tighter around her and pulled her up against his heaving chest. Her lips were shaking. She was kissing him back.

"I love you," he whispered. "No man will ever love you the way I do. But I won't beg. God damn it, I won't beg."

His mouth was on hers again, and she felt herself weakening, surrendering, as she looked up into his flashing black eyes. Her head was swimming, her knees buckling, her heart thumping about wildly in her breast, and she knew that in another minute she would be completely under his spell.

She pushed him away. She felt ashamed of how little resistance she had.

"Stop. Don't, Peter. Please don't."

His arms released her slowly, but his eyes continued to hold her under his spell. They were wild, blazing with anger.

"Go then; go to d'Artois, and think of *me* when he kisses you, your precious d'Artois! For all you know he's a raving faggot—I've never seen him with a woman, ever! You'll come running back to me when he kisses you, and it fizzes like a stale beer. I'll wait for you to come to me. I'll wait, you hear? I won't come to *you*."

His loud shouting echoed down Sixty-third Street. Someone came to the window in the building across the street and peered out to see what was going on.

A cry escaped Rosalie's lips as she fled past Peter into the building and the waiting elevator.

Peter swore out loud as the elevator doors closed shut, and he rammed his fist into the door in angry frustration.

"Fucking Duke Faggot—I hope he rots in hell!"

He climbed into the Morgan. His fist was bleeding and dripping on his trousers. He licked some of the blood from his cuts and tore away from the curb with a loud roar.

Rosalie cried herself to sleep that night, alone in her bed, aching inside for the man she loved. She had pride. She could not let him treat her like that. No man had hit her before. She fell asleep thinking about Peter and Jean, wondering why they could not be friends.

For five days she stayed inside, writing letters and answering the many invitations she received each day in the mail, sometimes from people she did not even know, to dinners and cocktails and galas and premierés and benefits. She declined them all, spending her time instead hungering for Peter.

On the sixth day, she was ready to call him. She wanted to go back to him. She missed him so much that she could not stand being away from him any longer. She was sitting in the living room in her favorite seat, perched up on the windowsill, eating an apple, looking down at the park. It was mid-November. More than eight months had passed since she had met Peter that rainy night in the park. The weather outside was cloudy. It looked as if it might rain, as it had that night. She kept remembering his kisses, his strong, roving hands, his wild eyes.

I love him because he is filled with excitement, she thought. Wild and crazy, but I love him.

She expected to see d'Artois that night and decided to explain to him that she was going back to Peter and so could not see him anymore. It would be hard to do, but she loved Peter, and Jean would have to understand.

She jumped down and walked over to the phone on the coffee table. She took a big bite out of her apple and sat down on the sofa. She wriggled herself into a comfortable position and pulled her feet up under her. She reached for the telephone and held it with one hand while she dialed with the other, the apple clenched between her teeth. She listened. It was busy. She hung up and waited awhile, finishing her apple. As she was about to pick up the receiver for the second time, the phone rang, and she jumped, a little startled by it.

"Hello? Who is it?"

Peter's voice over the phone was melodious. "It's me. Your love. Peter."

"Peter!" She sprang to her feet, knocking the phone off the table in her excitement.

"What was that?" came his voice.

"Oh, just the phone. I . . . ah . . . dropped it. I thought you weren't going to call," she said softly, only a slight hint of gloating to her tone. "Well? Why did you?"

"I tried not to, but then I just couldn't go any longer without talking to you. So here I am."

"I was just about to call you, too. We must have been dialing each other at the same time."

He snorted a little on the other end. "Am I supposed to believe that? I don't think you would have called me in a year if I hadn't called you first."

She was getting annoyed at him and could feel her temper rising. "Don't call me a liar, Peter. I rang your number, and it was busy. I hung up and was about to call you again when the phone rang."

"All right, I believe you. The reason I'm calling is to tell you that I miss you, and that I want you to come home where you belong. I've decided I want to marry you, if you'll have me. I'm not rich, but I can offer you love. That's more than any amount of money can buy. What do you say?"

She was dumbfounded. "Oh, Peter!"

It was all she could say. She was crying into the phone, sobbing and laughing at the same time.

"Of course I'll come home! I've missed you terribly."

"How about my coming over to your apartment in half an hour to help you pack your things?"

"Why sure, come on over. Oh, damn! Peter?"

"Yes? What is it?"

"I'm expecting someone in a little while. After he leaves, I'll call you, and you can come over."

"Is it Jean?"

She hesitated for a moment. "Yes, it's Jean, but—"

She heard the phone slam down on the other end and then silence. He had hung up on her. The doorbell was ringing and Tomó was hurrying to answer it.

Rosalie knew it would be futile to call Peter back. He would just hang up again.

I'll call him in the morning, she thought. By then he'll have calmed down.

Tomó's voice came to her from the entrance hall.

"Ah, Monsieur d'Artois," came the young voice floating into the living room. "How nice to see you, and without your bandages."

She heard d'Artois say thank you and ask where she was. She glanced quickly in the mirror and smoothed back her hair with her hands.

"Tomó, show Monsieur d'Artois into the living room, will you?"

D'Artois came in looking bright and cheery.

"You're looking well, Rosalie, as always. I was sorry to hear that you and Peter broke up."

He came toward her, and she let him kiss her on the cheek. He sensed her aloofness.

"Is something wrong, my dear? You aren't letting that young scoundrel get to you, are you?"

"No, Jean, it's not anything he did. Would you care for a drink? Come and sit down on the sofa. Tomó, bring Monsieur d'Artois his usual, will you? And bring us some caviar and lemon."

The servant bowed and left.

She came right to the point. "What I have to tell you, Jean, is not at all pleasant for me. It's not easy, but I have no other choice."

A look of concern came over his face as he leaned back to listen. "Yes? Go on."

"Well, as you know, Peter thinks you're in love with me. He thinks you have some kind of hold or power over me, and he wants me not to see you anymore. I have fought him for eight months now on this subject, and I have got exactly nowhere. The facts are simple. I love him. I don't want to live without him." She paused and smiled wanly. "No matter how stubborn and pigheaded he is, I still love him, and I'm asking you as a dear friend to understand why I have to say this. I can't see you again, Jean. He made it quite clear; it's him or you. And well, he's asked me to marry him."

"Marry him? Who the hell does Mr. Peter Brian think he is? He doesn't have a dime. He's crude and can be violent at times, *and* he threw you out."

"He didn't *throw* me out, Jean. He asked me to choose. I couldn't, not then, because we've been so close, you and I. So I left, but I just talked to him. He's mad at me right now because I told him you were coming here tonight; but tomorrow I'm going to talk to Philip about selling this place, and I'm going to pack up and move back in with Peter. He's good at what he does. He paints exceptionally well, and he believes in his work. I believe he'll be great one day." As she spoke these last words, her eyes were shining.

Following Rosalie's declaration, d'Artois engaged her in some small talk and left an hour later, without having tried to change her mind.

The following morning Rosalie called up Philip Buchin, James Buchin's son, who handled most of her business affairs in New York. She invited him to come for lunch and to discuss the sale of the Fifth Avenue apartment. He was surprised but offered no contrary advice. He knew her well enough to know that, if she had already made up her mind to sell, there was nothing he or anyone else could do to change it. He could visualize well the gentle curve of her lips, turned down slightly, as she firmly said, "Philip, I want this place sold, and that's that."

As a boy, Philip had known her father and from what he had heard from his own father and from what he had had the opportunity to observe for himself, it was incredible just how much like Armand La Farge she was. She was strong and decisive, imposing in everything she did.

He was in love with her. He had been ever since they had been children together in Martinique.

He arrived at her apartment at one o'clock sharp, was shown to her study off the living room and asked by Tomó to wait. A few minutes later, Rosalie appeared from her bedroom. Philip had removed his coat and was looking up at the portrait of her father in the white planter's suit. It was as if La Farge were alive, and merely waiting inside the painting to be set free by the wave of some magic wand.

Rosalie stood by the door in a white satin pajama outfit, which shimmered in the soft light of the glowing fireplace. Philip had not heard her come in and she watched as he stood in front of the portrait transfixed, his head upward, hands on his hips, legs wide apart.

She studied his lean physique and the striking shock of jet black hair. She had so often heard her father say to the senator, "Thank God that boy takes after his grandfather Buchin, for with your plumpness and Katherine's fair skin and red hair, he might have been a cherub."

"Philip?" Her voice was like a soft purr.

He turned. "Oh, Rosalie, my dear, I didn't hear you come in. I'm sorry."

"Don't,"' she said, waving a hand for him to sit down. "I had a chance to admire you admiring my father."

"A totally admirable man," he said. "Now, what's this about wanting to sell the apartment?"

"I don't *want* to sell the apartment, Philip; I'm *going* to sell it. My mind's made up."

Her lips turned down at the corner, a telltale sign, but Philip thought he should try one little argument.

"Do you think if your father were alive he would approve of your selling this place? You certainly don't need the money."

"Look, Philip, I don't want to get into a long discussion about this, and I don't want to seem unfeeling, but I don't think Papa would have cared one way or another. It's mine, and I can do with it as I please."

He shrugged and sat back in his seat. He retrieved a Gauloise cigarette from between the cushions.

"Did you give up cigars?" he asked, smiling.

"It's Jean's," she said simply. "He was here last night. He must have dropped it there. And, *no*, I haven't given up cigars. I wish you wouldn't act so damned square sometimes, Philip. Why should it be all right for a man to smoke cigars and not for a woman?"

She reached for the rosewood humidor on the coffee table and held it out to him.

"Here, try one. They're quite good. You might find that somewhere inside that boyish shell of yours lurks a manly cigar smoker."

He fingered the delicate, thin cigar and took one. He twirled it under his nose and held it there for a moment. "I'll save it for later. Maybe you are right, and I'm just too self-contained."

She took one herself, and he stood up to light it for her.

"I must say, you make one hell of a *femme-fatale* impression with that. Not that without the damn thing you aren't devastating."

She laughed. "Maybe. Now, did you bring those papers for me to sign?"

"I have them right here."

The lunch that followed was a simple poached fish in a white wine sauce accompanied by lukewarm asparagus, with lemon sherbet for dessert. They reminisced about the days when they were children together in the islands, about their "wild romance," and teased each other about the time they shared their first kiss behind the frangipani tree in the little cemetery overlooking the bluff.

Philip told her that he and his wife, Claire, were talking about getting a divorce. Although he did not disclose the reasons, they both shared the knowledge that it was because of Claire's excessive jealousy over Philip, as one of Rosalie's lawyers and closest friends, spending too much time catering to his client. Rosalie expressed her sorrow over the news and offered to get another lawyer to replace Philip, if he thought it might help.

"It's too far gone," he replied, almost too quickly. "Things have been festering between us for a long time, but now they've deteriorated completely." He shrugged, looking helpless. "I guess Mother sees herself in Claire. From what I heard, Dad wasn't very understanding when she was carrying my brother and me, and she blames me for everything."

"Does she blame me at all?"

"No. She doesn't believe you have anything to do with it. And you haven't," he hurried to say. "It's I who was in love with you, not the other way around." He sighed. "How could I ever have competed with Ahmed? He had everything."

"Yes," she said, sighing. "Everything."

A look of gloom appeared on Rosalie's face and lingered for a moment. "Oh well," she said, getting suddenly to her feet. Her eyes were misty. "Then it's all set. In the next two days I'll pack up and move out, and you can see to the storage of all the paintings and my other personal belongings. I don't want most of the furniture, so perhaps you can also contact an antique dealer. Anything he doesn't want, auction off and send the proceeds to whatever charity you'd like."

She went over to stand by the closed window. She stood in front of it, peering down at the avenue. From the coldness outside and the crackling fire inside, the glass panes were misty. She moved her finger along the pane, drawing out a heart. Her back was turned to Philip as she spoke. "I'm going back to Peter." She said it simply. "You probably don't approve," she continued, this time turning to face him, "but in the past doing the right thing hasn't made for lasting happiness. I was a good daughter; so I lost both my parents. I married my first lover, the man I loved, the man I wanted to be with for the rest of my life, and look what happened. So Peter . . . well, he's different. The very fact that nobody thinks he's right for me leads me to believe he's just the man for me. This time, if I'm lucky, I won't lose him."

She walked over to the Louis XVI commode and removed one of the small white roses in the Lalique vase. She stood looking down at Philip, sitting on the edge of his chair.

"I'm not going to marry Peter, Phil. He asked me, but I can't; it would ruin everything."

"Oh Rosalie, Rosalie." Philip came over to her and put his arms around her shoulders. He hugged her tightly. "Don't throw your life away. Some day you'll get over your hurt and be able to trust and love completely once again. In the meantime, go to Peter, if you think he can fill the gap." His tone softened to a mere whisper. "I only wish I could have been the one."

She pushed him away, gently. "Don't, Philip, don't talk like that. Go home to Claire. Tell her you love her, and that there's nothing between you and me."

His arms dropped to his sides. "I've tried; I'll try again, but it won't work with Claire. I'll be all right. I'll see you in a couple of days to go over whatever has to be put in storage."

He nodded and leaned to kiss her on the cheek. She extended her hand instead.

During the next two days Rosalie continued to call Peter's apartment. There was no answer. She was frantic. Had he left town? Had he moved? Could something be wrong? Why wouldn't he even pick up the phone? She decided to go over to the apartment and see for herself what was going on. She tried calling one more time before leaving, and this time his line was busy. Her heart did a somersault. He was home. She tried again with no success. The line was still busy. She peered out the window and looked out over the park. It was pouring. A cold, late November downpour. Nevertheless, she decided to go.

She dressed in boots, jeans and a sheepskin coat, the one Peter had bought for her on her birthday. He had got some money from selling one of his paintings.

She was remembering that day. She had awakened stiff and tired from the night before. They had been celebrating and had gone to bed late. She had found Peter missing from beside her. She had got up and dressed in a lilac dress, the one with the tiny straps and scalloped hem, a favorite of Peter's. She had been arranging her hair in front of the shell-framed mirror over her dressing table, the one Peter had built for her, and he had sneaked up behind her like a little boy and grabbed her, twirling her around and around until she was giddy, and they had fallen together on the bedroom floor, laughing and wanting each other. She remembered how wonderful their lovemaking had been that day. Then he had gone back to the living room and had returned with her birthday present, a beautiful hand-tailored sheepskin coat with colorful flowers on the front, embroidered onto the leather. She had loved it. Later she missed one of Peter's favorite paintings from the wall of his studio, and found out that he had sold it to buy her the coat. She had had to drag the information out of him, and he had been embarrassed about the whole thing. She had thrown her arms around him and had made love to him all over again to show her appreciation.

She checked herself in the hallway mirror as she passed by and stooped to pick up the small suitcase she had packed to take with her. In the morning she would call Tomó and have him bring over the rest. She reached for her gray umbrella from the stand in the entry and buzzed for the elevator.

Downstairs she stuck her head out the door and got a blast of ice-cold wind in her face. The weather was even worse than it had seemed from upstairs. She closed the door and hesitated. Should she ring Tomó and ask him to send Max with the Rolls? It would be a half hour at least before Max could get the car there from the garage. What would she do until then? No, she decided to take a cab.

Minutes later she pulled up in front of the brownstone that housed Peter's apartment. She paid the driver and got out onto the sidewalk. In one hand she held the suitcase and in the other her umbrella and a silver key chain with two keys on it. She tucked the umbrella under her arm, climbed the steps to the front door, and rang the buzzer to the apartment. No one answered. She used her key, and made her way up the stairs to the third floor. Again she rang the buzzer and got no answer; she let herself in with the second key.

She walked into the dark living room. The shades were drawn. The room had a musty smell, as if it had been closed up for a long time and needed airing. She tripped over a stack of magazines and newspapers carelessly left in the middle of the floor. She switched on the light and rested her suitcase and umbrella on the floor next to a chair. The place looked as if it had not been cleaned since she had left. Ashtrays were stuffed and running over; tables and chairs were strewn with magazines and beer cans. Several marijuana roaches were lying on the coffee table. The beautiful stone fireplace was filled with crumpled pieces of paper, soiled paper plates, and empty cigarette packets.

She could see a faint light coming from the hallway where the bedroom was. Her hand flew instinctively to her mouth, and her eyes widened in fear.

Oh, my God, she thought, he's dead. He's killed himself because of me!

Heart pounding with fright, eyes burning with welling tears, she rushed into the bedroom prepared for the worst.

"Peter?" It was both an exclamation and a question. Her throat felt dry, her lips parched; her hands were shaking as she came near the bed. Peter was lying, naked, stretched out across the bed on his stomach, facedown on the pillow. His right hand was hanging down to the floor next to the buzzing telephone receiver. It was off the hook.

The blue light bulbs in the room did not offer much illumination. She could not make out if he was breathing. She reached out a trembling hand and touched his brow. He was warm—warm and sweaty.

"Poor baby," she crooned, lowering herself to sit on the edge of the bed next to him. She reached out to pull the sheets up over him. Something moved beside him underneath the yellow blanket. Rosalie let out a startled scream as a curly black head peeped out from under the blanket and blinked up at her. It was a girl in her mid-twenties or so, small and skinny with large, deep-set eyes and bad skin.

Rosalie screamed again and backed away. Only this time, her scream was like a hoarse whisper. Her mind was exploding, and her heart stabbing with pain as she took in the scene. A jar of petroleum jelly lay open on the floor, and vials of blue and red pills were scattered on the table and floor, along with some discarded condoms. On the night table by Peter were two half-empty bottles, bourbon and gin, shoved up against the Indian lamp.

Rosalie felt sick as the impact of the room hit her. She turned to flee, and slipped on an empty bourbon bottle lying in her path. She almost fell, but held onto a chair. She grabbed the bottle as it skidded across the floor in front of her, and hurled it with violent rage into the mirror over the bed. The bottle broke and the mirror shattered and glass fell down onto the bed, on Peter and the girl.

The shattering sound and the shower of falling glass jolted Peter out of his drunken stupor. He saw Rosalie, and a look of horror came over his face.

She darted for the doorway leading out of the bedroom, and stopped a moment in the threshold to look back over her shoulder at him. She stood there, catching her breath in her rage, clinging to the doorframe.

He came toward her, holding the sheet in front of him. Part of the sheet was still wrapped around the girl in bed, and as it came loose Peter plunged forward, losing his balance. He banged his shin into a chair and bent over, howling with pain.

Rosalie glared at him. Tears were streaming down her face. "Why, Peter? I called you, I came to you. Why didn't you answer? *Why?*"

He reached out for her, his eyes dazed from a mixture of drugs and despair.

She let go of the doorframe and raced to the front door, almost tripping over her umbrella which had slid down onto the floor. Peter came after her, banging into furniture as he ran. She reached for the doorknob and jerked the heavy green door open.

"Stop! Don't go. It's all a mistake," he called out.

He clasped his hand over hers as she held the knob.

"Don't be a fool, Rosalie. I'm sorry, I'll make it up to you, she doesn't mean a thing. Not a damn thing, do you hear?" He was yelling. His eyes were flashing wildly as he held her back. "Stay! I'll throw her out. I swear it."

Rosalie turned her head and looked up at him. Through teary eyes she saw his handsome face, his tousled hair, his flaring nostrils and the space between his two front teeth. A sob escaped her. She still loved him. "Oh, God, after this . . ."

He tried to kiss her.

She could not speak to him. His breath was foul, smelling of alcohol and stale tobacco. She wrenched herself away from him and half fell, half ran down the three flights of stairs and out the front door.

It was still raining. She had left her umbrella, but did not care. She pulled the lapels of the sheepskin coat up around her face and darted down the stone steps out onto the street. She bumped into a man, almost knocking him over. She stopped for a moment to steady herself.

The man—of medium height, wearing a trench coat with the collar turned up and dark glasses and a hat pulled down over his face—turned and hurried away swiftly without a word.

For a second she thought he reminded her of someone but, in the fog and rain, she could not tell whom. She set off once again down the street around the square and onto Seventh Avenue. She ran until she could not run any more. Her lungs were stinging, her chest heaving in convulsions. She leaned up against the corner of a building, her head spinning for lack of oxygen. Her salty tears mingled with the raindrops and trickled into the corners of her mouth. Her mascara had run down her cheeks and her hair clung to her face and neck like strands of waterlogged straw.

She began to walk again, slowly at first, dragging her feet along the sidewalk, stepping in the muddy puddles.

A gray and white pigeon with its chest puffed out walked beside her and slightly ahead, making mocking sounds. She charged after it menacingly, making it fly away. She slowed down again, wanting to cross to the other side of the street. As she was about to cross she looked back and caught a full-length view of herself in the glass door of a building.

"Oh, God! Look at me." She sobbed once again, and then she began to laugh. "I look like a cross between a clown and a drowned scarecrow."

Tears were streaming down her face still, but she was now laughing wildly. Somewhat over an hour later, she reached the Fifty-ninth Street entrance to the park, across the street from the Plaza Hotel, and walked to the lake. There she sat, huddled over on a park bench, her sheepskin coat pulled up around her neck and face, crying out her anguish and remembering the rainy night she had first met Peter.

It was after two by the time Rosalie finally arrived at her apartment. The doorman was shocked to see the state she was in. He kept asking if she was all right, but she was not able to answer him.

The alarm exploded into strident sound as she went in; she

had forgotten in her despair that she had activated it before leaving. She called the security service and gave her code number, apologizing for the accidental tripping of the device. Then she called Philip.

Claire answered the phone.

"I'm sorry to disturb you at such a late hour, Claire, but it's very urgent. May I speak to Philip, please?"

Philip's voice came clearly over the phone. "Rosalie? Are you in some kind of trouble? Is something wrong?"

By now Rosalie had regained control of herself. "I'm sorry I got you out of bed at this hour. What time is it, anyway?"

There was a silent pause on the other end, and then Philip's voice came over the receiver again. "It's almost three o'clock. Where are you? Where are you calling from?"

"I'm at home. I'll explain everything to you in the morning. For now I just want to tell you to try to get reservations for me on the earliest flight possible to Martinique. I can't stay here another day. Peter and I are through—finished!"

He did not say anything.

"Come to my apartment in the morning around eight. I'll explain then."

"Will do. You're sure you're all right, now?"

"I'm fine. See you in the morning, and—oh, please tell Claire I'm sorry I called so late. I know she needs her sleep, with the baby and all."

"That's all right. We weren't asleep, just . . ." His voice trailed off. "Don't worry about it."

Rosalie hung up.

Three days of tropic sun, of Maman Rose's solicitude, of perpetual reminders of her heritage through Armand and Jacqueline La Farge, had restored Rosalie to a state of acceptance, if not of content. Waking on her third morning at La Rose, she was able to consider her relationship to Peter more calmly than on the night she had fled from the apartment they had shared for eight months.

She organized her thoughts by speaking aloud. "He's a man, after all. And he has this obsession about Jean. It must have cost him something to call me; and then, to find that he had to be disappointed yet another time because I felt Jean had a claim on me for that evening, well . . . I can see that he might respond that way—a wallow in the mud, as a kind of revenge on me. But he wouldn't do that, would he, unless he genuinely cared for me? That one, the girl with him, pimples and no tits, that's not Peter's style. Poor slut, she's a tool of his anger, not a betrayal of me. . . ."

She stretched in the bed, turning over in her mind what she might say if she decided to call Peter in New York. With his hair-trigger temper, the words would have to be carefully chosen—no reproaches, certainly. But no apologies, either. A delicate matter, but she would work it out. And then, once she was back with him . . . Her thighs tingled as she pictured their reunion.

She glanced at her wristwatch. Eight o'clock—he wouldn't have started work yet. She didn't have everything she meant to say organized, but it would come to her as she spoke, she was sure. Then why not call now and have done with it? Perhaps she could persuade Peter to join her here at La Rose—yes, that was it, the blazing colors of the tropics would add a new dimension to his painting, that might be the thing to tempt him.

She drew her peignoir around her and padded downstairs to the telephone. As she reached for it, it rang. She smiled broadly—perhaps, once again, Peter had called her just as she was on the point of calling him!

At the sound of the voice on the telephone she experienced a sharp pang of disappointment, which suddenly shaded into fear. "Philip? Why are you calling me?"

It was, as she had sensed, bad news. Peter Brian, after neighbors in his Morton Street brownstone had reported a strong smell of gas, had been discovered nearly dead in his apartment. An unidentified girl with him was dead. A woman known to have been living with Brian had been seen leaving the apartment shortly before the accident—if it had been an accident. After two days, it had been discovered that Brian's roommate had been one Rosalie La Farge Farahet—and the police would very much like to have the benefit of Mme Farahet's information.

"You don't have to come back, Rosalie," Philip said. "There's no charge against you, so it's not a matter that would call for extradition. It's just—"

"Of course, I'll come back, Philip," Rosalie managed to say. She was breathing shallowly, assailed by visions of the still, dead faces of Armand and Jacqueline La Farge, of the tormented cinder that had been her husband— Whom I love, dies, she thought distractedly. But, God be thanked, Peter *isn't* dead. "Philip, how is he?"

The pause before Philip answered told her the import of what he had to say. "It's . . . Rosalie, love, they're just not very hopeful, that's the best I can put it. Listen, I've checked out the flights—I can get down there no later than one this afternoon, and we can catch a plane back here at four. I don't want you to come back to all this alone."

I *am* alone, Rosalie thought. Rosalie La Farge Farahet, widow. I don't know if Philip coming down will help me. I suppose it will help him. Maybe that's what people like me are good for—to make the others feel good when they think they're helping you. "I'll . . . be grateful for that, Philip."

Chapter Twenty-three

New York, November 1965

The plane made a bumpy landing at J.F.K. Rosalie was on her feet before the plane had come to a full stop at the terminal. Despite the pleas of the stewardess to remain seated, she was already grappling her way to the coat closet.

The door finally opened and Philip, who was standing directly behind her, took hold of her arm. The stewardess smiled and said good-bye as they left the cabin.

As they came down the ramp, Rosalie reached for Philip's hand and squeezed it.

People were shoving from behind, their hand luggage bumping in their backs. Others were trying to elbow their way past them, hurrying to wait at the baggage claim area.

Max was there to meet them with the Rolls. Philip had wired him of their arrival. As they came through the door to the baggage claim area, they could see Max's blond head towering above everyone else's, and beside him, d'Artois.

Rosalie rushed into d'Artois's outstretched arms, her eyes filling with tears.

"Jean, oh, Jean. Isn't it awful?"

Philip nodded his hello to d'Artois, and motioned to Max to follow him to get the luggage. "I'll see you out front," he said to Rosalie and d'Artois as he turned to leave. "Wait till Max pulls up outside. I'm sure there'll be a mass of press people waiting as soon as you get past these doors."

D'Artois led Rosalie over to the side of the room and sat down with her.

"Don't cry, Zalie," he crooned, cradling her trembling body in his arms and following Philip with his eyes. "Everything will work itself out, believe me." He watched and smiled slyly over her shoulder as Philip disappeared down the corridor.

D'Artois's thoughts wandered back to the night of Peter's "tragedy." He had arrived at Rosalie's building that night to pay her a surprise visit, and had seen her hail a cab. He had called out to her, but she had not heard him. He had decided to follow her and he had waited downstairs in the rain, out of sight, while she had been upstairs in Peter's apartment. He had heard Rosalie's scream, and the commotion coming from upstairs. He had waited a while, and when he had not seen her come down right away, he had started up the steps. At that very moment she had come bursting through the front door, down the steps, and had almost knocked him over. Fortunately, she had not recognized him.

He had waited across the street for a while in the event someone else might be coming down the steps. Then, after a safe period, he had entered the building, picked the lock and gone into the apartment, to find Peter and a girl passed out on the bed, with empty liquor bottles and pills lying about.

He had closed all the doors and windows airtight, blown out the stove's pilot light, and turned all four burners on full. Then he had made sure the coast was clear and had left. He had then driven to the airport and had got on a plane to Switzerland. He was there when he received a call from Philip telling him what had happened.

Philip reappeared just then, a worried look on his face.

"Come on, let's go. Just as I thought, it's a fucking circus out there."

Philip grabbed Rosalie by her arm. "Come on, Jean, stay close to her. We are going to have to fight our way through that mob."

As they threw the doors open, a loud roar went up at the other side of the lobby.

Someone shouted at the top of their lungs, "There she is, over there. She's with her lawyer."

Someone else shouted, "It's her! Rosalie Farahet. Come on."

"Quick, Max," Philip muttered, as they hurried across the room. "Take her to the car. I'll get the luggage."

Reporters came running like a stampeding herd of bulls, flashing away with their cameras, yelling and shouting questions.

"Did your boyfriend kill the girl, Mrs. Farahet?"

"Are you aware that he has suffered a stroke?"

"Did he try to kill himself because you found him with the girl?"

"What's going to happen now, Princess?"

"Why did you go to Martinique?"

A couple of guards held back the crowd, as Philip and d'Artois pushed Rosalie into the backseat of the Rolls and pulled the shades down. The Rolls lurched forward and they drove off.

That night, instead of going to Rosalie's apartment, they all checked into a small hotel on East Fifty-second Street, incognito. Philip had thought it the prudent thing to do; now that the press knew Rosalie was back in New York, they would be plaguing her for interviews and pictures. As soon as they were safely in their hotel suites, Philip picked up the phone and called the police officer in charge of the Brian case.

He informed the lieutenant that his client, Madame Ahmed Farahet, was in town, and that she would be available in the morning for questioning.

The following morning at ten, Rosalie, accompanied by Philip, arrived at the Broome Street station. After close to an hour of questioning, the police allowed her to leave. She was still technically under suspicion, but there was no evidence against her other than the fact that she had been Peter Brian's girl friend and that she had seen him and quarreled with him just before he had been gassed.

The investigation went on for five weeks, until it dwindled away. Rosalie was free, at least as far as the law was concerned; she would never be truly free of her memories of Peter.

Philip took her arm as they came out of the courthouse for the last time.

It was snowing. The sky was putty-colored and there was a distant rumbling of thunder.

"It's going to rain," Rosalie said, as though the weather were a topic of great consequence. "I hate it when it rains and snows at the same time. Manhattan becomes a mud puddle." She seemed in a daze as Philip guided her along the sidewalk to where Max was waiting with the car.

For the first time in weeks, there were no *paparazzi* storming behind them, no reporters badgering them, pushing pads and pencils in their faces. Only one television van was parked across the street. Although the mystery of the gassing of the girl and Peter Brian was not solved, at least Rosalie La Farge Farahet was not responsible.

Evidence helpful to Rosalie had been given by two people: one who had seen Rosalie leaving the apartment crying and then had seen Peter Brian at the door only a few moments later with a towel wrapped around him; and another who had seen a man leaving the building at approximately one-thirty in the morning.

The police had not got Rosalie's name until the next day. Everyone knew a girl had lived with Peter, but no one knew her last name. It was not until the third day that they had finally traced her, and then had got to her attorney, Philip Buchin, who had convinced them that Rosalie had not run away and that she would return at once to New York for questioning.

The press had not been kind to her during the inquiry. It had been a long and trying five weeks, and Rosalie was glad that it was finally over at last.

Rosalie felt someone's eyes digging into her back. As she was about to get into the backseat of the car, she turned to look.

A man was standing in the doorway of the courthouse. His brown suit hung loosely on his lean frame. In his hand he held a crumpled hat. For a moment her eyes met his and she felt as if she had seen him before. His dark eyes were intense, almost bold, in their stare. She wondered who he was.

Philip touched her arm lightly.

"Come on, Rosalie, let's get out of here. I know I'm a lawyer, but courthouses give me the creeps."

She climbed into the car and pulled him in beside her.

"I know. You should have been a priest instead."

Philip threw back his head and laughed.

"A priest? Me?"

"Where to, madame?" Max asked, as he closed the car door. "To the apartment?"

"No, Max," said Philip. "We're going to the hospital. You have the address."

Max nodded. "Yes, sir," and made a sharp right turn heading west.

The man standing in the doorway turned, put on his hat, and went back inside. His shoulders were slumped, his steps slow and heavy. C.C. Youngblood had followed the Peter Brian case closely in the hope that it might reveal something bearing on the von Witte business. It had not, and Rosalie La Farge had walked away again leaving another tragedy behind. He fumbled in his pocket for a dime. He had to make a call.

Minutes later, as the car pulled up in front of the hospital, people coming out of the dingy building stopped to see who was arriving. Rosalie was dressed in a black wool pantsuit with dark sunglasses and a black felt hat. Her eyes looked sunken; and her lips, a little pale, contrasted with the otherwise healthy tan of her face.

"It's that woman," somebody whispered as Rosalie and Philip climbed the hospital steps, "the one in that murder case in the Village."

Philip whisked Rosalie by hurriedly, ignoring the stares and the whispers. At the information desk Philip asked to see Dr. Kaiser, in charge of Peter's case. They were shown to an elevator and then whisked into a small, private waiting room.

"The doctor will be with you in just a moment; he's with Mr. Brian now." The nurse closed the door behind her as she left.

The doctor came and warned Rosalie that she might be in for a shock. Philip tried to get her to go home and come back another time, but she would not have it.

"Dr. Kaiser," she said, just before going into Peter's room. "There's one thing I *must* know before I see him."

The doctor looked quizzical. "Yes? What is it?"

"Is he going to die?"

The doctor looked at Philip, who lowered his eyes to avoid having to respond, and then back at Rosalie.

"He came out of it much better than we expected, and I certainly think at this time that I can say he'll live, but . . ." He paused for a moment, wiping his mustache with his fingers before continuing. "His brain has been damaged. A lack of oxygen for too long. That, I'm afraid, we can't do anything about."

"You mean, he'll be a . . . vegetable, doctor? Alive, but unable to understand or think?"

The doctor patted Rosalie on the back and nodded. "I'm afraid so. There's nothing we can do." He opened the door and they went in.

Peter was lying on his back, propped up in the hospital bed. His eyes were open and staring blankly at the ceiling.

Rosalie walked over and stood by the bed. Her hands were trembling as she reached out and touched him. She lowered her face over his and spoke to him in a soft, almost shy tone. "Peter? Peter, darling, can you hear me?"

His eyes shifted from the ceiling and focused on her face. His look softened; for a moment she thought he recognized her, but then his face broke into a foolish grin and he began babbling incoherently and whimpering like a lost child. Her hands flew to her mouth to choke back her sobs, but tears were already welling up in her eyes as she rested her cheek against his.

"Peter, oh, Peter, darling, who did this to you? Oh, God—God—why?"

Philip came over and placed his arm around her shoulders.

He pulled her away gently. "Don't, Rosalie, you'll only frighten him more."

She looked pleadingly at the doctor. "Would an operation help, doctor? Can't something, anything be done for him? I will pay for it. I will give everything I have if you can get me someone who can help him."

The doctor looked helplessly at her. His eyes were filled with compassion. "There's nothing that can be done for him that hasn't already been done. He'll be like this for the rest of his life."

"Oh, God, no!" she cried out. "Not like this, not *Peter*, please God, no!" As she broke into a new outburst of sobs, Peter raised his head from the pillow and he babbled something. He seemed to be trying to talk. Rosalie saw his wide shoulders shake and he stuck out his lower lip like a child about to cry. She watched him pityingly, but her pity changed to anguish and fright as she watched the big man lying in the bed crying helplessly. "Why is he crying, doctor? Does he know it's me, you think? Does he understand anything at all?"

The doctor shook his head solemnly. "I'm sure he doesn't know who you are. He doesn't even know who *he* is. It may be that he has some vague sense of recognition. I'm sure that's all it is."

She sat down on the bed beside Peter, and pulled him to her breast. "Please, doctor, Philip? Could I be left alone with him for just a little while? Please?"

The doctor nodded yes, and he and Philip stepped outside the room into the hallway.

She began to stroke Peter's head gently. "There, darling, there, my baby, I still love you, no matter what, don't cry anymore. I can't bear it."

His cries subsided as she stroked him, and he sighed and closed his eyes completely, relaxed now in her arms.

"I love you, Peter," she whispered. "I only wish I could make you know that. Go to sleep now, Peter. I'll take care of you. I'll see that you have your exhibition. You deserve it, and if I can't give you anything else, I'll give you the fame you always wanted." She looked down at his handsome face. The features were drawn and his skin yellowish from the medication and the lack of sunshine. "You won't know it, but I'll always be here for you. You can count on it." She kissed him lightly on the lips and pressed her cheek against him tenderly. "I'll see you again soon."

The door opened a crack and the doctor motioned to Rosalie that Peter should be left alone now. A nurse came in and gave him an injection and he dozed off to sleep, smiling innocently, like a baby. Still dabbing at her eyes with a corner of Philip's handkerchief, she was ushered out of the room into the bright fluorescently lit hallway. Her eyes fell on the small artificial Christmas tree on the nurse's desk, with small presents under it wrapped in gold paper and tied with red ribbon. On a bench in the hallway, a family of Puerto Ricans sat, obviously waiting to see someone. One of the men was holding a small transistor radio up to his ear, listening to Bing Crosby sing "White Christmas." A little girl was sitting on the man's lap, sucking her thumb. She was stroking his hair with her other hand. Someone was paging a Dr. Koombagh over the intercom, and a man's body was being wheeled down the hallway on a stretcher. His face was covered. Rosalie's head was spinning, everything was beginning to blur before her. She felt a blackness enveloping her as if she were being sucked under by quicksand. She cried out Peter's name and her legs gave way under her as she lost consciousness. She came to minutes later in the doctor's office. She gagged at the odor of the smelling salts he was passing under her nose.

"There you are," the doctor said, beaming. "You had us worried." His round, cheerful face was smiling down at her the way her father used to when she was a little girl.

"I—I felt faint. I couldn't see. The next thing I knew I was falling."

"You'll be okay. Just a little nerves and fatigue. I'll give you some pills to take before you go to bed tonight, and again in the morning, and then I want you to see your doctor for a checkup. You've been through a lot, young lady. You'll need to take it easy for a while, or you'll have a breakdown." He smiled and patted her reassuringly on the shoulder. "Mr. Buchin here has promised me he'll see you get some rest and solid food in your stomach. When did you last eat, young lady?"

"I—I ate yesterday."

"Just a cup of coffee and a piece of toast," said Philip. "I'm taking you straight home where Madeleine will fix you up a juicy steak and a salad, and I won't take no for an answer."

Doctor Kaiser nodded approvingly. "You do that and you'll feel much better in the morning, but don't forget, see your own physician for a checkup. You're a little thin, and you might be a little run-down."

She made a face. "I don't feel very hungry, but I'll try."

When Rosalie was strong enough to stand on her feet, the doctor helped Philip take her out to the car. Max was unnerved by her pallor.

"Is madame all right?" he asked. He kept looking at her in the rearview mirror.

"Madame is fine, Max," Philip said, "just a little tired from a very exhausting day. We're going to the apartment; Tomó is expecting us. We don't have to worry about the press anymore. You can pick up our baggage at the hotel in the morning. They'll be expecting you."

"Yes, sir. I'm glad for madame that it is all over."

Rosalie turned to Philip. "Is it, Philip? Is it all over, I mean?"

He nodded and squeezed her hand.

Chapter Twenty-four

New York, December 1965

Christmas was two days away and Rosalie was beside herself with loneliness and despair. Philip was in Washington at his father's side. The senator had been accused of misappropriating certain government funds and although the Senate committee was having a hard time actually proving it, the press was slaughtering him. It was certain he would not get reelected. Philip had called earlier to see if she was all right. Knowing how worried Philip was already with his father, she reassured him that she was fine, and that she was looking forward to seeing him when he returned to New York the following week. Solange had called that morning to invite Rosalie to join her and her boyfriend in Connecticut for the holidays; at first Rosalie had said yes, but later had called back and said she had changed her mind about going. Solange had tried her best to persuade her friend, but the best she had got out of Rosalie was a promise to drive up herself later if she felt like it. She was pacing the floor back and forth, smoking cigar after cigar, when the phone rang and jolted her out of her deep concentration.

"Allô—oui?"

"It's Jean" came the voice on the other end. "I just got in a little while ago. I'm staying at the Sherry-Netherland. I thought I would give you a ring and see if you wanted to have dinner with me."

"Jean! My God, it's been a while. I haven't seen you since a week before the inquiry ended. You said you'd be back in a few days. What happened? I tried calling you, but I got no answer. I even sent you a telegram. You had me worried," she ended with a little laugh. "Where have you been?"

"Well, as I told you," d'Artois said, "I had to go to Geneva on some business, and then something unexpected came up, and I had to go to Lausanne as well." He lowered his voice. "I hate to admit this, but I fell asleep at the wheel and drove my car off the road into a ditch. I was pretty banged up and had to stay in the hospital for a while. I didn't call you because I didn't want to worry you, you had enough trouble without that. I only found out the outcome of the inquiry last night when I got back to my apartment in Geneva and found your picture plastered over every American newspaper. I wanted to call, but I thought a visit would be more appropriate. I'm glad it's all over for you. I want to hear all about it when I see you. Will you have dinner with me tonight?"

Rosalie gave a strained laugh. "I don't know if I want to go out, Jean, but I certainly could use company."

Twenty minutes later, dressed in a black tailored jump suit, her hair parted in the middle and pinned high at the temples, Rosalie greeted d'Artois.

As she entered the living room, d'Artois rose to his feet. "Rosalie, my darling, you look as ravishing as ever. I'm so glad you're over the hump. God knows I've been worried about you."

As she floated into the room with her arms held out she looked as fresh as a schoolgirl. "Jean! I'm so glad to see you." She was fighting tears as he took her in his arms.

"Come, get your coat, and let's go out to dinner. You look beautiful. Let me show you off to the city."

"Couldn't we just sit and talk a bit, Jean? I'm really not myself yet, and sometimes I just start bawling for no reason at all. I wouldn't want to embarrass you."

"Nonsense," he scoffed, tweaking her chin as if she were a little girl. "You could never embarrass me. Rosalie, do it for me. It's almost Christmas—get out and enjoy the bustle. We'll go some place nice. We'll relax, have a drink, have dinner, and then perhaps even a late movie. How does that sound to you, eh?"

She was smiling through her tears. "Oh, Jean, you *are* kind. I know you must have a million more interesting things to do in New York than take me to dinner; it's like taking a ghost to dinner." She laughed a little shakily. "Are you sure you can see me, Jean?"

He laughed and hugged her to him. "See you? Why, you are like the blinding light of the morning sun coming over the horizon. You are a vision of beauty and poise and grace, and everything rare and exquisite. You bet I can see you. Now come along. Let's go before the clock strikes twelve and you turn into a pumpkin."

Rosalie laughed and threw him a kiss over her shoulder as she hurried to get her coat. "Which one should I wear, Jean? The sable or the leopard?"

"The leopard, wear the leopard one. It will look great with what you're wearing. Black suits you."

The restaurant they chose for dinner that night was La Grenouille. Robert, the maitre d'hotel, greeted Rosalie with much ado. He picked a flower from the gigantic bouquet near the bar and brought it to her along with the menu.

"Une jolie fleur, pour une belle dame," he said. He sent the sommelier over to their table.

"What would you like, Rosalie?" d'Artois asked, as his eyes took in the room and the people in it.

"I think I'd like some champagne, Jean. I'll just stick with that, and I'd like the filet of sole, and strawberries for dessert, no cream, just lemon juice and a little sugar."

D'Artois studied the wine list a minute. "I think I'll have champagne too, then, and let me see, what shall I have to eat? Ah, yes, I'll have the fish too, and a salad to start, but I think I'll skip the dessert." He passed his palm along the front of his stomach. "At my age, dessert goes to one spot only—right to the waistline. I envy you your youth; you don't have to worry about things like that yet."

"I should think I have quite enough to worry about as it is. I'm glad I don't have to worry about my weight as well."

He patted her hand and waved for Robert.

Rosalie's nose was itching, and she realized she had to blow it more enthusiastically than would be seemly at the table. "Excuse me a minute, Jean. I'll be right back." She was heading for the power room when a man moving back from the bar bumped into her from the side, almost sending her sprawling. He caught her as she reeled backward, stopping her from falling.

"God, I'm sorry," the man blurted in the naive way only an American can make convincing. "I didn't see you behind me."

She looked up as she tried to steady herself. Her eyes locked with his and she felt she knew him from somewhere. But where? Where had she seen those eyes before? And that voice, where had she heard it before?

There was suddenly an excitement in the man's eyes as he recognized her. "Rosalie, Rosalie La Farge, right?"

"I . . . I've been married. It is now Rosalie Farahet. Do I know you from somewhere, monsieur? Have we met?"

He bent his head and kissed her hand, which he was still holding. As he raised his eyes again he said: "Jeffrey Alan Guthrow at your service, madame."

Her heart stopped, did a flip-flop, and then stopped again. "It's so nice to see you again, Mr. Guthrow. I'm sorry I didn't recognize you right away, but it—it's been a long time."

"Three years and four months to be exact."

She smiled, surprised that he had kept track. She was a little embarrassed by the way he was looking at her. She pointed with her finger to where d'Artois was sitting—waiting. "I must be getting back to my table. My friend is waiting for me."

Jeffrey turned his head in the direction of the table. "Ah yes, Monsieur d'Artois, your escort. A mite old for you, wouldn't you say, Miss La Farge?"

"Madame Farahet," she corrected him. Her words had a sharp edge to them.

"Ah, yes, I'm sorry. It's just that I never can picture you as having been married."

She gave an angry little snort. "I see. Well, from now on I wish you would change your 'picture' of me."

He smiled and took her elbow, steering her toward her table. "Never in a million years, but I will remember to call you by your proper name from now on, I promise."

The duke got to his feet as they approached the table. He had a scowl on his face and his lips were white with anger.

"Jean, this is Mr. Guthrow—Jeffrey Alan Guthrow, an acquaintance from years back."

Jeffrey extended his hand to the duke. D'Artois took it with great disdain, and stood waiting for Guthrow to leave.

Rosalie spoke. "Mr. Guthrow, why don't you join us for an aperitif, or perhaps for dinner?" She looked questioningly at d'Artois, waiting for him to extend the invitation as well. He said nothing and Jeffrey sat down.

"I'll only stay for a drink. I'm expecting someone to meet me here shortly, but I'd love it if you would both join us later in my suite at the Pierre for a nightcap. I'm having a little get-together there after dinner."

"I'm afraid that would be entirely impossible, Mr. . . . eh . . . Guthrow; Madame Farahet is not feeling herself this evening and plans to retire early."

"Oh, really? She looks great to me. I don't see any sign of sickness in the lady's eyes. Just sadness, perhaps. Sometimes getting out and meeting people is the best thing for the blues."

Rosalie gaped at him wide-eyed. Hadn't he read about her misfortune? About her hardships? Could he be so callous as to think she would be in a partying mood after all that had happened?

They sipped their champagne and tried to make small talk, but the duke made it clear in every possible way that he had not invited Jeffrey to his table, and that it would please him immensely if he left.

The door to the restaurant opened and a woman wearing a pearl gray tweed coat and hood entered; Robert went to greet her. The woman looked around the room momentarily, and then her face lit up.

"Là-bas," she said, pointing to Jeffrey.

"Ah," said Robert. *"C'est Monsieur Guthrow que vous cherchez, mais, il faillait me dire toute suite."*

He led her across the room to their table.

"Jeffree-ey," she squealed. "I'm so sorry I'm late, please forgive me?"

Jeffrey rose and kissed her hand in greeting. "Ah, Andrea, my dear, you are late and beautiful as ever."

She giggled girlishly and kissed him fondly on the cheek. "You're always such a kidder. I can never tell if you're serious or joking."

The duke stood up again and bowed his hello. "Will you be joining us also, madame?" His tone was polite, but cool.

Andrea smiled nervously. "Aren't you going to ask me to sit down, Jeff?"

Rosalie winced mockingly at the way the woman said Jeffrey's name. She was remembering the night they had met Jeffrey in Monte Carlo. Visions of that night so long ago floated before her eyes. How happy everyone had been that night! How young and inexperienced I was then, she thought; and how old and empty I feel now. It seems a lifetime has passed since that night. The sound of his voice jarred her back to the present. Jeffrey was holding her hand, bending his head to kiss the back of it.

"Thank you for the drink," he was saying, turning his head slightly to address the duke as well. "It's been nice bumping into you again." He smiled slyly, his eyes were warm and direct.

D'Artois stood up to say good-bye. Jeffrey extended his hand. "*Au revoir*, monsieur. Thank you for allowing me to join you. I would be delighted if you would stop by later at my suite. I shall hope to see you."

Andrea was tugging at his arm. "Let's go, darling, we've intruded long enough on these poor people. Their dinner is getting ruined."

Robert was motioning.

Jeffrey straightened up and smiled again. "I hope you enjoy your dinner," he said and turned to leave.

Robert seated them at the table next to Rosalie and d'Artois, and handed them a menu. D'Artois immediately launched into a torrent of conversation on how the world was getting smaller and smaller and soon no one would have any privacy left. Rosalie pretended to be listening, but her thoughts were elsewhere.

She was back to that summer night sitting with Ahmed and Jeffrey Guthrow in Monte Carlo in the barroom of the Café de Paris. She was seeing the then-bearded American kissing the back of her hand, and she smiled as she remembered how brazenly he had licked the martini off her finger. He had stared boldly into her eyes, and his gaze had had a strange effect on her. She had never quite forgotten it. Even tonight the first thing she had remembered were those eyes, which seemed to pry into her very soul. He fascinated her all over again, just as he had that night, and his self-assurance angered her as much tonight as it had then. What was it about this American that frightened her so, yet also left her spellbound? Even now as thoughts raced through her mind, she could feel him watching her, like a cat watching a mouse. Watching and waiting for something, only she wasn't quite sure what. She stole a glance once over to his table. She thought she was being discreet, but he turned his head just then and caught her looking at him. She jerked her head away, but not before catching the tiny smile at the corner of his mouth, letting her know that he was aware of her watching him. She tried to cover up her embarrassement by launching into the conversation with d'Artois, who was still complaining about man's disappearing privacy. They talked through the first and second course and by the time her strawberries were set down before her she had a splitting headache, caused by too much champagne, and the fact that she had not had very much to eat that day. The scent from the bouquets of flowers throughout the room seemed to be overwhelming. A feeling of nausea seeped into her stomach. She felt that any minute now she would have to rush for the ladies' room. She nudged d'Artois with her elbow. Her face was white, her jaw twitching nervously.

"Let's leave right away, Jean. I feel as though I'm going to throw up."

His face showed concern. "You think you can make it home? Don't you think it would be better if you went to the ladies' room before we leave? I'll have the hat-check girl help you."

She shook her head rapidly from side to side. "No, I don't want to make a spectacle of myself. Please, Jean, just do as I say. Now!" Her voice cracked as she spoke, and her hands were shaking as she reached across the seat for her purse.

The duke motioned to Robert, who hurried over to the table. "Quick, Robert, help me get madame out to the car; she is ill. You may put the dinner on my account."

Robert pulled the table out for them and took one of Rosalie's arms as the duke took the other, and they led her out the door. Jeffrey saw the commotion and sensed that something was wrong.

He followed them outside to the duke's waiting limousine. "Is . . . is she all right? Can I do anything?" Jeffrey asked as he caught up with them.

Rosalie shook her head. "I'll be all right, it's just a headache and a queasy stomach." She looked at the maitre d'hotel apologetically. "It has nothing to do with your lovely dinner, Robert. It's just that I've been taking medication, and I shouldn't have mixed it with as much champagne as I've had tonight. Please excuse me if I've caused you any embarrassment."

Robert shook his head and frowned at her reproachfully. "Never in a million years, Madame Farahet, could you cause me or anyone else the slightest embarrassment. I just hope you feel better soon."

Jeffrey ran around to the other side of the limousine and

stuck his head in the window. D'Artois, getting ready to get into the car, asked Jeffrey to move.

"Fritz, roll up the windows, please," d'Artois said. "I don't want madame to catch cold."

The chauffeur pressed the button and rolled up the windows. Rosalie sank back in the backseat, and closed her eyes. She felt drowsy from the mixture of champagne and medicine. She could faintly hear d'Artois talking to Jeffrey, but she couldn't focus on what he was saying.

"She will be fine when she gets home and relaxes," d'Artois was saying. "She has been through a lot lately. She is just tired. I'm afraid we won't be able to accept your invitation for a nightcap; perhaps another time, another place."

Jeffrey stepped away from the car as the duke got in the backseat with Rosalie and the car began to move. Was it his imagination, or had there been a mocking smile in the duke's eyes as they had driven off? Jeffrey shrugged and together with Robert walked back into the restaurant.

"I have known her since she was a little girl and used to come here with her father," Robert said. "She has suffered a lot, that one."

Jeffrey nodded. "Yes, she has."

D'Artois stayed at the apartment until Rosalie was feeling better; at first he had insisted that she let him call her doctor, but she had convinced him that it was unnecessary.

"I'm feeling fine now, Jean. As you said yourself earlier, I'm just a little tired."

He left after making her promise that she would call her doctor in the morning, and that if she needed anything at all during the night, she would call him at his hotel.

D'Artois had been gone for a little more than half an hour when the doorbell rang. There was a delivery, the doorman said, and Tomó asked him to bring it up. The buzzer buzzed again. Tomó hurried to answer it. It was the elevator man with a note. A chauffeur in a silver Mercedes-Benz, he said, was waiting downstairs for an answer. Tomó asked the elevator man to wait, and walked in his soft slippers across the white marble floor to the living room door. The living room was dark. He knocked lightly on the glass doors.

"Yes, Tomó, what is it?"

"A message, madame; they are waiting downstairs for your reply."

"A message, from they? Who are *they?* Who would send me a message this time of night?"

"I not know, madame. Chauffeur is waiting downstairs."

Rosalie turned on the light on the table near her. She blinked and squinted at Tomó. He handed her the small white envelope on an oval sterling tray. She looked to see if there was a name on the back of the envelope; there was none. She opened it up and removed the small green card. She read the scribbled words. The handwriting was big and bold.

"I thought your watchdog friend would have left by now, and I can tell you won't be able to sleep tonight. Please come and have a nightcap with me at my hotel. If you are afraid of how it might look, don't worry, there'll be lots of people here, except Andrea. You may bring your Doberman pinscher if you think it's necessary, but I'm as harmless as a lamb. I promise you—all we'll do is talk. Please?"

The gall, Rosalie thought, as she read the message over and over again. The absolute gall of the man! Who does he think he is? She asked Tomó to have the elevator man wait, and then went into her study for a piece of paper and a pen.

"Dear Mr. Balls," she wrote. "It's nice to know that the world still holds such marvels as you, but I am in no mood to play games with you, or any other man—not now or ever—so if you want me to be your friend, please stay away from me. I assure you, I'm bad luck!" She signed it: "Rosalie."

She gave the note to Tomó and told him to give it to the waiting elevator man, then took a hot bath and got ready for bed. About an hour later, as she put out the bedside light, she heard the downstairs buzzer once more. She waited for Tomó to answer it, and turned over on her side to go to sleep. There was a light rapping on her bedroom door. She listened; it came again. "Yes? Who is it?"

"Tomó, madame, there is someone here to see you. He says he is your doctor."

"My doctor? Which one?"

"I don't know, madame, I have not see him before. He says it is urgent that he sees you. He says Monsieur d'Artois sent him."

"Oh, all right, Tomó. Show him into the living room, and stay with him will you? I'll be right out."

"Yes, madame," came Tomó's voice from the hallway.

She flicked on the bedside light and rubbed her eyes, which had already become used to the darkened room. She yawned and placed her hand over her mouth as she got out of bed. "I must have a talk with Jean in the morning," she muttered. "He must think I'm dying or something just because I made him bring me home early. All I had was a headache." She donned a peach silk dressing gown, with matching slippers and brushed her hair a few times, back away from her face. She stopped as she was going out the door, and dabbed a touch of cologne behind her ears.

I wonder if the doctor's going to be persistent and insist on taking my temperature; or giving me shots; or whatever a midnight doctor does. She checked her reflection in the shell mirror over her dressing table and passed through the study to the living room, rehearsing what to say that would send the good doctor away without hurting his feelings. She saw him at once, standing with his back turned, looking out the window onto the avenue below. He was wearing a black, expensive-looking wool coat, and a white wool scarf around his neck. The collar of the coat was pulled upward over his ears, hiding most of his face.

She cleared her throat. "Doctor?" He did not turn around. She looked at Tomó standing in the archway between the living room and hallway entrance. The servant raised his eyes and shoulders simultaneously, and then walked over to the man standing by the open window.

"Excuse me, sir, but Madame Farahet is here."

The man nodded and turned around to face her. Her mouth dropped open, and she gave a little gasp of surprise.

"You—you—impostor—you liar! What are you doing here?"

Tomó's expression was one of complete bewilderment. "Shall I show the gentleman out, madame?" he asked.

Jeffrey spoke in a quiet commanding tone. "I don't think so, my lad, but why don't you make madame a cup of tea? I'll have some brandy if you have any." He dismissed Tomó with a wave of his hand, as if he were his employer. Tomó looked at Rosalie for a sign, but she was just standing glaring at the intruder. "Madame?" Tomó finally said. "Shall I bring you some tea? Or shall I show monsieur out?"

"Tea," Jeffrey commanded and made a step forward. "Go on!"

Tomó threw up his hands and walked off to do as he was told. The door closed softly as he left the room. Rosalie sank down on the sofa, stunned by Jeffrey's boldness. Jeffrey removed his hat and coat and rested them on the arm of a chair. He sat down in another chair directly across from her.

"Well, are we ready to be examined now?" He was smiling wickedly as he said it.

"What? Are you crazy? First you send your chauffeur over here to take up my time with your childish notes; next you come barging in here, posing as a doctor, and now you want to examine me! I think *you* are the one who should be examined, and the sooner the better." Rosalie was rising to her feet. "I think you had better leave—now, while I'm still calm. In another minute, I'll lose my temper and call the police. It wouldn't look very nice for you, sneaking into a woman's apartment at this ungodly hour in the morning!" She headed for the telephone on the table by the window. As she clasped the receiver, he sprang to his feet and clamped his hand over hers. The hand was big and strong, and his fingers were long and wiry. He squeezed down firmly on her clenched hand.

"Don't do that," he whispered. "I'll leave if that's what you really want."

Her eyes were full of fire as she spoke. "Why did you come here in the first place? Did you think because you kissed my hand once three years ago in Monte Carlo that I would be ready and willing to throw myself at your feet? Or is it the fact that I'm a woman alone, a widow, and a grieving, silly fool, that you think I would go to bed with the first man, any man, who showed up on my doorstep at two o'clock in the morning?" Her eyes were wild and moist as she spoke, and her lower lip was quivering violently as she fought to control herself.

"No," he said simply, looking down into her eyes. "I just thought you needed a friend, a *real* friend, someone to talk to, someone who, perhaps, might be able to help you."

Her eyes flashed, angrier than before. She opened her mouth to speak again, but he stopped her.

"Ssh! For once shut up and listen. What you need is a man, a real man, not like the lover boys you've had so far, and certainly not an old man like d'Artois, who has the hots for you, but probably wouldn't know what to do with you once he had you in his clutches." He was leaning her against the wall, his palm clasped over her mouth to prevent her from speaking.

"It's the morning before Christmas, Rosalie. Christmas, a day of birth and joy and new beginnings. A time for forgiveness and love. Don't throw your life away on men like d'Artois. He's evil. He's old, too old for you. Come away from here, from the eyes of the press, from this apartment. Free yourself once and for all from the ghosts of your past. Learn to forget. Accept what has happened to you and let yourself live again. Let yourself go, for God's sake, before it's too late." He took his hand away from her mouth and lifted her chin so that her face was tilted upward to meet his. "If you are the woman I think you are, you deserve to find happiness again, and love."

She sighed aloud. "Love. You make it sound as if it is hanging on a tree just waiting for me to pick, but I know that the tree is bare, at least for me. I've already picked all that there was."

Jeffrey stooped and gathered up his hat and coat. "I don't believe that, Rosalie. There is love if you look, only this time it will be up to you to find it, not the other way around." He took her hand in his. He was smiling now as he kissed it gently. "I had to come here tonight. I felt I had to tell you this. Look around you, Rosalie, and see your friends as they are. Set a new goal for yourself and fulfill it. Find the love that's yours and take it, for a life without love is like a flower that never blooms. And you, I know, are a flower that should bloom." He smiled again. "I hope something I've said will be of some use to you, and perhaps—if you *wish,* that is, we might have dinner together one evening, when I'm back this way."

She did not answer, but kept looking into his warm brown eyes. They were sincere; there was no reason for her not to believe he was speaking the truth.

He turned to leave. "I'll show myself out; no need to bother you any more than I already have."

She stood rigid, watching him leave. She wanted to say something, but she couldn't. Something, some hidden force was holding her back.

BANG!

There was an immense crash. Jeffrey, still looking back over his shoulder at her, and Tomó coming through the doorway, balancing a teapot, cup and saucer, and a bottle of brandy and a snifter on a tray collided.

The tea and brandy went everywhere. Broken bits of glass and china scattered over the marble floor in the hallway entrance, and Jeffrey, who had tried to catch the falling brandy bottle, was doused from head to toe as the bottle hit the floor and the liquid splashed all over him. Tomó blurted out apologies and ran to the kitchen to get a mop and dustpan. Rosalie took one look at Jeffrey's face and collapsed with laughter.

"Twice in an evening is really too much," he said. "You must think I'm an awfully clumsy fellow. Would you believe it's never happened to me before?"

Rosalie motioned to him to follow her, and led the way into her bathroom. "You had better take a shower before you return to your hotel, or your reputation as an alcoholic will be established in all the morning papers. I'll have Tomó see what he can do about your clothes."

It was three-thirty in the morning by the time Jeffrey finally left the apartment, smelling strongly of cologne and the cleaning fluid with which Tomó had tried to clean his suit and coat.

Jeffrey's chauffeur gave his employer a knowing look as he opened the car door for him.

"Where to, sir?" he asked, trying to keep upwind from the fumes.

"To the Pierre, of course, Serge. Where the hell else do you think I'd be going at three-thirty in the morning smelling like a damn whorehouse?"

The silver Mercedes turned the corner onto Fifth Avenue. The light was red. The car slowed down and came to a stop behind another car. In an apartment above, a woman's face was pressed against the windowpane, looking down. Jeffrey turned and looked up through the back window of the car. He saw Rosalie just for a second—then the light changed, and the car shot forward like a silver bullet into the night.

[illegible]
and the [illegible]
Peter and the gas.

Chapter Twenty-five

New York, December 1965

Later in the day a giant bouquet of red and yellow tulips arrived with a card. Rosalie's fingers fluttered eagerly as she opened the tiny white envelope. It smelled of brandy. She smiled, seeing that the end of the card had been dipped in brandy, making the ink run. She read the card aloud.

"Rosalie. While I don't have a medical degree, I do hope you will follow my prescription! I'm leaving today for Los Angeles. I hear you have a place in Malibu. Perhaps on your next visit there you will give me a ring. I look forward to seeing you again and determining how carefully you have followed my 'professional advice.'

Au Revoir!

P.S. I hope you like tulips."

That day, Rosalie sat in her bedroom contemplating the flowers and sipping glass after glass of white wine. Outside, it was snowing heavily. The leafless trees along the avenue were swaying wildly, like skeletons on Halloween. An old woman, with a gray coat flapping in the gale, was leading a poodle on a leash. The woman and her dog were being blown backward by the wind as they tried to cross the street.

The day did not feel like Christmas. Except for the blazing fire in the fireplace and the bright yellows and reds of the tulips, everything was quiet and normal. Rosalie did not have a tree. This was the fourth year in a row she had not had one. She had given everyone the day off except Max. Max was replacing Tomó for the day, and was standing by with the car in case Rosalie decided to go out that afternoon.

Rosalie stood up once again and began pacing the floor. She could do anything she pleased, go anywhere she wanted, buy anything she fancied; yet nothing appealed to her. Jean had called her up that morning to see how she was feeling, and to see if she would like to go to a ball with him. She had declined, mainly because she did not feel like having to make conversation with Jean over her health. She knew he would bring up the subject of the "clumsy American," as he had already referred to Jeffrey the night before on their way home. Rosalie did not feel like discussing Guthrow, and her feelings puzzled her. Max brought in a tray with half a grapefruit and a pot of tea.

"Are you sure, madame, that this is all I can get you? A mouse wouldn't survive on this."

"I don't have any mice living in, Max, so you don't have to worry. Thank you, you may go now."

Max bowed, clicked his heels and turned to leave. She was reminded of the times Max would do that in front of her father, and how her father would chastise him for it. "Max?"

He stopped and turned. "Yes, madame?"

"Perhaps later this afternoon you can have some time off. I don't think I'll be going out. Perhaps you would like to take the car and go somewhere on your own—enjoy the Christmas spirit. I feel awful keeping you here doing nothing."

"If you insist, madame, but as I already told you this morning, I wouldn't enjoy myself knowing you were in the apartment all alone."

"I see. In other words, Max, you don't trust me. Am I

right? You are afraid I might jump out the window, or something?"

"No, madame, that's not what I meant. If I had meant that I would have said so. What I meant was I don't like your being in this big apartment on the day before Christmas with no one here."

"I see. Very well, Max. I won't force you, but if you change your mind in the course of the day,"—she turned her back to him and sat down to eat—"my offer still stands."

Max clicked his heels once again and left without another word.

After she had eaten most of her grapefruit and drunk most of her tea and honey, Rosalie took two of the sleeping pills her doctor had prescribed for her. The dosage on the bottle was for one pill, but she felt she needed the extra one. Later, Max came in to remove the tray. He found Rosalie curled up on the chaise lounge, sound asleep. He put her to bed, tucked the comforter in around her, and pulled the white wolf throw over her. He checked the fire in the fireplace, placed the bouquet of tulips on the commode by her bed and took the tray on his way out.

It was already eleven o'clock the following morning, Christmas day, and Madeleine and Tomó and the other servants were busying themselves with their chores. Max had not left since the day before. He had not been dismissed and did not think he should leave until he was. The doorman was buzzing the intercom. Several packages and some flowers, he said, had just arrived for Madame Farahet. He wanted to know if he could bring them up.

In her bedroom, Rosalie was stirring for the first time since she had gone to bed the night before. Her arms and legs felt stiff and tired, as if she had been doing a lot of exercise. She stretched and yawned lazily, and threw back the covers to get up.

There was a knocking on her door.

"Madame, are you awake? It is I, Max. You have a special delivery of flowers and several parcels. Should I take them into your study? Or would you prefer I bring them in to you?"

Rosalie stifled a yawn. "Just a minute, Max, let me put something on. It'll only take me a minute." She sat up and dangled her legs over the side of the bed for a moment. "God, I feel as though I've been asleep for a week." She yawned again, this time aloud and got up and went into her dressing room. "Come in, Max, and put the packages down anywhere. I'll be out in a minute." She gave a little groan when she saw herself in the mirror. "Good God, I look awful this morning. I won't take any more of those pills again."

The door to the dressing room opened, and Rosalie came out dressed in a silver green dressing gown. She was barefoot, and her hair was brushed all to one side of her head and resting on one shoulder. She wore no makeup except for a dab of red lip gloss. Max's eyes widened as he realized that for the first time since she had returned to New York, she was wearing something other than black or white or lavender. She looked fresh and relaxed. His heart seemed to turn over with joy and relief.

"Good morning, madame," he said, when he could finally find his tongue. "I see . . ." He paused for a moment to rephrase his sentence. "You look very well this morning, madame. Very well, indeed."

She cocked an eyebrow at him and came toward him. "Max, when was it that you stopped calling me by my first name?"

Max smiled fondly at her. "I don't exactly recall the day. I guess one day you just grew up, and I couldn't very well go on calling you by your first name as if you were still a little girl. Monsieur Farahet would not have stood for it. I'm sorry, madame," he blurted out. "I'm sorry I'm such a . . . a . . ."

"Nice man, Max?" She smiled and squeezed his arm affectionately. "It's all right to mention Monsieur Farahet, Max. I've decided to stop feeling sorry for myself. Today is Christmas, a day for rejoicing, and I've decided to try and rebuild my life." As she said it, she thought of the bold American, "Mr. Balls," and smiled, amused by the name she had given him.

A tear was running down Max's cheek as Rosalie looked at him. She pretended not to notice, and turned away.

"Get me a pair of scissors, Max, and a letter opener, will you? I would like to find out who these packages are from, and oh, Max? Didn't you say there were flowers delivered, as well? Are they tulips by any chance?" Her voice held anticipation.

"The flowers are in the hall, madame. I'll have Tomó bring them in right away, but they are not tulips. They are white roses, dozens of madame's favorite kind."

Rosalie's face fell. The light went out of her eyes. Oh? I wonder who they are from? she thought. Probably from Jean, trying to perk me up. She went and sat down on the chaise. She looked at the labels on the packages. Tiffany's . . . hmmm . . . I wonder who sent these?

Max reentered the bedroom carrying a pair of scissors, a letter opener, and a large chrome wastebasket. "For the wrappings," he said.

"What happened to the flowers, Max? I thought you said you would have Tomó bring them in."

"He's bringing them, but you know Tomó. It takes him an hour and a half to get from point A to point B even if point A is only thirty feet away from point B."

Rosalie laughed. "Oh come on, Max. Don't be mean. He isn't that bad. He's short; he doesn't have your long legs."

Max chortled. "I guess you must be right; that's what it is. I'll try not to be so hard on him from now on."

"Good, Max, that's a very good resolution. I only hope it lasts until the New Year."

Max was kneeling on the carpet beside Rosalie, opening one of the packages. He stopped for a moment, and looked up at her. "I hope all resolutions made today last through the New Year, madame."

She looked away. She knew he was including hers. "Hurry, Max." A touch of impatience crept into her voice. "How long does it take you to open up a package, anyway?"

Max ripped the package open with one sharp pull, and at that moment Tomó entered, almost completely hidden by the enormous bouquet of white roses. He was struggling so as not to buckle under its weight.

"My God," Rosalie yelled, as she beheld the bouquet. Max rushed to prevent the roses from crashing to the floor.

There was a small card attached to the basket in which they had come. Max handed it to Rosalie.

As she slid the letter opener under the flap, she smelled the familiar smell of brandy. He had done it again!

"Rosalie: By the time these get to you I will have left. I hope by now you have received the packages from Tiffany, and the brandy. I felt guilty about my collision with Tomó, and I am salving my guilty conscience by replacing the broken items. Tell Tomó I accept full responsibility. P.S. I remembered reading somewhere that you liked roses. These were all I could find in New York."

By now, Max had the three packages opened. On the coffee table, he placed a teapot, a cup and saucer in the exact Flora Danica pattern of the ones broken, and a large Baccarat crystal brandy snifter, also an exact match.

The intercom was buzzing again. Tomó went to answer it. It was the elevator man, wanting to know if he could bring up a package. Minutes later, Tomó reenetered the bedroom carrying a large, rectangular box.

"Another package, madame," he said, as he handed it to Rosalie.

"My God, this certainly has started out as a busy day. This must be the brandy." It was exactly that: a bottle of hundred-year-old Napoleon brandy.

Rosalie appeared mesmerized; her eyes were shining and there was a small, sultry smile on her lips.

Max motioned to Tomó to follow him, and the two men slipped out of the bedroom, taking all the wrappings with them. The door closed softly behind them, and once again Rosalie was alone.

Alone with her flowers and her note from Jeffrey, she leaned over and smelled the roses. What a man, she thought. What a crazy, clumsy, annoying, considerate, generous, incredible man. She would see him again, she knew, and this time . . .

That afternoon, she called Berthe in Paris. Berthe was still living in and caring for the apartment on avenue Montaigne, where Rosalie and Ahmed had lived until his death.

"I've decided to go to California for a while," Rosalie announced as Berthe answered. "I would like you to leave Hamdu and Jusif in charge of the apartment, and join me in Malibu on the fifth. That's in eleven days. I have a few things to take care of here, and I must settle my affairs. Also, I must visit someone in Connecticut before I leave. I want you to bring Diablo with you, too. I've missed him."

Berthe's response was enthusiastic. "It will be so nice to see you again, Rosalie. It has been difficult being away from you this long. I'm glad you want me to come. I hope I'll be a comfort to you." She went on at great length about how she had missed Rosalie, and how she would help Rosalie pick up the pieces of her life again.

Rosalie interrupted her. "I've got to go now, Berthe, but I'll be seeing you soon. That'll be time enough for you to tell me everything that's happened in Paris since I left." She laughed and said good-bye to her old governess, then hung up and dialed again. This time the call was to Connecticut. She listened patiently as the phone rang and rang at the other end. By the ninth or tenth ring, she heard the click of the receiver being taken off the hook.

"Hello, Forest Lane," a voice said.

"Yes, hello. May I speak to Dr. Gates, please? Yes, Dr. Helen Gates. It's Mrs. Farahet calling. Yes, I'll wait, thank you."

Rosalie waited a moment for the doctor to come on the phone. She heard the familiar voice.

"Hello, Mrs. Farahet. How nice to hear from you. What can I do for you? Is it about our patient, Mr. Brian?"

"Yes, it is. I wanted you to know, I'll be coming up this Saturday to see him. I do hope you'll be there that afternoon. I would like to discuss a few things with you concerning Peter—I mean, Mr. Brian."

As Rosalie corrected herself, she wondered why she had done so. Everyone knew they had been lovers. What was wrong with referring to Peter by his first name? She realized the reason at once. "Mr. Brian" made him sound like a man—instead of Peter, "the child," "the vegetable." Then she realized the doctor was talking to her, and just barely head the last words: ". . . make a point of being here then, so that we can talk."

"Very well," Rosalie said, "I'll see you on Saturday then. I believe we have a little accounting to do. I will be leaving New York in a week or so and I will want to make sure everything is in order before I leave."

"You have already taken care of everything for the next two months at least, Madame Farahet. There is no accounting necessary."

"Perhaps. We'll discuss that when I see you Saturday. Good-bye then and thank you again, and—oh, doctor? Give Peter my love, will you? Tell him . . . just give him my love. Good-bye."

Rosalie rested the receiver back into the cradle.

"Madeleine?" she called out. "Madeleine?"

"Yes, madame, coming. What is it? What can I do for you?"

"Get me Monsieur Philip on the phone in Washington, will you? And then, get Monsieur d'Artois on the other line. He's at the—"

"At the Sherry-Netherland. Yes, madame, I know. What shall I tell them?"

"Tell them nothing, just get them on the phone. I'll tell them myself, and while I'm waiting I'll tell you the good news. We're going to California, to the beach house in Malibu. I hope you'll like it there." She got up and walked out of the room to her bathroom. She called over her shoulder to the secretary, "If you get one or both of them before I'm out, ask them to hold a minute, will you?"

Philip was the first to be reached. He was just coming to the phone as Rosalie came out of the bathroom.

Madeleine covered the mouthpiece with her palm and whispered to Rosalie, "I have Mr. Buchin on the phone, madame, in Washington."

"Why are you whispering, Madeleine? It's all right if you

think Mister Buchin has terrible taste in clothes. Say it out loud. He won't mind. Mr. Buchin likes a woman who speaks her mind *openly*"—Rosalie was half shouting into the phone—"even if it *does* pain him to know he is a bad dresser."

Madeleine could not believe what she was hearing. Her face turned white and her eyes widened until Rosalie thought they would pop right out of the woman's head. Madeleine stood there shaking her head and slapping her hands against the sides of her cheeks. "I didn't," Madeleine finally said softly.

Rosalie by now was in a fit of giggles, sprawled across her bed, balancing one of her slippers on the ends of her toes.

"Hey, what's this? What's this I hear about being a bad dresser?" It was Philip on the phone. He was laughing too.

"Oh, it's nothing serious. Madeleine just confided in me that she thought you should spend a little of that Buchin money your granddaddy left you on some lessons on how to dress."

That was the last straw. Madeleine threw up her hands and stomped out of the room, saying over and over again, "I don't believe it, I really don't believe it."

Rosalie broke up again. This time she was near tears. "God, Philip, you should've seen Madeleine's face. She almost died."

Philip's voice came over the phone. "Did she really say that? About me being a bad dresser, I mean. Why that little . . ."

"No, no, she didn't say anything. That's why it's so funny. All *she* said was, 'I have Mr. Buchin on the phone in Washington,' and then she passed me the phone."

"But," came Philip's puzzled voice, "I thought . . ."

"No, dope! *I* said it. She was acting so funny, clamping her hand over the mouthpiece, whispering, so you couldn't hear her say she had you."

Philip burst out laughing on the other end. "You are bad, Rosalie, you know that? I mean, did anybody ever tell you you were *bad?*"

"Yes."

"Who?"

"You!"

They broke up laughing again. When they finally stopped, Philip asked, "Rosalie?"

"Yes?"

"What blessed angel gave you back your laughter? It's wonderful to hear you laugh again. It's unbelievable. Tell me, what happened? What brought this on? I want to know."

"Oh Philip, dear, dear Philip, if only I could answer that question as simply as you ask it, but I can't. It's very complicated. Even I don't know the whole answer."

"The whole answer? Then, give me the part that you do know. Come on, spill it, I'm overwhelmed by all of this. You've got me curious."

"Oh, you'll live. You are one of those indestructible people who always survive, no matter what."

"Like you, Rosalie. Indestructible, like you."

Madeleine came back into the room. Her head was high, her nose in the air, her glasses perched dangerously low on her freckled nose. "Monsieur d'Artois is on the other line, madame. Shall I ask him to hold on?" She said it so loud this time that Rosalie broke up again. Only this time Madeleine laughed too, leaving Philip on the other end trying to puzzle out what was going on.

"Philip?" It was Rosalie back on the phone. "I want you to see if you can come to New York a day earlier than you planned. Something has happened to me. I can't explain it, but I'll try to when I see you. I want you to bring all the papers you have concerning Peter's affairs, and the papers for the apartment, this apartment."

"Oh no," Philip groaned. "Don't tell me you are going to sell the apartment again. I don't believe it."

"I'm not telling you anything. That way I'm sure your raging curiosity will hurry you back to New York. Oh, Philip, there's just one more thing I forgot. Get hold of that architect who's been in the news so much lately. The one chosen by the President to do that monument. You know who I mean. We even talked about him once. Remember?"

"Yeah, I remember, David Hawley, but what do you want with an architect? Are you going to try to build a house in

Central Park, or maybe your own private bridge to Long Island? I give up."

"I'll tell you when I see you in New York, but please arrange for the architect to fly in with you. I don't have very much time. I'm going to be leaving for California soon. In about ten days or so."

"California? Just like that? Why?"

"I won't tell you anything more until I see you in New York. Let Madeleine know your flight number and what airline you're coming in on. I'll have Max pick you up. Well, I have to go now. I have someone holding on the other line. Jean, to be exact, and if you know Jean, he doesn't like waiting for anybody!"

"He's in town? Where was he when you could have used a friend? Out hunting grouse, or bull-whipping four-year-olds in a nursery school?"

"Oh, Philip, you're impossible. He was in Europe, to answer your question; and as for having a friend when I needed one, I had *you*, didn't I?" She blew a kiss to him into the receiver. "See you. 'Bye."

" 'Bye."

Rosalie pressed the flashing button on the phone. "Hello, Jean?"

"Rosalie, my dear, I'm so glad you called. How are you feeling?"

"Just fine, Jean. I called to accept your invitation to the ball. I'll see you at eight. I'll have some news for you." Before he could answer, she hung up. "Madeleine? Let's go find something for me to wear tonight. I'm going to that ball, after all."

That was on Monday night.

On Wednesday, Philip, and David Hawley, the architect, arrived on the morning flight from Washington. Hawley was esepecially eager to meet the famous Madame Farahet, whose name, like her father's before her, was already a legend.

The meeting took place at Rosalie's apartment.

It started a little after 1:00 P.M. and lasted almost until midnight, with time out only for a quick lunch and dinner prepared by Tomó. The subjects discussed varied from Rosalie's wish to sell the apartment to establishing the Peter Brian Foundation. Rosalie explained to Philip that she wanted the proceeds from the apartment to go toward the start of the foundation. The exhibition she had planned for Peter's paintings on the fourth of January would bring a lot, she thought, what with all the publicity he had received. The foundation building would be staffed with the best art instructors money could buy, and she wanted Hawley to design it for her. The proceeds from the exhibition would be added to whatever they got for the apartment, and she would then donate three million dollars for the building.

"My God, Rosalie!" Philip shouted. "*Three* million bucks? Aren't you going a little overboard? A million would do, I'm sure. Get some of your rich friends to put in a few hundred thou of their spare change. I'll throw in something for good luck, but Jesus Christ, Rosalie, three million fucking dollars?"

Rosalie gave Philip an annoyed look. "In life, Peter had no other friend but me; in death, or whatever you call his state, I don't think he needs anybody but me. I want to do this for him. Maybe I'm doing it as much for myself, to help ease the guilty feeling I have inside."

Hawley cocked an eyebrow and shifted uncomfortably in his chair.

"If Peter and I had never met, this . . . this horrible thing would perhaps never have happened to him. Look at my past. All the men I've ever loved, all the men I've ever touched, have been doomed." Rosalie's eyes found Philip's and held them.

Philip threw his hands up in frustration. "Very well, then, three million it is for the Peter Brian Foundation." Philip shrugged, convinced that nothing he or anyone else could say would make Rosalie budge. He turned to Hawley, who was sitting on the edge of his seat, drumming his fingers nervously on his briefcase. "I guess that means you are now officially working for the lady."

Hawley looked pleased. His lips broadened into a smile and he stood up and extended his hand to Rosalie, sitting across the table from him. "I'm sure it will be a pleasure working with you."

Rosalie extended her hand to be kissed, but Hawley, a thorough Midwesterner, grasped it and pumped it heartily up and down.

Philip noticed the slightly confused but mostly amused look on Rosalie's face, and burst out laughing.

Everything was arranged for the Peter Brian Foundation to be set into motion. Hawley would see Rosalie in a month in Los Angeles with rough sketches, and in the meantime, he would consult with Philip and Sean Chase, Rosalie's accountant, about the finances.

Philip saw Hawley to the door and the two men shook hands.

"I'll be contacting you in a few days, then, Mr. Buchin. As you know, I'm quite booked up for the next week with meetings in Washington, but as soon as that's out of the way, I will be sure to get in touch with you. I would also appreciate you sending some copies of Mrs. Farahet's sketches to me. I would like to follow her ideas as closely as possible." Hawley leaned forward and lowered his tone so that Rosalie could not hear him through the open doorway. "She is really quite a woman, every bit as fascinating as you said. Wonderful woman and bright, too."

Philip nodded politely. "Yes, Rosalie has everything, depending on how you look at it."

Hawley thanked him again and stepped into the waiting elevator. Philip closed the door, and went back into the library to join Rosalie.

"Now," Rosalie said, as Philip entered the room, "all we have to do is decide how much I want for this place and which moving and storage company to use, and then you can go home and I can go to bed. I'm bushed, and I have a long day ahead of me tomorrow. I have to make sure the gallery doesn't screw up the arrangements for the exhibition next Thursday. You know these galleries. By the way, you haven't told me yet, Philip. Are you coming?"

"You mean to the exhibition?"

"Of course, I mean the exhibition. I haven't invited you to anything else I know of, except my funeral. . . ." Her voice trailed off. Her face took on an air of seriousness. "Really, Philip, are you coming or not?"

"Of course I'm coming, Rosalie. From the few paintings you have shown me, I find Peter quite a good artist. He has a style all his own. There's one in particular I'd like to buy, if I can afford it." He laughed a little and added, "I'm just kidding, but I'm sincere about buying this painting. I think one day it might be worth a hell of a lot more than whatever I'll have to pay for it."

Rosalie smiled. "You mean the one of me in the lavender dress?"

"No, I knew you'd be keeping that one, you told me so. I'm talking about the other one, the one of you in profile with your hair draped over your shoulders. I thought you might want to keep that one too, but then I found out it was for sale."

"Oh, well, the reason I'm not keeping that one is because it was never a favorite of Peter's. I was angry the day he sketched it, and he says it shows up on the canvas; a little like Dorian Gray," she giggled. "I think Peter was right. I can't see why you'd want it. I've priced it high because it's the only other portrait he's done, and quite good in its way. Selling your own portrait is somehow like selling a part of yourself, don't you think? I couldn't sell it too cheaply. I mean, what would people think?"

Philip frowned and rolled his eyes incredulously. Rosalie laughed, and he came over and bent his head down to hers.

"I forgot to tell you what I love most about you."

"Yes? What is it?"

"Your lack of vanity."

They looked at each other and broke up laughing once again. Rosalie rang for Tomó to bring them coffee and brandy. They still had a couple of hours' work to do.

Rosalie, Philip and Madeleine spent the following two days seeing to all the arrangements for Rosalie's move to Los

Angeles, including the packing and storage of her things from the apartment.

By Saturday everything had been taken care of. Solange wanted to buy the apartment. She and her boyfriend of over two years had decided to get married and were looking for a place. That morning Solange made her an offer. Rosalie turned it down. It was close, but not enough. Rosalie was firm. The price was seven hundred fifty thousand and not a penny less. Solange promised to get back to her in a week or two.

"Well, I hope it isn't sold by then," was Rosalie's reply. "You should understand that this apartment does not belong to me anymore. I have already signed it over to the Peter Brian Foundation, and that's the price we're asking. I'm sure we'll get it, too. I do hope you and Louis can see your way to paying it; the place sould suit you perfectly."

The ride up to Connecticut promised to be boring. The weather was bad, the skies gray and cloudy. Rosalie nestled herself into the backseat of the big old Rolls with a bottle of Dom Pérignon, a newspaper and some fashion magazines.

"Take it easy, Max," she had ordered as they were getting out of Manhattan. "The streets are terribly slippery, and I get sick if you drive too fast while I'm reading."

Max had nodded and smiled to himself. Just like her father, he thought, exactly the same, down to the Dom Pérignon—only it's not my driving that made them ill, but the champagne.

By the time they pulled up in front of the big electric gates of Forest Lane, it was three o'clock in the afternoon. The weather had cleared, but it was still freezing cold. Rosalie slipped on her camel's-hair coat and gloves as the gates opened and the Rolls ascended the slope to the converted Victorian mansion.

Rosalie had called before leaving her apartment and had told Dr. Gates that she would be arriving between three and three-thirty in the afternoon. The doctor and Peter were waiting together on the enclosed terrace, which was heated during the winter months.

Rosalie saw Peter at once, standing looking out onto the

frozen lake with his palms and face pressed against the glass wall which enclosed the terrace. On his left wrist Rosalie could see the watch she had given him for his birthday. His hair was a lot shorter than when she had last seen him. It looked as if he had had a haircut that morning.

Everything about the handsome man looking out the window was normal. A lump stuck in Rosalie's throat as she watched him. Dr. Gates, who had temporarily stepped outside to pick a pine cone Peter had been pointing to on a spurce tree, came in shaking her head and stamping her feet to rid herself of the snow which she had collected outside.

"Ah, Mrs. Farahet, you're here. How was your drive up?" She motioned for Rosalie to sit down.

Peter had still not turned around. He remained staring out over the lake. Rosalie removed her coat and gloves, and placed them on a chair. "Brrr, so far this has been a cold winter."

Dr. Gates smiled warmly. "I guess you must be quite anxious to hear about Peter's progress." She motioned to Rosalie to sit down.

On hearing his name, Peter turned around. His eyes stared at Rosalie, but the stare was empty.

Dr. Gates was about to continue, but stopped as she saw Peter take a step forward.

Peter came toward them slowly, with his hands outstretched before him like a blind man feeling his way.

The two women sat motionless, waiting to see what Peter would do.

He came up beside Rosalie and placed his hands on her shoulders. He looked down at her, his eyes wide and innocent like a child's. He smiled and pointed out over the frozen lake, shaking her shoulder with his other hand. "Shee," he said with a lisp. "Shee?"

Rosalie jumped up, completely taken aback by the fact that Peter had spoken. "Peter, Peter darling, you can talk!" She threw her arms around his neck and hugged him to her. "He can talk, doctor. Why wasn't I told?"

Dr. Gates stood up and placed a hand on Rosalie's arm. Rosalie was shaking from emotion as she held on to Peter.

"He only says three words, and he doesn't really know what they mean."

Rosalie looked around. "But that means there's hope, doesn't it? If he can say three words, doesn't that mean he might be able to learn more in time?"

Doctor Gates motioned to Rosalie to sit down. "Don't get him too excited. He's like a child, only more vulnerable. He tends to go into a deep depression after your visits. We don't know why, but it happened after both your other visits."

Rosalie sat down, and Peter sat down right beside her. Rosalie continued to hold his hand.

Dr. Gates continued, "We—that is, my colleagues and I—believe that somewhere in his damaged mind there is a tiny spark of memory left. Only it's so small, so insignificant, that he can't make much use of it. The combination of the drugs and the gas, plus the lack of oxygen for such a long time, completely and permanently damaged his brain. We are positive that he will not progress much further, but we are hoping that with the right care and attention, he will be reasonably happy. As happy as anyone can be in his condition."

"I see," Rosalie said simply. "What are the other two words he says?"

Doctor Gates cleared her throat. "*Rosalie* is one, *Peter* is the other."

"Rosalie, Peter," Peter repeated, shaking his head and pointing out over the lake once again. "Shee?" he said once again. "Shee?"

Rosalie looked pityingly at Peter, and then turned to the doctor sitting beside her. "Would you please leave us alone for a little while? I would like to be alone with him. I . . ." Her voice faltered.

The doctor nodded. "I have to make my rounds anyway. I will be back in half an hour. There's nothing to worry about. He is not dangerous, or violent in any way, but should you need anything, just buzz."

Rosalie nodded, and the doctor left.

Almost at once, the door opened, and Dr. Gates stuck her head in. "I almost forgot Peter's cone." She rested the pine cone down on the coffee table and left quietly.

Peter picked up the cone and put it in his pants pocket, and pointed again to the lake.

"Peter?" Rosalie said. He did not turn around. She called his name again, "Peter?" and tugged at his sleeve.

He ignored her.

She tried again. "Would you like to go for a walk by the lake, Peter?" She pointed to the spot by the lake he had been pointing to before. His face lit up. Rosalie jumped up. "Okay, let's go for a walk. I'll check and see if it's all right with Dr. Gates."

When Dr. Gates came out half an hour later, they were sitting together on a park bench at the edge of the lake, holding hands. Rosalie was singing a song, and Peter was sitting quietly, listening, or at least seeming to listen. It was a patois song, one he had liked to hear her sing when they had lived together.

Dr. Gates stood apart for a while, just listening. Rosalie and Peter were in a world of their own. The doctor's heart reached out to the young couple, and she hated to interrupt them. "Well, there you are!" Dr. Gates said when Rosalie reached the end of her song. "I thought I would find you here."

Peter pointed to the large pine tree nearby. "Shee?" he said. "Shee?"

Rosalie looked up at the doctor. "He is fascinated by that tree. I wonder why?" Rosalie said. Her eyes were moist.

Dr. Gates shrugged. "I don't know, but ever since he arrived, he has been in love with the lake, and that tree in particular. My colleagues and I feel that perhaps this setting, the lake and the tree, brings back a childhood memory of a place he lived once or visited when he was a little boy." Dr. Gates leaned over and took hold of one of Peter's arms. "That's why we had him moved from his former room to this side of the building. So he could look out from his window." She spoke to Peter in a low, gentle tone. "Come, Peter. Let's go in now. It's time for your medicine."

Peter did not understand, but he responded to the gentle tug on his arm. He stood up and walked around the bench.

"We don't usually put patients on this side of the building. It's really for the staff, but we feel that Peter is gentle and predictable enough, so we've made an exception." Dr. Gates smiled and patted Peter's arm fondly. "We are all very fond of Peter, and feel that if it makes him happy to be able to look out over the lake, we should certainly oblige him."

Rosalie nodded and smiled and took Peter's other arm. "I'm glad you feel that way, doctor." She reached across and touched the doctor's hand lightly. "At least I know he is in good hands when I'm away and can't visit him as often. Thank you."

The doctor smiled and squeezed Rosalie's hand reassuringly. "He will be given every possible attention. *I* will see to that, Mrs. Farahet, you can be certain."

Peter was given his medication and his dinner and then it was time for Rosalie to start back. She arranged for his care and gave instructions that no reporters be allowed near him during or after his exhibition.

"I will not have him ridiculed or pitied. I want him to keep his dignity as a man and a serious artist. No one must *ever* be permitted to see him like this."

Rosalie was allowed to say good-night to Peter before he was put to bed, and after giving details of how she could be reached in an emergency, she said good-bye to the doctors in charge and left.

Chapter Twenty-six

New York, January 1966

On the morning of January 5th, 1966, a black-and-silver Lockheed jet bearing the black head of a leopard on the silver stripe with the initials *A. La F.* was in the Butler Aviation section at La Guardia Airport preparing for takeoff.

Rosalie, Madeleine, Tomó, and Max were getting ready to board.

At the same time, at J.F.K., at the TWA counter, a man with dark, longish hair, dressed in an ill-fitting brown suit with a gray coat hanging over his left arm, was standing in line for his ticket on the next flight to Los Angeles.

As he stood shifting his weight from one leg to the other, wiping the perspiration from his brow, C.C. remembered the endless times he had stood in line waiting for a plane, a bus, a cab, in the hope it would take him to something or someone who would lead him to his goal: von Witte. He wiped his brow with an already wet and soiled handkerchief and rested his bag and coat on the floor beside him. He felt ready to pass out.

The last several weeks had been rough for him. He had been "retired" from the Company three days after Rosalie La Farge had been cleared. He remembered that morning well. He had argued, pleaded for more time, but he had been denied.

C.C. had put the case for continuing on von Witte's trail vehemently—the political advantages, the moral necessity to get one of the major surviving war criminals, the money. He had, in fact, put his arguments in the form of an ultimatum—keep him on the case or throw him out.

"Now, *there's* a thought," the gray-flanneled man across the desk had said. "I am getting some flak from the Hill about some of the stuff we've been up to. Pork Chop Beach"—he used the Company slang term for the Bay of Pigs misadventure—"didn't do us any good, and it wouldn't be the worst idea in the world to have a head to show some of the mouthier congressmen. You weren't in on that one, but who's to know? You've fucked this assignment up enough so there's cause for termination, and I believe we can spread enough shit around so that we can suggest you had a hand in about everything that hasn't worked out the way the *New York Times* would like. Good thinking, C.C.

"Youngblood," he had been told, "in two and a half years you haven't uncovered a single trace of von Witte. More years won't make a goddamn bit of difference. You're off the project, period."

Now, weeks later, C.C. was continuing the chase on his own. Coming out of that office in Langley, he had sworn to himself that nothing would stop him from accomplishing his goal. He would not give up until he had found the Nazi bastard and, if necessary, had squeezed the life out of him with his own hands.

C.C. caught a glimpse of himself in the glass door at the far side of the boarding area. This case had taken a lot out of him. He was thinner, his shoulders, once broad and straight, now hunched slightly, and his face looked worn and lined from sleepless nights. He looked much older than his forty years.

The last person in line before him walked away, and C.C. shuffled heavily up to the counter, shoving his luggage with his foot in front of him. The ticket agent looked up at him with concern. C.C.'s face was dead white. His teeth chattered loudly, as if he were freezing from the cold. He had a fever.

At Butler Aviation, the doors to the cabin of the Lockheed closed and the ramp was wheeled away. Rosalie's personal pilot, Jean-Paul Petit, and his co-pilot, Gary Armstrong, radioed the tower for permission to take off.

The plane began accelerating down the assigned runway. From the balcony above the edge of the runway, a man in a black cashmere coat and a hat with the brim turned down stood watching. His eyes were glued to the moving plane.

D'Artois stood rigid as always, his hand shielding his eyes from the glare.

Rosalie was waving to him one last time from the plane.

"Good-bye, Rosalie," he whispered, as he waved back. "I shall see you soon."

As the plane lifted off the ground, Rosalie pulled the curtains of the cabin window shut, and lay back in her seat. She closed her eyes and sighed. Her thoughts were on two men, the one she was leaving behind; and the one she was going to find, the man she felt she needed—Jeffrey Alan Guthrow. Rosalie repeated his name over and over to herself, imagining his face before her. What is it about him, she wondered, that makes him so different, so special?

Rosalie opened the book she was reading, a novel by Françoise Sagan, and touched the white rosebud she had pressed between the pages. Her face took on a look of great tenderness and she brought the flower to her nose and sniffed it daintily. A small card slid out from between the pages and fluttered to the floor. She picked it up and replaced it, together with the rose, in the center of the book.

The pilot's voice came over the intercom on the cabin wall next to her seat. "Madame, you may now remove your seat belt and move around as you wish. The weather reports are excellent, the wind velocity is low, and we have a clear sky ahead of us. You can expect a smooth ride all the way."

Rosalie thumbed the "reply" button. "Then that is what I

will expect, Jean-Paul, a smooth ride all the way. I am very tired now and will be resting for a while, but I'll join you later in the main cabin. It has been so long since I have been up there . . ." Her voice trailed off. She switched the intercom off, then buzzed for her secretary. Madeleine came almost at once with her pad and pencil. Rosalie motioned for her to sit in the seat facing her. "Take a letter, Madeleine. It's personal. Dear Mr. Guthrow . . ."

Chapter Twenty-seven

Malibu, January 1966

Three days after Rosalie's arrival at the redwood beach house in Malibu, the phone rang; Tomó hurried to answer it.

"Hello, Madame Farahet's residence. Who is calling, please?"

Tomó paused to listen.

"Ah, yes, Mistah Guthrow, madame outside in garden. Hold on moment, please? I let her know you on the phone." Tomó rested the phone on the limestone table and hurried out the door onto the terrace.

Rosalie was in the rose garden, bending over a small bush with a pair of clippers in one hand, and a basket of cut roses hung over her opposite arm.

Tomó came up beside her. "Phone call for you, madame."

Rosalie turned to look up at him. "Yes, Tomó? Who is it?"

"Mistah Guthrow, madame. He on the line waiting."

Rosalie's eyes widened slightly and the corners of her mouth curled into a smile. "I'll take it on the terrace."

"Yes, madame."

Tomó hurried ahead of Rosalie and picked up the phone on the table on the terrace, handing Rosalie the receiver.

Rosalie rested the basket of roses on the table and wiped her palms on her bush jacket. Tomó went in to hang up the other phone. She sat down on the driftwood chaise and arranged herself comfortably on the salmon-colored pad. She fluffed up her hair and pushed back the strands from her face. She smiled impishly and brought the receiver to her ear.

"Hello," she drawled, "Mr. Guthrow?"

"Hello," came the voice on the other end. "I thought I would have to wait forever to talk to you. How big is your place, anyway?"

"Why?"

"Because it took you so long."

"Not too big, but what can I do for you, Mr. Guthrow? I'm sure you didn't call to discuss the size of my property."

"Well for one thing, I called to congratulate you on your friend's New York success. I was impressed by the reviews I read. It was incredible what you did."

"I didn't do very much, Mr. Guthrow. Peter did the work. He is a very talented artist."

"Well, it was really something. I hear everybody was there, and every painting was bought, if I can go by what I read in the newspapers. You must be very pleased."

"Well, it's true, and yes I am, but you weren't there, so I guess *everybody,* as you put it, didn't show up after all. Didn't you get the invitation we sent you?"

"We? Who's we?"

"My secretary and I."

"I see. Well, I did get it, but unfortunately I couldn't attend. I'm sorry. I should have let you know. But after all, it was just an invitation sent in hundreds, a formality; I didn't think I had to—"

Rosalie cut him off. "You didn't. I didn't think you'd come. I just sent you an invitation so as not to appear rude—a formality, as you so nicely put it." There was a pause as they both remained silent for a moment.

He spoke first. "I received your letter this morning. Why didn't you call? You've been here three days already, and I didn't even know. It's a shameful waste."

"Of what?"

"Of good time, that's what. What are you doing tonight? No midnight gardening, I hope." His voice was teasing.

"No, no midnight gardening. I'll probably call up some friends later and have a little get-together. You are invited, if you wish, and you may bring someone with you, of course."

"Oh? Like whom, for instance? My tailor?"

"Don't be ridiculous. A friend, a girl, a woman, whomever you wish."

He whistled into the phone. "Now, that is the most insincere invitation I've ever heard. You don't mean a word of it, I can tell."

Rosalie laughed, amused by his tone. "Think what you like. I'm inviting you. If you want to come alone, fine, if you want to bring someone, fine too, and if—"

"And if I *don't* want to come, fine as well?"

Rosalie laughed again. "Why did you call me up? Just to be funny?"

"No, but I'm glad you at least think I'm funny. When I last saw you in New York I had the distinct impression you didn't think very much of me, period. Maybe there's hope after all, but," he added quickly before she could reply "I did call to ask you to dinner tonight. I had another engagement, a business engagement, but I canceled it when I opened your letter and discovered you were in town. Well? Can I pick you up? Say seven-thirty or eight?"

She took time to answer. "Where would we be going?"

He made a clucking sound into the receiver. "Don't you know it's impolite to be so curious? You aren't supposed to ask me where I'm taking you for dinner. It's downright *gauche*," he chuckled. "Don't you know that, Madame Social Butterfly?"

"I know, but I have to know where I'm going so I know

what to wear. This is California, not Paris, where you always get dressed up to go out to dinner. Here it's anything from barefoot in jeans to gala attire."

"Oh, I see. Well, perhaps you should get *very* dressed up in that case."

"Oh? Where did you have in mind?"

"Well, I think for our first date we should go somewhere special."

"Yes?"

"I made reservations for nine at the Bistro. We can't be late, or we'll have to go to McDonald's instead."

"Well, the Bistro *is* a very popular place, but I don't think I want to go out tonight, even for a hamburger. Perhaps another night. As I told you, I was going to call up—"

"Well, is it set then? I'll pick you up between seven-thirty and eight."

"I don't remember having accepted your invitation. You certainly have an air about you. I told you, I—"

"Yes, I know, you were going to call up some friends later and have a very boring evening."

"Think what you like, Mr. Guthrow, but I . . . oh, all right, I'll see you then."

"I'll be looking forward to it." Guthrow's voice did not show the slightest surprise at her acceptance. "Till tonight then, and—oh, I sent you a corsage. I knew I would see you tonight. Wear it in your hair, will you? I love the smell of gardenias." He hung up before she could say a word.

"The gall that man has, the absolute male impudence, the . . . the . . . the balls!" Rosalie slammed the phone down.

Tomó was passing through the living room just then, and overheard Rosalie muttering to herself. "Are we expecting Mistah Guthrow for dinner tonight, madame?"

She gave him a stern look. "No, why?"

"Sorry, madame, I just thought—"

"Stop thinking, Tomó, and get cooking! I'm starved and it's way past lunch time. Why are you so late today?"

"I not the one late, madame. Your lunch ready and waiting on the terrace. Shall I set an extra place for Mistah Guthrow?"

"No!" Rosalie was aware that her vehemence was excessive.

Tomó went out to the terrace, a broad smile on his brown face. Rosalie followed him out, and sat down to a lunch of poached cold sea bass, asparagus tips, and marinated cucumbers.

She undid her napkin and waved a hand at Tomó to dismiss him. "I'll call you if I need you, Tomó. Why don't you go and have some lunch yourself? I have some things to think over."

Tomó bowed his head graciously. "Yes, madame, I understand." An unmistakable smile was still on his face as he turned to leave.

"Tomó, I would appreciate it if you would keep your mind more on your cooking, and less on my phone calls." Rosalie looked up at him with half a scowl on her face. She looked down at her plate "It looks delicious."

The gall, Rosalie thought, as she helped herself to some fish. "Who does Jeffrey Guthrow think he is anyway—Don Juan? I should call him up and tell him I've changed my mind. But I won't, and that's the worst part. He knows I won't."

Tomó interrupted Rosalie's tête-à-tête with herself. "Package delivered for you, madame. From Mistah Guthrow!"

Rosalie threw Tomó an exasperated look and took the box from him. There was no name or note attached to it. "How do you know it's from 'Mistah Guthrow'? Oriental intuition?"

"No, madame. Mistah Guthrow's chauffeur say so."

"Ah so!" Rosalie said. "I see! Is he still waiting?"

"Mistah Guthrow?"

"No, his chauffeur. You did say he brought the package, didn't you?"

"I said he said package from Mistah Guthrow. Yes, he brought it."

She threw up her hands in exasperation. "Well? Is he still waiting?"

"Oh, no, madame," Tomó said. "Mistah Guthrow did not tell him to wait for answer."

"I see! Very well, then run along. I don't want you breathing down my back when I open it."

"Yes, madame. I bring dessert in little while?"

"Bring it later. No, on second thought, skip it. I'm going out to dinner tonight, and I don't want to eat too much now."

Tomó gave her a knowing smile, "Yes, madame." He turned and left.

Rosalie opened the box. It was from a Beverly Hills florist. A lone, creamy white, perfect gardenia was pinned to a piece of white, crinkled satin. Taped to the inside of the box was a small white card. She detached it and opened it. She recognized at once the bold handwriting. It read:

"I went to a lot of trouble to find the perfect flower for a near-perfect lady, who is having dinner with me tonight. Wear it in your hair. *À ce soir*."

Rosalie threw the card down. "Ha, the perfect flower indeed! 'Near-perfect,' am I? I'll show that . . . that . . . Oh, what's the use? I don't have a thing to wear tonight. Even so, I don't *know* what to wear. Something long? Short?"

Tomó returned, carrying a tray with steaming coffee and some macaroons.

"Tomó, send Madeleine out to me, will you? And tell Berthe I would like to see her too for a moment. Where is she, by the way? And Diablo? Ever since that animal arrived, he's been hiding inside all the time. Bring him out. Let him get some fresh air, he needs it." She could see the negative expression on Tomó's face. "Oh, all right, have Max or Berthe do it, but you had better start getting used to poor old Diablo. You'll be seeing a lot of each other from now on."

The servant nodded and hurried back inside to do as he was told.

Rosalie sat back against the cushion of the wicker chair and sniffed the flower. What shall I wear tonight? she mused.

At ten minutes to eight the doorbell rang. Tomó answered it.

"Ah, Mr. Guthrow," Tomó exclaimed. "Come in. Madame Farahet upstairs. Soon ready." He gestured for Jeffrey to pass in front of him. "Please come in living room and wait. I tell Miss Madeleine tell madame you here."

"Very well, Tomó, but please remind madame that our reservations won't wait."

"Yes, sah!" Tomó turned and went into the study where Madeleine was typing out a letter for Rosalie. "Mistah Guthrow here," he announced, "an' he says tell madame their reservations won' wait."

"Is that so? Overbearing sort, isn't he?" Madeleine got up and peeked cautiously around the doorway. Jeffrey was looking straight at her, a smile on his face. Madeleine cleared her throat and laughed nervously. "Oh, Mr. Guthrow, I *am* sorry. I thought you were somebody else. Tomó's English isn't the very best; I misunderstood him completely."

Tomó looked flabbergasted. Jeffrey roared with laughter. Madeleine excused herself hurriedly to escape her embarrassment and went upstairs to inform her mistress that Guthrow was downstairs. Tomó shook his head from side to side. "Women!" he said in a tired tone of voice. "You never know what they gonna say. My English pretty good."

Jeffrey chuckled. "Right you are, Tomó. You never can predict women, and as for your English—why, I think it's near perfect."

The sound of voices coming from upstairs made Jeffrey and Tomó turn to look. Rosalie and Madeleine were just coming around the circular balcony to the stairs.

Berthe came out of the bedroom and walked to the wrought iron balustrade to look down. There was a look of disapproval on her face as Jeffrey took Rosalie's hand and kissed it.

As Jeffrey looked up, he saw Berthe standing there. Her eyes were cold and piercing. He nodded hello to her and then turned to Rosalie and asked in a low voice, "Who is she? The woman on the balcony?"

"Berthe? She is my governess-companion. Why?"

"I thought she reminded me of someone. Someone I know."

"Oh? And who might *that* be?"

"Oh, no one I guess. It's just her eyes. They are so . . . so lifeless: like she hates the world, or doesn't care if someone blows it up with an atomic bomb."

"You're crazy. She is the nicest, kindest person. Berthe has been like a second mother to me. It's just the way she is. Reserved."

"You're probably right. Well, shall we go?"

"Go? Aren't you going to stay for a drink or something?"

He looked at his watch. "I'd be delighted. What are you serving?"

Rosalie was somewhat taken back.

Jeffrey grinned mischievously. "If it's fair for you to ask me where I'm taking you to dinner on our very first date, I think I can allow myself a similar privilege, don't you?"

"I'm sure you're right," Rosalie said, "but I agreed to go out to dinner with you, not to go out on a date. I don't *date*, except when I sign checks." Her tone was severe, but her face was smiling. Jeffrey, however, could not see that. Rosalie's back was turned to him, as she led him out to the enclosed bar, overlooking the ocean.

An hour and a half later, they arrived at the Bistro well past the time of their reservation. They were welcomed, nevertheless, and treated with a great deal of care.

Rosalie was amazed at the deferential attention bestowed on Jeffrey.

"I can see this must be one of your favorite places," Rosalie said. "After all, where else do the merely rich get treated like nobility?"

"How about a drink, Rosalie?" Jeffrey asked, ignoring her remark. "Some champagne or a little wine, perhaps?"

She shook her head. "I'm not in the habit of having more than one drink in an evening, and," she added, her voice taking on a more arrogant tone, "I'm not about to become an alcoholic just to please you."

"I'm glad to hear that, although it wouldn't make much difference to me if you were. I'd like you no matter what your faults were." Jeffrey's voice trailed off as the sommelier brought him the wine list. Jeffrey took it and waved the man away.

"So no champagne or wine for you, eh? Well, I guess you

are right not to have any. I would hate to have to carry you out of this place drunk.'' His lips spread into a devilish grin. ''People might talk.''

''I don't care what people say. I'm surprised you do. I should think you wouldn't, the way you go strutting around like a peacock in heat.''

''Me? Strut? I've always been told I had a lanky Texan stroll.''

Her face showed amusement. ''Really? I guess that's because you're so bowlegged. I hear all Texans are bowlegged from too much riding. I guess you must do a lot of that.''

Jeffrey smiled. ''Well, now, that depends. Are you talkin' about outdoor riding or the indoor kind?'' He imitated a Texan: ''Ah could teach you if you wanted—''

''I don't.''

Jeffrey motioned for the captain, who came over to the table with the menu, written on a large blackboard. Jeffrey asked Rosalie, ''What would you like to eat? Would you like something to start with?''

Rosalie scanned the menu with him. ''I don't know. I don't see anything I want. I'm sorry. Maybe it wasn't a very good idea, coming here with you tonight. I feel strange. I mean, here we are, practically strangers, and we're arguing all the time.'' She looked around the room. There were several faces she recognized, and in the far corner across from where they were sitting, Mona Farret, the Hollywood gossip columist, was watching her. Rosalie leaned over the table toward Jeffrey, ''By tomorrow afternoon,'' she whispered, ''our names will be plastered all over.''

Jeffrey leaned forward to meet her and silenced her with a kiss. It was unexpected, and it took her by surprise.

''Why did you do that?''

''Because I wanted to. Your lips were very tempting and much too close.''

A small group of people at the next table were whispering and pointing at them. A man and woman came in and stopped to say hello to Jeffrey as they passed by. Jeffrey introduced them to Rosalie. The woman recognized her on sight, Rosalie could tell.

Rosalie noticed other people staring at her from different tables. Their eyes all seemed to be passing judgment.

"Please, Jeffrey, take me home. I don't feel very comfortable," she whispered, her voice rasping, as if she were about to cry. Her eyes pleaded with him. "I guess I can't stand people staring at me anymore. I shouldn't be out dining with a man so soon after Peter's . . ." She left the sentence unfinished.

Jeffrey studied Rosalie's face intently for a moment, then motioned for the captain to come over to their table.

"All right," Jeffrey said, his voice soft and reassuring, "we'll leave, but I think it's silly to let a bunch of stupid people ruin our evening. You're a famous person and a beautiful woman. People are bound to talk and stare, today or next year. You might as well get used to it."

The captain leaned over. "Yes, sir, Mr. Guthrow, what have you and the lady decided on?"

Jeffrey placed his hand over Rosalie's. "Jimmy, bring us a magnum of Dom Pérignon, will you? And two filet mignon doggie bags to go. The lady wants to leave."

Jimmy gave Rosalie a queer look, and then grinned at Jeffrey. "You're kidding, Mr. Guthrow, right?"

Jeffrey looked up. "Extra salt and pepper, Jimmy—and oh, throw in a couple of napkins."

"But, sir—"

"Never mind, man, I'll borrow these two." He took his and Rosalie's napkins and stuffed them into Rosalie's small black Chanel purse. She watched in amazement, not believing what she was seeing or hearing.

"Doggie bags, here? This is crazy," she said.

"No, it isn't; they'll do it, you'll see. Want to bet?"

She shook her head. "No."

Jimmy came out carrying a linen-wrapped bundle, and handed it to Jeffrey.

"Thank you, Jimmy, thank you very much." Jeffrey rose from the table and extended his hand to help Rosalie up.

"Where are we going?" she wanted to know, as they were getting into his car. "Are you taking me home?"

"We are going on a picnic," he mused. "Just you and me and the stars. I know *just* the spot."

As she got in the car, Rosalie recognized Charles Mansfield getting out of the backseat of a brand-new Rolls-Royce. He did not see her. She was glad. It was not easy getting away from Mansfield once he got hold of you. Jeffrey saw her looking at the Rolls.

"You know Mansfield?"

"Huh? What?" Her thoughts had been so far away right then, his voice had startled her.

"I said—"

"I heard you. Yes, I know Mansfield. You can say he is sort of a business partner of mine." She smiled.

"Oh? How so? Or am I being too inquisitive?"

"No, not really, but I don't think it would be nice to take away any of Charley's glory right now. I—"

"Charley, is it? Well, that must mean one or two things and it has to be the second, since the first is unquestionably out. You're probably the backer for his last film. I heard he had a very wealthy woman backer. So it's you? Well, what do you know, and I hear it's one hell of a success, too. Tell me, how did you two ever meet?"

"It's a long story. My father knew him. I knew him. He needed help. I helped, and look at him now." She pointed with her head as Mansfield disappeared into the restaurant with his usual entourage of stars. "But I'm glad the picture was a success."

"I can bet," said Jeffrey, half sarcastically. "I heard the picture grossed thirty-five million, and all it cost was three million. I should say you should be glad, it was a damn good investment."

Rosalie threw him an annoyed look. "I didn't do it for the money. I did it for Charles. He was very nice to me once. I wanted to repay him."

"That must have been one hell of a niceness, to be worth a three-million-dollar risk. What did he do? I can't imagine Charley being nice to his own mother."

Rosalie thought Jeffrey was suggesting that she and Mansfield had had an affair; she glared at him. ''And what is that supposed to mean?''

He smiled and threw up his arms. ''What does *what* mean? Why are you so touchy?''

''I don't like people insinuating things about me.''

''Who's insinuating things about you?''

Her eyes flashed angrily. ''You are, and I resent it. You have a dirty mind, and I don't like people with small, dirty minds. Please take me home.''

''Home? Just because I asked you a simple question? What about our picnic?''

She glared at him. ''I think, Mr. Guthrow,'' she said, ''that if you don't want to hear a few of your choicer American expressions, you had better take me home as I say.''

He glared back at her. ''Let me tell *you* something Miss . . . Miss . . .''

''Yes?'' Rosalie's tone was icy. Her eyes flashed dangerously. ''Miss what?''

''Miss Spoiled Rotten Little Brat, Miss Arrogant, Miss Pompous, Miss . . .'' He stopped, searching for the final word, the last lash. His eyes cut into her like daggers.

Rosalie's eyes welled with tears. Her lower lip began shaking, trembling with rage and frustration, as she fought to keep her composure. She hated Jeffrey, hated his guts right then; yet as he degraded her, she had a horrible and insane feeling of love for this man who was whipping her with his tongue, slashing her with his harsh words.

Jeffrey's attack continued: ''Oh, what the hell difference does it make what I say you are? You're too cold, too lost in the past to recognize that there could be a future. You're letting your past devour you completely.'' He looked at her, and was stricken with remorse. Rosalie's trembling, quivering face was too much for him; he touched his fingers to her cheek and lifted her face so that she was forced to look directly into his eyes.

''I'm sorry,'' he said. ''Sorry I've been so hard on you. I . . .''

She turned her head and looked away. A tear rolled down her cheek and fell into the palm of his hand.

"Take me home," she said. "I don't feel very well."

Jeffrey's fingers clasped shut over the speck of dampness in his palm, and his knuckles grew white, as he squeezed his fist tight. He hated himself for having been so rough with her.

He thought: I love her, yet I allow myself to hurt her. Why? He started the car engine. Because I expect her to love me back and she doesn't. He swung the car away from the curb and in his frustrated anger, almost hit a pedestrian. As he swung the car to one side to avoid hitting the man, the brown paper bag fell off the seat onto the floor between his feet. A real picnic, Jeffrey thought, and kicked the bag with the heel of his shoe.

Rosalie's eyes were glued to the streets of Beverly Hills. Her expression was cold and aloof, but inside her heart was breaking, and she felt as if she were drowning in the well of tears remaining inside her.

I thought he was someone special, she thought, someone who could help me find a way to a new life, but he is cruel and uncaring. I hate him! They sat in silence, not uttering a word to each other, as the car sped along the Pacific Coast Highway heading in the direction of Malibu.

At twenty to eleven, Jeffrey's Mercedes pulled into Rosalie's Malibu driveway. Gravel flew everywhere as the car came to a screeching halt and lurched, throwing both of them forward in their seats.

"Here we are, Princess," Jeffrey said, the faintest touch of sarcasm in his voice. "And well before twelve, so you won't miss your beauty sleep. If you're not going to let yourself live, you'd better take care of your looks at least." He got out and went around on the other side to open her door.

Rosalie walked past him without a word or a look. He stood holding the door open for a moment, watching Rosalie climb the three steps to the flagstone landing.

Except for the width of her shoulders, which were broad and held back proudly, Rosalie's figure looked very small—too small, Jeffrey thought, and too frail. An invisible force seemed to push him forward as he leaped up the stone steps after her. Rosalie was reaching for the doorbell. Jeffrey grabbed her before she could press the button. His arms went around her with lightning swiftness, and, with the expertise of a practiced lover, he brought his lips down hard on hers, silencing her before she could speak. He crushed her soft body against his chest and kissed her with an insatiable passion, as she fought to free herself from the prison of his towering frame. He let her go.

"I love you, Rosalie. I'm sorry I said what I did earlier, but you made me so angry—the way you flew off the handle and tore into me, just because I asked you a simple question."

Rosalie looked up at him. Her lips were reddish pink and quivering still from his bruising kiss. The pungent perfume of her gardenia was hypnotizing. Her bruised lips looked even more tantalizing than before. He bent his head over hers again.

"I love you," he whispered. "I want you for my wife."

She moved her head to one side to avoid his oncoming lips. But he lifted her up off the ground and kissed her hard once again, then he put her down gently, as if she were a china doll.

"Go to sleep now," he said. "You look tired. I'll call you in the morning."

Jeffrey turned and left without a backward glance; he climbed into his car, and backed out of the driveway like a wildcat, spraying gravel everywhere once again.

Rosalie stood on the landing, her fingertips gently pressed against her lips. "Jeff," she whispered as the silver car shot through the open gates onto the highway. "Jeff." She leaned against the carved wooden door and cried.

The next morning, she discovered she had left her purse in his car. Jeffrey telephoned at around ten o'clock; she did not take the call. Again at twelve, and then at four in the afternoon, he phoned, and still she did not take the call. The next time, I'll talk to him, she decided; but he did not call again.

Days passed, then weeks, and still Jeffrey did not call her. Every time the telephone rang, Rosalie's heart would race wildly, and she would wait and hope; but it would always be somebody else, calling to invite her somewhere, to a charity benefit, a party, a dinner—or it would be the press, requesting an interview.

Ever since she had catapulated Peter Brian into fame, the press had been unable to get hold of her. Each time a reporter called, Rosalie had Madeleine tell him not to bother her; but the next day or the day after that, the phone would ring, and there would be some pushy young reporter begging to speak to her, if only for a moment. One reporter even called and said that he knew from a good source that she was Jeffrey Guthrow's mistress, and that if she did not grant him an interview, his paper would print the story. She called Philip, and he took care of it.

As time went by, Rosalie got accustomed to the idea that Jeffrey would probably never call her again, not after the way she had treated him. She began once again to shut herself off from the world, from everyone except those in her employ. She became thin, even thinner than after her parents' death, and wan for lack of sunshine. For, although she lived at the ocean's doorstep, she hardly ever went outside except to sit and watch the stars at night, alone, when all was quiet in the house. Dr. Bridges, who had been summoned by Berthe, pleaded with Rosalie to get some sunshine, or get out and have fun and see people.

"I don't like people," Rosalie would say. "They are not real, people. One minute they are here; then, pouf, they're gone forever. They don't care. People are mean and cruel and selfish." She would sit in the rocking chair and rock for hours, staring blankly into the flames of the fireplace.

Dr. Bridges scolded Berthe for allowing Rosalie to lock herself away from the world, and pleaded with her to keep trying to get Rosalie to break out of her isolation. "I fear for her sanity," he said. "No one can lock himself up forever! Something has got to give, sooner or later. Get that girl out in the sun," he would say to Berthe each time he left, "or you'll have me to reckon with if she falls ill."

"I can't do very much with Rosalie," Berthe would say.

"After all, she is a grown woman, and I cannot order her about. It is the other way around, doctor. She tells *me* what to do, and I do it."

"You know, Miss Giraud," he would reply, "I don't believe a word of that. I know Rosalie is stubborn as a mule when she wants to be, but I have the feeling you can be twice as stubborn if you want to be. That girl is pining away for somebody, and I'm telling you, whoever it is had better show up fast, or God knows what'll become of her."

On a Sunday night, exactly six weeks after the fight with Jeffrey, the doorbell rang. Rosalie was sitting alone on the terrace, having some coffee. She had just finished dinner and was relaxing, under the stars, listening to the surf pounding on the beach. The doorbell rang again.

"Tomó?" Rosalie called through the open door to the living room. "Tomó, would you please see who is at the door?"

Tomó did not answer; he did not hear her. He was already heading from the kitchen toward the front door. A few moments passed, and Rosalie dismissed the ringing as having come from another intrusive newspaperman. She stood up and walked over to the glass divider and pressed her face against its dampness, damp from the dew and salty air. She did not hear Tomó come out to the terrace. Her mind was far away, wondering where Jeffrey was—what he was doing.

"Madame, excuse me, but you have a visitor. I told him I not know if you in."

Rosalie turned slowly to look at the servant. "A visitor, you say? A man? At this hour?"

"Yes, madame, he waiting in study."

"You mean you let him in? Who is he, this phantom of the night?"

"Mistah Guthrow. He says see if you in. If you not in, he wait till you in."

Rosalie's face grew white, and she swallowed hard. She was suddenly very thirsty. The coffee cup she held in her hand teetered dangerously on the edge of the saucer.

Her voice was a mere croak. "Mr. Guthrow, did you say?"

Tomó reached out and took the cup and saucer from her trembling hands. "Yes, madame, he waiting in study."

Her hands flew instinctively to her face. She was not wearing any makeup. She smoothed back her hair with her hands and straightened the belt of her long, sweeping, wraparound gown.

"Tell him that I am in, and show him out to the terrace, will you?"

Tomó bowed gracefully and went inside.

Rosalie held on to the side of the railing to steady herself. Her heart was racing, her legs felt weak, like putty, under her weight. She braced herself and squared her shoulders, and turned to look out over the sea as if to find courage from it. She heard footsteps coming towards her, *his* and Tomó's.

Jeffrey spoke her name. "Rosalie?"

She turned to look at him, half holding her breath, lest she burst out into a fit of tears of joy at seeing him again.

"Hello, Jeffrey," she managed to say, after a lapse of several seconds. "This is quite a surprise."

"Pleasant, I hope?" His face was calm and relaxed, his tone gentle.

"Yes, it is a pleasant surprise." She waved her hand for him to sit down as Tomó disappeared once again inside, leaving them alone.

"How have you been, Rosalie?" Jeffrey asked. "I tried calling, but—"

"I know," she said quickly. "I didn't want to talk to you. I'm sorry. It was childish of me." She glanced at the box he had been carrying, which now rested on the chaise beside him.

Jeffrey saw her glance. "Your purse," he said. He handed the neatly wrapped package to her. "Your passport is in it. I thought I should return it."

Rosalie took the package from him. Their hands touched, and she jerked her hand back as if stung by a bee. Jeffrey noticed, but said nothing.

"I'm leaving for Europe in the morning," he said casually. "I've decided to spend a few months in Italy and France. I thought I should see you before I left."

Her eyes widened, and a cold hand seemed to clasp over her heart. "Leaving? You're leaving in the morning?"

He nodded. "Yes, I'll be gone for three or four months."

She clasped her hands together and wrung them nervously. "I . . . I'm sorry to hear that." She lowered her eyes, but not before he saw the despair in them.

"Are you, Rosalie?" His tone was urgent.

She looked up. "I'm sorry I behaved so childishly that evening. I don't know what came over me. I guess I was just very nervous about going out with a man again—a strange man." She corrected herself: "Well, a man I don't know very well, anyway. I just thought you were being rude and I got carried away. I'm sorry." She turned her head away so as not to let him see that she was crying.

Jeffrey stood up to leave. "I have to go now. I just came to say good-bye, to return your purse, and to say I'm sorry I was so hard on you."

She nodded her head, but did not speak. She was so heartbroken, she could not. Even more than his angry words of that night, his casualness now cut deep into the all-too-raw wounds of her heart.

He touched her shoulder. "Maybe some day we'll see each other again. I read in the paper that you were leaving for Switzerland to spend some time at d'Artois's new mansion. Is that true?"

Rosalie did not answer, for by now her frame was shaking with silent sobs as she huddled over, head bent down, arms clutched about her shoulder.

"Rosalie, darling, you're crying. Oh, God, what have I said now?" He bent down over her and lifted her up in his arms. He pressed his cheek against hers. "I didn't come here to upset you. I'll leave, and I won't bother you again." As he said these words, her arms went round his neck.

"Don't leave me, Jeffrey. Don't leave for Europe in the morning." She paused for a moment to catch her breath. "I love you," she said simply. "I don't want you to go."

He hugged her to him.

"I won't go."

Chapter Twenty-eight

Malibu, February 1966

Four days later, they were married.

The ceremony was held at sea on Jeffrey's yacht, the *Spartan II*. Standing together, side by side, she in a tailored white linen suit, he in navy and white, looking like the ship's captain, they were joined together in marriage by Archbishop Lernier, who had flown in for the ceremony.

Only a few close friends of the bride and groom were present. Jeffrey's parents had died when he was a child. He was sole heir to their sizable fortune in oil properties, land and cattle. An aunt, his father's older sister, had raised him; she was present, together with Gregory, his valet, and his close friend and attorney, Harold Brooks.

Among the other guests were d'Artois and Berthe.

Jeffrey slipped the narrow diamond circle over Rosalie's finger and arranged a small white orchid in her hair. He kissed her. ''Hello, Mrs. Guthrow. How does it feel to be a *new* woman?''

She looked shyly up at him. "I don't know. It terrifies me somehow. I guess I'm just gun-shy. It will take time."

"I know. I understand," Jeffrey said.

D'Artois was standing close by. A forced smile appeared on his lips as he stepped up to shake hands with Jeffrey.

I can wait, d'Artois thought. I will simply sit by and wait. It won't last long. He turned away from Jeffrey and held out his arms to Rosalie. Berthe was standing directly behind d'Artois. She noticed d'Artois's smirk, and in a nervous attempt to move away, stumbled forward, spilling her drink over the duke's white suit. He wheeled around, his face livid with anger, and glared furiously at her. Rosalie caught the look and was amazed at d'Artois's hostility. That's not like Jean, she thought, puzzled even more by Berthe's fearful expression.

Berthe hastily picked up the fallen glass and retreated within the cabin.

D'Artois knew Rosalie had caught the look on his face and hurried to cover it up.

"The poor woman," d'Artois said. "I might have been kinder." He sounded somewhat abashed. "Should I go after her?"

Rosalie smiled and shook her head. "No need. I'm sure Berthe will be all right."

D'Artois held out his arms to her. "I never did get to kiss the bride," he said.

That night the newlyweds did not make love. Jeffrey slept in the master cabin; Rosalie in one of the cabins reserved for guests.

A week later, the *Spartan II* and its passengers returned from their voyage at sea. The honeymoon couple was browner than when they had left, and to the unknowning world, seemingly happier, but the marriage had not yet been consummated.

Mr. and Mrs. Jeffrey Alan Guthrow drove through the massive electric gates of the Guthrow mansion in Holmby Hills at three o'clock on a March day, ready to begin their new life together.

That night, after Rosalie had bathed and changed in the

guest suite adjoining the master suite, she joined Jeffrey downstairs in his study. He was waiting for her in a wine-colored velvet suit with piqué shirt and black velvet tie.

He is so handsome, Rosalie thought, as she approached him. She was wearing a lavender silk Dior hostess-pajama outfit.

Jeffrey's eyes swept over Rosalie critically, trying to find fault with this perfect creature who was now his wife. Her usually composed face was smiling. She looked impossibly beautiful and tempting. Her green eyes searched his face for a sign of approval. He could tell she was waiting for him to comment on her outfit. He walked over to her and lifted her hands to his lips. She trembled slightly under his touch, like a frail flower in a gentle breeze. He kissed her hands and led her over to where he had been sitting by the window, overlooking the pool and gardens.

"Come and sit down, darling. You look and smell better than all the gardens out there." He pointed outside. "I've missed you all afternoon. Where have you been all this time? Not moping around, I hope?"

Rosalie shook her head. "No, I was showing Madeleine where to put all my things. I'm sorry it took me so long."

Jeffrey brought her left hand up to his lips once again, and kissed her ring finger. "Shall I tell you that I want to take you upstairs right now to my bedroom and make wild, passionate love to you? Do you know what it's like to look at you, to smell and touch you, to have you so close to me"—he ran a lean bony finger along the contour of her cheek—"and not make love to you?" He finished the sentence in a whisper.

Rosalie turned her head and looked out the window. "Don't make me feel any worse than I already do, Jeffrey." She turned her head once again, and looked directly at him. His face, although stern, was loving. "I don't know why, Jeffrey. I love you; yet, every time I'm faced with going to bed with you . . . I freeze." Her eyes were pleading. "Please be patient with me, Jeff. I'm trying, really I am."

The butler came in to announce that dinner was being served in the dining room. Jeffrey stood up and reached out his hand to help Rosalie up. She squared her shoulders, and rose to her feet, a wan smile on her face.

"I love you, Jeffrey. Isn't that what really counts?"

He nodded. "Yes, of course."

Together they walked out of the study into the marble hallway and through the huge arched doors into the dining room. Back in the study, a bottle of Dom Pérignon and two glasses remained untouched and forgotten.

That night after dinner and coffee and anisette on the terrace, Rosalie and Jeffrey went upstairs to get ready for bed, he to his room, she to hers. Half an hour passed, and then there was a knock on her door. She froze. Her heart was beating wildly. She felt weak, panic-stricken, as she imagined Jeffrey pushing his way into her room and taking her by force.

He knocked once more. "Rosalie?"

She sprinted across the room and climbed into bed, pulling the covers up over her.

"Come in," she said finally, almost too softly for him to hear.

"Are you decent?" came his voice once again.

"Yes, come in."

The doorknob turned and the heavy door opened back into the bedroom. Jeffrey looked around the room and saw Rosalie in bed. He came closer. The covers were pulled up almost under her chin, and he could hardly see her face in the dark. He switched on the night-light and sat down on the edge of the bed beside her.

Rosalie moved over slightly to give him more room.

"You didn't have to run for cover. I won't force you to make love to me." Jeffrey leaned over and kissed her cheek lightly. "I won't even kiss you, if you don't want me to." He brushed his lips lightly over her face. She twitched, and closed her eyes. "Too many ghosts hover between us," he said softly. "Too many husbands and lovers, too many disappointments. I'll wait until you're ready, until you *want* me to make love to you, not as a substitute for some lost lover, but as the only man you'll ever want to touch you again. Until then . . ." His hand cupped her chin lightly, gently, as if it were made of porcelain and would break under the slightest pressure.

"I want you, Rosalie. As I look down at your heavenly face and body . . ." He rolled back the covers. She was nude, her skin smooth and tanned from their week in the sun, and still damp from her bath. "I could take you now; after all, you *are* my wife, but I want you to tell me that you want me to and mean it. I want you to need me as a lover. Not only as a friend, or someone to lean on. Do you understand, Rosalie?"

Rosalie shifted her eyes away from Jeffrey's and glanced at his maleness, which was pressing boldly against the light blue silk fabric of his dressing gown. She could tell he wanted her, she could *see*. She felt weak. She had never yet seen Jeffrey naked. Her mouth felt dry. She felt a yearning, burning sensation within her, as she imagined him taking her. The sight of his lean, strong body rippling under the light fabric made her grow warm and tight inside, as she imagined him standing nude before her.

Jeffrey lifted himself off the bed and pulled the loose belt of his robe tight around his waist. He stood away from the bed and smoothed his hair back away from his forehead with his hands. He had teased her, tempted her with his maleness, and he had succeeded in reawakening her womanhood. He could tell from her rapid breathing, from the tiny beads of perspiration forming around her upper lip, and from the way she was looking up at him, her face completely unveiled.

It was the face of a woman wanting a man, and yet, he could tell she was not ready. Her pride still formed an insurmountable wall.

I'll wait, Jeffrey thought, as he fought his urge to throw himself up on her.

He could feel himself weakening as he watched the rise and fall of her tanned breasts above her ribs, and the smooth flow, like honey, of tanned curves against the ivory silk sheets. He leaned over, feeling drained and weak, and kissed her softly on the lips. He pulled the covers up over her and tucked her in for the night.

"Good night," Jeffrey whispered, turning out the night-light. "If you feel lonely or cold during the night . . ." He did not finish his sentence, just smiled and closed the door behind him.

For several hours, Rosalie tossed in her bed, trying to blot Jeffrey out of her mind. "He's my husband. I'm married to him. I have every right to him; then why am I punishing myself like this?"

It was not pride holding her back, but fear. Fear of being hurt again like all those times before. She had come to feel that if she loved a man, he would die; or, if he did not die, somehow he would be taken away from her. She fought with her emotions. "Do I have a right to ask him to love me without loving him back? Do I have the right to love a man when death and doom have taken all those whom I've loved before?"

Rosalie's face was hot and sticky, the sheets damp from her perspiration. She pushed the covers back and climbed out of bed. She was naked. She turned on the night-light and went to stand in front of her full-length mirror.

She studied her figure critically. The small, round breasts . . . were they too small for Jeffrey, she wondered? The flat stomach and narrow waistline—too frail, perhaps? Her hands moved gently over her body, exploring every curve, every hill and hollow. She held her breasts in her hands and felt a rush of pleasure engulfing her body. She could feel herself getting moist. "I am a woman, a *married* woman. I need a man. I need Jeffrey," she whispered. She tiptoed across the carpeted floor to the dressing room and chose a lavender, slightly transparent dressing gown with soft wide ruffles around the plunging neckline. She put it on and dabbed a touch of perfume behind her earlobes and on the back of her neck. She went and stood in front of the large door which separated her bedroom from Jeffrey's. She felt like a gawky schoolgirl hesitating outside the classroom before going in to throw herself at the schoolmaster's feet.

"Rosalie La Farge, you are a fool," she whispered to herself. "He's yours—go get him." She raised her hand to knock on the door, but stopped.

Damn it. What's the matter with me? Why can't I just walk

right in? Then, before she could change her mind, she turned the doorknob and stole in.

Jeffrey was sitting in the dark, smoking a pipe in front of the fireplace, his legs propped up and crossed on an ottoman.

Rosalie wanted to turn and run, but Jeffrey saw her in the mirror over the mantel and stood up to greet her.

"Come in," he said, offering her a chair. "Come in and sit awhile by the fire."

She went and sat beside him by the fire.

"Couldn't you sleep?" he asked, puffing on his pipe while gazing into the crackling fire.

"No, I was hot— *Warm,*" she corrected herself hastily. "It was very warm in my room." She sat on the edge of her chair, knees tight together, hands folded in her lap. She kept her eyes fixed on her toes which curled up and down nervously.

"I can check the air conditioning in your room if you like, but I'm pretty sure it's working." He was not making it easy for her. "Do you want me to open a window for you?"

She shook her head. "No." Her voice croacked. "I . . . I want to talk to you."

He bent down and checked his watch in the light from the flames. "At three-thirty in the morning? Why don't you admit the truth? You are dying for me to make love to you and you came to find me. Well? Am I right?"

His shameless arrogance made her want to kick him in the place where her father had always told her to kick such men. He was standing inches away from her, towering over her, reeking of sex and impudence. She could not stand being putty in his hands, and yet, if she let her pride take over . . . She thought of leaving, but could not. All she could think of was touching him, holding him, having him devour her with his lovemaking. She chased her pride away and swallowed hard, determined to get what she had come for.

"I . . . I came, like you said." Her voice was so low he could hardly hear her.

"Like I said?" Jeffrey repeated. He looked down into her eyes, and saw the fire reflected in them, like flames of passion, and he felt like pouncing on her at that moment, but he held back. She is going to have to ask for it, he thought to himself. I won't be toyed with like a puppet, leaping whenever *she* decides to pull the strings.

Jeffrey felt Rosalie's hands on his body, running up along his hips and waist, tempting him with her caresses. She came closer, pressing herself against him. She parted the upper part of his dressing gown and began running her tongue up along the muscular curves of his stomach and chest. She stood on tiptoe, continuing her kisses along his throat to his ears. He felt his knees weakening, his body becoming hot. His vital parts seemed to be disintegrating, such was the mixture of pain and ecstasy in his resistance.

"Jeffrey?" Rosalie whispered, while darting her tongue into his ear. "Pick me up. Hold me. I need you." Jeffrey picked her up and swung her into his arms.

"You came for me to love you?" he asked.

"Yes." Her eyes were still looking straight into his.

"Then say it, Rosalie. Say 'I want you, Jeffrey.' " His arms were like a cradle, his breath like a summer breeze, as he squeezed her against him. His mouth was an inch from hers, poised and waiting. A lock of his blond hair had fallen forward and now hung over one eye. She liked him this way, slightly disheveled.

He lowered his face closer to hers. "Say it, Rosalie. Say it."

Rosalie could feel Jeffrey's heart beating fast against hers, could hear it pounding like a beaten drum. She felt a rush of helplessness, a surging tide of love and warmth that sent prickly shivers up her spine and left her limp. *"I want you,"* she said urgently. "Now."

Jeffrey lowered her onto the huge bed and began to undress her. His hands worked swiftly with the sash of her dressing gown, expertly lifting her body with one hand and disrobing her with the other. Then he let his own dressing gown slide to the floor and climbed onto the bed beside her. "I'm glad," he said. "I would have waited, but I wouldn't have got much sleep in the meantime."

Rosalie looked up at Jeffrey, her face tremulous with love. He looked down at her with desire, and whispered, "Tonight, my love, I will love you in such a way that for as long as you live, you will remember this night with joy."

They laughed together and kissed, and he showered her with love all night, until the early morning light lit up the room and bathed their suntanned bodies with its golden rays. They spent the night wrapped in each other's arms, making up for the lost time since their wedding. He had left her limp and giddy, wild and content, all at the same time.

That morning, Rosalie and Jeffrey had breakfast on the terrace overlooking the rose gardens, and laughed and talked about the future. Rosalie found her man, the only man who was big enough, old enough, loving enough—and *strong* enough to deal with her emotions and hurts and bad memories of the past.

Time passed, and Jeffrey's and Rosalie's love grew stronger and stronger, but the haunting shadows of Rosalie's past still hovered over her, filling her dreams, and casting shadows on her otherwise joyful days.

One morning, as Rosalie slept in the huge bed in the master suite at their Holmby Hills estate, Jeffrey sat up watching her. He raised himself on his elbow and moved his eyes slowly along the curves of her slender body. She appeared frail against the stark white sheets. He felt like picking her up in his arms and cradling her.

The week before, Diablo had died, and Rosalie had still not got over it. D'Artois had been visiting them, as was his custom. appearing for a few days' stay once every month since their marriage. Rosalie had seemed happier and more relaxed then usual. Then one morning, d'Artois arrived at breakfast and announced that Diablo had been found dead. The cat, he said, had slipped from the ledge above where he slept every morning, and had fallen onto the pavement below. The animal's death seemed to open up every wound Jeffrey had thought healed. His heart reached out to her. Her small body was draped across the bed, her back pressed up against his chest, her leg brought up high and wrapped around a pillow. Her blond hair was mussed and curly from a night's sleep. He touched her lightly. Her skin was moist and smooth.

Rosalie felt the caress, and instinctively snuggled closer, pressing her hard young buttocks up against his groin. Jeffrey's arms went around her, and his voice caught a little as he spoke. "Rosalie, my darling, I love you so much."

"Me too," Rosalie whispered, stifling a yawn and arching her back. "I love you too." She smiled wryly and looked up at her husband. His expression was that of an adoring husband, a man rapturously in love. "If anything ever happened to you, I would cut out my heart and bury it with you, I swear," Rosalie said. Her voice sent a chill through Jeffrey's body. She began to cry softly, her body shaking as she sobbed out her words. "Don't die before me, Jeffrey; please don't ever leave me behind. I couldn't take it. I couldn't take losing *you*."

Jeffrey's arms wrapped around her. "Don't worry, darling. I won't die. I promise I'll live to be as old as the mountains and as wise as a redwood tree, and I will love you more each day. I'll never leave your side. I promise." He smiled. "You are my whole world, you know. You are everything to me. Without you the sun would no longer rise in the sky, the water wouldn't run in the brook, and the birds would never sing again outside my window. I promise you, I'll never leave you as long as I live; and even after, I'll still be there."

He had never before wanted her so desperately, so completely, without restraint of any kind. He clasped her curves against his hollows, pressing her hard to him, molding her warm flesh to his.

Her body bloomed under his gentle caresses, and she returned his kisses and caresses with all the burning passion she possessed.

That morning, it was as if they had never made love before; as if in their wildest fantasies, each sea was parted, each multitude fed, each child comforted; each in turn was vanquished by the other's passion.

That warm June morning, a child was conceived, their

first. Nine months later, a son was born, Armand Olivier Guthrow, a tiny replica of his handsome father. Hurts and sorrows mellowed, dreams faded away, and Rosalie rejoiced in the new love she had found in Jeffrey and in the child she had borne.

Chapter Twenty-nine

Côte d'Azur, France, June 1974

Seven years passed, and life for Rosalie was now filled only with joy and laughter, and the happiness she shared with Jeffrey and their children.

She had borne him two more sons; Sacha, now six, and Jeremy, now four years old. The years had been good ones, but the future held yet another promise. Rosalie was expecting her fourth child—a girl, they hoped. Rosalie was four and a half months along when they decided to return, after a lapse of years, to France. In the beginning of their marriage, Rosalie had been against it. "Too much happened to me there," she had said. "I couldn't bear to go back. Please, Jeffrey, if you love me, *please* understand."

He had understood, and had not pushed her; and as the years passed and the children arrived, they had much to do, and many other places to go. But now Jeffrey felt it was time for Rosalie to face her past. Enough time had elapsed. He felt she was ready and could handle it.

They received an invitation from Monaco to attend the *Bal de la Croix-Rouge*, the Red Cross Charity Ball, in Monte Carlo, and Jeffrey thought it the perfect excuse to get Rosalie to return to Europe.

Rosalie was reluctant at first, but after much cajoling and some pressure from Jeffrey, she gave in.

When the day to leave for France finally arrived, the bustle at the Holmby Hills mansion was unlike any in years, as everyone—servants, as well as master, mistress and children—prepared for their two-month stay in Europe.

The plan was to stay one week at the Hotel de Paris, for old times' sake—that was where Rosalie and Jeffrey had first met—and then to on to St. Tropez, to Colombier, which was being readied for their arrival, and then on to Paris for a few days.

A few close friends—Solange and her husband and their two children, Philip and his new wife, and d'Artois—were invited to meet them at Colombier.

As their plane landed in Nice and came to a full stop, the first person Rosalie spotted in the crowd was d'Artois. He had flown from New York on a commercial flight, arriving the day before.

D'Artois waved to Rosalie as she came down the ramp. Rosalie led the way, with Jeffrey next, Armand and Sacha close behind, and Jeremy leading his governess, Chantale, by the hand, and screaming at the top of his lungs that he had to go *pipi* at once.

"Welcome to Nice once again, Jeffrey, and you too, Rosalie," d'Artois exclaimed as he first pumped Jeffrey's hand up and down and then wrapped his arms around Rosalie. "I'm glad you have finally returned, my dear. The Côte hasn't been the same since you left it.'

Jeffrey made a grimace and, turning away from d'Artois, took hold of Rosalie's arm. "Come along, darling. I see Jules waiting for us. Max?" Max appeared from behind.

"Yes, monsieur."

"See that the trunks are handled with care during the unloading, will you? And call ahead and make sure our suites at the Hotel de Paris are ready. I would hate it if I arrived there and had to wait in the lobby, just because we're half a day early."

"Yes, monsieur." Max turned on his heel and went to see to his duties.

"Well, my dear," Jeffrey said, turning to Rosalie. "What would you like to do while the trunks are being unloaded?"

Rosalie looked up at him and smiled. Her face was radiant, her cheeks flushed from the heat. "Well, why don't we go have a drink while we wait? We can send the children on first with Jules and Chantale; and we can wait for the Rolls to return. Jules will have to make an extra trip anyway for most of the luggage."

"Frankly, my dear, I think he'll have to make at least three extra trips for your bags alone." He laughed at the expression on her face. "Oh come on, I'm just teasing. Actually, I can hardly wait to see you in all those lovely dresses, not that you wouldn't look good in a potato sack or naked, for that matter." He raised his eyebrows and crossed his eyes a little in a boyish way. "*Especially* naked!"

"Oh, shut up, Jeffrey, and stop looking at me that way. Everyone is staring at you; you're embarrassing me."

He grinned. "Why don't I undress you right here, and really give them something to stare at?" He pretended to lunge for her.

"Oh stop it, Jeffrey Guthrow, you big oaf. You . . . ."

"*Goon* is the word you're looking for, pretty lady, and I don't mind being one as long as I'm married to you."

"Well, if you don't let go of my blouse, I'll—"

He bent over and kissed her on the mouth. "Yes? You'll what?"

"Oh, never mind, undress me if you want, I don't care."

He removed his hands from the delicate pearl buttons of her lavender shirt. "Well, now, I don't like a prude, but on the other hand I'm not sure I like a loose woman either."

She rolled her eyes in their sockets. "Jeffrey Guthrow, you are the most impossible man I've ever known."

"That's easy," he retorted, "since I'm the only *man* you've ever known."

D'Artois was busy helping Chantale herd the three boys into the backseat of the limousine.

Jeffrey glanced toward d'Artois.

"The way d'Artois muddles about, poking his nose into everything, I swear he's beginning to remind me of an old-maid aunt."

Rosalie scowled at her husband. "Oh, Jeffrey, don't be so mean. He's all right, really he is. He is just a little affected by whatever happened to him during the war. It isn't fair to make fun of him. He's our friend."

D'Artois closed the car door and started toward Rosalie and Jeffrey.

"I still think he's queer," Jeffrey replied, his voice coming out a bit louder than he had intended. "Why else is he never with a woman?"

"Hush!" Rosalie squeezed his hand. "He'll hear you."

Jeffrey shrugged.

The boys were waving and conducting a personal riot in the backseat as the car pulled away.

"Poor Jules," Jeffrey laughed, as the car disappeared. "He'll have a splitting headache by the time they get to Cannes."

"I hope they behave themselves when they get to the hotel." Rosalie sighed, her face a mirror of her love for her boys.

"Well, I don't know, you can't expect too much out of those boys. They take after their mother."

Rosalie poked Jeffrey playfully in the ribs and turned to d'Artois, standing nearby.

"Jean, tell this big oaf of mine what a fine young lady I used to be *before* I married him."

D'Artois opened his mouth to speak, but seeing Jeffrey's severe look, changed his mind.

Rosalie and Jeffrey decided to go for a drink while their luggage was being unloaded, and Rosalie asked d'Artois to join them. They went to the airport lounge and sat around the small, square table drinking champagne cocktails.

D'Artois told Rosalie about the changes that had taken place on the Côte since she had left, and Jeffrey sat silently smoking his pipe, studying the man who seemed to hover close by wherever they went. He watched d'Artois gesture with his bony, scarred fingers, waving them in the air as he spoke.

What a fake d'Artois is, he thought. What a louse—but with the cunning and swagger of a panther.

"You *must* go to the Red Cross Ball," d'Artois said emphatically. "The press has already announced you will be there, and everyone will be looking for you. It is the perfect forum for your reappearance in European society. It will be the biggest turnout ever. Everyone is curious. They all want to see the new Rosalie Guthrow."

"I don't know," Rosalie said, her voice almost tremulous, "I may not be ready to face the press." She reached across the table into her purse and took out a long, thin Havana cigar.

"When I was little, I used to tell myself that as long as Papa was around I could do anything. . . ." Her voice trailed off. She lit the cigar, took a puff, and looked up at Jeffrey. "But now I have Jeffrey, and I guess I can do now whatever I could do then." Jeffrey smiled, his face warm and tender.

"I'm sure you can, my darling, and I do agree you should begin going out again." Jeffrey squeezed Rosalie tightly. "I can hardly wait to see you in that red dress you had made for for the occasion." He lowered his lips to her ear and whispered, so that only she could hear. "And I can hardly wait to get you to Monte Carlo, so that I can see how you look in my arms."

She gave him a loving look. "You're getting me all excited, Jeffrey. Behave yourself. Isn't it enough that we've had four children in six years?"

"Three and a half," he corrected her and placed his hand under the table on her stomach. "I know it's going to be a girl," he said, "a girl just like you."

D'Artois cleared his throat. Jeffrey wished the duke would disappear.

"Yes?" Jeffrey asked, annoyance showing in his voice.

Artois spoke softly. "It's Max, Jeffrey, he has been motioning to us. I think everything is unloaded, and the Rolls is ready."

Jeffrey paid the bill, and they left.

A week later the Guthrow family and guests were ensconced at Colombier. It was the day before the ball, and Jeffrey was preparing to leave for London that night on a business trip. He had to be in London early the next morning and had promised Rosalie to be back in time for the ball the following evening.

"If I'm a little late," he had said, "go on with Solange and the gang. I'll meet you there."

"Oh sure," she had said, pouting a little. "Everyone will be with their husbands, and Orphan Annie in her red dress will come in all alone and stick out like a sore thumb."

"Don't be silly," Jeffrey said. "You'll look ravishing as always, the belle of the ball, and then I'll come riding in at the last moment on my white charger, and I'll make love to you right there, and everyone will go wild with envy. The women will envy you because I'm such an expert lover, and the men will envy me because you're such a delectable morsel. Actually," he said, pretending to be critical, "you are more than a mere morsel lately. You are, if I may say so, one hell of a mouth-watering mouthful." He patted her belly.

"I don't even *show* yet, you . . . If you're trying to say I'm fat, I'm not."

He laughed. She pouted and scowled up at him.

"Jeff?" She said his name tenderly.

"Uh-huh?"

"I thought this was supposed to be a vacation. We're hardly here eight days, and you are already all wrapped up in business. I thought this was going to be our second honeymoon."

"Well, now," he joked, "look who's talking about a second honeymoon. You are a very pregnant woman, a mother of three, an old lady. You shouldn't be talking about honeymoons at all. What would people think?" He grinned wickedly. "Pregnant ladies don't have honeymoons. They have babies."

"And sex?" she asked.

"Yes, that too."

"Well, then, I guess it's time for me to get myself a lover. After all, husbands are *supposed* to be dull."

"Dull, am I?" he growled as he lunged forward, grabbing Rosalie and placing her back on the bed. He stood looking down at her laughing face, radiant with blooming motherhood.

Rosalie stopped laughing and looked up at her husband, looming over her. She felt their child flutter inside her and she wanted him to make love to her, to be as close as possible before he left.

Jeffrey felt her mood, and struck a match, lighting the candle on the night table by the bed. In the soft light, his face seemed overwhelmingly handsome to Rosalie. She felt her need growing, as she admired his lanky body.

A breeze was blowing through the one open window. The sheer white curtains lifted and danced along the sides of the window frames, looking like slender ghosts in the dim-lit room. In spite of the breeze, it was a hot, humid night. Rosalie could see Jeffrey's chest, brown from the sun, the golden hairs glistening with perspiration. How strong and tempting he looked standing there against the pale shadows!

"I want you, Jeffrey, before you go."

"Oh, baby, I . . ." Jeffrey said swiftly, bending toward her. "How can I resist you? Come here." He bent and picked her up and took her over to stand with him by the open window. Only the tiniest sliver of a moon could be seen, hanging in the purple black sky. The stars were few, and far apart. Outside the window a giant fig tree was rubbing up against the windowsill. They heard a little squeaking sound, as a thin branch scraped along the glass panes.

"Our own violinist," Jeffrey said softly, nuzzling Rosalie's ear. "I feel like dancing with you right now." He pressed his cheek against hers and cradled her body lovingly with his own.

"Jeff? Make love to me. Right now. It won't hurt the baby." Her eyes were ablaze with desire. "I wish you didn't have to be away tomorrow. Can't you cancel your trip to London? Put it off?"

"No, I can't, my darling, but I promise you I'll hop on that plane and be back just as soon as I'm done with my business." He kissed her underneath her chin, and nudged the strap of her nightgown away from her shoulder. "I'll be very gentle, darling. I'll remember there's a tiny little person inside you. Someone I'm very fond of."

Rosalie smiled and passed her fingers lightly over Jeffrey's face.

"Jeff, darling. I know I probably shouldn't say this, but I could never love another man after you."

"You won't have the chance," he teased. "I'll still be around when I'm a hundred, keeping an eye on you, and after that, you'll be too old for anybody else to want you."

She snuggled closer to him and whispered in his ear, "I hope you look as good when you are a hundred."

Jeffrey placed Rosalie on the bed once more, and propped her head up on a pillow. He began to undress, swiftly, but with ease and grace. His broad chest was heaving in anticipation of the pleasure of the woman he loved. The muscles in his legs rippled, as he climbed onto the bed. He lifted her easily with one hand and slipped off her silky gown.

Jeffrey trailed a finger up Rosalie's side and down between her breasts. Her skin was moist from the summer heat, yielding under his touch. He cupped one of her breasts in the palm of his hand, and felt it quiver.

"Hold your other breast, darling," he whispered coaxingly. "Touch your own body and let me love you with my eyes." His voice was like a drug, sweet and deep and hypnotizing. He bent and kissed her small rounded stomach. He felt the baby flutter inside her and laid his head on her belly in awe of the miracle of life within.

Rosalie writhed under his touch.

"Jeff, Jeff, darling, you're driving me crazy. I can't stand you teasing me like this."

"I'm not teasing you. I'm just admiring my wife, my pregnant, sensuous wife, swollen with my child." He moaned and kissed the tip of her breast. He flicked his tongue across the pink tip, as if he were tasting a ripe plum. He moaned his pleasure as he felt the nipple grown hard under his tongue. "When you're pregnant you get fat in all the right places. I'm considering keeping you like this forever. I want to remember you always as Eve, a pregnant Eve in my garden of love." He touched her between the legs, at the beginning of her thighs, and she moaned her pleasure at his touch. She was soft and moist inside. Her whole being cried out in anticipation, as she waited for him to take her.

"I'll be gentle," he whispered. "I'll be so gentle you won't even know I'm there."

Rosalie sank her head back deeper into the pillow, and heaved her breast forward. She wrapped her legs around him tightly. "Not tonight, Jeffrey, I don't want you to be gentle tonight. I want to feel you, deeper and harder tonight than I've ever felt you before. I don't care how rough you are." She cried out his name as he thrust himself into her.

Jeffrey moved slowly, plunging himself deeper and deeper into the moist, warm depths of her throbbing body, and he shivered with pleasure, as he watched her breasts, full and round, and golden-colored in the soft light, bouncing freely in rhythm with each thrust.

Jeffrey slid his left arm around Rosalie's waist and rolled over with her, letting her lie on top of him. She raised herself up, placing her palms on the bed on either side of him. As she straddled him, she looked down at his face, and her hair fell forward like a waterfall, long and golden, and came to rest on his chest and neck. Jeffrey could feel Rosalie's warm breath. He could feel her passion as she moved on top of him. He cupped her breasts in his hands and squeezed them gently.

"I'm coming," he said simply, writhing with pleasure as he watched her move. He pulled her to him, crushing her against his chest and stomach, and wrapped his legs around hers tightly. "I love you," he panted as they moved together rapidly in a last heated rush, and he exploded inside her. They remained clamped together, their bodies trembling and quivering, as every raw nerve cried out to be soothed. Rosalie whimpered like a hurt puppy, and Jeffrey kissed her and held her close until she fell asleep.

Later, in the dark, for the wind had blown the candle out, Jeffrey dressed and then stood over the bed for a moment, looking down at Rosalie's sleeping face. He smiled and brushed a lock of hair away from her eye. He checked his watch. It was very late, after eleven, and he had to leave. The door closed softly shut behind him as he left the room and hurried down the corridor and down the steps to find Jules to drive him to the airport.

Chapter Thirty

Côte d'Azur, June 1974

Rosalie sat in her upstairs bedroom, nervously twitching on the stool in front of her dressing table. She had just received a call from Jeffrey, the third one of the day, telling her he was detained, and this time telling her to go on ahead to the Red Cross Ball in Monte Carlo with Solange and d'Artois and their other guests. Rosalie had been terribly upset and disappointed that he would not be home in time to escort her to the ball; but he had promised to meet her there, no matter how late.

Rosalie was apprehensive. She and Jeffrey had never gone and place without each other since their marriage.

There was a knock on her bedroom door, first soft, then louder. It was Germaine, bringing in her dress, still warm from having been just pressed.

The narrow-faced maid smiled pleasantly as she entered and asked Rosalie where to put the dress.

"Just lay it on the bed, Germaine. In a little while, Mademoiselle Madeleine or Berthe will come for it."

The woman looked at her questioningly. "Come for it, madame? I thought you were going to wear it to the ball tonight. I guess I misunderstood."

"No, you didn't, but I'm certainly not going to put it on and sit on it for all the time it takes to drive up to Monte Carlo. It would be completely crushed and rumpled by the time I got there."

The maid nodded, still amazed by the ways of the rich. "I see, madame. I hope madame has a fine time tonight. I'm sorry monsieur isn't here." Upon mentioning Jeffrey, the maid's face lit up into a broad smile. The staff loved him. All the older servants, who had been with the La Farge family since Rosalie was a child, had welcomed him with open hearts.

Berthe came in just as Germaine was leaving, and then looked down her nose as the maid passed her in the doorway. "I hope you didn't burn madame's dress, Germaine, or put a shine to it."

Germaine looked back over her shoulder at her mistress sitting now on the edge of the bed beside the dress. Rosalie winked and nodded, signaling the maid to ignore Berthe.

"Run along, Germaine; the dress looks perfect, thank you very much," Rosalie said.

Berthe walked over to the bed and sat down in the straight-backed chair across from Rosalie. "Rosalie, I wish you would be a little more formal with the servants. These girls are already so lazy, and with the slightest sign of leniency from you, the next thing you know, they'll be trying to run things themselves."

Rosalie cocked an eyebrow at Berthe. "You can't be serious, Berthe. Why, ever since I can remember, you've been trying to boss me around. You aren't telling me," she said, clucking her tongue disapprovingly, "that I've been that easy to boss around." She smiled and patted Berthe's hand. "They've all been with me for years, Berthe, with *us*." She pointed to Berthe and to herself. "I'm not going to start putting them all through the grinder just because Germaine is ten minutes late with my dress. Maybe she wasn't feeling well today. Maybe it just slipped her mind; about the time, I mean."

Berthe looked up at the ceiling and crossed her legs. "I say she's just plain lazy, and too slow. I should have a talk with her."

Rosalie shook her head. "Let it go, Berthe, all right?"

"Very well, if that's what you want," Berthe said, lowering her eyes.

"That's what I want, Berthe—and, speaking of people being late, where is Max? Go get him, will you? We'll have to be leaving in five minutes if I'm going to make my appointment with Alexandre. Ask Madeleine to call the Hotel de Paris and tell them to have Alexandre wait if I'm a few minutes late."

Berthe stood up. "I shall take your dress downstairs, and hang it in the garment bag in the car. Is everything else already in the car?"

"Yes, there's just the dress now. I'll be down in a jiffy."

Berthe turned and left the room, her head held high in an indignant manner.

Shortly after Rosalie arrived at the Hotel de Paris for her appointment with Alexandre, Madeleine entered Rosalie's suite with a note. It was from d'Artois.

He was writing to say he could not attend the ball. He had come down with a bad case of the flu, and had been ordered by his doctor to stay in bed for twenty-four hours until it passed.

"Oh damn," Rosalie muttered as she finished reading the note. "He *would* have to get sick tonight, of all nights. Now I don't even have Jean as an escort." Oh well, she thought, I might as well call him and see if there's anything I can do for him. Damn!

She rang d'Artois's villa. The butler answered. "Monsieur le Duc has gone to bed, madame. I cannot disturb him. He said to tell you if you called that he will be fine and not to worry. He will probably be fully recovered by the morning; and oh yes, madame, Monsieur le Duc also said for me to tell you to 'have a good time and knock them dead at the ball.' "

"Thank you, Fernand, I hope Monsieur le Duc is feeling better in the morning. Tell him I'll call around ten to see how he is." She hung up. Someone was at the door.

"Berthe? Madeleine?"

"It's Solange."

"Solange? Come in. Is it time to go already?" Rosalie embraced her old friend.

"Already?" Solange said. "If we don't leave now, we might as well not go. After all, we don't want to arrive *after* Princess Grace and Prince Rainier."

"Oh? Why not?"

"Because it isn't done, that's why. They are supposed to come in last, after everyone else is there and seated."

"I see."

"No you don't, but anyway, we had better be going."

"Where's Sergio?"

"Who?"

"Your husband, woman, your husband, Sergio. Or has he changed his name since this afternoon?"

"You mumbled, I didn't hear you."

"I *never* mumble."

"Oh, come on, let's go. We'll be late."

"Oh, all right, I'm coming. I wish Jeffrey were here with me right now, though. I'll feel funny walking in all alone."

"You won't be alone. You'll be with Sergio and me, and Jean."

"Jean isn't coming."

"He isn't? Why?"

"He has the flu."

"Damn him!" Solange said. "Of all times to get sick. Some friend he is!"

There was a knock on the door and Rosalie beckoned the caller in. It was Sergio, dark and handsome in his tuxedo, a wide smile on his tanned face.

"Well, are you two ready?" he said.

"Rosalie is ready," Solange said, "that is, all except for her shoes. You aren't planning on going barefoot, Rosalie, are you?"

Rosalie looked down at her naked feet and laughed. "You're so short, Solange, I always think I'm wearing high heels, even when I'm barefoot—if I'm standing next to you!"

Sergio laughed. "Sometimes I have trouble finding her myself. Only last night I had to shake the sheets to find her."

Rosalie burst into a fit of giggles upon seeing Solange's exasperated expression.

Rosalie went into the dressing room and slipped on red satin sandals. "Don't worry, Solange," Rosalie called through the open door. "There've been some very famous short people. Napoleon was short, for instance."

"And Tom Thumb," Sergio piped up.

"Now look here, you," Solange said. "Without a head you could be even shorter than I am." She pretended to throw a vase of roses at Sergio, who was still standing in the doorway to the living room. As Solange lifted the vase, she noticed a card was attached to one of the rose stems. "Jeffrey send you these as a peace offering?" she asked, as Rosalie came out of the dressing room, still adjusting the thin straps of her shoes.

"No, Jean sent them."

"Jean? I thought sick people were supposed to *receive* flowers, not *send* them."

"Oh, well, I guess he felt guilty about not being able to escort me tonight." Rosalie smiled and threw up her hands. "You know how Jean is."

"Well, I've known him for years, but I can't say I really know him, if you know what I mean. He just isn't a very easy person to get to know."

Rosalie gave her friend a reprimanding look. "Oh come on, he's okay."

Sergio stood back to admire the two women as they came out into the hallway. He whistled approvingly, and complimented Rosalie on her stunning red dress.

"You remind me of a vision," he said, as he took their elbows and led them down the hall to the elevator.

"Yes, of Jezebel!" said Solange.

Rosalie laughed. "I hope you don't mean that, Solange, or I might think you were a prude."

"A prude? Me? Ha, I'm certainly not that. But I can tell you, walking between you and Sergio, I not only feel small tonight, I also feel deprived."

"Deprived?" exclaimed Rosalie. "Why?"

Solange patted her chest with the palms of her hands. "I wish *I* could wear a red dress with a *décolletée* so low that my navel was showing." She pulled out the bosom of her dress. "What I wouldn't give for a size C cup." Solange looked up at Rosalie, laughter in her eyes. "I've even tried bumping into big pieces of furniture, but I have the kind of body that doesn't swell up when I get hit. All I get are black and blue marks."

"Really?" said Sergio. "How come I never notice them?"

"Because you never look at me between the waist and the neck. Even if you did, you're so nearsighted you'd think the marks were freckles."

Sergio and Rosalie burst out laughing. Solange pretended to be upset by their laughter.

Rosalie and her party descended the steps of the Hotel de Paris and crossed the street to the International Summer Sporting Club where the ball was being held. People were filing by, two by two, heading toward the vast terrace now packed with guests in gala attire. The newspapers had announced that the famous French millionairess, Rosalie La Farge Guthrow, who had left her country over ten years ago, had at last returned, and would make her first appearance in European society at the Red Cross Ball.

As Rosalie began walking down the steps to the terrace, photographers and reporters swarmed around her, taking pictures, throwing questions, shoving microphones in her face. In a corner of the terrace, facing a TV camera, a fashion commentator was announcing that Rosalie's stunning red dress had been a creation of none other than the now superstar designer, Henri la Tour, who in September of 1962 had designed the famous wedding gown which at the time had created such worldwide publicity.

"Yes," Rosalie answered pleasantly, as a woman TV

reporter shoved a microphone under her nose. "I discovered Henri, but I did not make him famous. Only his talent could have done that."

Someone was coming toward Rosalie. She smiled as she recognized the dark, chiseled face she had not seen for so long. "Sheikh!" she exclaimed. "I didn't know you would be here tonight. I knew Jeffrey had invited you, but I didn't think you were well enough." She held the old man away from her, her eyes moist, her heart heavy with feelings of joy and sadness. They embraced, tears streaming down their faces. The photographers and reporters went wild. Before their very eyes one of the world's most fascinating and intriguing women, the mysterious Rosalie, a legend, stood openly crying on the shoulder of her ex-father-in-law, the oil billionaire, Sheikh Farahet.

People in the crowd were whispering; "Where is her husband?"

"Why isn't he here tonight?"

"Yes, why isn't he with her?"

"Do you think they're getting a divorce?"

The sheikh, along with Sergio and Solange, managed to get Rosalie past the crowd to their table.

"My God, Sheikh, it's been so dreadfully long since I last saw you." Rosalie's eyes were still moist. She took a napkin from the table and dabbed at her eyes.

"Ten years it's been," Sheikh Farahet said. "The last time I saw you was early in 1964. You had already moved to New York."

Rosalie looked at the old man and placed her hand on the table on top of his. "I wish I had been a stronger person. I wish I hadn't run away the way I did."

Sheikh Farahet smiled and leaned over and kissed her on the cheek. "Oh, Rosalie, my dear child, you haven't changed. More beautiful, perhaps, if it is possible you could be more beautiful than that day eleven years ago, when your father and I stood watching you and my son . . ." His huge black eyes misted once again and he squeezed her hand tightly. "It's a good thing you were not stronger, as you say, for if you had not gone away, you would not have met your new husband. I hear he is a wonderful man, much admired by his friends and the public."

"Yes, he is, Sheikh, so wonderful sometimes, I think I don't deserve him." She took a sip of her champagne. "He's coming in from London tonight; he will be joining us in a little while, I hope. He will be pleased to meet you. I've spoken to him often of you.

The sheikh nodded. "Yes, I'm looking forward to meeting him. I hear you have three sons, and that you are expecting again."

Rosalie nodded. "Yes, I'm four and a half months along."

The sheikh had a faraway look in his eyes as he said, "Allah works in mysterious ways. Perhaps it was best that you and Ahmed did not have children."

Rosalie felt so sorry for the old sheikh. Since Ahmed's death he had deteriorated terribly. He had had several heart attacks, the last of which had almost been fatal.

Dinner was being served, and Rosalie began to wonder where Jeffrey was. She glanced at the sheikh's watch.

My God, where is Jeffrey? she thought. What's keeping him so long? I'll kill him if he doesn't show up!

Solange, sitting across the table, had been watching her friend. She could sense Rosalie's anxiety. Solange's lips formed the words: "Don't worry, he'll be here soon," and then she smiled at Rosalie reassuringly across the elegant table.

Rosalie smiled back. A black American singer, Dionne Warwick, was singing a soulful melody. Rosalie's mind was wandering. The sound of the woman's voice was taking her back to the night before, when she and Jeffrey had made love. The faces around Rosalie blurred as she slipped into a world of her own. . . .

A gray Continental limousine, driven by Jules, pulled into the driveway at Colombier. Jeffrey was in the backseat, in the same taupe-colored suit he had worn the night before.

"Jules, Alain will be here in fifteen minutes with the 'copter. Tell him I'll be right down. I'll just run upstairs and change. My wife would kill me if I showed up looking like this." Jeffrey sprinted up the curving stone steps to the main landing. He was earlier than he had thought—five past eleven. He could still shower and dress and make it in the helicopter to Monte Carlo in time for at least part of the ball.

As Jeffrey ran down the marble hallway alongside the bedrooms, his eye caught a gleam of light showing under the door of the study. He wondered if Rosalie had been there earlier and had forgotten to turn out the light. It couldn't have been a guest. No one went into La Farge's old study but Rosalie; or the servants to dust. No one would be dusting at this time of the night, he thought, as he approached the study door.

For no definite reason, but perhaps because he thought he heard a noise inside the room, Jeffrey decided to enter the study through La Farge's bedroom. He knew that all the guests had left for Monte Carlo earlier that evening, and that the servants were alseep—all, that is, except the new gate watchman, Felix, who had opened the gates of the estate for him and Jules just minutes before. Jeffrey suspected there was someone in the room up to no good, perhaps a burglar. The door was unlocked. He stole on tiptoe into the bedroom, then removed his shoes. He walked across the soft shaggy carpet to behind the door leading to the study. He pressed his head up against the wooden door and listened. He heard a sound again, like someone opening and closing a drawer. He walked over and grabbed the poker leaning up against the black marble fireplace. Then he slowly turned the knob to the wooden door, trying his best not to make a sound, as, inch by inch, he pushed the door open. The door creaked; he pulled back his hand, and waited. He held the poker in the air, waiting. Seconds ticked by and nothing happened. He wondered if perhaps the burglar had outsmarted him and slipped out the hall door. Holding his breath, he gave the door one more push, this time with force. It swung back into the study and slammed loudly against the wall. He looked around, but there was nobody in sight. He could see, however, that someone had been in the room.

Jeffrey walked over to the window and leaned out to see if the person had escaped by taking the beach elevator. He looked down and saw that the elevator was still at the top of the shaft. Whoever it was didn't escape that way, Jeffrey thought, unless he was one hell of an acrobat. As he was about to pull his head back in, his eyes was caught by the light over the elevator shaft reflecting on something metallic showing through the pine branches below. He leaned further out the window to get a better look. It was a boat, tied up to a small pine tree growing out of the side of the cliff. "Shit, I better go down and check that out," he said to himself.

Jeffrey's mind flashed to Rosalie and all the tragedies that had followed her. A feeling of apprehension came over him, as he ran out the door next to the window and descended the small wrought iron stairwell—strung practically in midair from the study terrace—to the small steel platform below leading to the elevator.

He got in the elevator, pressed the "down" button and the small circular car began its rapid descent to the main platform. He reached the platform and went over to investigate the boat tied up alongside the elevator shaft. He did not recognize the boat, but it had a name written on it. He lit a match and leaned closer to read the lettering: A-N-G-E-L-E.

Angèle, he recalled, was the name of d'Artois's boat. What the hell was going on?

Prompted by an instinct he did not understand, Jeffrey looked up. A man leaped out at him and grabbed him around the throat from behind. The man's muscular arm was strong, and cut into his flesh like steel as Jeffrey fought to free himself. Jeffrey yelled and kicked backward, then he felt a stinging, sickening pain as his attacker slid the blade of a knife into his spine. His knees weakened and his legs crumbled under him as the man twisted the blade of the knife sideways in Jeffrey's back, cutting the spinal cord.

Jeffrey fell to the platform facedown, unable to move. "D'Artois," he murmured as the man slid the tip of a black leather boot under Jeffrey's ribs and rolled him over on his side. A stream of blood was oozing out of the hole in Jeffrey's back, settling in a pool around his writhing body.

The moon was shining down through the branches of the

trees growing out from crevices in the cliff. It shone down on d'Artois's face, lighting it up. D'Artois lit a cigarette and took a puff from it.

"Why did you have to show up here tonight, Jeffrey?" he asked, his voice sounding almost petulant. "Why couldn't you have stayed away?" He scowled as he looked down at Jeffrey's bloody back.

"If you hadn't shown up when you did, things might never have come to this. I never wanted to kill you, although for seven years you had the woman I wanted. Yes, for seven long years, I've stood by and watched you possess the woman I think of as mine." D'Artois leaned closer. His voice blazoned his suffering.

"Do you know how hard that was, to see you in my place? Yet somehow I managed to live with it. I hoped that in time the marriage would dissolve. I always knew you despised me, but you were never a threat, not like the others."

Jeffrey grunted, trying to speak, but the pain was too great.

D'Artois stiffened. "Now I must kill you, something I hate to do." His voice croaked. "All I can expect from this is trouble. But I have no choice—like the times before—I have no choice."

D'Artois had the bloody knife still clutched in his left hand. He looked at his watch and put the package of cigarettes back into his breast pocket. He was wearing black trousers and a black shirt, with the sleeves rolled up just above his elbows.

Jeffrey's arm shot out and grabbed d'Artois by the pants leg. D'Artois lost his balance and fell backward, hitting his head on the wall of the cliff. Jeffrey tried to move, but was completely paralyzed from the waist down. He tried rolling over to grab d'Artois again, but d'Artois recovered quickly and sprang to his feet like an enraged animal.

D'Artois picked up a rock which had come loose from the cliff when he had fallen against it, and lifted it over his head. For a few seconds d'Artois held the rock in midair as he watched Jeffrey's eyes staring in fear of the blow to come. D'Artois's lips curled into a vicious smile, and he brought the rock down and smashed it into Jeffrey's face. Blood spurted wildly.

Downstairs in the library, the young cheetahs Jeffrey had given Rosalie as a present after Diablo had died, chased through the room and screamed shrilly into the night. At the front gate of the estate, Igor and Samson, the two Dobermans, howled plaintively. The smell of death was everywhere.

D'Artois cursed the animals as he took the elevator back up to the study. A pity I can't do away with all these beasts like I did that black demon, he thought to himself. It hated me. Animals can tell too much about people.

He reached the terrace and looked around to make sure no one was about, and tiptoed down the corridor back to the study, to continue the search Jeffrey had interrupted.

D'Artois had waited all these years for this moment, always wondering if the secret hidden in the study would be discovered and mean his end. Colombier had been closed and well-guarded ever since the deaths of Armand and Jacqueline La Farge. D'Artois put his hand in his pocket and retrieved a key—the key La Farge had pointed to before he died—the key La Farge used to bargain for Rosalie's life. In the moonlight shining through the study window, d'Artois's hair looked like a silver cap. Against the wall, his profile stamped its shadow like an evil gargoyle.

D'Artois searched rapidly, his hands feeling under the desk, searching for a secret panel. His fingers slid along the sides of the polished wooden desk, his knuckles rapping softly from time to time.

The loud ticking of the antique clock on the mantel drummed in his ears; the sound was driving him to distraction. He tried to remain calm. He glanced up at the clock—11:55. He did not have much more time. He knew that in a little while the chauffeur would be coming upstairs to see what was keeping Jeffrey. He wiped the perspiration from his brow with the back of his hand.

His eyes, squinting, scanned the room.

"Where is the damned vault?" he muttered. He studied the elaborate bar against the wall. He began to walk toward the bar, his hands sweeping the wall as if he were on a cliff and needed to steady himself.

A sound from outside startled him. He froze, listening like a cat. Again he heard the sound. Footsteps. Someone was coming up the marble stairs.

His pulse was racing. The tension was unbearable.

He quickly sized up the room.

"I mustn't leave anything behind. Did I set anything down?"

The footsteps were coming closer. In a minute, whoever it was would be upon him.

D'Artois darted quickly behind the doorjamb. The door opened, and d'Artois leaped out from behind it. There was a scuffling noise, then a loud thud. Then the muffled sound of a body being dragged across the carpet. Then everything was once again still.

At her table at the Summer Sporting Club, Rosalie was sipping her coffee. She had given up hope that Jeffrey would arrive.

Something very urgent must have come up at the last minute, she thought, and he couldn't make it. In a few moments I'll excuse myself and leave. I don't feel very much like going to a night club afterward. I'll go home and wait for Jeffrey.

Solange motioned to her that she was going to the ladies' room and Rosalie decided to go along. Once there, Rosalie told Solange she felt like going home.

"I'm not feeling myself tonight," she said apologetically. "I just wish Jeffrey could have been here with me tonight. I can't stand being without him."

"You lean too much on Jeffrey, Rosalie. It isn't good. You shouldn't depend so much on him for everything. What if something happened to him? What would you do then?"

"I don't lean on him, as you put it, Solange. I love him. He's my husband. I love having him with me. There's nothing wrong with that."

"Come on, Rosalie, honey, let's go get Sergio and let's go home, okay? My heart isn't in staying anyway, knowing how you feel."

"You don't have to leave because of me. I'll take the Rolls; you and Sergio have your car."

"I know we don't have to, Rosalie, but I want to, and I'm sure Sergio will feel the same way. Come on, let's get back to the table."

They bade good-bye to their friends and Rosalie hugged

the sheikh and kissed him before she left, promising that she and Jeffrey would get together with him before he returned to Saudi Arabia.

For the trip back to Colombier, Rosalie rode in the Rolls with Max and Berthe; Sergio and Solange followed behind in their limousine with Madeleine and Philip and his wife.

Felix, the guardian, was asleep when they pulled up in front of the estate gates. Max let himself into the gate house with his key, and then opened the gates for them to pass through.

The heavy gates slammed shut with a loud bang as the steel bolt fell into place once again and locked.

As they drove up and stopped in front of the house, they saw the helicopter sitting on the front lawn.

Rosalie did not wait for Max to open the door for her. She jumped out of the car and ran up the stairs. "Is my husband home?" Rosalie asked the pilot, Alain, who was standing on the front steps. "Did he just get in?" She stopped to wait for his answer.

"I don't know for sure, madame. He called me from London, and said to be here at eleven-fifteen or so; I was to take him to Monte Carlo, where you were expecting him. I had some problems with the engine and arrived a little late. He wasn't here and neither was the limousine or Jules—unless the limo is in the garage, but the garage is locked, so I can't tell."

Rosalie frowned and paused for a moment. "You say he called you from London and told you to pick him up here tonight at eleven-fifteen? Why didn't he have you pick him up in London, and have you fly him directly into Monte Carlo? I don't understand; it doesn't make sense."

"Well, you see, he did ask me to do exactly that, but as I said, I was having problems with the engine and I couldn't get it fixed in time, so he told me he would go in a friend's private plane to Nice, and then have Jules drive him here to meet me. He said it was just as well, as he hadn't brought along the proper clothes to wear to the ball."

"I see," Rosalie said simply, "but where is he, then? And where is Jules?"

"I don't know, madame. I've been here for over two hours

now." Alain looked at his watch. "I've been here since twelve. It's now ten past two. I don't know what happened. Perhaps he didn't get a ride with his friend after all, and had to take a commercial flight. If that's the case, he's probably on his way now from Nice."

Rosalie looked from Solange to Sergio to Philip, who had been standing on the steps listening. Madeleine, Berthe, and Philip's wife had gone up to bed almost immediately.

"Well," Rosalie sighed. "I guess you can go home, Alain. My husband certainly won't be needing you when he gets here; I don't think he'll be going anywhere but to bed." She stifled a yawn with her hand, and addressed herself to the others. "I'm bushed. If you people will excuse me, I'm going right up to bed. Jeffrey will wake me when he gets in, whenever that is." She rolled her eyes and made a face at Solange. "Men! If Jeffrey ever found out how miserable I was tonight without him, his ego would puff up so, I'd have to hang an anchor on him to keep him on the ground!" Rosalie laughed and blew a kiss to her friends. "Good night, everyone—I'll see you all in the morning—late." She disappeared into the house and climbed the marble steps to the second floor.

As Rosalie walked down the wide corridor, her thoughts were of Jeffrey and the children. On the spur of the moment, she turned around and walked back the other way to the nursery.

Rosalie turned the doorknob and peered in. Armand and Sacha were sound asleep. She went over to stand between their beds and bent down and kissed each one tenderly on the cheek; then she left and went into Jeremy's room. Jeremy shared a suite with the governess. He was asleep facedown with his bottom raised in the air and his knees pulled up under him. His pajama bottoms were in a crumpled up ball on the floor where he had thrown them after taking them off; the moment, no doubt, Chantale had left the room.

Rosalie chuckled and stooped to pick the pants up. She pressed them to her face and smelled the sweet smell of baby powder on them. She laid them on the bureau beside Jeremy's crib, and covered his naked little bottom with the sheet. She smoothed back a curl from his forehead and thought: He's as bad as you probably were, Papa, as bad and as impossible, but just as lovable.

Rosalie closed the door carefully, so as not to wake her son, and started down the hallway again to her room. She was about to enter her bedroom, when she noticed the light coming from under the study door. She froze and her hands came up to her mouth. Her knuckles grew white as she pressed them up against her teeth.

What's a light doing on in Papa's study? she thought. No one ever goes in there, but me or the servants to clean. She walked into the room and looked around, anticipating finding someone there. The door, she noticed, had been unlocked.

The window on the ocean side was wide open and the shutters were pounding against the outside wall, as if about to break. An empty vase had fallen off the table on the foor. Rosalie stooped to pick up the vase and discovered it was cracked. She rested it down on the table and went to close the window. She stood with her back to the window and her hand on her hips, surveying the room.

Something was wrong. She could feel it. She ran to the open door and screamed into the hallway for Solange and Sergio to come. Philip and Stephanie were in the guest wing; they would not be able to hear her.

Solange and Sergio came running into the room. Rosalie was standing on the small balcony, looking down at the landing below.

"Someone's been in this room," she whispered softly, as if she didn't want someone to hear her. "In my father's room."

Sergio pointed to the elevator down below. "It's true. Whoever it was took the elevator. It was up here earlier, I'm sure. I saw it when I looked out my window this afternoon just before we left."

Rosalie grew pale at the mention of the elevator. She had been so preoccupied with the open window and door that she had not noticed that the elevator was down below. Her shoulders trembled, and she pulled her black feather shawl tightly around herself.

"Since Papa died, no one has ever used that elevator or this room. Even I have come here only twice before tonight, and I did not leave the door and window open,'' she said.

Sergio came over and put his arms around her. ''Perhaps there's a logical explanation. Why don't we look around and see if there's anything missing, and if there is, we'll call the gendarmes, and they can have a look around the place.''

Solange backed away from the window.

''I think I'm going to call the police right now,'' she said. ''Suppose there's some lunatic out there on the loose. I'm not taking any chances.'' As she crossed the room to pick up the phone, she spotted something.

The door to the bedroom was open, and a pair of men's shoes were near the bed. Solange turned on the light in the bedroom and went in. On the floor beside the shoes was a suitcase, light brown, with small, gold lettering: *J.A Guthrow*. Beside the suitcase was a small white box.

Solange's face lit up in a smile. She ran back into the study. ''It's Jeffrey, Rosalie, he's home! His things are in there''—she pointed to the bedroom—''on the floor.''

Rosalie's lips broadened into a happy smile. ''Oh shit, and here I am getting hysterical; thinking there's been a burglar in the house, and all the time it's that . . . that . . . *goon* of a husband of mine!'' She was headed out the doorway. ''I'll bet you anything he's in bed, asleep. I know what happened,'' she said, laughing. ''He came home tired, a little earlier than expected, and went to take a little nap before Alain came, and he never woke up.'' She threw back her head and laughed and blew Solange and Sergio a good-night kiss. ''Good night, you two. I'll see you in the morning at breakfast, if I can tear myself away from my husband's arms.''

''He'll be too tired,'' Sergio laughed.

''Oh no, he won't,'' Rosalie laughed back. ''The way I've missed him all day, if he were a corpse, I'd make him come to life.'' She waved on her way to the bedroom.

Sergio put his arm around Solange's shoulders as they left the room. ''Say, how come you don't miss me like that when I go away and leave you alone? Eh?''

''Because you never go anywhere, that's why. If you did

go somewhere, perhaps I would miss you, but you'll never know until you try."

Sergio was about to respond, when suddenly a chilling scream rang through the house.

Solange and Sergio froze in their tracks.

The scream came again, as if someone were being burned to death.

"It's Rosalie," Solange cried out. "Oh my God, it's Rosalie! She's in her bedroom."

Solange and Sergio ran to Rosalie's bedroom at the end of the hall, and threw the door open. "Rosalie," they shouted as they raced inside. "What's the matter? What's wrong?"

Rosalie did not seem to hear them. She was at the window, her body leaning half out; whimpering like a small hurt animal. She looked as if she were about to jump.

Sergio and Solange rushed to her and tried to pull her back inside. At the same time, footsteps were running down the hallway, coming toward them. Sergio held tightly to Rosalie, while Solange ran to the door to see who was coming. It was Philip and Stephanie, half naked with towels wrapped around them haphazardly, and Chantale in the rear, in her nightgown. They saw Solange in the doorway and yelled out.

"What's wrong? Who screamed?" the three said all at once.

Solange motioned for them to come in and pointed to Rosalie, who was kicking and scratching at Sergio as if she thought he was attacking her.

Thinking that Sergio might have had too much to drink that evening and had come in to make a pass at Rosalie, Philip sprang to Rosalie's aid, grabbing Sergio away from her and throwing him across the room to land on the floor at the foot of the bed.

A stunned Solange rushed to Sergio's side.

Stephanie stood rooted to the floor. Her orange towel had fallen away from most of her body, and was now clenched between her trembling knees. She did not know what was going on.

Philip reeled around to face Rosalie, and as he did, she stepped backward. Her hands flew to her horrified face and she let out another piercing scream, her eyes flashing like crazed dog's.

"*Ai-i-i-i!*" Rosalie screamed, stepping back one more time. Everyone in the room gasped, as Rosalie fell backward, over the low windowsill of the open window, and plunged through the air. Her long flaming red dress ripped loudly, tearing off in Philip's hands as he attempted to grab hold of her. Rosalie landed on the pavement below with a sickening thud.

Philip turned his head and vomited on the rug. Solange and Stephanie began screaming hysterically. In a state of shock, Sergio ran down the hallway calling for help.

Footsteps came running up the marble stairs, voices began shouting. Max, Berthe, Madeleine, and several other servants, some in their nightclothes, some half-dressed, came charging toward Sergio.

Before Max could speak, Sergio shouted, "Quick, Max, the elevator, bring up the elevator! There's been a horrible accident. Rosalie—it's Rosalie. She fell . . ."

Max's face grew pale. His eyelids and hands began to quiver nervously. "Madame? Oh, God, no!"

The two men ran toward the study. Sergio screamed over his shoulder, "Somebody call an ambulance and the police. Hurry!"

Max was like lightning. He sprinted down the staircase to the landing and pushed the button for the elevator. Sergio came up beside him, panting. Across the way from Rosalie's and Jeffrey's bedroom, the two men could hear Solange's and Stephanie's wailing cries. The thudding, clanking sound of the metal elevator coming to a sudden stop beside the platform was chilling in the night. Max shuddered and pushed the elevator doors open. Sergio reluctantly followed Max into the elevator.

"I can't see her," Max said, looking through the wrought iron bars. "Where did she fall?"

Sergio did not look down. He pointed blindly to the landing. His insides were churning, both at the thought of finding

Rosalie with her beautiful face all smashed in and from his fear of heights. The open elevator shooting down along the side of the rocky cliff was terrifying for him beyond words.

The elevator stopped abruptly. Max jumped out and pulled a shaky Sergio out after him.

"Where did she fall, man? Please? Where is Rosalie?" In his anxiety, Max had called Rosalie by her first name, the way he had when she was a little girl. Sergio opened his eyes finally and pointed to behind a huge boulder at the far end of the platform. When the platform was being built, the boulder had remained despite several dynamite blastings. La Farge had laughed at the time, and said, "Anything that stubborn should be left alone." He had ordered the platform built around the boulder.

Max remembered that the Nazis had put the elevator in during the war, for what purpose nobody knew. When he bought the place years later, La Farge decided to update it and use it as his own private escape to the sea for fishing, swimming, or snorkeling, without constant intrusions by guests.

Max and Sergio rounded the huge boulder. They both gasped in horror at the scene before them.

Max closed his eyes for a second, as he gathered his strength to move forward. He heard Sergio's vomiting, and his own guts curled up and rumbled in his belly. He felt his insides were going to burst out of him, like a tidal wave, and spew out on the pavement.

"Mein Gott," Max muttered, *"Mein Gott."*

He heard Sergio groan and say, "Oh Lord, it's Jeffrey. *He* was what Rosalie saw from the window."

Max walked woodenly up to the two hideously wrecked bodies.

Rosalie was lying, face sideways, her neck at an awkward angle, her legs sprawled over Jeffrey's bloody body. One of her arms was bent under her, with a piece of bone from her elbow protruding through the flesh. Max could see that one of her cheeks was indented where the cheekbone had given way. There was blood oozing from her nostrils. One of her legs was broken just above the knee, and was now sagging in two directions over Jeffrey's body. Max fell down on his knees, fighting the urge to be sick. He reached for Rosalie's pulse. It was not until that moment, that he saw for the first time Jeffrey's smashed face and skull. Max's insides heaved once more, and his brain went numb with revulsion.

"Is she alive?" Sergio asked pleadingly. "And Jeffrey?"

Max looked up at Sergio. Tears were streaming down his lined face. His voice came in rasps. Sergio felt the man's agony.

"She's alive," Max muttered, "probably because she fell partly on top of him, but he is dead. He has been for some time."

Voices were calling down from the upper platform, telling Max and Sergio that the doctor and the police had been notified and were on their way.

Philip remained in the bedroom with Solange and Stephanie, trying to calm them down. One of the servants had gone to alert Felix to be ready to open the gates for the ambulance and the police. Others were searching the premises for any possible signs of the burglar.

Several minutes later, the doctor and the ambulance and the police arrived in congregation. The doctor, his assistant, and the police inspector were the first to come down the elevator.

The doctor was a huge man with a goatee and a thin, scraggly mustache. He moved with a limp toward the bodies; he checked Jeffrey's pulse and went directly to Rosalie.

"He's dead, that one," the doctor said casually, as if he were not talking about a human being.

Rosalie lay slack. Her breathing now seemed more forced, more ragged. The doctor felt her pulse and gave her a quick examination. He motioned to his assistant to hand him his bag, and took a hypodermic needle from it. He injected Rosalie in the upper arm.

"This is for the pain," he said. "I'll have to get her to the hospital in Nice at once. They have the facilities." He filled another needle and injected again, into the same arm. Then he made a tourniquet around her arm, above where the broken bone protruded. "Get her on that stretcher," the doctor ordered, as it was being lowered down the elevator. "And be damned careful. She may have a concussion. I'll try to patch her up a bit in the ambulance."

Somebody yelled that the helicopter was still there.

"Then get her in it; it's quicker." The doctor turned to the police inspector. "Who in hell did this? Who would do something like this to a beautiful woman?"

"We don't know, but we'll find him, whoever he is."

"I hope you do. Anyone who would do something like this isn't fit to live." He spat on the ground in disgust. "God, that poor man—what he must have suffered before he died!"

The police examined the bodies, and questioned Max and Sergio for the details.

Rosalie's breathing was still heavy, but slower and more even. The doctor and his attendant lifted her carefully onto the stretcher. The police photographer kept clicking away, taking pictures of Rosalie and Jeffrey together, then of each of them separately.

The police inspector turned his head away and wiped his face with his handkerchief. "God," he said to Max, who was leaning up against the cliff weeping like a child, "I've seen some pretty bad cases in my life, but none like this." The inspector took a deep breath of fresh air. He spit the butt of his Gitane into the black water and loosened his tie.

They were hoisting Jeffrey's battered body up now. The elevator clanked and creaked under the weight of the corpse and the two police officers.

"Come on," the inspector called to Max, "we're next."

Rosalie was rushed to the hospital in Nice, and Jeffrey to the morgue for an autopsy.

Later, as the police continued their search of the premises, they found the limousine locked in the garage, but Jules could not be found. The police concluded that when Alain arrived, and Jeffrey hadn't come downstairs, Jules decided to go up and see what was keeping his master. Jules somehow came face to face with the intruder, was killed, and his body probably thrown into the sea. The next day the police sent divers down but the chauffeur's body was not found.

The doctors had given out a report to the press that Rosalie had a concussion and that she had suffered several broken bones. She was threatening to miscarry, but as yet she had not lost the baby, and she was holding her own in the intensive care unit. Archbishop Lernier got on a plane to Nice the moment he heard the news. He, and Dr. Labans, the family physician, and Dr. Laurent, a bone specialist, flew in from Paris.

As Rosalie lay in her hospital bed, phantoms in white hovered around her everywhere. Strange lights and whispering voices seemed always to be approaching her. She wondered if she were having another one of her terrible dreams. She blinked her eyes and licked her parched, dry lips. Her throat was even dryer than her lips, and her arms ached. So did her legs, and her head. Her hand reached up and touched the bandages wrapped around her head, and those on her cheek. A long, yellowish tube dangled from her left arm. The long needle in her arm stung like a small knife stuck in her flesh.

More whispering, more phantoms in white; and then another light, a small bright light staring straight into her eyeball, coming closer. Rosalie screamed and pulled her head away to one side. As she screamed, new visions appeared before her even though her eyes were squeezed shut. . . . visions of Jeffrey lying on the platform at the bottom of the cliff with his head smashed in and his eyeballs beside him on the pavement.

"*Aiiiiiii.*" Rosalie screamed again and again, and thrashed wildly about on the hospital bed. Then hands were grabbing her, figures in white were strapping belts around her arms and legs. Strapping her to the bed.

A tall, looming figure with a smiling face came toward her with a long, menacing syringe. She recognized the doctor as he grabbed hold of her arm and inserted a needle.

"Doctor," Rosalie said, her body already relaxing from the injection. "Doctor Laurent."

Archbishop Lernier was outside her door. Dr. Laurent asked him to come in. The archbishop came and sat down beside Rosalie's bed and took her small silky hand in his big hairy one.

His face was as she had always remembered it, red and puffy, and slightly effeminate, but kind and caring.

Rosalie wanted to tell him to go away, to take his God and peddle him someplace else. That she had had enough of God's cruelty. But sleep was drifting over her like a black cloud, making it impossible for her to speak, or think. Her mind was going blank. The phantoms were all going away. She felt warm and sleepy.

Chapter Thirty-one

Côte d'Azur and California, August 1974

Seven weeks later, Rosalie was permitted to leave the hospital. She was pronounced in good enough health to return to the United States with the body of her husband.

On the morning before beginning the trip back to America, Rosalie sat on a Louis XVI banquette in her bedroom in the Carleton in Cannes. The window was wide open, and she was watching the ocean. In the distance a huge yacht was passing, heading in the direction of Monte Carlo.

Rosalie wondered if it was the *Créole*, heading back to its berth. The boat had been berthed at St. Tropez all this time, the captain waiting to be told what to do. That morning Rosalie had called him, and had told him to take the *Créole* home. She would decide later what to do with her.

As the gentle seabreeze blew through the open window on her face, Rosalie thought of her father and mother, of Ahmed, of Peter, and of Jeffrey. A tear rolled down her pale cheek, and she placed her hands tenderly over her belly and stroked it.

"Jeff, oh, Jeff, my darling," she wailed softly, still looking out the window. "You broke your promise to me; but you couldn't help it. I know you couldn't."

Footsteps were coming toward her. She heard them, but did not turn around. A hand reached out and touched her lightly on the shoulder.

"Rosalie?"

She did not answer. Her pain was like a sword, cutting away at her womb, slicing her heart and piercing her soul. She sat there crying pitifully for her lost love, her Jeffrey.

"Rosalie?" the voice called once again. "It's time. We must go."

She looked up this time, a blank, dazed look on her face. "Go?" she said, as if she really did not know why she had to go anywhere. "Go where?"

"The plane. Alain says everything is ready. He is ready to take off anytime you want to." Solange took her friend's arm, and Philip the other, and together they ushered Rosalie out through the door, down into the elevator, through the lobby and out into the waiting Rolls.

"Let's go, Max," Philip said as they got in, and the car pulled out of the driveway and onto the Croisette, picking up speed. It vanished in the traffic of the morning rush hour.

The scene was more than just sad, as Rosalie, Solange, Philip, Berthe, Max, and the rest of Rosalie's entourage prepared to board the private aircraft.

Rosalie wore black, a simple dress with a small gardenia pinned to her bosom, her blond hair slicked back in a chic twist around the curve of her skull. Under one arm she clutched a black snakeskin bag, while in her hand she held a lavender scarf. She stood rigid, stiff as a board, her three children at her side, and watched in reverent silence as Jeffrey's casket was carried onto the aircraft.

The two younger children did not understand what was happening. They stood and watched as their mother did, and shuffled their feet in childish boredom. But, Armand, now seven, held on tightly to his mother's hand and wept with her as he watched his father's remains being carried aboard.

D'Artois stepped forward from the line of friends who had come to say good-bye, and held out his arms to Rosalie. She blew her nose and made a step forward to meet him, to say good-bye, but Armand stepped between his mother and the duke, wrapping his arms around his mother's waist, and said, "Let's go, Maman, let's go."

Rosalie extended her hand to d'Artois, while hugging her son to her, trying to comfort the boy.

D'Artois took her hand and leaned over the boy to kiss Rosalie. "Good-bye, Rosalie, my dear. I will see you soon in Los Angeles."

She nodded and started to walk to the plane.

"Good-bye Armand," d'Artois called, as the boy, still clutching his mother around the waist, looked around and glared at him. "Perhaps, when I see you again, we can go fishing, you and me. You would like it, I'm sure."

The child did not answer. He turned and looked ahead and smiled up at his mother. "Don't worry, Maman, I'll take care of you. I'll never leave you."

Rosalie and her children walked up the ramp without a backward glance and disappeared into the gaping hole in the plane. The door slid shut. The engines roared as Paul, the steward, made sure everyone was strapped in. The plane lifted off the ground.

Rosalie glanced out the porthole of her cabin and looked down at the people, her friends, waving good-bye from the ground. Her eye caught d'Artois, standing alone, apart from the rest. She felt a strange sensation, and turned to look at her young son. Like his father, she thought, Armand can't stand Jean. . . .

The plane lifted in the air, and far beneath, a lone figure stood watching, hand over his eyes, shielding them from the sun, his face the everlasting shadow of death. "The waiting's almost over, Rosalie," he whispered as the plane disappeared into the clouds. "I know that now I shall possess you—at last."

Jeffrey was laid to rest on a rainy Sunday morning. Only a handful of close friends and relatives were present, huddled under gray and black umbrellas, praying softly as the casket was lowered into the ground.

Rosalie stood near the open grave under a tree. Her eyes were fixed on the wreath of white roses on the casket, and in her hands she clutched a dried up flower, the brown remnants of the last gardenia Jeffrey had brought her on the night he was killed, and had never had the chance to give her. She clutched the flower tightly to her breast and a sob escaped her lips as she stooped to throw a handful of dirt into the grave.

The priest was speaking haltingly. "I am the resurrection and the life. Whosoever believeth in me shall dwell forever, though he be dead . . ."

The cries and whispers of the crowd drowned out the priest's voice and Rosalie began to speak softly, reciting Jeffrey's favorite poem, Robert Louis Steveson's "Requiem." "Home is the sailor, home from the sea, and the hunter home from the hill."

As she finished reciting, Rosalie stooped once again, picking up a rose which had fallen from the wreath as the coffin was being lowered. She stood up and motioned to the men standing with their shovels to close the grave, and she stepped back.

D'Artois nudged her. "Come, Rosalie, my dear, you must be brave. It is time to go."

Rosalie followed d'Artois listlessly to the waiting car. In the front seat beside Max sat Armand, wearing a gray suit and tie, much too somber for a seven-year-old boy. He was wrapping one of his father's monogrammed handkerchiefs around one hand. He did not look around as Rosalie and d'Artois got in the car, but turned to Max and in a grown-up voice said:

"Let's go home, Max. Papa is gone. There's nothing left here."

Rosalie leaned forward and touched her small son's shoulder pityingly. "We have each other, Armand. There are you and me and your brothers, and perhaps soon a new little sister, and as long as I have my children, I can survive."

The car turned out of the cemetery heading home, and

Rosalie turned to d'Artois and said, "You are welcome to stay at the house, Jean."

He nodded and took her small, trembling hand in his. He squeezed it tight. "I'm glad you suggested it, Rosalie. If you hadn't, I would have. What you need now is a friend, a good friend."

Rosalie turned and looked up at him through red, puffy eyes. "Yes, Jean. I need you."

Eight days later, at the break of dawn, Rosalie was rushed to a hospital in Beverly Hills with severe abdominal pains. Two hours after her arrival at the hospital, a five-pound baby girl was born ten weeks prematurely. She was christened Rosalie Aline Guthrow. The child died six hours after birth from a defect the doctors said was caused by the fall Rosalie had endured.

Baby Rosalie was buried beside her father; but, unlike him, on a bright sunny day. On that September morning, Rosalie stood watching, standing under the same tree where she had mourned for Jeffrey, as the small white casket was placed on the straps to be lowered into the ground.

Rosalie turned and walked away, her eyes dry, her face listless and forlorn, and she smiled wanly at her three little boys. She whispered, "Don't feel sad for your sister, my little men. She is with your father. He will watch over her."

Six months later, Rosalie stood in the same spot once again, as two identical pink marble headstones were placed at the head of each grave, and the temporary headstones were cast into the back of the truck.

After the two workers dusted the stones off and gestured to Rosalie that they had finished, she stood back and read the inscribed words. She read Jeffrey's headstone first: "I promised to bury my heart with you. Here it lies beside you—our daughter. Jeffrey Allan Guthrow. Born September 5, 1928. Died June 20, 1974."

She read the other one: "Rest in peace beside he whose love will always keep you warm and sheltered—your father. Baby Rosalie Aline Guthrow. Born Morning, August 19, 1974. Died Afternoon, August 19, 1974."

Rosalie nodded her silent approval to the men putting up the stones, then placed a wreath of tiny white roses on each grave, and headed back to the waiting car. Her arms and legs were heavy from the reawakened agony of her many painful memories.

Max held the door open for her. She got in and they drove off.

On the hour-long return trip to the Guthrow estate in Holmby Hills, Rosalie's mind drifted back to the scene of that morning, before she had left for the cemetery.

D'Artois had brought her breakfast in bed, with a red rose in a vase on the tray. He had sat down beside her, nibbled a little off her tray, and then—suddenly, out of the blue, had reached for her hand and proposed marriage to her.

"Zalie, my darling," he had blurted out, squeezing her hand in his, "marry me and let me take care of you. I know I cannot take Jeffrey's place but I can try to make you happy again."

Rosalie had been both shocked and touched by d'Artois's proposal. She had never suspected d'Artois felt this way about her. Even now she could not clearly capture how she had felt then. It was as if she were seeing Jean as she had never seen him before. When suddenly he kissed her on the mouth, she had been even more taken aback.

Berthe had come in just then and had saved Rosalie from having to answer d'Artois. She wondered now, did Berthe hear him? Did she hear him ask me to marry him? God, I wonder what she must think—I must talk to her.

Back at the house and settled in her bedroom, Rosalie buzzed for Berthe. She waited a few minutes, but Berthe did not come. She rang again and waited. Then she slipped into a white silk dressing gown and a pair of soft white silk mules and made her way out the door and down the hallway to the opposite wing, to Berthe's room.

Rosalie came to the door and knocked. There was no answer. It was not like Berthe, not to be in her room at this hour. Berthe's habit was to remain upstairs during the time Rosalie had her dinner, after which she would help Rosalie get ready for bed. Rosalie had lost a lot of weight during the last six months and it was not uncommon for her to become dizzy and faint. The doctor had ordered that someone be with her at all times. Today had been one of the rare occasions that Rosalie had gone out. The three times before had been to the church and one other time to the cemetery six weeks before.

Rosalie knocked again, and then opened the door. The severe blue-and-beige room reflected Berthe's aloofness and drab personality. Rosalie looked around. "Berthe?" She walked across the bedroom into the dressing room and looked into the bathroom. Berthe was not there, but the smell of her lemony cologne still lingered faintly in the room. She had been there not long ago. She must have gone downstairs for something; Rosalie thought, she was about to leave when something on the floor by the toilet caught her eye. It was a small fragment of a glossy black-and-white photograph. Rosalie picked it up and looked at it curiously. Half of a girl's face was visible. The picture had been torn off just under the girl's nose and a pair of limpid eyes stared back at Rosalie from the small piece of photograph. She brought it up closer to the light, and studied it closely. Something about the eyes seemed very familiar.

I wonder who it is? Rosalie asked herself. Berthe doesn't have any close friends that I know of, and no relatives.

Feeling a little dizzy again, Rosalie made her way toward the little wing across the hall. As Berthe was the only staff member living upstairs, Rosalie had told her to use it for herself.

Rosalie lifted her hand to knock. She heard a soft, sobbing sound. She hesitated for a few seconds and listened. The sobbing was coming from inside the room. She thought: Berthe crying? What on earth for?

Rosalie knocked on the door, lightly at first; then louder. There was no answer. "Berthe? Are you in there? Answer me." Still there was no answer, only more sobbing.

Rosalie decided to go in. The room was dark. She ran her hand up along the wall, feeling for the light switch. She found it and switched it on.

The room was filled suddenly with light from the ceiling fixture.

"Berthe!" she exclaimed. Berthe was slumped over on the floor, against a chair, sobbing her heart out. "What's wrong, Berthe? Why are you so upset?" Rosalie hurried over to the older woman's side and stooped down. "What is it, Berthe? Please tell me. I've never seen you like this before!"

Berthe continued to sob, her body shaking.

Rosalie pushed back the hair from around Berthe's eyes. Berthe's graying hair had come loose from its usual stern twist, and was hanging loosely about her shoulders.

Berthe shook her head. "No, go away. Leave me alone. He killed my child. Oh, God, he killed her, my own brother!"

A group of photographs lying on the floor between Berthe and the chair caught Rosalie's attention. Berthe's hands were stroking the photographs as if they were living things.

"What child, Berthe? You don't have any children, and *he*, who is *he?* I don't understand." Rosalie reached out and put her arms around Berthe's shoulders. "Here, let me help you up. I'll help you to your room, and call the doctor. You're probably on the edge of a nervous breakdown because of me. I've been too dependent on you. I've leaned too much on you and Jean."

At the mention of the name Jean, Berthe began to howl. Her eyes bulged out of her head and her face was like a mummy's mask. "He's a devil," she said, in a rasping, fearful voice. "He will be your end. I hear him telling you how much he loves you. I see him falling in love with you. Yes, in *love* with you."

Rosalie's mind was racing, her heart beating faster and faster, as she saw something worse than death in Berthe's eyes.

"What are you trying to tell me? Berthe, for God's sake, I don't understand! What's put you in such a state?"

"It's not a state, Rosalie, it's *me*. It's the *real* me, the way I've been ever since I let Heinz persuade me to help him. I'm a monster, a vicious, evil monster—like my brother! You must go to the police, Rosalie. Kill him if you have to, but you must be rid of him, or you will be just another of his victims. like all the others and Margot." Berthe clasped her hands tightly against her chest, and began moving her body back and forth, as if rocking a child to sleep.

"Who is Heinz, Berthe?" Rosalie asked. "Who is this man you call Heinz?"

"He is my brother, a Nazi murderer. He kills everyone who gets in his way. He killed your father and your mother—*and all the rest.*" She ended her sentence with a groan. "He is mad. He has to be stopped."

Rosalie's insides were like the pit of a bubbling volcano, while her hands were ice-cold, and her eyes were burning. She reached out, picked up the photographs and held them up to the light. There were two; one was yellow and ragged from age and much handling. It was a picture of a little girl about three or four in the arms of her mother, a smiling woman with long, dark hair and a wide mouth. Rosalie stared at it, holding her breath in. Her lungs felt as if they were on fire. The woman in the picture was Berthe, much younger and a lot prettier, but definitely Berthe.

"That's me and my baby," Berthe said, stifling sobs, "and that's her when she was sixteen." She pointed to the other photograph, a more recent one.

There was a certain mischief in the girl's eyes, an evil almost, Rosalie thought, as she examined the photo closely. It seemed familiar, but she could not place the face. I'm living a nightmare, Rosalie thought, another horrible nightmare. This can't be real; I must be going crazy.

The photographs slid to the floor. Berthe reached for them and clutched them to her breast. Thoughts were exploding in Rosalie's mind, as if forced through a strainer, and the strainer kept getting smaller and smaller, and the thoughts kept coming faster and faster, until she couldn't bear it anymore. I must wake up, Rosalie thought, before this dream becomes reality. I must find Jean. He'll help me.

She stood up on her feet in a daze. "I'll get Jean. He'll know what to do."

"No!" Berthe screamed. "No! He'll kill you."

Rosalie had not heard her. She was already half running, half stumbling down the hallway heading for Jean's suite at the opposite end of the hall. "Jean," she called, as she pushed his door open. "It's Berthe. She's gone crazy. She thinks she's somebody else. She thinks her brother killed my parents."

D'Artois seemed to appear out of nowhere. He grabbed Rosalie's arms. "What's this about Berthe? What's wrong?" His fingers dug into Rosalie's arms, and he led her over to the sofa in the small sitting room of his bedroom. "Wait here, I'll go see what's happening with Berthe." He lifted Rosalie up and laid her on the sofa and placed a cushion under her feet. "You stay here. You look as though you are going to pass out." He went into the bathroom, opened a small vial, removed a pill, and filled a glass of water from the faucet.

He came back into the room. "Here take this. It'll relax you. Where can I find Berthe?"

Rosalie pointed down the hall. "In the sitting room across from her quarters. She looks terrible."

D'Artois raced out the door and ran down the hall. He reached the sitting room and threw open the door. Berthe was no longer sitting on the floor. He ran to the closed bathroom door and threw it open. Berthe was kneeling on the floor with her arms and head hanging over the tub. There was blood everywhere, and the sweet, sickening smell of it was overpowering in the small room. She still clutched a razor blade tightly in one fist, and in the other she clutched the two photographs.

D'Artois grabbed her under the armpits, lifting her up, and sat her down on the *chaise percée*.

"Heinz," Berthe said as she recognized him, "if you came to kill me, you're too late. You shouldn't have killed Margot, Heinz. She was all I had. I would never have helped you if it hadn't been for Margot. I wanted to protect her. I trusted you. I thought the one person you would never betray was me—not after what I've done for you, Heinz. I knew you had killed her—from the moment I received that newspaper clipping in the mail. I knew it was you. You said the girl in the story wasn't Margot, but then the private investigator sent the other clipping and it told of the ring on the dead girl's finger. The ring I had given you to give Margot. You weren't so smart this time, Heinz. You forgot to remove the ring from Margot's finger." Berthe's bleeding body slumped to the floor between the toilet and the tub. She grasped, "I've told Rosalie everything. She knows you are the murderer. It's best that she be the one to destroy you. I don't have the right."

D'Artois's eyes were glassy and crazed. He took Berthe's hand and brought it up to underneath her throat, slashing the throat with the razor blade. Berthe made a strange, gurgling sound as d'Artois cut her windpipe and her head fell forward. She was dead. D'Artois let go of Berthe's hand and wiped his own clean with some toilet paper.

He lifted Berthe's other hand, which was still clutching the photographs, and pried the fingers apart. He ripped up the photos and threw them into the toilet. Then, taking Berthe's limp hand in his, he closed the fingers around the toilet handle, pushing it down. He watched the small bits of paper swirl around and around in the bowl and disappear. Then he let go of Berthe's hand.

D'Artois slammed the toilet seat down with his knee and stood looking down at the woman who was his sister. "You fool," he snarled. "You goddamn ignorant fool! Yes, I lied to you. I did kill her, but I couldn't help it. I *had* to. She tried to blackmail me. She threw herself at me, and when I rejected her, she spied on me. She saw me coming in that night, the night I killed Guthrow. I *had* to kill her."

D'Artois turned and walked out of the room. He went to the telephone on the table by the sofa and dialed the police. "Hello," he said, "there's been an accident. A woman cut her throat." D'Artois gave the address and phone number, and identified himself to the police officer. He hung up and walked slowly back to his suite, as if he were taking an afternoon stroll.

Rosalie lay glassy-eyed on the sofa, in the same position in which he had left her. "Jean, how is Berthe?" she asked as he came through the door. "Did you call the doctor?"

D'Artois nodded. "Yes, I did. He'll be here in a little while. Berthe is resting." He went and sat down in a chair beside her. He touched her shoulder. "I want you to relax, try to get some rest. That pill I gave you should take effect soon."

Rosalie yawned sleepily, fighting the drowsiness that was beginning to flood her. "Oh, I'm so tired, Jean, so tired. Are you sure Berthe will be all right? I'm so worried about her. I thought it was because of me, because of all the tension I have around me always. I thought maybe . . ."

D'Artois flicked his forefinger over Rosalie's lips and then over her eyelids. "Shh, go to sleep. When the doctor comes, I will take care of everything."

D'Artois buzzed for Max. Rosalie was asleep. He buzzed again and went to meet Max at the head of the stairs. "Something horrible has happened Max, it's—"

"Madame?" Max's face went white. "Is it madame? Did something happen to her?"

"No, Max, it is not madame. It is Berthe. She has killed herself in the bathroom." He pointed in the direction of the sitting room. "The one at the end of the hall."

Max's jaw dropped open. His pale blue eyes, yellowed with age, blinked wildly, and his prominent Adam's apple bobbed up and down in his throat. "Killed herself, you say, sir," he finally blurted. "You must be joking, sir—not Berthe!"

D'Artois nodded. "Yes, Max, Berthe. It's horrible. Madame rang for her. When Berthe didn't come, she went to Berthe's room. Madame found Berthe lying on the floor, holding a razor blade and carrying on like a crazy woman. She came to find me. I was in my suite. Madame was extremely distraught. She told me what she saw, and I had to give her one of her pills. She was about to pass out. At first I thought maybe she had been dreaming again. You know how every night she has those nightmares. Anyway, I went to see for myself. By the time I got to the room, Berthe wasn't there. I was about to leave when I heard a strange noise coming from the bathroom. I went in . . . ." D'Artois made a face as if he were going to be sick. "Berthe was lying on the floor, her wrists and throat slashed with a razor blade. I called the police, and the ambulance, but I might as well not have. She was already dead. I checked her pulse."

Max sank down on the steps. He did not say a word.

D'Artois resumed speaking. "I buzzed you for quite a while before you answered me. Where were you?"

"I was asleep, sir. I had been watching the news, and must have fallen asleep. The buzzer woke me up."

Shortly thereafter, the police arrived with an ambulance. The police photographer took several pictures of the body from different angles. A police officer marked with chalk around the body lying on the floor in the pool of blood; then the body was bagged and taken down the back way.

"Where are they taking the body, officer?" d'Artois wanted to know, as he watched the large plastic bag, tied at the top like a garbage bag, being taken downstairs.

"To the coroner. A death like this, we do an autopsy."

The police officer questioned d'Artois in detail, then thanked him for his patient and thorough answers and asked to be allowed to see the mistress of the house.

"She is very distraught, officer," d'Artois said as he led the police officer to his suite. "As you know," he said, lowering his voice, "she has been through a lot in the last year. She was on the verge of collapse when she came into my room. She was staggering and looked as if she had seen a ghost." D'Artois looked directly at the police officer, and shook his head from side to side. In his eyes shone an apparent mixture of sadness and concern. D'Artois said, "She has seen so much blood shed in the last few years—I thought she was just having another bad dream."

"But you checked anyway," the policeman said.

"Yes, I gave Madame Guthrow one of the pills her doctor prescribed, helped her to the couch, and went to see what had happened."

Rosalie was asleep on d'Artois's sofa. One of her legs dangled over the edge. D'Artois gently placed Rosalie's leg back on the sofa.

"I would like to speak to her," the officer said. "My report wouldn't be complete without that."

D'Artois leaned over, placed his hands on Rosalie's shoulders, and shook her gently.

"Rosalie, wake up. There's someone here to see you. It's about Berthe." Rosalie sighed in her sleep and moaned softly.

"Wake up, Rosalie. Come on, you can do it. Up, come on." D'Artois lifted Rosalie upright on the sofa.

Her hands flew instinctively to her eyes, shielding them

from the overhead light. "Jean?" she said, as if she were not sure who was standing over her. "Who are you?" she asked, staring in bewilderment at the lieutenant, standing behind the sofa.

"I'm Lieutenant Wells," the police officer said, extending his hand. Rosalie did not take it. "I would like a statement from you."

She moaned a soft, sighing moan.

"I'll make it brief, Mrs. Guthrow, but a woman is dead, and I would like to have certain facts from you."

"Dead, did you say? Who is dead?"

"Your governess, ma'am. She killed herself. You saw, didn't you?"

Rosalie's already pale face turned at least ten shades whiter. She clasped her hands around her throat. "Berthe killed herself, Berthe? How?"

D'Artois sat down on the couch beside her and put his arm around her shoulders. She was shaking like a leaf in a storm.

Lieutenant Wells cleared his throat and said, "She cut her wrists and her throat."

Rosalie's knuckles grew white as she pressed them against her teeth to hold back a scream. Tears sprang from the corners of her eyes and she said in a small voice, like a child's, "Berthe thought she was somebody else, a Nazi. She kept telling me she had a child, and some other Nazi, a Hans or Heinz somebody, I don't remember the other name, had killed it. I . . . I . . ." Rosalie collapsed forward. Her hands clasped over her face. Her elbows were resting on her knees, and her throat rattled as she cried out, "No! Oh, God, not *again*, and not *another?*"

"Calm yourself, Rosalie, it's all right, don't worry, just calm down." D'Artois looked up at the lieutenant, standing with his pad and pen ready. "Make it as brief as possible, please. I don't think Madame Guthrow is in any condition to do much talking."

The lieutenant nodded. "Ma'am, could you tell me, please, in your own words what happened between the time you went to find your governess, and the time you went to get Mister d'Artois here? Take your time, please."

Rosalie lifted her head up slowly, and in a soft, weak voice described finding Berthe on the floor, sobbing, the photographs on the floor.

"We didn't find the photographs you mentioned, Mrs. Guthrow, or the piece you said you found. Are you sure of what you saw, madam?"

Rosalie looked up at the lieutenant. "I . . . I don't know exactly anymore." Rosalie clutched d'Artois's arm tightly. "I don't remember, Jean. It's like a dream." She pressed the palms of her hands against her temples as if preventing her head from exploding.

Lieutenant Wells felt sympathy for the frail woman before him. He was well aware of all the past tragedies in her life.

"I think this is all I need to know for now, but I will need your permission, ma'am, to search the house and premises for any clues, or prints, which might shed some light on Miss Giraud's death."

Rosalie nodded.

"The one thing which puzzles me though," the lieutenant went on, "if Mrs. Guthrow *really* did see those photographs—" He paused for a moment. "What could have happened to them?" He shrugged. "It looks like a suicide, but you never know." He turned and called out to one of his assistants waiting outside: "Harley, get on the phone. Call headquarters. Tell them to send out a crew. With as much ground as this to cover"—he made a wide gesture with his hands—"we'll need more men."

After two weeks of investigating the case, the police concluded that for reasons unknown to anyone, Berthe Giraud had taken her own life and that between the time Rosalie saw her, and the time d'Artois found her, she had moved from one place to the other, had flushed the photographs down the toilet, and had slashed her wrist and throat. The case was closed as an obvious suicide.

Chapter Thirty-two

Holmby Hills, California, February 1975

Six months passed, and Rosalie began to put the shock of Berthe's death in the past, accepting it as something she would never understand. For the sake of her children, Rosalie tried to pick up the pieces and go on.

She was sitting in the garden sipping her tea, thinking of Jeffrey and her approaching thirtieth birthday. She wondered what they would have done to celebrate.

"Oh, Jeff," Rosalie whispered, as she fingered the locket she wore around her throat, "how I miss you still!" As she opened the locket, a tear rolled down her cheek and fell on the picture of her dead husband.

D'Artois's face came into her mind. She wondered how she would handle him. He had left the week before, on the pretext of a business trip, with the expectation that when he returned, Rosalie would give him her answer to his marriage proposal.

How will I say no without hurting his feelings? Rosalie

wondered. Her face grew solemn as she imagined how d'Artois would react.

Jean is a dear friend, someone I trust and love, perhaps more than anyone alive today—except my children, of course—but I love him as a friend, not as a woman loves a man.

Rosalie's thoughts flashed back to Peter, to the times he had told her d'Artois was in love with her. Jean is just a lonely, aging man, she thought. He sees me suffering because I'm alone now, and he has convinced himself that his fondness for me is love.

Tomó came outside to clear away the tea.

"Tomó? How is Max feeling this morning? Is he any better?" Max had been feeling low ever since Berthe's death, which had hit him very hard.

Tomó smiled and nodded. "Yes, madame. He is up and working on car, since early in the morning."

Rosalie smiled. "That's good. When you see him later, during lunch, tell him to stop upstairs and see me. I think I might feel like a drive this afternoon. I feel I have to get out for a while."

The doorbell was ringing. "I wonder who it could be, at this hour. Are we expecting anybody?" Rosalie asked.

Tomó shook his head, "No madame, not that I know, unless it Mr. d'Artois back from trip."

"No, it can't be Jean. I'm not expecting him for two days yet. He would have called if he were returning sooner."

Tomó shrugged his shoulders. "Then I dunno who at door, but I betta go see before go 'way." He hurried across the flagstone patio through the open French doors of the garden room into the hallway and raced to the front door.

A man in a plain gray suit, carrying a briefcase under his arm, stood on the landing. "Good afternoon," the stranger said to Tomó.

"Good afternoon, sah!" said Tomó. "An' what can I do you, sah?"

"I'm sorry I came without calling first, but I couldn't get your phone number."

Tomó nodded affirmatively. "Yes, sah, madame phone unlist."

"Yes," said the man in the gray suit, "I know, but I had to see her. You see," he said, "I have a very important letter to deliver to her in person. I was supposed to have delivered it two weeks ago, when I first learned of Miss Giraud's death from her attorney, but when I came to call then, I was told Madame Guthrow wasn't well and wasn't seeing anyone. The letter is from Miss Giraud. Is she in?"

"Miss Giraud?" Tomó looked stupefied. "No, she dead. She very damn not in."

The man smiled woodenly. "No, not Miss Giraud. I know she is dead. I meant Mrs. Guthrow. Is *she* at home? May I see her?"

"I dunno, I have to go see. You wait here." Tomó pointed to a leopard-upholstered banquette inside the door. "You sit here. Won't bite. I go see if madame at home."

Rosalie was somewhat apprehensive.

"He says he has lettah for you," Tomó said, "*Verah* important, from Miss Giraud. She must write it before she died. He says, verah, verah important."

Rosalie gave Tomó an exasperated look. "All right, Tomó, you can show him in. And don't forget to tell Max to stop by later."

"Yes, madame. I mean, no, madame. I mean—"

"For God's sakes, Tomó, stop babbling and go let the man in."

"Erik Rumbaugh at your service, madame," the man said as he stood before Rosalie.

"What can I do for you, sir?" she said, seemingly quite relaxed, except for the telltale sign of her fingers, stiff and taut, clasping the edge of the table. "My servant tells me you have a letter for me. A letter of importance?" She sat down.

Rumbaugh nodded and handed Rosalie a long, thick, white envelope. It was heavy, as if there were something besides a letter inside. "Miss Giraud came to see me on the evening before she died," Rumbaugh began. "She seemed terribly distraught, but did not volunteer any information to me as to the cause. She entrusted this letter to me for safekeeping, and paid me to deliver it to you in person after her death. This sort of thing," he added, "is not uncommon."

Rosalie shifted nervously in her seat and crossed her legs. "Yes? Go on, Mr. . . . ?"

"Rumbaugh, Erik Rumbaugh, attorney-at-law."

"Yes, Mr. Rumbaugh, would you go on, please?" Rosalie motioned for him to sit down.

"I must apologize for my tardiness in bringing this letter to you, but—"

Rosalie interrupted him. "Yes, I know, my servant told me. You tried to see me and couldn't. I was not well for quite some time after the . . ." She stopped. "It hit me hard."

"I understand, such a terrible thing to happen. Well, as I was saying, I was paid to deliver this to you if anything happened to her. Now, that I have"—he pointed to the envelope clutched tightly in Rosalie's hands—"I don't think there's anything else I can do, or say, except that I hope that whatever it contains will explain in some way her reason for killing herself. It might help you to accept it."

Rosalie nodded and rang for Tomó. She extended her hand to Mr. Rumbaugh. "Good-bye, sir. Thank you for bringing me the letter."

As Rumbaugh turned to leave, Rosalie suddenly spoke. "Did you tell the police about this? The letter, I mean?"

He shook his head. "No, she didn't pay me to do that."

Rosalie nodded. "I understand."

Rumbaugh turned and followed Tomó into the house and left.

With shaking hands, Rosalie ripped the flap of the envelope open. She shook it, and the folded pages of a letter slid out onto the table before her. Between the pages was a small, flat envelope and inside this envelope was a key and a folded newspaper clipping. She read the newspaper clipping first.

It told of a woman's body found in a cement mixer in Marseilles in late June of the previous year. The face of the woman, it said, was mutilated beyond recognition. The teeth had been broken off short, and the skull was fractured, as if someone had almost beaten her to death, and then had decided to strangle her.

The article gave a general description of the woman, her approximate height, weight, and coloring, and said that the only clue to her identity was a ring found on her middle finger, a sort of friendship ring, as it was described, bearing the initials: "R.H.v.W." and "R.H."

The article ended there, but there was a scribbled note attached to the bottom of the newspaper article:

> Miss Giraud, I have reason to believe that this is the young woman I have been sending you information on. The last time she was seen alive was in Cannes, in mid-June. She was seen leaving the home of the Duc d'Artois with a man whom I was unable to identify. When I read this article, I knew, from the description of the ring, that this was the young woman you were looking for. You had described the ring to me the very first time you came to see me. All these years, I have kept you informed and you have paid me well for my services. I do not know why this young woman was so important to you, although I have my suspicions. Since our account is well up to date, I will not be getting in touch with you again. I hope I have satisfied you.
>
> Sincerely,
> Hans Wieller
> Private Investigator

An icy hand seemed to be squeezing Rosalie's heart. Mechanically, she placed the newspaper article on the table and picked up the pages of the letter. The handwriting was small and precise, the letters of each word carefully balanced.

> *Ma chère* Rosalie,
>
> This letter is the hardest thing I will ever have to do in my life, the hardest except for when I gave up

my child and decided to join my brother in his maniacal scheme.

It is a long story, and I have neither the time nor the will to tell it all. Therefore, my dear child—forgive me if I call you that, but I still think of you as such—I will explain only a few facts in this letter; the facts you need in order to protect yourself and your children from further disaster.

I only wish I had had the courage to do this long ago, after your father and mother were murdered, but I couldn't because of my child. I felt I could not ruin her life; even if protecting her meant that you and your whole family were destroyed in the process.

Rosalie swallowed hard, licked her lips, and continued:

My true name is Berta von Witte. I was born in Germany, not in Alsace. I had a daughter out of wedlock. She was the daughter of Reinhard Heydrich, Chief of the S.D.

I have a brother. His real name is Heinz von Witte. He was a Lieutenant General in the Wehrmacht. He is responsible for the destruction of a French town, Railleur-sur-Pelle.

He is the man you think of as your friend, the man you trust more than anyone else in the world. He now calls himself d'Artois.

A cry escaped Rosalie's lips. Her mouth felt dry. She felt her brain was about to force its way through the top of her skull. Jean? *Jean?* Jean, a murderer? My friend? My father's friend? The pages of the letter fluttered to the ground. Rosalie stooped to pick them up. She placed the sheets of light blue paper before her once more, but she was too stunned to read. The name Heinz von Witte kept flashing before her eyes on the paper. "Heinz," Rosalie whispered, "that was the name Berthe said to me the night . . ."

Rosalie sucked in her breath and tried to focus once more on the words before her. The letter continued:

It was d'Artois who murdered your father and your mother. It was d'Artois who killed Ahmed because Ahmed was pursuing him. And Peter Brian, the young artist. Only he didn't quite succeed in *killing* Brian. D'Artois killed Jeffrey, and must be held responsible for your child's death. And now he has killed *my* child, Margot. I want him to pay for all the horrible things he has done in his life, for all his hideous, unspeakable crimes.

I thought of going to the police and turning him in, but that would not be punishment enough for him. I thought of killing him myself, but I do not have the right, for I am as evil as he is.

You must be the one, Rosalie. You must destroy him. You must find a way to make him suffer as much as you have suffered because of him.

This key is to a bank deposit box in Paris. You must go there. You will find that the box contains a set of keys which, on the orders of my brother, I removed from your father's safe the night your father was murdered.

You will also find a manila envelope containing a complete set of files your father kept on my brother. I was ordered to destroy them, but I didn't. It contains the complete story of how your father came to suspect my brother. You will also find a red booklet, with a summary of his conclusions which I removed recently from your father's study in Colombier. Jeffrey was murdered when he surprised Heinz searching for it. Heinz was unable to find it and sent me back to look.

You will see in the files that your father had been very close to discovering my brother's true identity. I kept my brother informed of the progress of your father's investigation. I was Heinz's spy in your house, and because of this your father was murdered, your mother, and the rest.

You will also find in the box a list of my brother's Swiss accounts—the account numbers and the amounts deposited. The one mistake Heinz made was to have allowed me access, but he had no choice. I needed a guarantee that one day my daughter would, as he had promised, inherit the money, and the best way for me to be certain of this was to always have access to the money—"in case something ever happened" to him.

My heart is breaking as I write this—whatever heart I have, after all the cruel things I've done to you and your family.

I don't expect it, but I'm hoping against hope that you will find it in your gentle heart to forgive me for what I have done to you.

Adieu, Rosalie, yes, adieu—for when you read this, I will be dead, and gratefully so, for this way I shall never see in your eyes what I see in my own when I look into a mirror.

I am sorry, and I ask your forgiveness once again.

"Berthe"
Berta Hannelore von Witte

The word *mut*, meaning courage in German, was scrawled as an afterthought, and then Berthe had carefully printed the name and address of the bank in Paris where the safe-deposit box was, and the number of the box.

Rosalie's arms and legs seemed disjointed, as she lifelessly dragged her slippers along the stone patio and entered the house. She passed a mirror as she was heading for the stairs, and stopped and turned to look at herself. The woman who looked back at her was a stranger, cold and aloof, like a messenger of death. An upright corpse.

Rosalie stared into the reflection of her eyes and swore under her breath: "I will get you, d'Artois, my friend. I will do to you what you have done to me and worse, and if you kill me first I will come back from the grave to get you. I will never rest until I do.''

Rosalie turned and walked up the stairs, her back straight and stiff with new found strength. Her body suddenly came to life and by the time she was halfway up the stairs, she was running like the wind. As she reached the landing, she stopped and picked up the phone. She dialed a number and waited.

''Hello? Alain? I would like to leave for Paris this evening. I have urgent business there. When is the earliest we can leave?''

Chapter Thirty-three

Côte d'Azur, June 1975

From the moment Rosalie left for Paris, she had become entirely consumed by her thoughts of revenge. She thought of nothing else. She thought of all the years her father and mother had harbored a murderer within their home and how she herself had befriended d'Artois. She had been in Paris for two months and now was at Columbier. She went over in her mind the details of her plan.

It was seven-thirty. Rosalie was standing in the upstairs living room at Colombier, a tall glass of champagne in her left hand, a thin cigar in the other. She was wearing a red dress, similar in its uniqueness to the one she had worn to the ball the night of Jeffrey's death. She straightened her back, tensing for a brief moment, as she heard d'Artois talking at the front door. He had just arrived and was to be led to meet Rosalie in the private living room off her upstairs bedroom.

All the servants, save one had been dismissed for the night. Even Felix, the gate watchman, had been told he could take the night off, once Monsieur le Duc had arrived. The one remaining servant was to leave after he had served dinner. He was to leave with Felix in Felix's car.

Rosalie looked stunning in her red dress. It was long and tight-fitting, molding her curves with wicked accuracy. It had a slit on one side from her left hip to the floor. It had a high halter tied in the back of her neck under her knotted hair. On one arm, she was wearing the diamond bracelet her father had given her, and at the cleft of her throat where the strap of her halter top went around her neck, she had pinned a gardenia.

As d'Artois entered the room, Rosalie stood so he could not see her face. She pretended to be studying a painting, one of her mother as a young girl.

"Rosalie, my dear, how have you been?" D'Artois came toward her, and she could feel his eyes on her naked back.

Rosalie turned and smiled coolly. "Jean, it's nice to see you after all this time. I've missed you." She turned her cheek for him to kiss.

D'Artois took her arm and led her over to the bright green sofa in front of the fireplace. The fire was lit, the flames whipping wildly around the logs.

D'Artois said, "Tell me, my dear, how have you been, not that I have to ask, seeing how ravishing you look. You are really breathtaking tonight! Of course, I won't presume to think it has anything to do with the fact that you have accepted my proposal. Oh, Rosalie, my dear, I can hardly believe it. Even now that I'm here *with* you, I still can't believe you have said yes." D'Artois moved closer and kissed her hand tenderly.

As she watched the back of his head, bent over her hand, Rosalie's eyes shone with hatred and loathing.

D'Artois looked up and his eyes caught hers. He leaned his head closer, offering his lips.

Rosalie looked into d'Artois's small, cold, gray eyes and saw the devil in full dress, horns, hooves, tail, the very visage, stony and diabolical, of the statue he had presented to her father. Within the icy, frigid depths of his eyes, she seemed to see the fires of hell burning and she imagined she saw the screaming souls of the hundreds of men, women, and children he had murdered. There were many familiar faces among them. She saw her father, her mother, her husbands, her lover, and her child.

Now, d'Artois was after her too, but this time the situation was different.

D'Artois was looking for a lover, not a victim.

God help me, and forgive me for what I am about to do, Rosalie prayed silently.

D'Artois kissed her full on the mouth.

She closed her eyes tight in disgust, as d'Artois's dry, scarred, wrinkled lips touched hers.

A shudder went through her body, as she imagined Jeffrey's face before her, crushed against the pavement.

Today was June 20th, the anniversary of Jeffrey's murder. Rosalie had waited two months for this day.

D'Artois wrapped his arms around her, Rosalie's flesh cringed beneath his touch, and the lining of her stomach heaved upward, as she forced herself to be still.

"I love you," d'Artois said. "I can hardly believe we'll be married in less than a month."

He heard footsteps coming, and drew away from her abruptly. It was the footman, bringing in a tray of hors d'oeuvres.

Rosalie shuddered and rubbed her palms together as if warming them. "It's cold tonight," she said. "Would you close the door please, Manot?"

The servant complied.

"It's a little chilly," d'Artois said, helping himself to an hors d'oeuvre, "but I wouldn't say it's cold."

The cheetahs, roaming free in the gardens below, stood with their heads high and their noses sniffing the air. Their ears wriggled intently back and forth, and they paced up and down as they heard the sound coming off the sea on the wind, a rhythmical creak, gradually growing louder, coming closer. It was the sound of oars in oarlocks.

The big cats tried to jump over the high wall which confined them to the garden. The smell of a stranger was in the air. They reared up on their hind legs and screamed at the intruder below. The boat drifted up onto the beach, and the prow grated noisily on the sand as the boat came to a full stop.

The man in the boat shipped the oars and jumped out. He hauled the boat higher up into the shelter of a large boulder. His trouser legs were rolled up and he was barefoot.

C.C. Youngblood ran silently, in a hunched-over position along the beach, until he came to the stone steps leading up to the house and terraces. He felt his way swiftly up the steps, the moon lighting his path. He reached the top, the main patio, and stooped lower as he darted across it and melted against the wall of the house for cover.

He crept along cautiously, careful not to make a single sound. He came upon an open window, and looked in.

It was the dining room. Two large sterling candlesticks gleamed richly in the flickering light of the candles in them. Two chairs were pulled away from the table, and a pale pink napkin lay in a tiny heap on the floor under the table where it had fallen from somebody's lap. The table, however, was cleared. No sign of servants around. C.C. could hear the cats growling viciously. He knew the size of them, and shivered slightly as he stooped once more beneath the window. He slid his hand into his pocket and pulled out a .38 revolver. He checked to make sure it was loaded, replaced the safety catch and stuck it, muzzle down, in his belt. He continued to make his way along the stone wall and came to another set of steps, cut into the cliff, leading upstairs to a second terrace.

A stream of light was shining down on the steps from an open window above him. A shadow moved across the grass in front of him, and he drew back, blending into the wall in back of him.

He could hear voices, coming from the room upstairs. A man's and a woman's. It was Rosalie and d'Artois in the upstairs sitting room. C. C. listened carefully.

The woman was talking.

That's her, C.C. thought to himself.

"I'm very tired, Jean," Rosalie was saying. "Tired and sleepy. I'll see you in the morning."

C.C. could hear d'Artois's voice as well.

"Sleepy?" d'Artois was saying. "Why, it's only ten-thirty. You just had dinner, only an hour ago; you can't go to bed now. It isn't good for you to go lie down the minute you finish eating. I read somewhere that it's very bad for your health. If *you* don't care about your health, *I* do. I don't want you falling ill on me before our wedding."

Rosalie was standing next to the fireplace in the living room. She looked at d'Artois with revulsion. Oh, Jean, what a hypocritical fiend you are! What a convincing liar. She said aloud, "I'm sorry, Jean. I know you must be disappointed, but I'm really very, very tired, and if I go to sleep now, I will wake up feeling fine, and we can have a great day fishing tomorrow as we planned. Just you and me. But if I don't go to sleep now, I won't feel up to it in the morning. Five o'clock is awfully early to get up."

"All right," d'Artois said. "You win, as usual. I'll read in the study for a while before going to bed. I'll see you in the morning."

Rosalie stared at d'Artois, her eyes narrowing into slits. "Yes, Jean. I'll see you in the morning at five. No need to ring for the servants to wake you in the morning. I already instructed them." She feigned a smile. "I've had Manot put your things in the green room, the one next to mine. I thought you would be most comfortable there."

"And close to you," d'Artois said, smiling that smile she could no longer bear to watch.

"Yes," she said, "I'm sure I will sleep well tonight, knowing that you are close by." She gave him her hand to be kissed. "Good night."

"Good night, Rosalie; I'll see you in the morning. I love you."

Rosalie's eyes looked straight into his. "I know." She turned and left the room. She walked swiftly down the hall to her bedroom. She hesitated for a moment and glanced quickly back over her shoulder. She heard d'Artois going into the study. She slipped into her room and locked the bedroom door from the inside. Once she had done so, she walked over to the one closet that was in her room, opened it up, reached up on the top shelf for a large pink hatbox, and removed from inside a plastic vial, containing some small yellow pills.

They looked like throat pastilles in her hand, but she had it on what she hoped was the best authority that they were the real Borgia stuff. A succession of inquiries, from the fellow in charge of security for the La Farge empire, down, level by level, to the murky area where pale-eyed predators like Ganaud swam, had brought them to her.

Ganaud, looking like something that might study her from the other side of an aquarium tank, had been briskly business-like. "As specified, madame, these have been made up to resemble your ordinary nighttime sedative, as used by the gentry suffering from jangled nerves. Once down the gullet, the subject bends back like a bow, and then it's all up with him."

"Will it be very painful?" she had asked.

After studying her briefly, he had said, "Enough for what you might be wanting, I'd think. Nothing lingering, but, no, not an easy way to go. And all the same, nothing left in the system that'll arouse unworthy suspicions on the part of forensic-medicine specialists, eh? One of these, and the subject's out of it, and no awkward questions."

For an insomniac, as she knew Jean to be, it was the ideal method. A few of Ganaud's special items dropped into Jean's sleeping-tablet vial, and the job would be done. The servants would probably not hear the single strangled cry, and Jean, Duc d'Artois, would be found dead in his bed in the morning. Yet another victim of the strange curse hovering over Rosalie La Farge Farahet Guthrow, the newspapers might say—but they would have no way of knowing that the "curse" had finally been lifted with this last tragic death.

Jean—no, Heinz von Witte—would be an hour or so over his book in the study, and then would come to his room, undress, prepare for bed, settle between the sheets, and unsuspectingly take the pill which would make his sleep a final one. An hour after that would be the time to slip into his room and replace the lethal pills with the innocuous sedatives she had removed from the vial; the job would be done by then, and Armand and Jacqueline La Farge, Ahmed Farahet, Jeffrey Guthrow and Baby Rosalie Guthrow revenged. . . . Lord God, could *one* death pay for all those?

She showered, slipped into a robe, and crept to the bathroom connecting to his bedroom. Opening the medicine cabinet, she saw the squat vial of sleeping pills, with the blue-and-white label from the Paris pharmacy. She reached for it, thumbed the cap loose, and prepared to transfer the pills she carried in a twist of paper into it.

"You're licensed to dispense medicine then, *chérie?*" The words came silkily soft from behind her.

She whirled. "Jean—you—"

"I found that I had already read the book I had started on, and decided to abandon my literary endeavors in favor of getting another hour's sleep, so that I might be brisker company on our fishing trip," d'Artois said. "I admit that I had not counted on finding my fiancée playing pharmacist in my bathroom." He reached for the hand that held Ganaud's pills and twisted her wrist until she released what she held.

D'Artois rubbed one pill against the porcelain surface of the washbasin, then held it near his nose and sniffed delicately. "Cyanide, yes—you don't forget that smell, once you've encountered it. We used to hand pills like this out to low-level agents, for use in case of capture, and I believe many of them were silly enough to use them." He dropped the pills he had taken from Rosalie into the toilet and flushed it, then held his hands under a stream of hot water in the washbasin.

"It's done, then, isn't it?" he said. "You know."

Rosalie, sickly seeing that he was blocking her way from the bathroom, nodded slowly. "I know," she said hoarsely. "Who you are, and what you've done—not only my parents, my husbands, and—may your soul howl forever in the hottest flames of Hell!—my little daughter . . . but your own blood kin, your niece, your pathetic, treacherous fool of a sister, poor, torn Berthe. And now it's to be me, isn't it?"

He nodded slowly. "I loved you, Rosalie; I love you still. But I am not the self-sacrificing kind, do you see? If you are ready to kill me, as you have just tried to do, I would be simpleminded indeed to try to persuade myself that some accommodation could be worked out. You have set it up—I must die or you must die, there's no other solution. The choice seems to lie with me."

His hands darted out and clutched her around the throat in an agonizing grip. She emitted a strangled scream, which he quickly stifled.

Outside the study C.C. Youngblood was fumbling with the window, trying to open it. D'Artois had locked it when he had gone to bed.

"Shit. Goddamn asshole," C.C. muttered. "Why does he want to lock up a house on a night like this? Doesn't he know about the benefits of fresh air? God damn! Now I'm going to have to either climb around the ledge, or go back downstairs and try to get in some other way. Wish Harry was here. I could get him to go down the goddamn chimney."

C.C. sat down on the terrace for a minute; his back pressed up against the wall under the window. He was building up his courage to start his climb along the narrow ledge, which ran from the terrace along the house to a small balcony outside a door at the other end. He was not as young as he used to be, or as sure-footed. He adjusted his gun tighter in his belt, and removed his shirt. It was too noticeable in the moonlight.

Since December of 1965 when he had been terminated by the CIA, C.C. had continued on his own to pursue his search, to the point of becoming consumed entirely by the case. The break he had longed for came during the Berthe Giraud hearings. Rosalie La Farge had stated that when she found her governess sobbing on the floor in her room, she, Rosalie, had been under the influence of certain tranquilizing drugs, which at the time caused her to be confused as to what exactly Berthe was saying.

She remembered only that Berthe had admitted to being somebody else and that she had had a child—which somebody had killed.

Rosalie also said she thought she remembered Berthe telling her of a brother and that his name was Heinz. She thought Berthe said something about a Nazi, but she wasn't certain.

That had been C.C.'s clue—the brother named Heinz.

Rosalie La Farge's statements had been taken lightly, since her doctor attested to the fact that the drugs she was taking were strong enough to affect her mind and make it almost impossible for her to be sure of what she had heard her governess say.

C.C. had obtained, through bribery, the D.A.'s records on the case, and had immediately set out to find out whether Berthe Giraud was indeed Berthe Giraud, and if not, who. He had gone to Alsace, researched the records there, and had found out that a Berthe Giraud had existed, but had moved away when she was quite young. A priest remembered the girl and recalled that the young Berthe Giraud he had known in catechism class had later married a German and had moved to Germany. This Berthe Giraud, however, would have been at least twenty years older than Rosalie's governess.

The priest also told C.C. that when he saw Berthe Giraud again years later, she had a daughter, also named Berthe. He said she had married into wealth, a prosperous German family, but that was all he knew. He had been transferred soon after, he said, and only recently had returned to Alsace.

With this new information, C.C. had set out to find people who would have known Berthe Giraud, the mother. His search led him to Germany, to the von Witte family, into which Berthe Giraud had married, and had two children, Heinz and Berta.

The links of the chain had begun to join together. C.C. had guessed that Berthe-Berta had been planted in La Farge's home to make sure that La Farge never betrayed her brother. One mistake and La Farge's daughter would be in danger.

C.C. had always believed that d'Artois knew of the connection between La Farge and von Witte, and that all those years before La Farge's death, had been accumulating a fortune for himself by blackmailing La Farge.

Somehow, C.C. had figured, La Farge had gotten weary of his relationship with von Witte and had decided to put an end to it. D'Artois learned of La Farge's intentions and had had La Farge killed before La Farge could betray von Witte, or himself as a blackmailer.

D'Artois, C.C. had reasoned, then became the new connection to von Witte, but the only way he could cash in on the protection money was to marry Rosalie, heiress to La Farge's fortune. And the only way he could achieve that goal was by murdering her husbands, to free the way for himself.

Since C.C. had come to these conclusions concerning d'Artois, he had spent every moment, day and night, following him. C.C. had been convinced that d'Artois alone knew where von Witte was hiding and would inadvertently lead him to him.

Earlier that evening C.C. had been hiding outside in the garden of the duke's estate in Cannes, and had heard the duke talking to Rosalie on the phone.

"I will be there on time, my darling," d'Artois had crooned. "I can hardly wait to see you again."

D'Artois had hung up and had turned to his own reflection in the mirror over the console by the phone and had smiled. "When you are my wife, Rosalie," he had said to his reflection, "*I* will be the man the world envies. *I* will own everything my partner once did, and I will have achieved my goal!"

He had stood at attention, clicked his heels together loudly, and with mocking glee raised his right hand in the "Heil Hitler" salute. And at that moment the truth had burst on C.C.

D'Artois was Von Witte. After all these years of searching, following every possible lead, coming up with nothing, and then to find out that von Witte was right there all along!

C.C. bit hard on the inside of his cheek to keep from bursting into hysterical laughter.

He had waited, planning what to do. This was *his* business now, not the Company's. A head shot through the window would avenge the dead of Railleur; but von Witte's Swiss fortune remained, and it would be a damned poor return for his time not to work out a way to get some of it. He had watched d'Artois leave the villa in a black Aston Martin. D'Artois had taken a small suitcase with him, as if he would be gone for a few days. C.C. had overheard him say to his valet, as he was leaving, "Should I receive any phone calls, just say I'm out of town. I do not wish to be disturbed at Colombier."

C.C. had felt that something crucial was about to take place at Colombier—tonight would be his lucky night.

He had driven as far as St. Tropez and there he borrowed a boat for the last leg of the trip.

C.C. got to his feet, and crawled along the wall until he came to the edge of the terrace. He climbed over the wrought-iron balustrade and stood facing toward the ledge. He limbered up his body, relaxing his muscles, preparing to jump. As his body lurched through the air, he heard a scream. His foot caught the edge of the ledge and slipped. His hands flailed wildly, groping for something to hold on to. He felt himself falling. His fingers touched the ledge and grabbed on, his nails digging into the aged stone. Another scream rang out. C.C. began to move along the ledge. The weight of his body pulled heavily on his straining arms. He moved carefully along the ledge, edging his way, inch by inch, with his hands.

His gnarled, scarred fingers trailed from her throat to her jaw. He passed a bony finger along the curve of her lips. "I wanted you—so badly. It didn't start out that way. At first, all I was doing was protecting myself, my identity; then I found myself wanting you. Hating the men who could have you."

He leaned closer to her and pressed her half limp body up against his. "I'm going to have to kill you, Rosalie. I don't want to, but I know you will never forgive me. I must kill you, yet I love you so."

Rosalie had fainted. D'Artois picked her up and carried her to the bed.

At that moment the door to the bedroom off the small terrace burst open and a dark-visaged man burst into the room. His gun was pointed straight at d'Artois. D'Artois brought Rosalie's limp body up in front of him, and quickly snatched his .44 magnum from under his pillow.

C.C. made a step forward.

"Don't come any closer, or I'll blow the lady's brains out," d'Artois said. He held the pistol to Rosalie's head.

C.C. dropped his gun and raised his hands. At that moment, Rosalie regained consciousness. She saw C.C. and screamed. The noise threw d'Artois off guard for a moment, and C.C. dove behind a chair. Rosalie found new courage and went wild, kicking and screaming. She grabbed hold of d'Artois's arm and sank her teeth into it.

D'Artois screamed like an animal caught in the jaws of a steel trap and brought the butt of his gun down on Rosalie's skull. She groaned and slumped over.

C.C. pulled the lamp plug, the lights went out, and he jumped out from behind the chair and grabbed d'Artois from the side. They grappled in the dark, rolling together on the floor.

There was the sound of a fist cracking a jawbone, a moan, a shot, and yet the fists continued to fly. The gunshot woke Rosalie out of her daze, and she crawled to the door, pushed it open, and started running down the hall.

Her escape distracted d'Artois for a second, and C.C. wrenched himself away from the duke's grasp. Crouching, he tried to kick the gun out of d'Artois's hand, but d'Artois rolled away, cat-quick, and fired three shots in rapid succession.

C.C. Youngblood's obsessed search had come to an end, and so had his life.

Rosalie heard the shots and the dreadful finality of the thud of an inert body hitting the floor. The light went on in the hallway, and the sound of pursuing footsteps came to her.

She glanced over her shoulder as she placed her foot in midair to descend the staircase, and she tripped. D'Artois stood, aimed, and fired, but she was already slipping, falling on the slippery steps, and as the bullet sang past her Rosalie plunged forward.

She screamed and her arms flailed in the air. She fell against the wrought-iron balustrade, her body contorted and slid limply to the landing at the bottom of the stairs.

D'Artois ran to the top of the marble stairs and looked down. He saw Rosalie lying facedown, arms outstretched, as if on a crucifix. Blood was oozing from her face and head. D'Artois ran down the stairs, out through the garden and into the garage.

He came back running, carrying two large cans of gasoline, one in each hand. He ran upstairs, removed the ring from his finger, placed it on C.C.'s, and began dousing the room with gasoline. He drenched C.C.'s body with it, threw some on the bed, the carpet, the drapes, along the runner in the hallway, and down the steps.

He came to Rosalie's limp, unconscious body. He raised the almost empty can to pour gasoline on her, and then stopped. He could not do it. For the first time in his life d'Artois *could not*.

He turned to leave and lit a match. He held it in his hand for a brief moment as he surveyed the room and Rosalie's prostrate body. The flame burned his fingers and he let go of it. The fire caught with a loud sound and the rooms began to burn.

D'Artois headed out the front entrance, as flames began to lick the draperies.

He could hear dogs barking; and the sound was coming closer. He began to run, stumbling in the dark, crashing into tree branches as he glanced back every now and then at the burning mansion. He ran faster and faster until he reached the top of the stairs that led to the beach. He stood on the edge of the cliff for a moment, his heart pounding from his effort. He looked back and saw Colombier engulfed in flames, the sky above it streaked with crimson red and orange; around the mansion itself, giant flames were flickering and dancing, as the wind blew them higher and higher, like giant arms reaching for the sky. He heard a howl, a dog's haunting, blood-curdling, chilling howl. He saw the dog coming. He saw the open jaws, the gnashing teeth and fangs coming toward him, and he turned and ran in terror down the stairs, onto the sand, and toward the water, fleeing for his life.

The dog was gaining on him. He could hear the gnashing of its teeth, almost feel its hot breath.

Then d'Artois saw the boat, pulled up on the beach, hidden between the rocks. If I can get to the boat, he thought, I'll make it. Puffing, his lungs aching, he reached it and threw himself against it and pushed with all his strength.

The dog was halfway across the beach now; d'Artois had only seconds to get the boat in the water. He pushed again with every ounce of strength he had and the boat suddenly shifted, then shot into the water, leaving him sprawled on the sand. He sprang into the water and grabbed the oarlock to hoist himself up. He pushed with his feet and lifted himself over the edge, but as his legs came out of the water the dog was upon him.

The black beast's eyes flashed, its jaws opened wide and clamped shut on d'Artois's right leg, sinking its teeth into the bone.

D'Artois's agonizing scream echoed in the bay; then a shot rang out, and suddenly all was still except for the gentle lapping of the waves against the hull of the boat, and in the distance, the faint sound of sirens wailing.

Epilogue

On a nearby bluff, not too far from the ruins of Colombier, a man roams listlessly along the edge of the cliffs, his coat flapping loudly in the wind.

He carries a cane, and walks with a limp. His face is scarred and he wears a beard. He stops a moment as he reaches a spot where he must climb over a large boulder to reach the other side.

He lays down his cane, and leans up against the rocks. His gnarled hands reach down and rub his right leg. Beneath the gray trouser leg, his leg seems somewhat withered. It is plain that it pains him severely.

In the distance a church bell rings out, announcing the hour of noon.

The man fumbles in the pocket of his soiled gray jacket and pulls out two folded newspaper clippings.

He unfolds them carefully and spreads them out on a rock before him. He studies the first one. There is a picture of a woman under the headlines, a picture of Rosalie La Farge. The article is dated June 21st. His wary eyes scan the words.

• • •

Last night at the fabulous La Farge estate, Colombier, the famous mansion was burned to the ground.

The fire took the life of Jean Duc d'Artois, wealthy industrialist and partner of the late Armand La Farge. Rosalie La Farge Farahet Guthrow, only child and sole heir to the La Farge fortune, was miraculously saved, when one of the guard dogs led the gate watchman, Felix Segure, to her as she lay unconscious amid the flames. The watchman was able to rescue her in time. She suffered only minor burns.

She also sustained a slight head wound from a bullet that grazed her temple, presumed to have been fired by the intruder who also shot the Duc d'Artois.

The police have concluded that someone, probably a burglar, shot her and the duke, stole whatever they were looking for, and then set the mansion on fire. Felix Segure, the gate watchman, who had been off duty that night, as were the rest of the servants, had decided to return to the estate early. As he approached, he saw the flames and rushed to the gatehouse to phone for help. One of the watch dogs intercepted him, and, according to M. Segure, "dragged" him to the spot where the young heiress lay.

She was taken to the hospital in Nice, where she is now under the care of her personal physician, Dr. Etienne Labans of Paris.

The man unfolds the second clipping. It is dated four weeks later. He studies the article grimly.

Mme Jeffrey Guthrow, completely recovered from injuries sustained in the deadly fire of 20 June at Colombier, the estate of her late father, Armand La

Farge, announced today at a press conference, that she was donating fifty million dollars to a foundation established to help the victims of totalitarian regimes.

Mme Guthrow established the foundation in memory of her late friend, Jean, Duc d'Artois, killed by the intruder on the night of the Columbier fire, and to commemorate the residents of the town of Railleur-sur-Pelle, the duke's boyhood home, who were massacred by the Nazis on June 10, 1944.

"My money. *My* money," hissed the man, his face contorting.

"Everything I own. Everything I've lived and killed for . . . given away. Damn you, Berta. Damn your soul, and may you rot in hell for what you've done to me. What will I do now . . . without money . . . without a name? To the world I am dead. I do not exist. I am exiled from the world, from the living. How can I reclaim what is mine? There must be a way. There *has* to be. When I arranged for that man's body to be identified as mine, I counted on what I had in Switzerland to buy me a new name, a different face. I thought you would be dead, Rosalie."

He looked down at the second clipping again. He traced Rosalie's picture with his fingertip.

"You *know* I'm alive. You know it was not *my* body they found, and yet you have chosen to remain quiet. You are even cleverer than I imagined. You know that this state of living death you've forced on me is worse than execution."

An old man with a large yellow dog came up alongside and sat down on a rock. He greeted the man with the cane, and offered him a cigarette.

The man with the cane declined. "I don't smoke," he replied, "I quit a long time ago."

The newcomer's eyes caught the newspaper clippings. His eyes focused on the photograph.

"Terrible fire that was," he said, pointing with a tobacco-stained finger to the first article. "The worst one in these parts in years." He lit up a Gitane, and threw the match over the cliff into the water. He exhaled slowly as he searched the lame man's face.

"Why are you saving those articles after all this time? Did you know the La Farges?"

The man with the cane looked up, his scarred face a mask of wretchedness.

"Yes," his voice croaked. "I knew them once. I was a friend of the family."